SLIPSTREAM

SLIPSTREAM

a novel

Leslie Larson

Shaye Areheart Books • New York

Published in the United States by Shaye Areheart Books, an imprint of the Crown Publishing Group, a division of Random House, Inc., New York.

www.crownpublishing.com

SHAYE AREHEART BOOKS, and colophon are trademarks of Random House, Inc.

Library of Congress Cataloging-in-Publication Data

Larson, Leslie, 1956–
Slipstream: a novel/Leslie Larson.—1st ed.
1. Los Angeles International Airport—Fiction.   2. Los Angeles (Calif.)—Fiction.
3. Airports—Employees—Fiction.   4. Airports—Fiction.   I. Title.

PS3612.A7737S58   2006
813'.6—dc22   2005025399

ISBN-10: 0-307-33799-5
ISBN-13: 978-0-307-33799-3

Printed in the United States of America

Design by Lauren Dong

10 9 8 7 6 5 4 3 2 1

First Edition

For Carla

Where are we really going? Always home!

—Norvalis

Tuesday, November 19

1 Wylie's eye was acting up again. That and the wrist he'd broken forty years ago falling out of the back of his father's moving pickup. He'd been eleven; now it ached whenever it was going to rain, like a goddamn barometer. He squeezed a lime into a Bombay and tonic and looked out into the terminal where the morning business crowd was thinning out. The line at the security check had dwindled to a trickle. As he watched, a fleshy man whose gray suit made him look like an elephant bent awkwardly, removed his shoes, and passed through the metal detector. The security crew, in khaki uniforms and latex gloves, lounged behind the X-ray machine, chatting as they stacked the plastic bins and waited for the next rush of passengers. Wylie set the drink down in front of his customer, took the money, and rang up the sale. From behind the bar he had a good view of the travelers who streamed in from the ticket counters and passed through the pavilion where his bar stood along with a See's candy cart, an umbrella stand that sold espresso, a newspaper and gift shop, the La Paz Cantina, and a store that sold gifts for pets. The other end of the pavilion bottlenecked into the security check, where people were shunted through chutes, sifted through metal detectors, and discharged out the other side, where they gathered their belongings and disappeared toward their gates.

Wylie's eyelid fluttered and twitched like a bug was trapped under the skin. Stress, he figured, though he couldn't think of any particular reason for feeling edgy. A skinny woman with a too-dark tan ordered a screwdriver. Wylie counted the ice cubes as he dropped them into the glass, a bad sign. Not five, not nine. *Seven.* Otherwise, who knew what might happen? He added an extra one, eight, just to spite himself. To short-circuit the syndrome. But just before he served the drink, he took the extra cube out. When disaster struck, did he want his last thought to be *I should have stuck to seven*? Here we go, he told himself.

Across the pavilion, people waited in rows of black plastic chairs for arriving passengers to emerge from behind the barrier. At this hour, just before ten in the morning, the seats were almost empty. The professional travelers with their crisp suits and heavy smell of cologne, the occasional speck of dry blood on their freshly shaved faces, had flown off to San Francisco or New York. Soon families with whining kids would start straggling in, along with people on their way to weddings or funerals, honeymooners, and foreigners going back to their own countries after seeing Disneyland, Hollywood, the Pacific Ocean. The seats would fill with people who read newspapers and shushed their children as they waited, who looked up anxiously when a stream of people appeared, dragging suitcases and pushing strollers.

"Can I get a drink over here?" a scrawny white guy with a head shaped like a lightbulb called out. He tapped his money on the bar, one of Wylie's pet peeves.

"What can I do for you?" Wylie asked in a flat voice, placing a napkin in front of him.

"Dewar's on the rocks."

On the television over the bar, the weatherman announced that a storm was moving in from the south. It would hit late tonight. That explained Wylie's wrist, but he wondered about his eye. Not that you needed an excuse to feel jittery these days. You weren't safe anywhere—not in McDonald's, Safeway, or your own house. Not at your job or in your car or at school, and certainly not at the airport. The earth could heave and rip open. A plane could be heading for them this very minute, ready to explode in a fireball right here in the bar. Some nut could go ballistic and mow down the crowd with an automatic weapon. The only time you could relax, the only time you didn't have to worry about being maimed or killed, Wylie reflected as he poured the Scotch over ice, was when you were already dead.

"Six-fifty," he said, setting the drink down.

"I didn't ask for a double," Bulbhead replied.

Wylie clenched his jaw. "This is a single."

The guy made a big deal of pulling his wallet out of his back pocket and picking through the bills for the right amount. Just as he was putting his money on the bar, the phone rang.

Wylie took the money. It was going to be one of those days.

He answered the phone, expecting it to be one of the airport maintenance staff calling to say an electrician would be in to replace the light over the register that kept shorting out, or a manager from the concession he worked for wanting to know if he could cover somebody else's shift. He was surprised to hear Carolyn's voice.

"Is everything all right?" he asked anxiously. She'd never called him at work before. He pictured his house burned down, his dogs run over.

"Oh yeah. Everything's fine, Wylie. I'm sorry to bug you at work, but listen—"

"What is it, then?" he interrupted. Once the scare was gone, he was annoyed. They had their routine.

"Well, listen. I'd like to talk to you," Carolyn said uncertainly.

A flight crew bustled by like a flock of blackbirds. The bar was filling up. The Amber Ale had sputtered empty a few minutes before. The sink was full of dirty glasses, and the tables over by the big-screen TV needed to be bussed.

"Listen, Carolyn. Can I call you back in a few minutes?" Wylie asked. "It's kinda crazy in here right now."

"Sure," she said. "Okay."

"I just need to catch up a little. I'll call you right back."

He cleared the empty glasses off the bar and plunged them in the steaming water in the stainless-steel sink. He replenished the piles of cocktail napkins and stocked the containers of olives, lime wedges, and maraschino cherries. He liked the fluorescent lights of the airport, the low buzz of canned air, the garish purple and gold carpet. Outside, the sun was fighting to come out. Lurid, milky light streamed through the big windows, turning the people walking by into silhouettes, overwhelming the fluorescent tubes overhead, dimming the screens that listed arrivals and departures. Newspapers and paper cups were starting to collect on the black plastic seats in the waiting area. Big planes nosed up to the jetways, fuel lines dangling from their undersides like umbilical cords.

"Ketel One over," a guy who looked like a professional basketball player called out. He wore chunky diamond studs in his ears, garlands of gold chains. His buddy was tall and flashy, too. He ordered a cosmo.

Wylie spotted a handful of potential deathtraps as he made the drinks. The unattended sports bag against the wall, the package on the seat next to the glass case where pretzels twirled under heat lamps, the guy with the too-big overcoat looking around shifty-eyed as he stood with his hands in his pockets. Meanwhile they were taking away people's toenail clippers, confiscating penknives and tweezers. What a joke. People here had no idea what it felt like to think twice every time you touched anything, every time you raised your foot and set it down. It had been thirty years since Wylie was in Vietnam, but he was *still* looking for booby traps, *still* keeping an eye out for mines. People didn't know what it felt like always to be wondering if you were going to lose your legs, your balls, your life. Wylie had seen a nineteen-year-old from Tulsa, Oklahoma, step on a Bouncing Betty, do a double flip like an acrobat, and land gracefully in the limb of a tree.

A small woman with highlighted hair sat down at the corner of the bar where hot dogs rolled on metal rods. Early thirties, Wylie figured. Painted nails; neat, quick features. A little scar on her upper lip. She scanned the bottles behind him, eyed the beer taps.

Wylie nodded a greeting, wiped the counter, placed a napkin in front of her. "What can I get you?" he asked.

"Those what you have on draft?"

"Except the Amber Ale. That one's not working."

She touched each corner of her mouth with her fingertip, as if to wipe something away. Wylie waited quietly, his hands behind his back. He wondered if he should card her. In the old days, hell. But this was the airport. Everything by the book. Who would have guessed he'd end up here?

"I guess I'll have a margarita. On the rocks, no salt. And a shot on the side."

"Could I see some ID, please?"

She rolled her eyes and dug around in an oversized purse. She was twelve years over drinking age. First name Emily. Wylie thanked her and handed back her driver's license.

She watched him pour the tequila, then the mix. He imagined what she must see: a clean-shaven, average-height guy with a pock-marked face and a slight paunch, his brown hair—worn a little long as a nod to his past—graying around the edges.

"I'm not a drunk," she said when he set the glasses down. "Just afraid to fly."

He nodded. He saw it all the time. Macho guys with pulses racing like rabbits' in their necks. Society women sloshing down Chardonnay like it was water. Shots slammed one after another. People stumbling away from the bar like they were headed for the gas chamber.

"Odds are you'll make it," he said.

"I know. It's not rational." She did the shooter first, just a quick little flip of her wrist like she was downing cough syrup. "Wylie?" She pointed to his name tag. "Like the coyote?"

"Excuse me?" He didn't make a habit of getting chatty with customers.

"The coyote. You know, from the *Road Runner* cartoon. Wile E. Coyote."

She was talkative. Fear could do that to people, he'd seen it happen.

"Oh, that. Wylie's my *last* name. People just call me that."

"What's your first name?"

"Tom. Thomas. But nobody calls me that. Just my family. Well, they call me Tommy."

His eyelid flickered. He wondered if he should see a doctor about it. The woman smiled at him and picked up the margarita. Sometimes it was hard for him to remember he was middle-aged, fifty-one to be exact, and that women like her probably thought of him as a father, if at all. He picked up the rag and moved toward the cash register.

"I'm headed to Denver to see my new niece," the woman called out. The booze must be getting to her. "My brother's daughter. She's the first grandkid in the family."

"That's nice."

"I just hope it's not snowing there. Or a thunderstorm. Turbulence, you know. It kills me."

"Naw, it's a piece of cake."

Another customer sat down at the other end of the bar. Clean-shaven, with very short hair. His skin looked tight, like it would pop if you stuck a fork in it. Possibly military, or maybe a cop.

Wylie put a napkin down in front of him. "What can I get you?"

The guy was too busy checking out the woman to look at Wylie. Sizing her up. Same old story. "What would you like to drink?" Wylie asked more emphatically.

The guy gave Wylie a quick once-over. Summed him up and kissed him off. The uniform probably had a lot to do with it, Wylie thought—the black slacks and the putty-colored polo shirt that said TOP HAT ENTERPRISES over the breast pocket. The guy didn't know that Wylie had pulled two years as a foot soldier in Vietnam, that he'd gone to college—graduated, in fact—with a degree in political science. He didn't know that after doing a stint at a small newspaper in Bakersfield, Wylie had hitchhiked to San Francisco, flower power and all that, and had lived in the top flat of a trashed Victorian on Alamo Square. He didn't know that Wylie had worked in some of the best rock-'n'-roll bars on the West Coast, that he'd seen the hottest acts, that he'd married and divorced two women.

He didn't suspect that Wylie could play slide guitar, frame a house, smoke a salmon to perfection. Had no idea that it had been seven years since a drop of liquor or any drug stronger than aspirin had passed Wylie's lips. Didn't know and didn't care. All he saw was an over-the-hill guy with bad skin and a dead-end job.

"JB over," the guy ordered, keeping his eyes on the woman. "How you doing?" he called to her as Wylie filled a glass with ice.

"Okay," she said in a bored voice.

For once Wylie was glad for the plastic cap on the bottle that measured each drink. That sucker wasn't getting one drop more than the standard shot. As he served him, an older couple showed up—a black guy with a fringe of white hair and a white woman with an overbite and thick glasses. Vodka tonic for him, Bloody Mary for her. By the time Wylie had set up their drinks, three more people were waiting.

That's how it was at the airport. They came and they went. The fearful flyers, wannabe actors, losers on the make. Cokeheads who'd just burned through the last dime of their paychecks. Businessmen swaggering home after closing a big deal. Couples who'd met at conferences, spent the night together, and who—red-eyed and dazed—shared one last drink before they headed back to their families.

In the old days, at the other bars, there were the regulars, the ones whose life stories he knew, who cried and laughed and threatened to crack his skull if he didn't give them one more drink. Here, with a few exceptions, the people were always new. From Florida, Mexico, or China. The anonymity was a comfort. Wylie worked from seven in the morning until three in the afternoon, got on the road before rush hour, made it up to the hills where his rickety house with the pepper tree out front and the two dogs on the porch waited. It was easier this way, now that he'd stopped drinking.

He wiped down the bar and straightened the stools. He needed to call Carolyn back, but for some reason he dreaded it. He made sure the change drawer was full. She wasn't the type who'd call for no reason. He refilled the juice bottles, promising himself that he'd phone her back as soon as he finished. But then two executive types sat down and ordered Chivas on the rocks. Wylie wished he could shake the feeling that something bad was coming his way.

He was filling a glass with ice when a huge crash exploded on the other side of the bar. He leapt in the air. The glass he was holding smashed on the ground. There it was, the thing he'd been waiting for. Customers spun around. Somebody gasped. A hot spurt of adrenaline pumped through Wylie's body. Flashing bars of black and white blinded him. He forced himself to breathe, to resist diving onto the floor behind the bar and covering his head with his hands. Crunching broken glass underfoot, he ran. Out from behind the bar, past the pretzel case, into the bar's lounge where passengers who had been watching the big-screen TV spun toward Wylie as he charged over to the corner where the commotion was.

Seven or eight young people in red T-shirts were bending over something. Wylie pushed into the middle of them. "What the hell's going on?" he yelled.

A big kid with a face full of acne laughed. "It's just a barstool, man," he said. "There was too much luggage and it tipped over."

Wylie looked down. There it was, the offending barstool. Chrome legs, red vinyl seat. A barstool, just a barstool. The damn things made a hell of a racket when they went over. Like a machine gun, or a bomb exploding.

Wylie jerked it upright, kicked the baggage out of the way, and got in the pimply kid's face. One thing he'd inherited from his father was a temper. In the old days he would have swung first and asked questions later, but this was the airport, and he was on the straight and narrow.

"Sorry, man," the kid said, the color draining from his face. He held up his hands, took a few steps backward. "It was just an accident."

"Jesus, get a grip," one of the smartass girls in the group said. "A chair tipped over, dude. Big deal."

Wylie took a deep breath. People at the nearby tables were staring at him. His hands were shaking. The girl was right, he had to get a grip. "All right, then," he said, picking up a camera case and shoving it toward the kid. "Just be careful." He made an effort to slow his breathing down, to relax the muscles in his neck and shoulders. He rolled his head. "Take it easy, then," he mumbled.

He felt everyone's eyes on him as he walked back to the bar.

"Could I settle up?" asked the woman who was afraid to fly as Wylie swept up the shards of broken glass. She held up a twenty.

Her admirer had managed to maneuver into the seat next to her. "Get you one more?" he pleaded.

She raised her eyebrows at Wylie. "How about a shot for the road, in case it's a rocky flight?"

"What would you like?" Wylie asked with a smile.

"Tequila's fine."

He gave her the premium, since the jerk was paying. She tossed it back, shouldered her bag, and walked off.

"Gimme another," the guy said, tapping his glass.

A women's golf tournament came up on the sports channel. Amber Ale, Wylie reminded himself. He'd have to go downstairs and hook up a fresh keg before the noon rush. He carried out the empties and made a list of what needed to be reordered. When he ran out of ways to stall, he dialed Carolyn.

"So, can you come over tonight?" she asked.

Here it comes, he thought. The where-is-this-thing-headed talk. He'd hoped with her it might be different. What he'd liked was her independence, the fact that she seemed just as happy with the whole arrangement as he was. She had her own life. A good business renovating furniture that she picked up at garage sales and flea markets. She stripped, painted, and reupholstered it, then sold it for big bucks to people in West Hollywood and Santa Monica.

"Well, today's Tuesday," he said. "We're still on for tomorrow, right? Can it wait until then?"

She cleared her throat.

"Are you sure everything's all right?" he blurted, blindsided by the old fear. Panic that he'd done something he couldn't remember, that he'd blacked out and was about to be told the things he'd done and said, things he just couldn't believe. He had to remind himself that he didn't do that anymore, that those days were over. Now there were no surprises.

"Nothing's wrong. I'd just like to talk to you. I need to tell you something."

"Oh, *Jesus*. That sounds bad," Wylie groaned, running his hand through his hair. "Just tell me."

"No, not now. Don't worry. Just come over, will you? It's no big deal. But could you drop by?"

"Tonight?"

He glanced around the bar. Customers were glaring at him, tapping their money on the counter.

"Yeah, if you can."

"Okay, I will. What, around seven or so?"

"Yeah, that's fine."

"Okay. Look, I gotta go. A lot of thirsty travelers are here, giving me the evil eye. I'll see you tonight."

"Okay, see you then."

Something in her voice made his heart pick up, like the split second before you're rear-ended by a car.

"Are you *sure* everything's okay?"

"Depends," she said with a laugh. "It depends."

2 | While Wylie hooked up a new keg of Amber Ale, Rudy Cullen boarded a 737 just in from Orlando and started in business class, picking up magazines, blankets, what-have-you. He grunted as he bent down and felt a warning hitch in his back. God, don't let it go out again, he thought as he squeezed his pear-shaped body into the third row and grappled with a wad of napkins and empty peanut packets wedged between two seats. His small, dainty hands sweated in the latex gloves. In the next row, someone had stuck three crushed plastic glasses in the seat-back pocket. Whoever was sitting in the window seat had rolled pellets of chewed gum in a tissue, which they'd shoved between the armrest and the side of the cabin. Rudy dug it out. He blinked his colorless eyelashes and brushed crumbs out of the seat, then groaned as he bent to pick up a pile of newspaper on the floor. Someone had left a fuzzy gray sock. Boy, oh boy, the things he'd found in his years on the job—used condoms, toenail clippings, dirty diapers. People were pigs, no doubt about it.

But working on the planes was still great. Rudy had always loved them. As a kid he'd been crazy about model building: bombers, fighters, cargo planes, passenger jets. He'd spent a gazillion hours painstakingly constructing perfectly scaled gliders out of balsa wood and paper. He'd hung them from the ceiling of the room he shared with his older brother. He'd joined the navy right out of high school in hopes of becoming a pilot, but instead of training him to fly, they'd assigned him to a base in Virginia where he'd restocked shelves in the commissary. Just his luck, wasn't it? The story of his life.

Through one of the windows, he watched a loaded luggage cart zip off across the tarmac. After the navy, his chances for flight school were even more remote, and now, at thirty-seven, his dream seemed to be moving further and further away, until it was only a pinprick on the horizon. Outside, an L-1011 rolled toward its gate like a stately bird. Rudy felt a pang when he saw the tiny figures of the pilots in the cockpit. Even from this distance he could make out their white shirts, the black epaulets on their uniforms. One way or another, he swore he'd get his license. Even if it was a small, private plane, he'd learn to fly. Some day, somehow. He promised himself.

In the meantime, at least he spent every day around planes. *On* planes. He moved into coach class, pushing his cleaning cart in front of him. He loved the smell of jet fuel and the power of the aircraft as it stood tethered to its gate. He was part of the team that worked to keep it in top form, just like the crews that restocked the galley and cleaned the restrooms, or the guys down on the tarmac who wore headsets and knee pads while they refueled, unloaded, and checked out the landing gear. As he moved through the cabin, he thought of where the plane had been. The altitude it had reached, the velocity of its flight, the miles it had logged. He was part of it. *Ground support, airline industry,* he always answered when someone asked him what he did for a living.

There was a clatter at the front of the plane. Rudy looked up as Latasha McCain rolled her cart on board.

"How you doing?" she called out in a lazy voice, barely turning her head to look at him.

"Good morning, Latasha," he called. He waved at her, but she was already squeezing into the first row, spraying the armrests, wiping them clean. She straightened the seatbelts and pulled open the seat-back pockets to make sure they were stocked with in-flight magazines, safety instructions, and airsick bags.

Rudy suddenly felt sour. Still, he forced himself to ask, "How're you today?"

"Doing okay," Latasha mumbled, still not lifting her head.

Well, he'd tried, Rudy thought as he got back to work. The problem with Latasha was her attitude, and unfortunately hers wasn't the only one that could use some improvement. It was the same with all the women he supervised, what he called his *crew*. To them this was just a job, and they moved slowly, taking their own sweet time. They had no idea what it took to keep this big bird aloft. Didn't know and didn't care. They could be cleaning a house or a movie theater for all they cared. But *he* imagined the plane flying over the castles of the Rhine, the Wall of China, the Eiffel Tower. The pilots in the cockpit, the dome of the night sky, the air traffic controllers directing the web of routes that wrapped the globe.

"You want me to start at the front of coach or work back from the tail?" Latasha yelled. She gave him a look: her mouth off to one side, her eyes squinted up.

Rudy chewed his lips. It was important for him to stay professional. "At the front, Latasha," he said firmly and calmly. "Like always."

Boy, these people. They were different, that's all there was to it. Black and Mexican and Filipino. Not that he thought anything less of them, because he liked people, *all kinds* of people. He gave everyone a break. His *own wife* was from the Philippines, for goodness sake. But still, the looks they gave him. Like he didn't notice. Tittering behind his back, the way they met each other's eyes. Never his. And it wasn't like he'd had a whole lot of advantages; he'd started out just like the rest of them, as a cleaner. No easy breaks in *his* life—not that you'd ever convince *them* of that.

He bumped his head on the overhead compartment when he straightened up in Row 14. It figured, since if you added the two numbers together, one and four, you got five—his unlucky number. Plus, he was fourteen when he'd moved to L.A. from the small town in Nevada where he'd been born. That was when his troubles had started, when his mother had remarried and he'd been sent to a junior high where he felt out of step with everybody else. He watched Latasha out of the corner of his eye, her head bobbing up and down as she sprayed and wiped, her big behind poking into the aisle. Well, having his staff not like him was just part of the job, he reminded himself. That's the way it was when you were a supervisor. You weren't there to win a popularity contest.

"Hey, hey! Would you look at that," Latasha called out, more to the back of the plane than to Rudy. She held up a roll of bills she'd found in one of the seats, counted it right in front of him. "Three dollars!" Tucked it straight into her apron without a second thought, like it was her due. He'd found money himself: coins that fell out of people's pockets, singles given back as change for cocktails. Sometimes a ten, once in a while a twenty. He *always* turned it in.

"Not bad, huh Cap'n?" Latasha grinned.

Rudy scowled. He hated the nickname. It was bad enough when his crew used it, but other people at the airline had caught on, people who mattered, like the pilots. Some of them even saluted him when they saw him in the terminal, wheeling his cart of spray bottles and rags. "Morning, Cap'n," they said, a sparkle in their eyes.

Rudy moved to the seats behind the wing, picked up a pile of rumpled blankets, and pulled out a pillow that had been shoved between the seats. The flight attendants called him Cap'n, too. Hard to believe now, but he had actually considered being a flight attendant himself, had even begun the training. But he'd soon found out that being a fruit was practically a requirement for the job, so it was no wonder he only made it through one week of the two-month course. Those fairies talked and laughed with the women trainees like they were one of the girls, and the women talked and laughed right back, like they were the best buddies in the world. *He* was the one who couldn't get the time of day from any of the women! Like *he* was the fag! Go figure. Whatever. It had worked out for the best because now that he was married, with his wife's daughter to raise, he couldn't be running all over the globe. He was a family man who worked regular hours and came home for dinner every night.

"Hey, Rudolph! Mr. Red-Nose Reindeer! How goes it?"

Rudy turned toward the back of the plane, where Cage, one of the baggage handlers, had come up the rear stairs.

"How's life in housekeeping?" Cage shouted above the engine noise that flooded in from the tarmac. "How's Mr. Claus and all the elves?"

Rudy shook his head and pretended to laugh. Cage had the mental maturity of a five-year-old. Rudy watched while he reached into a compartment in the galley, took three Cokes, toasted Rudy with one, and headed back down to his buddies who were loading luggage for the next flight.

The baggage handlers were another bunch of losers. Dishonest as hell, slackers, and half the time they came to work drunk, stoned, or both. Rudy knew because he'd worked there, too. After six weeks on the job, one of the men—his supervisor, in fact—had shown him how to unzip the bags and slide his hand around to look for the stash of money so many people stupidly hid in their cases. But Rudy had higher standards than that. *Ethics.* Word got out fast that he'd refused to take money from the bags, and from that day on his life was in danger. Big bags came rushing at him whenever he turned his back. Packages dropped out of nowhere. The last straw came when the hatch was secured while he was still loading bags in the hold. In the pitch dark he screamed for all he was worth, pounding on the sides of the plane. He pictured himself suffocating somewhere over the Pacific. At the last minute the hatch had opened and he'd blinked out at his co-workers' laughing faces framed by the square of blinding light. He'd walked off the job and gone straight to the office to ask for a transfer.

Latasha was humming, working at a slow, steady pace, like she didn't have a care in the world. The airline had been cutting back the ground crews' hours since the terrorism threats, and unless things picked up and people started flying again, they'd lay off more people. You'd think that would matter to someone like

Latasha, but as he watched her she picked up a magazine, thumbed through the pages, and stuck it in her apron. She hummed a little louder, as if she was *trying* to get under his skin, to show him that—even though he was her supervisor—she didn't give a damn what he thought.

Rudy sighed. He'd almost reached the back of the plane. The day lay ahead: one more plane before lunch, when he'd eat the ham sandwich and the bag of potato chips that Inez had packed for him that morning. His stomach growled just thinking about it. Then the long afternoon followed by the drive home. His lower back twitched; his shoulders ached. Sometimes he felt so *old*, even though he was still nowhere near forty. He thought of Inez. His *wife*. He repeated her name and a kind of peacefulness came over him, a feeling that things were okay. He'd seen her for the very first time in church, standing in the pew with Vanessa, who was only six at the time. It was funny, but seeing the two of them like that—so serious, so quiet, as they listened to the sermon—he'd instantly spotted the empty space next to them just waiting to be filled. All he had to do was step into it. He realized then and there that he and Inez could complete each other, that he could stop being a single man and she could stop being a young, unwed mother with a daughter everybody wondered about. They could be a family. And that's what had happened, more or less. He thought of his happiness on a plane just like this one, when the two of them headed off to Hawaii for their honeymoon. It was a charter, sure, a package deal, and they had waited in the terminal through a four-hour delay while what the airline called the "equipment" was repaired. Still, once they were in the air, Rudy had looked out at the clouds that were as big as castles and felt that his life was finally getting on the right track, that things were about to take off.

And since then—well . . . Rudy pursed his lips. He thought of the stucco box the color of old bologna that he and Inez had rented for the entire eight years they'd been married. It was nothing like he wanted: bars on the windows, saggy screens, and a patchy yard. Tiny, so they were always bumping into each other.

The neighborhood was no place for Vanessa to grow up, with bums passing through all the time, eyeing the houses for anything they could steal. Kids throwing trash and hollering, lowlifes hanging out working on their cars on the weekends. No place for Inez, either. *Inez.* Rudy's heart sank. His moist hands itched in the latex gloves. Inez's silence grew and grew, filling the rental so that sometimes it was hard just to get a breath. She needed her own house, a place where she could have everything just the way she wanted it. Then things would be better. He was trying, he told himself, as he picked up pieces of a Disney World postcard someone had shredded all over the seat. He was doing his best.

When he finished the last row, he straightened up and stretched his stiff back. The cabin, which had looked like the scene of an overnight party when he got on board, now looked like a freshly cleaned hotel room. Latasha was halfway finished.

"I'm out next week, remember," she said as he squeezed past her cart on the way out.

"That's news to me, Latasha," Rudy responded. "I didn't hear anything about that." His crew was always taking time off: sick kids, vacations, colds, surgery. The latest was Imogene, one of his best workers, who claimed to have developed carpal tunnel syndrome.

Latasha shook her head. Rudy wished she'd look him in the eye. Just once. Was that asking too much?

"I told you. Two or three times," Latasha scolded. "I let you know a month ago that I needed the time off and I reminded you again last week." She put her spray bottle in a pocket of her apron and squeezed between the row of seats.

"Well, I didn't see it written down on the schedule," Rudy said, trying to keep his voice reasonable. Latasha went on working like he wasn't even there. "You know, Lula's off next week, too. I can't imagine that I'd give permission for both of you to be off the same week."

"My mother's having surgery!" Latasha snapped, finally looking up at him. "It's been scheduled for a month. I told you just as soon as I heard. She needs around-the-clock care for the first week. You'll just have to figure something out."

Rudy stumbled back a few steps, shocked by the look of rage on her face. The nerve of her, talking to him like that! He took a deep breath, ready to come back at her in no uncertain terms, but just as he was about to let loose, his own boss, Glenn Waller, appeared at the front of the plane.

"Rudy, could you step out here for a minute?" he said, motioning Rudy to the area near the cockpit. "I'd like to have a word with you."

Rudy gave Latasha an I'll-deal-with-you-later look and started down the aisle. "What's up, Glenn?" he said cheerfully when he reached the cockpit. He pulled off the latex gloves and looked down at his small, pink hands. For some reason his heart was pounding.

Waller took him by the elbow and guided him out the door and onto the jetway. A walrusy-looking man with pale skin, rumpled clothes, and a brush mustache, Waller steered Rudy into a corner next to a folded wheelchair. He stood too close to him, leaning down so that Rudy could smell the cigarettes and coffee on his breath.

"Listen, Rudy. I've got some kind of tough news for you."

"Is my wife all right?" Rudy gasped. His heart whirred. The wheelchair handle probed his spine.

"No, no. Nothing like that. Your wife's fine. I mean, as far as I know, she's fine." Waller thought a moment, brushing his mustache into shape with his index finger. He seemed to be looking at a place on top of Rudy's head. "What I was going to say is, well . . ." He cleared his throat. "The thing is, Rudy. We're going to have to lay you off. It's a hell of a thing and I hate to be the one who tells you. But you know how things have been around here. We just don't have the business. I'm sorry. Sorry as hell."

Across the jetway was a narrow, vertical window. Its glass was hazy, but Rudy could make out a plane pulling into the gate next to them, the flagman on the ground guiding it in. He watched it nose to a stop, watched the jetway push up to it, suction around the hatch like a lamprey eel. In the cabin everyone would be surging up, unsnapping seat belts, opening the overhead bins.

"When?" Rudy asked, his eyes still on the window.

"Well, that's the thing. Everything's happening so fast. This quarter was worse than we expected. We just got the word from upstairs: we have to cut back right away. So listen—"

Rudy's eyes shifted. He watched Waller's hand go to the back pocket of his ill-fitting gray slacks, watched him pull out a limp envelope curved to the shape of his oversized ass.

"I got a check for two weeks' pay here," Waller went on. He was looking at Rudy now, holding the envelope up so he could see. "We're giving you two weeks' notice, but you don't have to come in. Here's your check. Severance. You can have it now, but when you finish up today, that'll be it. It'll give you a chance to look around. A head start finding something else."

Rudy didn't catch much of what Waller was saying. Instead he studied Waller's face, noticed that one eye was a completely different shape than the other, that his incisors were the color of corn. Waller held out the envelope. Rudy hesitated. He didn't want to touch it because it might still be warm from Waller's body, from being cuddled up to his disgusting butt.

"Are you saying that this is *it*?" Rudy whispered. His throat was so dry, it was hard to talk. "Are you saying that this is my *last day*?"

Waller pinched his mustache nervously and patted Rudy limply on the shoulder. "I know it's hard, buddy. This is sudden, I know. I'm really sorry. There's nothing we can do about it, though." He held the envelope closer to Rudy's face, like he was trying to entice a dog with raw meat. "We're giving you two weeks up front, buddy. So you can get on your feet."

As if following an order, Rudy looked down at his feet. His black work shoes were run over on the sides, scuffed at the toe and heel. One lace was loose. Not untied, but almost.

"You can't," Rudy said. "You can't fire me just like that."

Waller nibbled the edge of his mustache.

"Not *fired,* Rudy. *Laid off.* And I'm afraid we can. We just need to give you two weeks' notice, and that's what we're doing. Again, I'm sorry."

He held out the envelope once more.

Rudy stared at it. His veins began to fizz: first the capillaries in his fingers, nose, and ears, then the bigger ones that fed his arms and legs. Finally the artery that passed through the middle of his body swelled and pounded until he felt his neck and chest would burst. His arms went numb from the elbow down.

"But I got a wife! A wife and daughter!" he sputtered. "They rely on me. They're my responsibility!"

Waller nodded like he understood, the schlub. "I know, Rudy. I know. It's a difficult thing, like I said—"

"And I'm the *supervisor!*" Rudy interrupted. "I've been here longer than anybody else! What about the others?" He gestured wildly toward the plane. "Some of them just came on. Why me? How can you do that?" A fleck of spit flew from his mouth and landed near Waller's lower lip.

"Hang on, hang on," Waller said, trying to pat Rudy on the shoulder. Rudy tore away from his hand. He panted, his chest heaving, his face turning a deeper shade of red with each moment.

"That's just it," Waller said in a soothing voice. "It's not you, it's the position. We have to eliminate some of the management positions, and yours is one of them. We're consolidating supervision to save money. We've examined everything, and this is one of the ways we've been able to streamline."

"You mean I worked all this time to make supervisor and now *that's* what's getting me fired?" Rudy screamed. "You mean if I was still a cleaner like the others, everything would be hunky-dory? I'd still have my job?"

"Well, in a nutshell—" Waller began.

"Are you kidding me?" Rudy bellowed, showering spit. "This is a joke, right?"

"It's not a joke, Rudy."

"This whole thing is a crock, and you know it," Rudy said in a low, menacing voice. He was starting to get what was happening. He squinted one eye and pointed his finger at Waller, pistol-style. "The truth is I'm *white*, isn't it? You know if you fired anybody else you'd have the ACLU up your ass in two seconds. *Discrimination.* You'd have a lawsuit on your hands before you could say Martin Luther King. But what about *me*? Huh? What am *I* supposed to do? I got no recourse."

"Wait a minute, here. Hold on a second. Calm down, now. Calm down." Waller put the palms of his hands on Rudy's shoulders as if he were trying to pat him down to normal size. He looked around nervously, whether to see if there was anyone around to help or to scope out an escape route, Rudy couldn't tell.

"Listen, there's a list for rehires. As soon as things take off again, we'll try to get you back on. When the scare blows over and people start flying again, we'll see what we can do. Just check in with the front office now and then."

"Don't touch me, Waller!" Rudy spat, knocking away Waller's hands. "Why don't you just admit it? Just admit it, Waller! *I'm* the one who's being discriminated against! Why don't you be honest for once in your life?"

Rudy couldn't believe this was happening, but in a way he could. His whole life he'd been misunderstood, treated unfairly. Why should anything be different now?

Waller took a step back and once again smoothed his mustache into shape with his forefinger. "You know what, Rudy?" he said in a quiet voice. "You just crossed the line, buddy. If you really want to know the truth, everything *hasn't* been perfect with your work. We've had a reasonable number of complaints from the people you work with. We've even talked to you about it in the past. So the best thing would be if you just take this check—"

"Why, because I was trying to do my *job*?" Rudy screeched. His voice caught; his throat burned. God, don't let him cry now. "Trying to get people to come in on time and do their work? Is that *discrimination*? Was I being *prejudiced*?"

He was about to grab the check out of Waller's hand and rip it up when he saw that Latasha was watching him from the entrance to the jetway. Her hands rested on the handle of her cart. Her eyes sparkled with curiosity, as if she were watching a good television show, a sitcom.

"I was just trying to get by you," Latasha said when the two men turned to look at her. "I'm finished here. I've gotta go do the next one."

"It's okay, Latasha. We're almost finished," Waller said, stepping aside so she could pass.

Rudy's tongue felt thick and dry, and for a minute he thought it might gag him. He wasn't imagining it: Latasha smirked as she walked by. She was *glad*. She'd been waiting for it, hadn't she? How many people had known that he was going to get the sack, how many had been in on it? He watched Latasha amble down the jetway until she disappeared into the terminal. When he turned back, Waller was holding out the check, still bent like a dead fish.

"Just take the check, Rudy. Take it and go on home."

The blood drained first from Rudy's head, then from his neck and shoulders, and finally from his arms and hands. He had to get out of there. He had to think. Things around him looked grainy, like a close-up of a photo in the newspaper.

"This isn't right," he said, taking the check because Waller was holding it out to him, because right then he needed something to hold on to, and even a piece of paper was better than nothing. "Someone's going to pay for this," he managed to mutter between clenched teeth.

Waller, the sap, just chewed his mustache and shook his head.

"It's not over!" Rudy called back as he stumbled down the jetway. "You're going to be sorry!"

Walking through the terminal was like flying through a wind tunnel. Rudy could hardly see, things flowed by so fast. He bumped into people who pulled luggage behind them, who pushed carts loaded with boxes and bags. A janitor was emptying the garbage in the waiting area, another swept debris into a long-handled pan. Women handed out pizza from behind a counter. They poured soda from a machine, made change from the register. With a pint of beer in each hand, the bartender with the pitted face whom Rudy passed every day looked up and nodded. Rudy rushed on. The security guard with bad false teeth, the scrawny old man who drove the electric courtesy cart, the ponytailed woman behind the desk at Gate 12, announcing the final boarding of a flight. It was just another day for them.

Rudy didn't have a plan, didn't know where he was going. He passed the gift shop with its display of key chains and coffee mugs, of stuffed bears wearing Hawaiian shirts. Racks of magazines; candy; T-shirts silk-screened with palm trees, the Hollywood sign, sunglasses. Beyond the gift shop, the blue-tiled entrance of the men's room beckoned like a quiet grotto. Rudy headed for it, but the janitor's yellow plastic sawhorse blocked the doorway. WET FLOOR. NO ENTRANCE.

Rudy stepped around it.

The bathroom was empty. The janitor's cart sat in the middle, stocked with cleaning supplies, rolls of toilet paper, stacks of paper towels. He glanced briefly at himself in the mirror, saw his wispy red hair, his wide hips and narrow shoulders, his small features. His ID tag still hung around his neck. At least they hadn't taken *that* away from him. He went into the last stall and locked the door.

The coolness of the tile and the echoing silence were comforting. He sat down on the toilet and put his head in his lap. His hands opened and closed. *Now what?* he thought.

What? What? What? What?

The floor was still wet, drying in places. Under the door, he could see the swipes the mop had made. He bent to retie his shoelace. He looked at his hands, his short, pointed fingers. His wife, he thought. Vanessa, her daughter. Waller. He smelled the disinfectant. The liquid soap in the containers near the sinks, the deodorant that measured itself into the toilets with each flush.

Though he couldn't seem to finish a thought, something was forming in his mind.

When the toilet got uncomfortable he unlocked the door and stepped outside. He went to the cart and examined the bottles on the second shelf. Unscrewed a lid, took a deep sniff, recoiled when it burned his nostrils and throat. He glanced at himself holding the bottle, then replaced the lid, put the bottle back.

Finally he took an armful of toilet paper and went to each stall, dropping three rolls into each toilet. When he left, the sound of flushing was like Niagara Falls. Walking through the terminal on his way to the exit, he imagined the choke and spray of water, the dramatic splash as the toilets brimmed and overflowed.

3 Jewell Wylie stuck a broomstick into the garbage disposal and thrust sharply as if she were harpooning fish, or churning butter. Tall and big-boned, wearing denim overalls, and with a thick brown braid that hung between her shoulder blades, she could have been a farm girl except for the silver hoops in her right nostril and left eyebrow, and the poker-chip-sized tattoo of a starburst on the back of her neck.

Breakfast trays rode the conveyer belt through the window in the wall, paraded jerkily in front of her, turned the corner, and piled up on the stainless-steel counter where the belt ended. The gutter was almost overflowing. Jewell cursed and gave one last jab with the broomstick. She held her breath and flipped the switch. The disposal groaned, and for a minute she thought it was going to spin free. When she smelled the motor overheating, she shut it off, leaned against the counter, and watched the water rise higher. Trays crashed into each other, tipping over glasses that rolled across the counter and fell into the gutter. A mess, out of control, just like her life. She set the broomstick down and pushed up her right sleeve.

What she was going to do was strictly forbidden: a sign near the switch said so. She plunged her hand into the tepid water, through the flotsam of wet napkins and soggy toast, until she felt the blades of the disposal. They were powerful, industrial strength, made to chew through bones and flesh. She'd seen what they could do to a spoon. Wincing, she stretched down as far as she could, until the backed-up water reached her armpit. Something sharp, with three prongs, was wedged against the blades. She pried at whatever it was, thinking that if the disposal went on now, that would be it. She closed her eyes, gave one last wrench, and the thing came free. It was a pork-chop bone from last night's dinner, soggy from the water, looking as if it had been gnawed by a dog.

She flipped the switch and the disposal churned, making a sucking sound. Trays came in hot and heavy. Jewell worked frantically, flipping the glasses and cups upside down into wire racks as orange juice, milk, and coffee flew in all directions. Big splashes of disinfectant sloshed out of the bucket as she tossed in handfuls of silverware. She blasted the dishes with the spray from an overhead flex. Scrambled eggs, pieces of pancake, swollen puffs of cereal, and sausage stubs floated down the trough to the disposal, which devoured them with a greedy gurgle. Jewell cursed. The stacks of dishes on the counter grew; the trays came in faster. Just before eleven, the rush came. Students in the dining room started stacking the trays on top of each other so that they came through the window in double-deck piles, sliding and falling, glasses rolling across the counter and exploding on the floor.

"Assholes!" Jewell yelled. "Jerks!"

She picked up a bowl and hurled it against the far wall where it shattered in a spray of thick white shards. Her arms were sticky with pancake syrup and orange juice; water ran off her face and apron. The spoiled brats, sitting on their cans while someone else did their dishes. Jewell jerked down the flex and blasted the spray out the window. There was a chorus of screams, some shouted curses.

"Read the fucking sign! Don't stack the trays!" Jewell yelled as she unleashed one last torrent to reinforce the message.

When the rush was over, the dish room was a wreck. Jewell's overalls were soaked from her neck to her knees; her high-top sneakers squelched when she walked. Still, she hadn't thought about Celeste for a good twenty minutes. That was something.

The relief didn't last long, though. As she got the squeegee mop and pushed the milky water toward the drain in the middle of the floor, the familiar hollow feeling filled her stomach again. She felt seasick. Her joints went cold and loose. She and Celeste had bickered that morning as soon as they woke up. It was the same old thing: Celeste's ex-girlfriend and the four-year-old girl the two of them were raising together. Jewell clenched her teeth as she bent to sweep the soggy napkins and broken dishes into the metal dustpan. She had never been the jealous type, until she met Celeste. Then it had sneaked up on her and clobbered her over the head. Now it ravaged her like a disease.

Keep busy, she told herself. She wiped down the counters and loaded the racks of glasses into the dish machine. The clock on the back wall where the plastic aprons hung said 11:15. Fifteen minutes until her shift was over, forty-five until her class. The dish machine belched a cloud of greasy, sugar-laden steam. "This isn't working," Celeste had said at the end of their argument, and Jewell knew it was true. The trouble was, the more hopeless the whole thing seemed, the more overpowering was the love she felt for Celeste. How twisted was that? Before her own eyes she'd become a jerk, a psycho. Always listening, watching for clues. On the alert for anything suspicious: the way Celeste chewed her bottom lip when she thought no one was looking, the way she carried the phone into the bedroom when Dana, her ex, called. There were plenty of signs, and they were everywhere.

Jewell was sorting the silverware into canisters when her phone rang. She fished it out of the front pocket of her overalls and watched the last few trays wobble in on the belt while she listened to Celeste explain that childcare for Rachel had fallen through that afternoon and that she and Dana had a meeting at Rachel's school that they just couldn't miss. Was there any chance that Jewell could pick Rachel up and watch her, just for a few hours?

"I was going to work on my project this afternoon," Jewell said. "It's due in less than two weeks and I'm really behind."

"I know, baby. I thought maybe you could put her down for a

nap and work while she's there. It's a real favor, I know. I wouldn't even ask you except—"

Jewell tried to ignore the words and just listen to the sound of Celeste's voice. She pictured Celeste at her desk, calling while the fifth-graders she taught were at recess. They had met at a party where Jewell hadn't known anyone. She had just wedged herself into an out-of-the-way corner, when Celeste had come in the door talking and laughing with a group of friends. She had walked straight to where Jewell was sitting, bent down, and said, "You're in my seat." She had reminded Jewell of the famous picture of Anne Frank: the same large, dark eyes, the same quizzical expression. They had whispered to each other all evening. Two days later they ran into each other in the toothpaste aisle at Rite Aid. "You again," Celeste had said. Jewell began to believe in fate.

"Can't Dana find anybody else to watch her?" Jewell asked. She hated even to say Dana's name.

"No, she wasn't able to," Celeste answered with conspicuous restraint.

Jewell sighed. "I'm at work, you know. I have class in a half hour."

"I know. I'm sorry. If it's too much trouble, it's okay. I'll just—"

"No, it's okay," Jewell said before Celeste could finish. "I'll pick her up on my way home."

Out in the serving bay a cook was cleaning the grill and breaking down the steam table. In the kitchen, another cook pulled metal pans of lasagna from huge ovens. Jewell had worked in the cafeteria since she started college four years ago; the lonesome smell of food cooked in too-large quantities was like home. She loaded a plate with sausage, eggs, and French toast and headed for the dining room.

Jewell's buddy Eli was eating and reading the paper at a table near the windows. He waved her over to the chair opposite him.

"How're you doing?" he asked.

Jewell shrugged and sat down.

Eli was probably the only student who put in more hours at the cafeteria than Jewell. He was Samoan, with rippled black hair that he wore in a ponytail. A second, sparser ponytail dangled from his chin. His big head and huge torso made him seem tall until he stood up, then you realized he was short. He always worked the pot room, the assignment all the other students in the cafeteria avoided because it meant leaning over a Jacuzzi-size vat of hot, greasy suds. Eli didn't mind. He scrubbed away on cookie sheets, baking pans, and mixing bowls while he listened to his Walkman and let sweat pour off his arms and face.

He and Jewell both worked full-time every summer, so they'd spent a lot of time together. They'd delivered coffee and doughnuts to seminar rooms in the morning, cheese and crackers in the after-noons. They'd flipped burgers at beach parties for incoming fresh-men, made thousands of sandwiches for the cheerleading camps that were housed in the dorms when classes weren't in session, drove the catering van all over town on university-related business. The two of them had a lot in common. Both were paying their own way through college. Both their fathers had spent time in prison. Neither of them could sit still. They shared the same dark humor, a love of kung-fu movies, and enormous appetites. Which was why Eli didn't blink while Jewell quickly demolished her heap-ing plate of food, then reached across the table for the tower of toast he'd stacked next to his own overflowing plate.

"How's your uptight girlfriend?" he asked.

Jewell held her napkin to her mouth. To her surprise, her eyes filled with tears.

"Uh-oh. Wrong question," Eli said.

Jewell grinned miserably and forced herself to talk. "I don't know. Things are messed up, I guess. It's mostly her ex-girlfriend. They're always talking on the phone, you know. Discussing Rachel, their kid. Making arrangements, dropping her off. Who's going to do this and who's going to do that. Maybe I'm paranoid, but I feel like something's going on. I mean, I know they have this kid and

all, but really." She searched Eli's face, embarrassed but also relieved to be talking. "I feel like there's still something between the
two of them. Like it never really ended."

Eli nodded. Jewell could tell he was freaked out that she was on
the verge of tears; she was usually so tough. He'd seen her go
through no small number of lovers over the past several years.
With the others, men and women both, Jewell had been more
than ready to move on when the time came, but it was different
with Celeste.

"You going to drink that?" Eli said, pointing to one of the four
glasses of milk she had lined up on her tray.

She pushed one toward him. He drained it solemnly, as if he
were downing a shot of whiskey to calm his nerves. "How long
have you and Celeste been together?" he asked, not bothering to
wipe the milk from his upper lip.

"About a year and a half."

Eli raised his eyebrows. "And how long was she with her girl—
the other woman?"

Jewell drank one of the glasses of milk herself. She felt relieved
yet nervous, as though she'd finally made a doctor's appointment
about an ailment she'd been ignoring.

"Four years," she said.

She leaned forward, eager for Eli's reply. He fingered the straggly hairs on his chin.

"I'm in over my head," Jewell prompted, since Eli didn't seem
to know what to say. "I don't know what it is about Celeste. I've
just never felt like this before. I keep making an ass out of myself.
Even *I* hate myself. I know I should just get out of there, but I
can't. I just can't see leaving."

Eli tugged so hard on his stringy beard that his chin stretched
like putty. "Celeste's a little self-centered," he said. "I don't think
she appreciates you."

"Really, you think so?"

Eli nodded solemnly. "Yeah, I do."

Jewell chewed her lips. How could she explain how wonderful it felt just to be in Celeste's presence, to watch her move and speak? What a miracle that they actually *lived* together, that Celeste came home every night and woke next to Jewell every morning?

"You're right, it's fucked up," Jewell said. She pushed one of the two remaining milk glasses toward him and took the other herself. "Cheers," she said grimly.

They clanged glasses and shot back the milk. "What's new in the news?" Jewell said, nodding toward the newspaper that was folded beside Eli's tray. "Read me something distracting."

"A big storm's supposed to move in tonight," Eli said, visibly grateful that the heavy part of their conversation was over. "The storm door is open and a series of systems is lined up across the Pacific."

He turned a few pages, reading to himself, while Jewell watched a student from the next shift wheel out a big bowl of fresh fruit for lunch.

"There was trouble out at the airport again yesterday," Eli said. "They had to close down a whole terminal."

"What happened?"

"Metal detector was unplugged and nobody knew it. Bunch of people went through before they figured it out, then they had to ground some planes because there were people on them who'd walked through without getting screened." Eli shook his head and smiled like the whole thing delighted him. "Big mess," he added. "People going crazy."

"My uncle works out at the airport," Jewell said absently.

"He a pilot?"

She laughed. "This is *my* family, remember? He's a bartender. Works one of the bars out there." She reached across and stabbed one of the extra sausages Eli had piled on a saucer. "What are you looking at?"

"Nothing. Just watching you eat."

"Why?"

"No reason. I just like to watch you pack it in."

She put the whole sausage in her mouth and grinned at him while she chewed.

"Impressive," Eli said.

"Thanks."

"I'll tell you what, all this tightened security is a bunch of shit," he said, turning back to the paper. "It's not going to do a damn bit of good. You watch. Something's going to happen. They're laying people off right and left, things like that. Well, it isn't so simple. You pull something loose over here, something else is going to give over there. It's all connected. Little things you don't see." He speared a sausage himself and chewed ferociously.

Jewell gazed vaguely over Eli's shoulder, out the window where students were passing on their way to class. "I think my dad's out now," she commented, switching gears without warning.

"Huh?"

"My dad. I think they released him. I think he's supposed to be out by now."

Eli nodded. Jewell didn't need to explain to him, since he, too, had complicated family connections as a result of several generations of wild and wayward hearts. Jewell had half-siblings she barely knew, more stepmothers and pseudo-uncles than she could remember, and a huge cast of indeterminate relatives who had played nothing but brief walk-on parts in her life. It was one of the things that Celeste, who came from a big but tightly-knit clan of Argentinean Jews, couldn't understand. Eli didn't blink an eye, though. He was living with his mother, his three young half-sisters, and the girls' aunt. His own father had spent the last eleven years in a Texas prison for assaulting a police officer.

"You going to see him?" Eli asked.

"Ah, jeez. I don't know." Jewell was her father's oldest, born when he was twenty-one, the same age she was now. "Probably not. It's been years since I've seen him. I have some good memories of him from a long time ago, but he's basically a fuckup. Probably by the time I got around to connecting with him he'd be back in jail anyway."

Eli used the last piece of toast to swab his plate clean. "You know how to get in touch with him if you decide you want to see him?" he asked before shoving the toast in his mouth.

"I guess I could call my uncle. He usually stays in touch with him."

"The same uncle who works at the airport?"

"Yeah, the same one. He's my half-uncle really. He and my dad have the same father, but my dad's a lot younger. They weren't brought up together. I think my uncle just bails my dad out of trouble every now and then."

"Doors are opening!" the cashier shouted from the front of the dining room. She unlocked the doors that had been closed after the breakfast shift, and a mob of students stampeded in.

"Animals," Eli said, shaking his head. "You going to class?"

"I don't think so. I need to work on my final project. Plus I have to pick up Celeste's kid this afternoon."

"What? Are you kidding?"

She smiled broadly. "Nope, we're one big happy family. Anything to help."

4

Logan Wylie didn't like the sound of the new ping his beat-up Toyota was making as he headed east on the Pasadena Freeway toward the San Gabriel Mountains. He backed off the gas, listened, stepped on it, listened again. Plus he was almost out of gas. He did a quick calculation of how much money he *should* have by the end of the week and figured, real fast, that he was going to come up short. Even if the engine *didn't* need work, which was unlikely considering it had over two hundred thousand miles on it and was burning oil like a motherfucker.

Still, it was a beautiful day. One of those late-fall mornings that could have been spring, the air was so bright and transparent. Everything sparkled. No smog at all. It was so clear the mountains rose up: right there. You could see all the details: the rivulets and canyons creasing the broad shoulders, the dark green scrub and white boulders. To the west, the city spread flat to the coast, the square blocks cut by the wider roads, all the buildings white and clean in this light. Even the fucking freeway looked beautiful, winding through the trees. Logan felt good.

Traffic was light. He passed a slow-moving pickup loaded with rakes, lawnmowers, and leaf blowers. Probably headed for the same ritzy San Marino neighborhood he was. He checked his watch, saw that his timing was perfect. His problem, he told himself, was that he was always getting sidetracked. Too much in the moment, which could be a good thing if you didn't take it to extremes. But everything interested him, got his attention. Always had, from the time he was a little boy. People and things, they just grabbed him. Which was why it was hard to keep his mind on track. Stick with the program. Stay clean, stay sober, one day at a time. Get a plan and stick to it. That's what he was working on.

The phone in the pocket of his jacket rang the first four notes of Beethoven's Fifth. For a minute he was flummoxed; he'd forgotten about this latest perk from the Salvettis, the client where he was headed. They needed to be able to get in touch with him if there was a problem. He fumbled with the buttons, his truck swerving as he steered with one hand. The phone kept ringing. He thought whoever had called him would hang up by the time he found the right button, but they were still there, breathing into the open line when he answered.

"Hello?" he said again. He felt the person waiting on the other end. A smartass, then, or somebody trying to trace him. Could they put a trace on a cell phone? Just when he was about to ask who the hell was calling, the person hung up. He drove for a while with the phone in his hand, disappointed.

The wind was picking up; the tall palms up ahead nodded and tossed. A bank of clouds sat offshore, blanketing the horizon. No reason he couldn't call someone himself. He'd spent an evening programming numbers on the speed-dial; now he just had to remember who was which number. The Salvettis were number one, that much he remembered. It was only fair, since they'd given him the phone. Two and three were his brother, at home and at work, though he didn't remember which was which. He'd programmed in his oldest daughter, a student at UCLA, as well as his second wife, who lived in Orange County with his son Stephen. His first wife lived in Northern California; she probably didn't even *have* a phone. His third wife was in rehab; he didn't have the number, not that he'd call her if he did. The kids he'd had with her, Tony and Heather, lived with their grandparents, her folks. He'd programmed his lawyer, his case officer, and the pizza joint down the street from the residence hotel where he was staying. Since that still didn't take up many spaces, he'd put in the weather and the time. He'd written down the names and corresponding numbers on a slip of paper at home, but it didn't do him any good now.

Logan eyed the gas gauge, the dented dash, the dirty windshield. He'd have to hit somebody up for a little advance, but who? He took a chance and pressed number three, listened to the phone ring five times before it picked up.

"Tommy?"

"Yeah, who's this?"

Logan could hear voices in the background. Glasses clinking, someone talking over a loudspeaker.

"It's me, man. Your bro. How you doing?"

"Hey, Logan. What's up?"

Logan heard the caution in his brother's voice. The problem with Tommy was he was so damn suspicious. Maybe because he was the oldest kid, but he was always expecting the worst. It'd been Tommy who'd picked Logan up from the facility when he was released two months ago, who'd driven him over to pick up his truck where it'd been parked all that time, and who'd set him up at the residence hotel.

"Nothing, man," Logan said. "Just tooling around. Thought I'd call up and say hi. Give my cell phone a little test drive. I'm heading up to San Marino for a job. Great day! I was just thinking about you, wondering what was up."

"That's twelve-fifty," Tommy said.

"What?"

"Hold on a sec," Tommy said. Logan heard him thank someone, heard water run and change rattle together.

"Okay," Tommy said when he came back to the phone. "What were you saying?"

"Well, I was just thinking how I need a plan," Logan replied. "How I need to find something and stick to it. Take a class or something. Maybe learn to repair something like copy machines or refrigerators, you know. Then I can save up and maybe move out of here, get a place in the foothills like I always wanted. I'm thirty-nine, man. Guess it's time to decide what I want to be when I grow up. What do you think?"

After a silence Tommy said, "Listen, Logan. I'm at work. Is everything okay?"

"Everything's fine, man. I just wanted to check in with you."

The phone broke up so that Tommy's voice was chopped off, like someone was playing with the button of a walkie-talkie. Logan only caught a few words. "You're not coming in," he shouted into the phone. "I can't hear you." His truck swerved. The car in the next lane honked.

"Call me later," Tommy said before his voice drowned in an ocean of static.

Logan tossed the phone onto the seat next to him. Tommy could be a good guy, but he could also be a dick. Self-absorbed, always worried about something. He tended to ride your ass, even though his own life had been far from perfect. Being a bartender in an airport wasn't exactly the pinnacle of success. Better not to rely on him too much. Logan gave himself a pep talk: get on your feet, get some money together, straighten things out. Take one day at a time, make all the appointments, go to the meetings. Stay clean. Stay on track. Keep your eye on the prize.

His exit came up and he curved off the freeway, onto the empty, quiet streets of San Marino. Jeez Louise, these people had money. The mansions were set far back from the street, their massive yards perfectly manicured by armies of Mexican gardeners. Logan checked out the tile roofs, the gated entrances, the expensive cars resting in the driveways. Everything cool, quiet, relaxed. That was the life.

The cleaning woman answered the door, gave him a look. Who was she to act like she owned the place, like she knew he was up to no good? Everything about this gig was just like the fucking movies. The fancy house, the maid, the frustrated wife, the rich but impotent husband. More than impotent, since the poor bastard couldn't move anything from the neck down. Logan fit in perfectly: the handsome con, the grifter on the make. Although he wasn't, really. Couldn't afford to be, though it sure was tempting.

"Wait here," the cleaning woman said. She'd been buffing the floor of the huge entryway. The tile was the creamy beige of pulled taffy, each one shiny and spotless. She frowned, like she thought he'd pocket something the minute her back was turned. He watched her short, squat body as she headed up the wide stairway.

Floor-to-ceiling windows opened to the garden, lush with banana trees, birds of paradise, jacarandas. The house was Spanish style, with open-beam ceilings, sparse furniture, area rugs in muted colors, big ceramic vases full of fresh flowers. Not bouquets of carnations or roses, but the fancy kinds of arrangements rich people had: huge things with bare branches and moss, flowers Logan had never seen before. Everything was spotlessly clean. After being locked up, the silence and the good smells were heaven. Even now, in the residence hotel, he got sick of other people's noises, of the looks they gave him and the smell of their bodies. If he lived here, he'd spend about three weeks just walking from room to room. He'd sit on the patio, take a cruise in the Jag, spend an evening by the fireplace. At night he'd lie down in one of the big beds upstairs and listen to the silence.

"She come down," the cleaning woman said. She started waxing again, ignoring Logan. Her husband, who did the yard work, was a lot friendlier. Fuck her. Logan cruised straight into the living room and sat down on a leather couch the color of buttery caramel.

Still, Logan wouldn't change places with the guy upstairs, Mr. Salvetti, for anything. Sure, the guy was loaded, but what good did it do him? His wife had explained: something had fallen on him at one of his construction sites, had severed his spine. The poor bastard couldn't feed himself, button his shirt, work the TV remote. Unlike Logan, he couldn't open a beer, play with his own dick, raise his finger to ask the waitress for a refill of coffee. He couldn't get up before dawn and head for the desert, couldn't throw down his sleeping bag and look up at the wide black sky and streaks of stars. Which was exactly what Logan had done as soon as he was released. Two days, just him and the coyotes. Nope, all Salvetti could do was lie on his back and stare at the ceiling.

"Logan, hello," Mrs. Salvetti said, sweeping into the room. She was looking a little rough that morning, but not bad. Not bad at all. Her white-blond hair was still damp, brushed back from her face. She reminded Logan of a greyhound, with her narrow face and sharp nose, the high-strung way she moved. She was thin the way a lot of rich women were, like she lived on salad and bottled water. Tan, with a jangle of gold bracelets on each wrist. Her eyes were a light, watery green.

It wasn't his imagination. She wanted him in the worst way.

"Everything's getting off to a late start this morning, I'm afraid," she said, smoothing back her hair. "Danny had a bad night and we had a crisis in the kitchen. Raccoons got in and ransacked all the cupboards. Christina spent the whole morning cleaning it up. And I have to be at an appointment in a half hour."

She looked nervously around the room, as if something else might go haywire. Finally her eyes rested on Logan, who had risen from the couch and stood with his hands in his pockets, smiling. She smiled back. "And how are you?" she said, touching him on the shoulder. "Can I get you anything?"

"I'm just fine."

Yep, she wanted it. Logan was used to it. All his life he'd been like that, catnip to the ladies. Despite all the speed he'd done, the time he'd spent inside, the week-long binges, he still had a fresh, boyish look. Maybe a few extra crinkles around the eyes and a crease or two down his cheeks, but that only added some spice. He'd never worked out a day in his life, but he had an athlete's build: broad shoulders, full chest, narrow hips. He looked cuddly, ready for fun. Women wanted to dress him in something soft and hide him in their rooms. And this one, Sylvia Salvetti, was no exception. Logan could see it in her eyes. She was just itching to get him all squeaky clean and good-smelling in her sunk-in whirlpool tub. Then she wanted him to climb between her 600-thread-count sheets and really put it to her. Uh-huh. Which he wouldn't mind doing, only it could get messy. Stay focused, he reminded himself. Eye on the prize.

"Well, let's go on up," she said. "Danny will be wondering what happened to us."

Logan walked in the contrail of her perfume as she led him up the stairs. Something floral, jasmine or gardenia. He eyed her butt, which swayed from side to side as she took the steps. Skinny, but not bad.

"I'm going to leave it to you," she said, motioning to the open door of her husband's bedroom when they reached the landing. "I've got to finish getting ready so I can get out of here."

"Sure, don't worry," Logan said. "We'll be fine. I'll see you to-morrow morning, then."

"Right. Do you have everything you need?"

Logan remembered his empty gas tank. If he didn't bring him-self to ask now, he'd be in a fix. But how could he? It wouldn't look good to admit he didn't have five bucks to put gas in his car. But it wouldn't look good not to show up at all, either, because he'd run out of gas. He'd be lucky if he even made it home. Sylvia watched him, waiting for him to answer. Friday, she paid him on Friday. Three more days.

She glanced at his crotch. Real fast, but he caught it.

"Everything's fine," he said. "Go ahead."

Salvetti's head was turned toward the door when Logan walked in. His body was hidden under the blankets.

"Good morning, how're you doing?" Logan said.

He was getting the hang of it. *Pancake flipping,* the guys at the residence hotel called it. Three or four of them did it for a living. They were the ones who'd turned Logan on to the job, who'd given him the name of the agency that had set him up with Salvetti and two others.

Logan didn't know why, but Salvetti couldn't talk, at least not in a way you could understand. Maybe he got hit on the head in the accident, too. It wasn't right to ask. Still, he made a sound that Logan understood as a greeting and nodded his head several times.

"Okay, I read your horoscope this morning and it said a bath's in the stars for you. We're going to get you all spiffed up, put on some clean drawers, and sit you up. Your missus had to go out. Did she tell you that?"

Salvetti's dark eyes followed Logan as he got ready to take him into the bathroom. Talking made things easier, Logan had found. At first the whole job had freaked him out, dealing with these guys. It was so personal, touching their bodies and all, seeing to their needs. Then he got to know them better and he loosened up a little. Now he pretty much just let his mouth go on automatic pilot, and the time went fast. The pay was shit and he wouldn't want to spend the rest of his life doing it, but right now it was better than nothing.

"Okay, you know what? Today I'm just going to carry you in there. We'll skip the wheelchair thing. I ate my Wheaties this morning and it'll save a little time. That okay? You all right with that?"

He pulled back the blankets and took off Salvetti's pajamas, careful with his arms and legs, which had pulled up around his body like a baby's. Salvetti kept his eyes on Logan's face as he lifted him, as his body slumped limply against Logan's chest. Logan wondered if Salvetti had his suspicions, if he thought Logan was already giving it to his wife. Or maybe the other guy was doing it, the guy who came at night and put Salvetti to bed. It was funny, but Logan felt jealous of him, even though he'd never met him. It occurred to Logan that Salvetti might not care if he was doing his wife, that he might even pay him to keep her happy. Wouldn't that be a sweet gig?

First the toilet routine, then the shower. "You're the best, you know it?" Logan said as he wiped Salvetti's ass. "This other guy I work for, he's in a chair, too, you know. Can't do much for himself. He's always trying to get me to do other stuff. Mop his damn floor, go get groceries. I keep telling him that isn't my job, but he keeps trying. He thinks I'm fucking around if I'm not working my ass off the whole time I'm there. Dude doesn't even pay me himself, government does. Those are always the guys, you know? The ones who act like *you're* the one leeching off the system. Know what I mean?"

If he did, Salvetti couldn't show it, since Logan had his head under his arm. He lifted him off the toilet and put him in the contraption they had in the shower. "Whereas you, you're a real class act," he said as he adjusted the temperature of the water. "This place, man. It's really something. I come here and I feel like I'm in a museum. It's so peaceful, and everything is really tasteful. I love the garden. That fountain is a killer. I told some of the guys where I'm staying about that and they just tripped. When I get some money, I'm going to remember that. I'm going to have a big fountain like yours because the sound of that water, you just can't beat it. When I wake up at night, I want to hear it, spattering away out there. Man, I bet you have the best dreams in the world listening to that."

The last thing he washed was Salvetti's face. It was funny, but of all the things Logan did, this was the hardest. It reminded him of when he was a kid, the smell of the Ivory soap and the warmth of the washcloth while his mother ran it tenderly over his nose and eyes, behind his ears, on the back of his neck. He felt her love. He'd never done it for his own kids, God knew why. Salvetti closed his eyes while Logan soaped up the rag, then gently bathed his face. It was the look in Salvetti's eyes when he opened them. Trusting, like a kid.

"That's it, buddy," Logan said. "You're all set."

It had to be tough for a guy who was used to telling everyone what to do to be like this now, Logan thought as he dressed Salvetti in the clothes his wife had laid out for him. Or maybe not, maybe it was a relief. Logan set him in his chair, adjusted the straps, opened the curtains, put on his socks. He wondered about the cleaning woman, if she was still downstairs. Too bad Salvetti wasn't holding the purse strings anymore, because it would have been pretty easy to hit him up for a little cash advance.

"You take it easy now," Logan said. Salvetti mumbled a thank-you. Logan closed the door and stood out on the landing, listening.

There was no one else upstairs, he was sure of it. He leaned over the railing and saw that Christina had finished in the entryway.

He didn't need much. Just a few bucks. Just enough to fill his tank, to get him to his gigs until Friday, when he'd be home free. What good would it do him to lose his jobs, shitty as they were? If he took a few bucks now he could keep his jobs, so in a way it was preventing him from resorting to more drastic means later. There was bound to be something lying around somewhere.

Sylvia's room was at the end of the hall. If he got caught, he could say that it seemed like Salvetti was trying to tell him to go in there and get something from her room. Logan walked quietly, swiftly, and knocked softly on the door. It was open a crack. He pushed it farther and peered inside. He'd never seen such a big bedroom. Huge windows, a sofa, even a round table in the middle of the room. The bed was a king, but the room was so big it didn't seem to take up much space. Clothes tossed everywhere. A big TV on a cabinet, videos thrown around on the unmade bed. Little Sylvia wasn't too tidy. Her smell wafted out, flowers in a rainstorm.

On the bedside table an arsenal of little brown vials.

Logan forgot about the cash. The drugs would bring a fair amount of money and be a little fun to boot. She was bound to have something good. He could take a few pills from each bottle, she'd never know. Which reminded him to check the bathroom. He could see it through a half-open door on the far side of the room. Marble walls, glass bricks, gleaming chrome. A mighty whirlpool, just like he'd thought.

He wished he knew where Christina was. Walk away, he told himself. Just turn around and leave. But it was so easy, the pills sitting there. Just a few. The old excitement was back, irresistible. In and out, he told himself. With a quick detour to the bathroom.

The plush carpet muffled his steps. Jesus! He couldn't believe he was doing this! Still, only a few more steps. But if someone came in! Quick, just grab them and run. Eureka! He could see the labels: Vicodin, Nembutol, Percocet.

He reached for them, and his phone rang. Logan almost

jumped out of his skin. He panicked, fumbled in his pocket. Shit! He had to get out of there. He left the bottles, rushed to the door.

Once he was on the landing, he came to his senses. Ludwig von! He laughed. What had he been *thinking*? He pulled Sylvia's door closed and walked quickly back past Salvetti's room. By the time he answered the phone, he was halfway down the stairs.

"Hey, it works," said his brother's voice.

Only then did Logan realize his heart was racing. He'd been so close, *so close.* "What works?" he said.

"Star-69. You punch it and get the last person who called you."

"Oh yeah? I'll have to remember that."

Logan reached the door. He hadn't done it. Eyes *still* on the prize. Now he was overjoyed, thrilled. What a lucky, lucky break.

"Listen, Logan. Sorry I couldn't talk before. Things quieted down a little, so I have a minute. I wanted to tell you, they need a greeter tonight if you want the job. Just meet these bigwigs at their gate and drive them to their hotel. You up for it?"

"You bet your ass, man. Can they pay me right away?"

"Cash, baby. On the spot. I can tell you where to pick up the car."

"Wow," Logan said with a laugh. "What do you know?"

The wind had picked up when Logan stepped outside. The trees made a rushing sound. He folded the phone and put it in his pocket.

Like the movies, he thought. Just like the fucking movies.

5

Inez Cullen stepped out onto her front porch, looked down the street for maybe the twentieth time that morning, and saw nothing. Just the wide black asphalt, the cars parked along the curb, the faded stucco of the crackerbox houses.

The rep said she'd drop the shipment off before noon. Inez was all set up: she'd cleared off the dinner table, taken out the bags, organized the orders she had collected over the past two weeks, readied her stapler and pens. Minutes dragged by. The street was quiet. The only people home at this hour were old Mrs. Thompson, two houses down, who put bleach bottles on her lawn to keep the dogs away, and the loudmouth white girl on the corner who'd just had another baby. The later the rep came, the less time Inez would have to get out there and deliver before Vanessa got home from school.

She shut the door and walked into the kitchen. She'd have to hurry with dinner once she got back, since Rudy liked it on the table as soon as he got home. She pressed her finger into the pound of ground chuck that was thawing on the counter. Still frozen. Delivery days always made her nervous. There was no way Rudy would find out, but she always worried. What if he got sick, came home unexpectedly, and found her like that, with everything spread out all over the place? Or while she was out, dropping off orders? Maybe she should put everything back until the shipment came. She gathered up the bags and orders and put them back in the cedar chest in Vanessa's room.

No use wasting time. Even though she'd cleaned the bathroom the day before, she went back and sprinkled cleanser in the sink and toilet. *God helps those who help themselves,* she thought as she scrubbed around the faucet and drain. Was that from the Bible, or just some saying? *Ask and you will receive.* The hot water handle leaked, weeping an orange stain down the side of the sink. *Knock and the door will open.* One of Vanessa's long, shiny hairs caught in the sponge Inez was using. She pulled it loose and examined it closely: the little bead of root at one end, the miracle of its molecules strung together. She wondered about her daughter, what she was doing at this exact moment. She pictured her sitting in class, her hands folded on her desk, her legs crossed at the ankle, her thick hair pushed back with a headband, hanging in a curve across her back.

She started on the toilet, scrubbing under the rim with the brush, plunging it in the water. *God will not give you a heavier burden than you can bear. God has a plan for you. Turn your life over to God.* Human will was a strong and devious thing. You always had to be on guard. She knew from experience, because her whole life she'd fought to have faith, to trust God, not to question His ways. But a part of her was always worrying, thinking, planning. Trying to figure things out. To decide what was best. What she should do. *Show me your will,* she prayed as she wiped the toilet seat with the sponge. Rudy never put it down when he was finished. *Please light my path.*

She straightened the towels. The day she got married, as she was walking down the aisle, she'd had a vision. A voice had spoken to her, as plain as day. *You're making a mistake.* But by then it was too late. She had thought she was doing God's will, that it was *His* plan that she and Rudy should marry. She kept it to herself as long as she could, hoping things would change, but not long after their first anniversary, it had exploded out of her one night as she watched Rudy step into his pajamas, his pink foot pointed as it slipped through the cuff.

"Rudy, something's wrong. I'm not happy."

He had pulled his pajamas over his underwear, had snapped the elastic around his wide waist. She had looked at the ring of long hairs around his bellybutton, at his tender-looking nipples. She had thought she would get used to him, but instead he got stranger as time went on: the way he slept on the very edge of the bed, his back to her; the way he always wanted the same thing, a hamburger and French fries, for dinner; the formal way he talked to her, even now—as if they'd just met.

"Happiness is overrated," he had said. "That's not what we're here for."

Something got the better of her then. His lies, the way he had misled her. How he had promised her countless things, but instead it was just this: a falling-down house that wasn't even theirs. The two tiny bedrooms. The kitchen with its scratched metal cupboards. The chewed-up linoleum and chipped counters, the dirt and mess left by all the people who'd come and gone, not caring. She wanted her own, something different. Better.

"I made a mistake," she said. "I want to leave."

She didn't know what he would do. She sat still on the edge of the bed while he walked over to her, put his hands around her throat. His thumbs pressed on either side of her windpipe. She froze, keeping her eyes fastened on the hairs inside his nose. They moved as he panted, quivered like leaves in a breeze.

"Don't you ever, ever leave me," he whispered close to her ear. "Don't even think about it. And don't you dare mention it, ever again."

Things got worse after that. Much worse. She felt Rudy's hatred growing day by day and with it her fear, but also her determination. She prayed, asking for direction. That's when her plan began to take shape. *For every one who asks receives.* And sure enough, God showed her. Because it was at the church that she met Clara Rice, who told her about Avon, who said she could get her own route and make her own money. Which she'd been saving for almost two years now in an envelope tucked beneath blankets at the bottom of the cedar chest. The one thing in the house that locked.

God's plan, not hers. All she had to do was wait, watch, listen. In the meantime, on the surface, everything went on as it had before. Like Rudy said, she never mentioned leaving him again.

Where *was* that woman? Inez drifted back to the living room and lifted the curtain one more time. No one on the porch. No one on the street. The television gave her a milky stare, like an eye clouded with cataract. When she was little, she thought the people on the screen lived inside the television and watched her go about her business just as she watched them go about theirs. She crossed the room, turned the set on, and flipped through the channels. There was the courtroom show, where you could tell people were lying through their teeth. The talk show where people hit each other over the head with chairs. Inez paused. A woman with bangs plastered to her forehead in little curlicues was complaining that her mother-in-law barged into her house whenever she felt like it, without even knocking. *Who Wants to Be a Millionaire?*, *The Young and the Restless.* Then commercials, lots of commercials. Which meant that it must be almost noon. Clara Rice was late. The news came on; Beth Fong announced that a storm would hit late that night, details to follow. But just as she was ready to move to the next story, the screen went blank.

Inez gave a puzzled frown. Static buzzed and a white bar rolled up the screen from the bottom to the top. A purple background flashed on. Inez's scalp prickled. A line of type inched its way across the bottom of the screen. What was happening? Inez fiddled with the remote, trying to increase the volume, but there were no words, only a menacing electronic tone.

She squinted at the type, trying to make out the message. PRO-GRAM INTERRUPTED . . . she read with rising alarm. EMERGENCY BROADCAST SYSTEM . . . PLEASE STAND BY.

6

Rudy stumbled on a grate in the airport's employee parking lot. He paused a minute, resting his hand on the fender of a yellow Jeep as he looked out over the sea of cars. He rubbed his eyes. Where the hell had he parked? It seemed like he'd been wandering here forever, up and down the rows, the black asphalt and the yellow lines pulsing up in his face. Jets roared overhead, landing gear dangling and wing flaps down. Rudy cursed Waller. That fucking son of a bitch. The asshole motherfucker. What a pathetic loser, hanging out in his flunky job so long he'd managed to get a little power over other people. And look how he used it! Brown-nosing the higher-ups by firing Rudy. Sucking ass to the Latashas and the Pilars and the Trinhs. The cocksucker. The fat, butt-licking deadbeat. The thought of Waller's hairy knuckles and livery lips turned Rudy's stomach.

Was that his car down at the end of the row, sticking out behind the pickup with the camper shell? Rudy dragged himself forward. God, he was tired. His legs felt like concrete. All these damn cars. Employees' cars. *They* still had jobs. Jobs, cars, houses, families. All of them would come out at the end of the day, just like always, take out their keys, start their engines, drive home. Eat their fancy dinners. Watch their big TVs. Go up to their master suites at night and brush their rotten teeth in marble-topped sinks.

It *was* his car! Thank God. He didn't feel like he could go another step. But it was still half a row away. How innocent he'd been when he'd gotten out of the car that morning! He'd had no idea, no inkling at all, that anything like this was going to happen. That any such thing was even possible! That ignoramus Waller! That pig of a dog shit! Jesus Christ, how much farther? How could it take so long to go so short a distance? Each bumper was the length of a football field. An airstrip! And the planes just kept coming over, clogging the air with jet fuel. Rudy's stomach bubbled with rage. His neck and arms were rigid with fury. Just get to the car, he told himself. A few more steps and he could sit down. He needed to get out from under the sky, away from the noise of the jets and the eyes of whoever might see him wandering around the parking lot.

Finally, there it was. The Buick that had once been a deep lacquered red but now had faded to the cheap orange of canned tomato soup. Specks of rust spangled the metal around the grille and windshield. A missing hubcap gave it a derelict look, like it had lost a tooth. Still, Rudy sighed with relief as he slipped the key into the lock, lugged open the door, and fell into the driver's seat.

It was hot inside, even though the sky was cloudy. Rudy turned on the motor and fiddled with the air conditioner. The radio came on to his favorite station. Light rock, less talk, ninety-four-point-nine. The Beatles were singing "Yesterday."

He closed his eyes and lowered his head. The moment his forehead touched the steering wheel, the music stopped. The usual programming was being interrupted, an announcer said. The clouds moved quickly, as if invisible hands were pushing them aside. *This is a test,* the voice went on, *of the emergency broadcast system.*

Jewell walked fast, her long legs eating up the distance between the cafeteria, where she'd just finished her shift, and her car. She weaved in and out of the clumps of students who strolled slowly or paused to talk. Walking was good because it was harder to think while your legs and arms were moving, while the pavement disappeared under your feet. At least it was harder to think about the *same thing.* To obsess, to brood.

Still, as she mounted the steps near Royce Hall two at a time, she thought again of how Celeste had pulled away impatiently that morning. She had been in the bathroom, her makeup spread out all over the sink, when Jewell had squeezed in behind her and watched her apply mascara with rapid flips of the wrist.

"It's weird that you buy Avon," Jewell said. "That you don't wear some fancier brand. You know, like Clinique or Lancôme or Shiseido or something."

"Family tradition," Celeste shrugged. "My aunt sold Avon and everybody bought it. Probably got a family discount, you know? Anyway, I'm into quantity, not quality. You know how much all this crap would cost if I bought it at Nordstrom? Besides, I like the Avon Lady."

"You're kidding! Why?"

Jewell couldn't remember the last time Celeste had smiled, but as she met Jewell's eyes in the mirror, a corner of her mouth drew up in the half-grin that Jewell found irresistible.

"I don't know what it is about her," Celeste said. "She has some secret quality. Or maybe it's just her name. *Inez.*"

The exchange seemed so friendly that Jewell, who was standing behind Celeste, took a step closer. She leaned forward so that she rested against Celeste's back and nestled her face in Celeste's hair.

"Don't," Celeste had said peevishly, shaking her off. "I'm late already."

The bells started chiming. It was twelve o'clock, that lost time between morning and afternoon. A crush of people crowded the walkway, a river of bobbing heads. The noon tide. Jewell counted the chimes. The moment the last one faded away, her cell phone rang. She fished it out of her overalls. It would be Celeste, calling to say that she was sorry, that she'd come to her senses.

It wasn't, though. It was Jewell's uncle. She hadn't spoken to him in several years, but she recognized the characteristic tinge of hoarseness in his voice that her father had, too, as if talking were a strain. Sometimes she even heard it in her own voice.

"How're you doing, Jewell?" Wylie asked. "How's it going?"

He sounded nervous, as though he hadn't called just to chat.

Jewell stepped out of the stream of people and leaned against a stone wall that divided the walkway from a group of trees. The clouds moved quickly across the sun, making bright patches glow and dim on the walkways and faces of buildings.

"What's up, Uncle Tommy?" she asked, trying to mask her disappointment that he wasn't Celeste. "Is something wrong?"

"No, no. Nothing like that."

"Where are you?"

"Oh, I'm out at LAX. Working, you know. This is my break. I mean, I got half an hour."

He hesitated, and Jewell sensed him struggling. A strange guy, her uncle. "Your dogs okay?" she asked to break the ice.

"Yeah, they're great." Wylie laughed. "Listen, I just wanted to tell you. To say that I talked to your dad today. He's out, you know."

"Oh?" Jewell felt herself go still, like an animal that relies on camouflage for protection. The last thing she needed right now was to get sucked into one of her father's dramas.

"I thought you might want to give him a call," Wylie suggested. "No big deal, you know. Just say hi or something. Just to check in, kinda."

Jewell pursed her lips. How many times had she been through this? Why couldn't her uncle call someone else?

"You there?" Wylie said.

"Yeah, I'm here. Okay," she said with resignation. "You got his number?"

"He's staying in a place downtown," Wylie answered. He sounded relieved that he was passing on the responsibility for Logan to someone else. "It's called the Morningstar, or something like that. Just a room, until he can find a better place. Okay, you got a pencil?"

"Just a minute. Hold on."

Jewell set the phone down so she could get a pen and paper from her backpack. The parade of students in front of her continued, passing to their classes or going to lunch. A lot of them had fathers who gave them career advice and paid for their educations, Jewell mused as she ripped a corner of lined paper from her notebook. Imagine that. She was still bent over her backpack when there was an electronic pop like the magic moment at a concert when the sound system comes on and the lights go down. The moment when the crowd comes to attention and the star steps on stage.

Jewell stood up and looked around. Another pop came from high above, from the sky and trees and roofs of the buildings. As if someone were tapping a celestial microphone, about to say *test, test.*

This is a test of our emergency broadcast system, a disembodied voice announced. *This is only a test.*

The words bounced off the buildings and plazas, the stairs and parking lots and hills. Jewell heard lagging versions of it echoing in the distance. Jesus Christ, what did they do, string up microphones in the trees? Mount speakers on the roofs? It was eerie, like the birds and trees were speaking in a human voice to warn people that the end of the world had come. And, most freaky of all, no one reacted. The students kept walking, chatting, sipping their Cokes on the lawn, reading beneath the trees. Where was Celeste? Where would she be if bombs rained down or missiles filled the air like swarms of insects? If L.A. became a charred-out hole on the edge of the continent?

The voice was counting backwards now, the echoes lagging as they boomed back toward where Jewell was standing. She looked down and spied her phone resting on the wall where she'd set it down.

"Sorry, Uncle Tommy," she said. "But this weird thing is happening. Can you hear it? It's like an air raid or something."

"An *air* raid?" Wylie said.

"Not a real air raid," Jewell said quickly, surprised at the alarm in his voice. "A test, you know. I remember now that they were going to install a new warning system, but this is the first time I've heard it. Anyway, it's just ending."

"Oh, it's noon," Wylie said, sounding relieved. "That's why."

"Yeah, that's it," Jewell agreed. As the last echoes died away, she realized her heart was pounding. "Okay, I've got the pen. What's his number?"

Wylie recited the number. "Thanks," he said. "I'm a little worried about him. I thought it might be good if you just said hi. You know, let him know you're thinking about him."

Jewell folded the paper with the number on it and stuffed it back in her bag. Whatever, she thought. She suddenly wanted to be off the phone.

"And maybe sometime, maybe we could—" Wylie began, stumbling over his words like a geek about to ask her out on a date. "Maybe we could get together sometime. Catch up, you know. Have a look at each other."

"That would be nice," Jewell said politely, though she knew that there was a good chance she wouldn't see Tommy or her father at all, maybe for years. Life would go on, theirs and hers, with no intersection.

"Okay, well, it was nice talking to you," Wylie said. "I better get back to the rockpile."

"'Bye, Uncle Tommy. Thanks for calling."

She dropped her phone in her pocket and shouldered her backpack. The PA system gave one last pop, like an electronic cough, before the trees and sky went silent.

Air raid? Wylie thought as he hung up and turned toward the pile of newspapers that littered the table in the break room. A vending machine hummed in the corner. He checked his watch. Less than ten minutes left of his break. He was a little hungry, and he had to pee. The can, then, he thought as he left the break room. He wouldn't get another chance before his shift was over.

As he walked down the corridor where the administrative offices were, he remembered the drills from elementary school. Air raid. Duck and cover. The clatter of chairs scraping the brown linoleum and the squeals and laughter from his classmates as they dove under their desks. The floor smelled of polish and pencil shavings. With his nose to the linoleum, his eyes squeezed shut, and his hands laced over the back of his head, he wondered—not if bombs were going to come crashing through the tall windows on one side of the class—but whether his teacher, bulky Mrs. Jackson whose ankles were the same thickness as her calves, was under her desk, too. Thinking of her squeezed into the cubbyhole of her wooden desk back near the bean plants that struggled in milk cartons, her big butt in the air and her face against her nubby plaid skirt, he had to smother his laughter.

In one of the offices along the corridor, the big guy with the walrus mustache and the Indian guy with the suit—the walrus's boss, Wylie presumed—were talking to a security guard. Wylie knew the first two by sight. The security guard was writing things down. As he pushed open the door and stepped out into the terminal near the cart where the kids from the alternative high school sold espresso, he suddenly remembered Jim Dunnigan, the kid who always emerged from under the desk with a wet spot that spread from his waistband to his knees. Front *and* back. Jesus, Wylie couldn't believe he still remembered the name. What was it, second grade? Every damn time. Fire drill or earthquake drill or air raid, it didn't matter. No wonder kids from his class were drugging themselves to the gills by the time they were in high school. The Cold War. The words still gave Wylie the jitters.

He hesitated near Baja Burritos. He could get one to eat later in the afternoon, when he knew he'd be hungry. The line was short, but it still took them awhile to make the burrito, and the guy who was relieving him back at the bar got pissy if he was late. No, better not. Instead he decided to grab one of the ready-made sandwiches at the cafeteria near the bathrooms.

The line there was miraculously short. He wondered about the alarm Jewell had heard and pictured the students at UCLA diving to their knees or scrambling for cover as he waited. Tuna, BLT, egg salad. Some kind of vegetarian thing with eggplant and cheese. It was too bad Jewell had grown up just like he had, scared shitless that some lunatic was going to push the button. He picked up a BLT, reminded himself how it was getting harder and harder to button his pants, set it down, and took a tuna instead.

It was a straight shot down to the pavilion where his bar was, and the bathroom was on the way. He'd be a little late, but Tony, the assistant manager who was spelling him, would just have to wait. Ambitious little fuck, always bustling around. Wylie glanced at the tuna sandwich. He should have chosen more carefully; this one was smashed on one side. How in the world had Logan managed to come up with a girl like Jewell? She hadn't been overjoyed to hear about Logan, and she hadn't exactly jumped at the offer to meet Wylie. But, really, who could blame her? With all the shit that had come down from the family, it made sense that she'd want to stay as far away as possible.

He was thinking so hard and he'd gone this route so many times that he almost walked straight into the tape. What the hell was this? He stopped, clutching the tuna sandwich. Yellow caution tape draped across the entrance to the men's restroom. Wylie's pulse ratcheted up, spun, whirred. A crime scene? He flashed on the barstool clattering over earlier that morning. The way his armpits had prickled when Logan had called. And then the air raid, the alarm in Jewell's voice. For a moment they all seemed connected. Wylie's mind did a dizzy spin as he had the disturbing sensation that he was remembering something that hadn't happened yet. It was just yellow tape, he reassured himself. A stool had fallen over. Big deal. They could be fixing a faucet or mopping the floor. Yet he sensed something lurking nearby. As the fear whistled through his nostrils, he turned and looked out at the terminal, where people still wheeled their bags toward the security check, still browsed at the newsstand, still bent to wipe a toddler's face.

Logan almost gunned it and jammed through the yellow, but at the last minute he decided to play it safe. The *very* last minute. Man, it almost put him through the windshield. Still, he felt good about it, especially since some granny came hobbling into the crosswalk with her little dog. He even put it in reverse, backed it up so the nose of his truck was behind the line. The law-abiding citizen. Mr. Clean. So it was no wonder he whipped around in shock when the siren sounded behind him.

What the fuck was going on? His first thought was to floor it. Take a right, get the hell out of there. But a stream of cars was moving through the intersection. Someone had pulled up behind him, too. Fuck! There was no way out. He checked the sideview, the rearview, swiveled his head around like an owl. No black-and-whites in sight. No unmarked, either, as far as he could tell. The shitheads! Where the hell were they?

Calm down, he told himself. Be cool, keep your head. He did a quick inventory. Wait, man, wait! Wonder of wonders.

Logan chuckled to himself, shook his head.

He was clean, man. Clean!

Okay, there was no insurance on his truck and his license was expired, but that was no big deal. So what was with the sirens? He stuck his head out the window and looked around. That's when he realized it was the noon whistle. The air-raid siren! The emergency notification system! Logan laughed. Christ, he was paranoid. It wasn't personal, man. It wasn't *him* they were after. Get a grip! It was noon, a Tuesday, the time they always tested these things. City-wide, man. No need to worry.

But why was the light taking so fucking long? The sound of the sirens filled the air, like a fucking buzz saw. He could hear other ones going off farther away, in the distance. A cloud of pigeons lifted off and whirled over the parking lot of the Safeway on the corner. They didn't like it either. They circled, soared, arched. A ball of birds. Logan tapped a nervous rhythm on the steering wheel. Hurry the fuck up. It's a siren, he told himself. No great shakes. Still, it bugged him. Jesus, was the light broken? Why did the damn thing keep blaring away? What if it was the real thing?

Come on, come on, come on, Logan chanted, tapping the steering wheel. *Let's get moving.* The sound was spooky, man. Annoying. It reminded him of fire drills. Gunshots, explosions, thunderstorms. *Ask not for whom the siren screams; it screams for you.* A million ways to die, some worse than others. Burning: he wouldn't like that. Or suffocating. It wouldn't be bad to freeze to death, from what he'd heard, or to go out in an OD haze, just drifting off to sleep. He glanced anxiously in the rearview. The siren made him feel like someone was tailing him, chasing him down. That it was only a matter of time.

Thank God! he told himself when it finally stopped. The light changed. The silence was such a relief, he felt like curling up and going to sleep in it. He began to hear the motors of the other cars again. The flapping of the pigeons' wings, the wind moving through the trees, the radio playing in the car to his left. The sky felt empty again, normal. The blood stopped pounding in his ears. Still, he was cautious as he pressed the gas, as he eased into the intersection.

"This completes our test of the emergency broadcast system," the smooth male voice said. One of *those* kinds of voices: Dan Rather or Peter Jennings. The guys with the thick, perfect hair, the kind everybody trusts. The type who never get their feathers ruffled. No one would ever show *them* the door, that was for sure, Rudy thought.

What if the alarm had been for real? he wondered as he looked out into the airport parking lot, where glass and chrome shimmered like the surface of a pond. He imagined everyone across the city stopping what they were doing: the woman changing her baby's diapers, the guy pumping gas, the office worker trying to decide whether to have sushi or soup for lunch. Everything that mattered the minute before would no longer make a difference. It was hot in the Buick, but Rudy didn't roll down the window. In the thick, fertile air of his car, something stirred in his brain. The radio emitted a long tone that could have been a submarine diving. It could have been an electronic whistle or a humming siren, or that word those yoga types said. *Om.* The sound of the universe. The sound of the truth, awakening in Rudy's mind.

The radio gave three short bongs. The test was over.

At that moment, in the warm car, Rudy's idea was born.

Right then, right there.

7

A test. It was only a test. Not a bomb, or a missile, or an earthquake. Not a tidal wave, as Inez imagined it could have been: a wall of water piling up out in the ocean, a mountainous wave gathering force before it swept into the basin of Los Angeles, where it would wash everything—parking meters, telephone poles, houses, the planes where Rudy worked, trees, and people—just like toys, like bits of broken wood and plastic, all out to sea. Like the flood and Noah's ark. *For behold, I will bring a flood of waters upon the earth, to destroy all flesh in which is the breath of life from under heaven; everything that is on earth shall die.*

Just as Inez was thinking that if Clara Rice didn't get there with the Avon soon, she might have to deliver it a different day, the doorbell rang. Inez switched off the TV and ran to the door. Clara was there with the box. The perfume wafted up, full of promise.

"Big order today," Clara said, trying to see around Inez into her house.

The sooner she left, the better, in case anyone should see. Not that Rudy ever talked to anyone in the neighborhood, but better safe than sorry. Inez smiled, nodded, took the box. "Okay, see you next time," she said, quickly closing the door.

She got right to work. Laid out her supplies, checked the shipment over, organized the invoices. Glanced at the clock. She divided everything up, carefully placed each order in a paper bag. Nail polish, foundation, lip gloss, facial mask, powder blush, eye shadow. Home decorations and jewelry. Candles. She added the free gifts to each bag: this month it was a sample-size lipstick of Very Cherry and a small vial of Spring Fling perfume. She stapled the receipts to the outsides of the bags, which she placed back in the box that Clara had brought. She went into the bathroom and touched up her own makeup, tied a scarf over her head, slipped on her loafers, and headed for the garage.

Rudy didn't think she should have a car, just like he didn't think she should have a job. *A woman's place is in the home.* She wasn't sure that was in the Bible, either, but there were plenty of other things that were: *Wives, be subject to your husbands, as to the Lord.* And, if that wasn't enough: *For the husband is the head of the wife as Christ is the head of the church.* But the ultimate authority, higher than Rudy, was God, and if God gave her the plan about Avon, her only choice was to obey.

The garage was tiny, crowded with Rudy's things. Tools, model airplanes from when he was a kid, newspapers, boxes whose contents were a mystery. He didn't like her out there, he'd told her so. His space, he said, where he could have a little privacy. When she started to wonder about him she stopped her mind, moved on to something else. Vanessa's burgundy mountain bike leaned against the wall near the light switch. Inez used bungee cords to attach the box to the rack over the back tire. She hung her purse on the handlebars, then wheeled the bike around to the side yard and out the gate.

The wind was whipping up. Eucalyptus leaves and smashed paper cups tumbled along the road. There was plenty of time. Inez took off. She smelled rain.

She pumped up the hill at the end of the street, where a vacant lot sparkled with broken glass, and headed for the neighborhood on the other side of the four-lane road. It was too risky to sell around her own house, in case Rudy got wind of it. Wild fennel gave off its licorice smell. The hill was steep, but Inez didn't mess with the gears. Vanessa might notice and, even though she'd never say anything to Rudy, it was better if she didn't know. That way she wouldn't have to lie, wouldn't have to have it on her conscience. *For whosoever condones a sin also commits it.* Or something like that.

At the top of the hill, at the corner with the dry cleaner and the eight-dollar haircuts, Inez stopped and caught her breath while she waited for a break in the traffic. It was all downhill from here. She liked to go fast, but the bottles on the rack behind her rattled, so she applied the brakes. It was silly how much she loved riding the bike. It brought back the one memory she had of her father: how, as a girl of four, right after he brought her over from the Philippines, she had ridden on the handlebars as her father steered them through streets so different from anything she had known. As she pushed through the intersection and started downhill, she remembered his brown hands on the handlebars and his voice close to her ear, talking in tight words because of the cigarette clenched between his teeth. The asphalt passing beneath them, the wind in her face, the handlebars bumping under her hips, his voice blending with the whistling of the wind. Her mother and brothers were supposed to join them in America later, but for a reason she never learned, they didn't. It was all foggy to her, even now. Then her father himself disappeared, and she went to stay in a series of foster homes until the Melberts adopted her and raised her along with their own three children.

The one picture she had of her father, which she kept in the cedar chest under the Avon products, showed him posed next to a bicycle, his hands on the handlebars and a cigarette between his lips, just like her memory of him. The photograph showed the deep creases in his cheeks, the dark hair that sprouted from his head like a bush and fell down over his forehead, hiding his eyes. Her dream, and part of her plan, was to find him, to find her whole family. *Ask, and you shall receive.* She knew it would happen, sooner or later. The one thing she had, that she knew, was her name. *Santos.* So beautiful, like a prayer. More than that, it was a clue, a step in the right direction. She repeated it now as she flew downhill, the bike jumping and skidding over the uneven pavement. She dreamed of this at night: riding tirelessly up and down hills, the miles falling away effortlessly as she passed through abandoned towns, seasides, jungles.

The fat family was the first stop. Brenda, the mother's name was, Brenda McNair. It was a corner house with a straggly loquat tree and a cyclone fence. Inez pushed her bike through the gate and knocked. The stink in there. Mercy. Inez couldn't understand it. Like they did their business right there in the living room. That and the smell of grease, everything they ate must have been fried. Dust and dirt stuck to the coat of grease, so everything was fuzzy. Walls, lamps, tables. All those big white people wallowing around in the tiny living room like a family of elephant seals, sisters and brothers and their girlfriends and boyfriends and kids and a couple of cousins thrown in, who knew *who* they all were?

They had a thing for angels, couldn't get enough of them. Angel candles, angel bells, angel music boxes. Angels sitting on the edges of tables and hanging off walls. You'd think with all those angels maybe they'd want to clean up a little, dust the furniture and clean the carpet, get rid of that smell. But no. Anyway, it was a good thing—for business at least. This time they'd ordered a pewter angel Christmas ornament and a wind chime dancing with little silver angels. They were impulse buyers, too. You could usually tempt them right on the spot with things they hadn't even seen before. Inez knocked again, louder this time.

One of the twin daughters answered. Both girls were no-goods, something wrong with them. Big girls, old enough to be married, who had dropped out of high school and were working at the Taco Loco up on Cesar Chavez. On their way to being as fat as their mother. Most of the time when she came by, they were side by side on the couch, staring at the TV.

"Avon," Inez announced. "A delivery for your mama."

"Mom!" the girl shouted toward the back of the house, not even saying hello, but looking down greedily at the bag Inez held.

Inez couldn't help thinking of her own daughter, so polite, so clean, so quiet. This one had dark circles under her eyes, like she did some kind of drug. Pimples she'd picked into scabs. Dirty house shoes.

Brenda McNair came waddling down the hall. "Come in, come in!" she yelled, motioning with her big arms. At least she had more manners than her daughter. Inez stepped inside. The other twin came in from the kitchen, the son's girlfriend from behind Brenda. Streaming in from everywhere, like animals at feeding time. Coming for their angels.

Inez gave them the order and waited for the oohs and ahs, the gasps and giggles and sighs as they passed around the wind chimes and Christmas ornament. "Buy forty dollars and get the free gift on this next order," she said, opening the catalog and pointing to the display of a carrying case, mascara, and fade cream. "If you buy sixty dollars' worth, you get the exclusive premium gift, worth thirty-five dollars itself."

They crowded around. The smell was getting to her. Pee and sweat and grease. Funny how every one of the houses she visited had its own smell, just like each person had her own personality. She could walk into any of her customers' houses with her eyes closed and know where she was.

"I want this!" one of the twins cried, just like a little girl.

"Mama, buy it for me," the other one pleaded, pushing her way into the circle to get closer to the catalog.

"Buy it yourself," Brenda said. "My God, you think I'm made of money?"

But she did end up buying them what they wanted. That and plenty else: the peaceful dove ceramic ornament, astringent cleanser, and Classic Coral powder blush. She bought after-shave splash for her son and Pearly Pink nail polish and matching lip gloss for his girlfriend. Cellulite control gel, moisturizing hand cream, and, finally, the spice-scented wax diffuser. Inez wondered where the money was coming from, but that wasn't her concern. She wrote the order down in her neat handwriting while the dollar amounts rolled in her head like miles on an odometer.

"Do we have enough for the free gift?" Brenda asked when the feeding frenzy was over.

"The *premium* gift," Inez pronounced.

Everyone clapped.

The next customer, Mrs. Betski, lived at the end of the same street. It was uphill; Inez stood on the pedals and pumped hard, squinting into the sun that was trying to pierce the high ceiling of overcast sky. A plane broke through the clouds, and for a moment, until it passed back into a thick bank of gray, she thought of Rudy, picturing his small, delicate hands and the fastidious way he cut his meat into uniform pieces before he ate. He might have cleaned that very plane up there now. Even with the noise from the freeway and the wind lashing the rasping fronds of the palms along the parking strip, she heard the roar of the jet's engines. She envied the people up there going somewhere far away.

Mrs. Betski opened the door the minute Inez knocked, like she'd been waiting. She wore shorts that showed her skinny noodle legs, big ugly sandals with thick men's socks. What a sight. Body lotion was all she ever bought. She took the bag and eyed Inez suspiciously. Her house smelled like the menthol rub Inez's foster mother used to massage into her chest when she had a cold.

"Same ting next month," Mrs. Betski said. She had an accent like Dracula. "Vhat are you?" she added before she handed over the money.

"Excuse me?"

"Vhat are you? Vhat are you?" she repeated impatiently, peering into Inez's face and gesturing with her big-knuckled hands.

Inez smiled like she always did when something unpleasant was coming.

"Chinese? Japanese? Vair you from?" Mrs. Betski scowled, as if Inez were playing stupid on purpose.

Love your neighbor as yourself, Inez reminded herself as she took a big breath. *For as you do unto them, so do you unto me.* "From

L.A.," she answered, pointing down at the porch as if she'd been born on that very spot.

After that was Carmen Miramonte, whose house smelled like cigarettes. Then Edith Lee, whose son was in a hospital bed in the living room. Mrs. Dilly, who decorated her windowsills and table-tops with the Avon bottles she'd been collecting since goodness knew when. And Joan Regosian, with all the cats. No surprise what her house smelled like. Big clumps of fur, too, stuck all over the furniture.

The orders rolled in. As she got back on her bike and pedaled past the little park where the neighborhood teenagers slumped around in their hoods and baggy pants, Inez imagined the enve-lope in the cedar chest growing fatter and fatter. There was noth-ing like feeling the money pile up. It was getting late, though, and a tingle of fear went through her as she imagined Rudy coming home a little early and finding the house empty. But why would he? All the same, she pumped faster, panting a little as she rounded the corner onto the street of one-story stucco duplexes where she'd make her last delivery. She'd have to hurry now to get home before Vanessa. The house where the two girls lived, *women* really, was in the middle of the block. She dismounted at the sidewalk and pushed her bike across the unkempt lawn.

The other one answered, not Celeste, her customer. This girl was big, tall, without a drop of makeup and a thick braid hanging down the middle of her back. Bare feet and bitten-down finger-nails. Faded jeans torn across the knees and a T-shirt that belonged in the rag bag.

"Yes?" she said, blinking like she'd just woke up. There was something shifty about her, restless. She fidgeted like a horse, shift-ing from one leg to the other while she looked Inez up and down.

"Is your *friend* home?" Inez guessed that was the word for it. Their place was small, a one-bedroom. She'd visited the bathroom on the last visit, had peeked in at the unmade bad. *Double* bed. Clothes tossed on the floor and over the chair.

"No, no. She's not here," the girl said.

"I have an order for her. Avon."

Inez held up the bag. The other one, Celeste, was one of her best customers, always ordering for her big family—sisters, mother, and nieces. A nice girl, and very pretty. Every hair in place with that one: makeup, nails, and clothes. South American, she had told Inez, but a Jew, too. Inez knew from her name, *Levy.*

"I can take it," the other one said, reaching for the bag.

She could be pretty, too, if she tried. Very pretty, in fact. Nice eyes, good bone structure. How had she turned out the way she had? An abomination. But it wasn't for Inez to judge. Still, when she thought of Vanessa around people like that, her blood ran cold.

"It's a big order," Inez said, keeping the bag out of her reach. "I need to collect the money."

"Come in, then. I'll write you a check."

Inez followed her into the house. The shades were down. It was a hippie-looking place, the lumpy furniture covered with Indian-print bedspreads and something woven hanging on the wall. It smelled of dried flowers and incense. Candles and carved wooden animals covered the coffee table; a brick-and-board bookshelf stood against one wall. The girl led her to a dining table at the side of the room near the kitchen. It was piled with books, newspapers, opened mail, and what looked like a half-built doll house made of balsa wood. A mess. Hanging on the wall over the table was a sketch of a naked woman leaning back in a chair. Right out in the open for everyone to see.

"How much is it?" the girl said, rummaging in her backpack.

"Seventy-seven eighty-four."

Inez felt exposed standing in the middle of the living room, alone in the house with a girl like that. She didn't want to get too close, although just looking at the girl you would never have guessed.

"I'll leave the first line blank and you can fill it out however you want," Celeste's friend said as she made out the check. Her braid fell over her shoulder while she wrote.

Inez couldn't help looking around. There were lots of photographs on the bookshelf of babies and kids and relatives. All Celeste's family, from the looks of them, clearly not this white girl's. There was Celeste herself, standing in front of a tree with her arms around what must be two of her sisters.

"Here you go."

When the girl smiled, her whole face changed. She looked like a child, innocent and happy. Inez's heart softened, she couldn't help it. *Jewell Wylie,* she read on the check. What kind of name was that? Would the check bounce? The girl watched her closely with a half-smile on her face, and for a moment Inez wondered if she should show her the catalog, encourage her to wear a little makeup. There was always hope. People could change. But it was getting late.

"I'll leave a catalog for Celeste. I'll call her in a week or so to see if there's something she wants to order."

"I can tell her to call you."

"No, don't call!" Inez blurted out before she could catch herself. "No bother," she added, forcing a smile. "*I'll* call *her.*"

It was early twilight, the saddest time, when Inez got on her bike and headed home. The dying moments of the day when she felt most alone. When she was a girl she'd thought that as the sun sunk into the horizon, it rose simultaneously in the place where she'd been born, waking her lost family who would get out of bed, have breakfast, and begin their day without her. Meanwhile she went home to eat the unfamiliar food of a foster family while she listened, bewildered, to their insider table talk, then went to sleep in a bed that smelled of strangers. Was it possible to be homesick for a place she no longer remembered? But at this time of day she longed for that place: for the humid island air, for the street sounds and smells of a city of millions who looked like her.

Her chest hurt when she took a deep breath. *Yea, though I walk through the valley of the shadow of death,* she recited as she pumped around the corner and up the hill. A gust of wind blasted grit into her eyes. The foster parents she'd had right before the Melberts adopted her, a man and woman who looked strangely alike, with protruding foreheads and no chins, had called her the Waif. Their kids picked it up and the name had spread to the other kids in the neighborhood. For a whole year she was known as "Waifie" or "Wafer."

Everyone was getting off work. The traffic made Inez feel like a leaf whirling in a surging torrent. There'd been an accident at the big intersection. A few spent flares, the rim of a headlight, pieces of plastic, and a puddle of broken glass littered the road. The last thing she needed right now was a flat. She steered carefully, remembering the Thanksgiving she'd spent with the family who called her Waifie. They'd gone to a relative's house where there were a lot of people: cousins, aunts, uncles, grandparents. People who'd known one another all their lives. They all—kids and adults alike—eyed her with curiosity, sneaking glances during dinner as if they were surprised she ate just like they did, cutting her turkey and ladling gravy over her mashed potatoes. After the meal, when the kids had gone outside to play, they had circled around her, shouting questions: Where are you from? How come you don't say nothing? Hey, can you hear me? Do? You? Understand? They'd made ape sounds at her, scratched under their arms like monkeys. Finally she had retreated to a corner of the yard with the family dog, a smelly beagle who pushed her head under Inez's hand the minute Inez stopped petting her. The dog had nestled close to her, sighing happily, until one of the kids noticed and alerted the others. "Hey, watch out!" he shouted. "She wants to eat your dog! She's making friends with it so she can have it for dinner!"

Why had God put her in this place where she always felt like a stranger, Inez wondered as a truck carrying bottled water rumbled by, forcing her to ride within inches of the curb. When was He going to lead her to her true home? *My days are like an evening shadow,* she mumbled. *I wither away like grass.* Someone honked at her as they sped by, belching a cloud of exhaust. It was hard to understand what you couldn't see, like God's love. But God was everywhere, Inez reminded herself. She glanced from side to side as if trying to find an example of it, something she'd overlooked, but all she spotted was a row of orange cones, a TV someone had abandoned at the bus stop, a pigeon with a curled foot.

As she got closer to home, guilt took the place of sadness. She was lying, deceiving everyone. Not even a small sin, but one of the Commandments. Then came fear. *Don't let him be there,* she prayed. *Please, please, please.* She pumped so fast she started to wheeze, her breath tearing her lungs like a sob. *Don't let his car be at the curb. Don't let him be standing on the porch, waiting.* Her calf muscles screamed, the bike jumped and jolted beneath her. She pedaled in a reckless panic, on the verge of tears. What had she been thinking? She was late, late, late.

His car wasn't there. Relief flooded her. Everything was okay, she'd pulled it off. Again. She got off the bike and wheeled it toward the garage. *Thank you,* she prayed as she leaned the bike exactly as it had been before and gathered her things together. *Thank you for your blessing.* She had doubted for a minute; there had been a hole in her trust of God. Who was she to question His plan?

She had asked, and now she was receiving.

8 Rudy squinted into the bleached light as he drove slowly in the right lane of Pico Avenue. People pulled out from the curb without even looking. If they felt like it, they double-parked. Rudy shook his head with disgust. That fat Waller. The nerve of him, calling Rudy in and firing him then and there. Rudy's hands felt rubbery, not at all like his own. He could hardly hold the steering wheel. His fingers tingled, almost numb. The whole airport. It had always been like that: a nest of lying, cheating vipers. If you were a hard worker and showed up on time, day after day, if you did your job the best you could, it didn't mean a damn thing.

Nope.

Stores slid by: windows with mattresses, washing machines, televisions. Rudy imagined the huge panes of glass shattering, shards blown in all directions. He wanted to know who was behind it: who had told lies about him in the first place, who had believed them like an idiot, who had made the decision to lay him off. He had his suspicions. It took all of his concentration to keep the right amount of space between his car and the one in front of it, to push the brake at the red light, to step on the accelerator when it turned green.

God, it would be nice just to go home, to go into the bedroom, close the curtains, and slide into bed. Rudy imagined the silky feel of the quilted, emerald green bedspread pulled up to his chin. He pictured himself the way he wanted to be: lying on his back, his eyes focused on the ceiling, the room quiet and dark. But he couldn't go home; Inez would be there. He thought of her again as she'd been on their honeymoon, when they'd gotten off the plane in Honolulu and the thick, moist air had enveloped them like a warm bath. It had made her jet black hair even more voluminous and she had laughed, trying to pat it back down to size. How strange it had been to have her things with him in the mildew-smelling hotel room: her small, patterned blouses hung up in the closet next to the short-sleeved shirts, size LARGE, that he'd bought at Mervyn's especially for the trip; her shoes—straw-colored woven pumps and sandals made of spaghetti-thin strips of colored leather—sharing space with his canvas flip-flops and the Nike sneakers, still gleaming white, that he'd bought half-price at a close-out sale right before they left.

He'd felt like a man, a real man who lived with a woman, one half of a whole. Inez had hung up all his clothes as soon as they got to their hotel room. She had buttoned the buttons and straightened the collars of his shirts. She had arranged his underwear in the top drawer of the little bureau that held the TV. When she had gone down to the lobby to ask about the luau, whose price was included in the cost of their package, he had slipped into the bathroom and picked up the cosmetics she'd arranged on the counter. He'd opened the creams and lotions, smelled them, had even rubbed a dab of something that smelled like coconut into the palm of his hand. *You can count on me,* he'd said into her hair that night after they'd made love—quietly and politely and, he worried, too quickly. He couldn't help but wonder about Vanessa's father while he moved inside her, her hands on his shoulders and his face buried in her neck. The sheets had smelled like mildew, too. Later, when he got up from the bed and went into the bathroom for a drink of water, a roach the size of a hummingbird had flown, *flown,* from the shower head to the light over the sink.

He was older, much older, Inez had told him when he'd asked about Vanessa's father. *A man at my church. Powerful in the church. Very respected. From the Philippines, like me.*

She had looked at Rudy, her large, steady eyes so like Vanessa's. Deep brown, almost black.

I was too young, she said. *I didn't know.*

There was no way he could go home right now. No way he could worry Inez by telling her what had happened. No reason to upset her, because he was going to straighten things out, get his job back. One way or another. He just had to think. *Think!* It was hard, though, with the glaring light and the cars starting and stopping, people pulling out in front of you like they were the only people in the world. A tiny old lady in a car the size of an aircraft carrier straddled the middle lane, her head barely showing over the steering wheel. God Almighty! No use mentioning a thing to Inez because before you knew it the whole thing would be straightened out.

Ahead, on the right, a shopping mall appeared. Rudy didn't know where he was or how he'd gotten there. An underground parking garage opened up like a cavern and, on a whim, Rudy turned and headed inside. He needed to think and it felt good to get out of the traffic and under the low ceiling where it was cool and dark. Besides, he was getting hungry. The smell of gas fumes in the garage was comforting. He drove up and down the aisles, his tires squeaking. There was a space next to a pillar painted with a large pink circle and the letter *B*, like in Bingo. Rudy parked, got out, and locked his car. Space 21, he noted. A very lucky number.

He hadn't been in a place like this in ages. As he waited for the elevator, he told himself there was no reason to panic. People lose their jobs all the time, and besides, he had two weeks' pay to hold him over. Not that he'd be out that long. It was a misunderstanding. He'd clear it up in no time once he calmed down a little. He was alone in the elevator. Someone had dropped what looked like chocolate ice cream on the floor and one of his shoes stuck when the doors opened. There was a sunny brick plaza surrounded by stores, knots of people walking with oversized shopping bags. The sky opened up above him like a vacuum that could suck him straight into space. He had to steady himself a moment before he headed toward a bench where he could sit and get his bearings.

That was better. There was no reason not to enjoy himself. To sit and just *be,* to figure things out. He'd lost his job. Okay, that much he got. Why? *That* was the nitty-gritty. The tough nut to crack. The million-dollar question. His stomach rumbled. Waller, that asshole. And Latasha, grinning at what was happening. Rudy ground his teeth. The story of his life. Bad enough that bad things happened, but there always had to be someone there to see it, to take pleasure in it. People hurried around him, so many and so fast they were almost a blur. He stared at details: a woman's painted toenails, a wristwatch on a hairy arm. His hands dangled between his legs. The sun felt good on his back.

A teenaged boy eating an ice cream cone sat down on the bench next to him. Black. He had the baggy, low-waisted pants they all wore, the same expensive tennis shoes. The boy licked the cone, looking out into the crowd.

"Where'd you get that ice cream?" Rudy asked.

"It's not ice cream," the kid said between licks. "It's frozen yogurt." He didn't look at Rudy. His tongue was brilliant pink against his dark skin. It swiped the ice cream in broad strokes, leaving paths like a snow plow.

"Is that any good?" Rudy asked.

The boy just nodded, still not looking at him.

"What time is it?" Rudy said.

The kid looked at his watch. "One-thirty," he said, not turning his head.

"I want to get me one of those. Where'd you get it?"

The boy lifted his hand and pointed, his arm outstretched like Columbus showing the way to the New World.

Rudy hurried over. He'd never had frozen yogurt before, and the flavors on the menu confused him. He wished he'd asked the boy what kind he had. There were two people in line ahead of him, taking their time. Rudy fidgeted. He wanted to get his cone and go back and sit down on the bench before the boy left. It would be nice to have *someone* to talk to.

"Did you see a kid come in here? Black kid? I want the same as he had," Rudy said when his turn came up.

The Mexican woman behind the counter gave him a blank look. Maybe she didn't speak English.

"A *black* kid," Rudy said loudly, with careful enunciation. But it was no use. The woman just stared. "Whatever. I'll take strawberry," he said in disgust, ordering the first flavor on the list.

The boy was gone when Rudy got back to the bench. In his place was a white girl, maybe seven years old, wearing a midriff top with sparkles in the shape of a heart. Rudy sat down next to her.

The yogurt was cold and tasty. Real strawberry flavor. He nibbled the edge of the cone and glanced at the little girl. Vanessa had been so quiet at her age, watchful and well behaved. This one's fingernails were painted deep purple, and several tiny braids ran through her straight blond hair. She gave off a sweet smell, like bubble gum. Rudy eyed her bare waist and glittery sandals. Who in their right mind would dress a kid like that? Like a whore, if you wanted to know the truth. And where was the mother? *Really.* Leaving a kid like that all alone. The black boy might still be lurking around, what if *he* saw her?

"What's your name?" Rudy asked the girl.

You'd think she'd seen a ghost. She looked at Rudy like *he* was the one who might do something to her. She scooted to the far end of the bench and scanned the mall for her mother.

"It's okay," he said. "My name's Rudy. I was just worried because I didn't see your mama and I want to make sure nothing bad happens to you."

The girl bolted across the walkway to a young heavyset woman in a tank top and shorts who was rushing toward the girl with a shopping bag in each hand. The girl threw her arms around the woman and buried her head in her blubbery belly. The woman bent down to talk to her. The girl turned and pointed toward Rudy, who suddenly felt skewered on the bench. He raised his half-eaten cone, as if that might explain everything.

As the two came toward him, Rudy debated whether to run or to stay and explain. He saw himself being taken away in handcuffs, pictured the police showing up at his doorstep, asking for Inez. He'd for sure never get his job back then, even though he hadn't done anything wrong. When the woman and girl reached the bench he stood, his feet apart, holding the frozen yogurt toward them like a microphone.

The girl had left her purse on the bench next to him.

"Get it and let's go," the woman said, shooting Rudy a dirty look. Though she was young, she had jowls already, a double chin. Her daughter, brave now that she held her mother's hand, looked at him like he was repulsive.

"She was here all alone," Rudy said. "You ought to be more careful."

"You loser," the woman said. "Why don't you get a life?"

Rudy dumped the rest of the squishy cone in the trash. Shake it off, he told himself. Pull yourself together. The world is a crazy place. He wandered toward the stores, concentrating on walking a straight line, on putting one foot ahead of the other. Everyone carried shopping bags—some white, some red, some with a large sun printed on them. When he got to one end of the mall, he let himself be carried by the stream of people through the glass doors of a department store. The stream split into smaller rivulets that flowed between the counters of perfume and watches, handbags, gloves, and sunglasses.

He thought of Inez. *His wife.* He pictured the blunt ends of her thick, dark hair. Her purposeful elbows and knees. Her powdery smell, the way she absently touched her fingertips to her lips when she was thinking. She wasn't like the usual women, who he thought of as *modern* women, who walked and talked like men. Bossy, hard, critical. The ones who always had an opinion and were never content with anything. He had proposed to her two months after they met because she was just what he was looking for. It didn't bother him that she already had a child, that people at the church where they met avoided talking about who Vanessa's father was, and why Inez had never been married to him. The whole situation made it easier for Rudy, less competition. And he had saved her, really, he had given her back her reputation. With him in the picture, no one could say a word about her or Vanessa.

Rudy stopped at a counter where gold bracelets hung like slinky snakes from the bare branch of a tree. Canned music poured down from the ceiling. Fluorescent lights reflected in milky pools on the white marble floor. Lately, Inez had been even quieter than usual. *Too* quiet. Spooky quiet. Watching him from the doorway while he dressed in the morning, as he finished his coffee or read the paper. Barely talking to him, just nodding at whatever he said. Losing his job was the last thing he needed right now—not that he'd lost it. There were racks of earrings on top of the counter and watches underneath in the glass cases. So many. Blue faces, gold faces, black faces. Looking at the jewelry, his heart expanded. He wondered if Inez knew that she was his home, his place in the world, the one and only body he wanted in the bed next to him.

One of the bracelets was spun of gold strands so fine he could barely feel its weight in his hand. It collapsed into a tiny heap in his palm, extended into a glittering web when he lifted it. Delicate, like Inez herself. Rudy looked at the price tag. Outrageous! He inspected a few more bracelets. Even the cheapest was far beyond his means, and all his credit cards were maxed out. Still, he wanted to give her something. To show her. To bring back the old feeling.

The clerk was on the other side of the counter, talking to a woman whose bronzed skin matched the color of her hair. He had heard that there were hidden cameras in the ceilings and undercover cops posing as shoppers. The thing to do was to avoid looking suspicious. The bracelet slid so quickly and easily into Rudy's pocket that it startled him, as if it had slithered there on its own. A jolt of terror shot up each arm. His armpits prickled. After glancing quickly to the left and right, he pretended to consider a few more bracelets before moving casually on, his face a study of nonchalance.

The purses and wallets were just a few counters over. No one seemed to be following him, and his heart gradually slowed to almost normal. The canned music, the fluorescent lights, the thick aroma of perfume made him feel giddy. He was proud of Inez, of having her as his wife. Other men envied him, he could tell. They were jealous of the quiet way she deferred to him, of the way she showed her respect. No question who was boss. He lifted a kidskin wallet, as light and pliable as paper, out of its box. It was a beautiful tawny color, with tiny stitching and a built-in change purse. And she took so much care with the way she looked: her hair and makeup, her clothes always perfect. For him, to please him. Slim hips and big breasts. His and his alone.

Rudy's pants fit loosely, and the pockets were big. He put the wallet back in the box and slipped it into his pocket with the bracelet. The jolts buzzed up his arms again, but not as strong as the last time. Might as well be hung for a sheep as a lamb, he laughed to himself. This was easy! He felt strangely excited, happy even.

Then there was Vanessa. Rudy didn't know what to make of her. Like her mother, only worse. Her silence, the way she watched him. As he strolled away from the handbags, he thought of how—at his insistence—Vanessa called him Dad, but in a way that made it sound like there were quotation marks around the word. There was never anything to scold her for: her grades were perfect, she never broke any of the rules he set, she dressed and spoke modestly. Still, something was wrong. It was like Inez and Vanessa had a secret code between them, like they talked in a completely different tongue when he wasn't around. There was no getting between them, they were thick as thieves.

He stopped at the scarf counter and ran his hand over the silk and knits. The colors made his head swim. He glanced at the price tags and chose the most expensive: a fuchsia scarf with initials at the bottom, one that would glow next to Vanessa's honey-colored skin. Beautiful! It was so light it crushed down to almost nothing as it slid into his left pocket.

"Could I help you, sir?"

Whoa! Rudy jumped. He stuffed the last corner of the scarf down farther and held it down with his fist as if it might climb back out. The clerk, a razor-faced woman with elaborately up-swept hair, had been bent down behind the counter. She straightened up and walked over to where Rudy was standing.

"You looking for something in particular?" she asked, eyeing him suspiciously. Before he could stop himself, Rudy glanced up at the ceiling, expecting to see a camera's eye trained on him. The woman tidied the counter between them, evening the space where the fuchsia scarf had been.

"No, no," Rudy said, holding on to the edge of the counter to steady himself. He smiled. "I'm just having a look."

"These are all designer scarves," she said, waving a withered hand over the piles in front of her. Her pale skin looked gray in the fluorescent light. "The ones down there are less expensive."

Was she trying to keep him there until security arrived? And who was she to decide what he could afford and what he couldn't? Fighting the urge to hurry away, Rudy fingered the corner of a scarf the color of dried blood. When he looked up, her eyes were fixed on his face.

"Like I said, I'm just looking," he huffed. "I'll let you know if I need help."

The clerk shrugged and turned away. Rudy pocketed the brownish red scarf and stalked away, his shoulders hunched with outrage. He passed mannequins with long necks and racks of sunglasses. He kept walking. When he was almost to the exit, he picked up a rectangular gold lighter, box and all, and placed it in the pocket of his jacket.

Was this really all there was to it, or were they just waiting until he got outside to nab him? He clenched his teeth as he neared the door, kept his fists in his jacket pockets. His chest felt tight and fluttery as he slowed to let the crowd make its way out through the doors ahead of him. Boy, did he want to push through, to run. A uniformed employee eyed everyone as they walked out. Holding his breath, Rudy smiled and nodded at him. The idiot!

Outside the sun was still beating down, the same current of people swam in a circle. He waited for someone to grab him from behind, for a voice to say in his ear, "Come with me," but there was nothing.

He didn't stop walking until he saw the pink circle with the letter *B.*

He leaned into the car and pulled the two scarves from his pocket, laid them on the passenger's seat. Spread the gold bracelet on top of them. Wow. He set the wallet beside them and checked his watch. Still a couple of hours before he could go home. Boy, was he tired. What a day! Maybe he could stop and buy wrapping paper on the way home, get a cup of coffee. Then take Inez and Vanessa out for a nice dinner. Why not? A man and wife didn't always have to be talking to each other, he told himself. A man and wife, in a true marriage, understood each other without a lot of explaining.

He suddenly felt optimistic, like the world was opening up to him. *Work smart, not hard,* his father used to say. Maybe he hadn't explored all of his options. He decided to look into things, maybe talk to a lawyer. The two weeks' pay would hold him over until he figured it out.

The lighter was the last thing he took out of his pocket. It was pleasantly heavy, etched with thin vertical grooves. It lit when he spun the little wheel with his thumb. He looked up at the garage ceiling, at the exposed concrete, the crisscrossing pipes. The stupid assholes. All of them. He got out and walked to the front of his car, stood on the bumper, and held the flame under one of the daisy-shaped spigots. See how they liked a taste of *this* medicine. They messed with him, he'd mess back.

It took longer than he expected. Just when he thought it wasn't going to work, the spigot sputtered, bubbled, and a blast of water shot down on him. As he ran to the open door of his car he saw identical cones of water spraying at regular intervals, like lawn sprinklers turned upside down. He slammed the door and started the engine as water hammered on his roof.

9 At five minutes to three, Georgette came into the bar wearing the same black pants and Band-Aid-colored polo shirt as Wylie. She ducked under the counter, stowed her purse on the shelf near the glasses, retrieved her name tag from the cash drawer, and took a quick, expert inventory of the bar.

"Hey, handsome. What's up?" she said.

Wylie just shook his head. Her smell of just-smoked cigarettes and way too much dime-store perfume was like nectar after his nerve-racking day. With Georgette you could relax.

"You see what happened down the hall?" she said, scooping money off the bar and dealing napkins out casino-style.

"Where?" Wylie asked anxiously.

"Down at the men's head."

"Oh yeah. I saw they had some tape up."

"Waterworks. All the toilets overflowed, so the rug's soaking wet all the way out to the gate." She'd been tending bar so long she took orders and made drinks as if she didn't notice she was doing it. "Felix, you know him? The janitor guy? Says they think somebody did it on purpose. Even got the cops in there in case it's some terrorist thing, like trying to distract attention away from something bigger."

"Great. What's next?" Wylie asked. He put on his jacket and watched Georgette fill three glasses with ice. Unlike him, she paid no attention to the number of cubes in each. He was so relieved to see her and so glad to be going home that he put his arm around her shoulders and gave her a peck on the cheek.

She shrugged. "Who knows? I guess we should be glad it's only a few plugged toilets. And, hey, what did I do to deserve that?"

"That's just for being you," Wylie said.

On his way out of the terminal a few minutes later, right before he got to the ticket counters, it happened. The streak across his peripheral vision, the impression that someone was running across the terminal toward him, about to ambush him. The sensation was so strong that he jumped to the side, whirled, and stood stunned, heart pounding. But there was only a row of newspaper racks. He looked around to make sure no one had seen him and stumbled toward the sliding doors, queasy with panic.

It happened again as he was opening his car door. A flash like a shooting star off to the right, almost out of his range of vision. When he turned his head it was gone, but he had the impression that someone, or something, was crouching behind the car next to him. It was a trick of the light, he told himself, the sun reflecting off a windshield or bumper. It was an acid flashback, or all that speed he'd done so many years ago. Some part of his brain misfiring, an electric impulse gone haywire, a psychotic flare-up.

Wylie made an effort to be rational, to pinpoint the cause. Speed, he finally decided. Dexedrine the army medics had handed out before the night patrols. Wylie didn't need it to stay awake, but if he took enough he felt like he could do anything, specifically avoid dying, or at least not care if he did. In that state, he was a listening machine. Everything was amplified, every little noise. When that got to be too much he reached into his other pocket, took one of the downers. He kept it up all night: ups in the right, downs in the left, fine tuning. If you went too far one way, you just balanced it out with something from the other side. A few nights or weeks of that and your nerves were fried. You were sighting down a long tube of whatever was right in front of you, but it was the stuff at the corners of your eyes that got you. Things moving. Tigers. Ghosts. Whole platoons of VC crouched down all around you, giggling in the brush.

He felt a little better once he was on the road, heading away from the airport. He wished he'd get over it. He'd hoped that as life evened out, the old stuff would go away. He accelerated onto the freeway and merged into traffic, heading east. Once he was home he'd feel better. He concentrated on breathing deeply, on relaxing the muscles in his arms and legs. Cars fed in from all the ramps. Traffic slowed. The sun was behind him. Clouds blew in from over the ocean.

What in the hell is wrong with you? he asked himself angrily, glancing in the rearview mirror. Exactly *what* is your problem?

Mr. Anxiety. It had been easier when he was drinking. At least that brought *some* relief, the reckless feel of the booze taking hold, that inner swagger that made him feel everything was okay. But there was hell to pay at night: waking up with the sweats and a pounding heart, all of it coming back to him double force, over and over. Maybe it was just his nature, he reflected as he signaled and switched lanes. He thought of himself as he appeared in his second-grade photo: shirt buttoned all the way to his neck, brush-cut sticking up in dual cowlicks. Eyes fixed nervously on the camera. Maybe he had a chemical imbalance. Maybe he should see about a prescription.

Forget it, he told himself as he reached his exit. Just chill. He braked, curved off the freeway, started up the two-lane road toward the hills. How long was he going to let this stuff bother him? He passed the little mall with the liquor store, Korean barbecue, video shop, and nail salon. Deep breath, he told himself. Deep breath, shake it off. *Jesus Christ, get over it already!* The guy who sold oranges out of the back of his pickup was there, parked next to the gas station. There was an old folks' trailer park, a public storage facility, a place where they rented U-Hauls. Then he was climbing, winding up the narrow road, no sidewalk on either side, the haphazard houses clinging to the sliding eucalyptus leaves and the thin earth, the sparse chaparral. It was more Appalachia than L.A., with fishing dinghies sitting on trailers in the yards, dogs tethered to porches and trees.

His driveway split from the road and ran up the hill to the house he rented. A long, narrow, no-frills prefab, just one step away from being a trailer. One bed, one bath, and a little kitchen. There was a metal shed at one end, a porch big enough for two beach chairs in front. Three trees: pepper, avocado, loquat. Straggly eucalyptus dotted the hillside behind it. The whole place would go up in seconds if there was a fire, but—fingers crossed—so far so good. Elsa, his collie mix, waggled down from the porch when Wylie got out of the car. Murphy, the lab, thumped his tail from where he lay under the pepper tree, still chewing the shin bone Wylie had given him that morning.

After chain-eating a couple of Snickers and downing a can of root beer, Wylie looked at the mail. He felt better: the plaid couch, the rag rugs, the dogs wolfing their kibble. So what if he saw things? He remembered one night, right before his hitch was up, when he had walked to the edge of the camp and looked at the supply road that drove straight out to nowhere. The full, frosty moon cast long shadows. As he stood there, the whole road moved: a swell that started at his feet and surged slowly toward the horizon like a monster wave rolling out to sea. The mail was all junk: a catalog for sports equipment, the latest sale at Mervyns, a circular for missing children. These things passed, Wylie told himself as he tossed it all in the recycling bin. They came and went. The thing to do was ride them out.

He shaved in the shower, put on a clean pair of Levi's, and ironed a cotton shirt with thin blue stripes, one of his favorites. He caught a look at himself in the mirror on his closet door. He sucked in his gut as far as he could, trying to prevent it from spilling over the waistband of his jeans. He'd weighed one-forty when he went into the army. Lean and mean. Now, who knew? It had been years since he'd been anywhere near a scale, but chances were pretty good he'd gained somewhere around fifty pounds since then. He turned, looked at himself from behind. His butt was no bigger, thank God, but two pillows of flesh just below his kidneys swelled his once-trim waist. The iron-warm shirt felt good on his skin. He experimented with tucking it in, but decided it looked better out. "I don't like those New-Agey guys," Carolyn had told him, wrinkling her freckled nose. "Their little goatees and linen pants. Ponytails. Soft on the outside. But on the inside, all dried up. Twigs, little sticks." She had grabbed a handful of his fleshy waist and said, "I'll take the meaty boys anytime. They're the *real* pussycats, even though they act tough. They might not put the toilet seat down, but they got a lot of heart."

He was whistling by the time he came into the living room to put his sneakers on. The dogs looked up expectantly. "You guys gotta stay here," he said. "Stay here and keep an eye on the place."

10

It was a miracle, but Logan made it home without running out of gas. On every hill he'd expected his pickup to sputter and stall, but by God he'd made it, though he must really be running on fumes now. Wonder of wonders, there was even a parking space on the same block as his residence hotel.

Use *isthmus* in a sentence, he challenged himself, then answered his own joke: Isthmus be my lucky day.

The Morningstar Hotel was on a downtown side street that wasn't too noisy. There was a check-cashing place on the corner, a cavernous Chinese restaurant that specialized in noodles, a liquor store run by two brothers from Lebanon, and a tropical-fish shop that was never open. Big goldfish with bulging eyes were painted on the side of the building. Three doors down from the hotel was the St. Vincent de Paul's where Logan had bought a camel-colored jacket that looked like something Humphrey Bogart would wear, Levi's perfectly broken in, two long-sleeved Brooks Brothers shirts, and a pair of Italian shoes with ivory-colored accents. He'd also bought a striped bowl for his morning cereal, two plates decorated with grapevines, a coffee mug with a lion on it, and a handful of silverware.

The front door was supposed to be locked, but someone had left it ajar, as usual. Salem, the old junkie with eyes that drooped like a bloodhound's, was in the little cage next to the elevator.

"How's it going?" Logan said.

Salem raised his head long enough to give his usual slow nod. The lobby was carpeted in something that looked like it had been torn out of a bowling alley, a green and red diamond affair with stains whose history you didn't want to know. Along one wall were two worn armchairs and a dusty rubber plant that you'd think was artificial, except who'd make such a lopsided thing on purpose? The place smelled of Lysol, cigarettes, and cinnamon rolls. The elevator was old-fashioned, with a metal grate you had to pull closed. It was so small you got jumpy if there was more than one person inside, plus it jerked and clanked in a way that Logan didn't like. He took the stairs.

He was on the third floor, room 312. Not a bad place, really. They changed the sheets once a week, the bathrooms were kept fairly clean, and some all-right guys lived at Logan's end of the hall. Adrian, a would-be writer who was basically a speed freak, had the room to the left. Only trouble with him was that he talked too much and kept his TV on 24/7. On the other side, in 314, was Damon, another ex-con in the same line of business as Logan. Mr. Whipple, an old man with a caved-in chest who always wore a hat and suit jacket, was across the hall. He'd lived at the Morningstar for thirty-two years.

The radiators were going full blast on Logan's floor, and the hall felt like a steam room. The carpet there was red and the hall was dark, lit by dim sconces that were supposed to look like torches. Disco music boomed from behind a door near the elevator, which clanked past as Logan headed toward his room.

He struggled with his door. You had to jiggle the key, lift up on the knob, and throw your shoulder against the door to open it. The heat in the hall was unbearable. The TV was turned all the way up in Adrian's room next door. Come on, baby, open up, Logan pleaded as he shook the knob. Had someone been fucking with it? He heaved himself against the door until it finally gave and he stumbled into the room. He'd left the curtains open and light streamed in, blinding him after the dark hallway. It smelled dusty. Traffic noise came through the window. He locked the door and sat on the foot of the bed near the window. The sun was low in the west. He looked out at the civic center and downtown buildings, small and quaint like a city within a city compared to the bigger skyscrapers to the west. The scuffed-up plazas and warehouses, the wide streets. A row of palms looked like they were sketched in black ink against the sky. He checked his watch. Almost four. Before long he'd have to leave again. Pick up the car and meet his group at the airport.

Hot plates weren't allowed in the room, but everyone had them anyway. Logan put on some water for coffee. There was a small scratched table next to the window where he ate and read the paper, and a chest of drawers where he kept his clothes neat and folded. After being inside, that seemed important. The double bed, sunken in the middle, was covered with a red corduroy bedspread that faded progressively pink toward the bottom, where the window was. In the corner, next to the radiator, was a sink that doubled as a urinal if he didn't feel like making the long trip down the hall. At night the cockroaches scurried over everything, but you never saw them during the day.

He dumped two heaping teaspoons of Folgers crystals into his coffee mug, along with packets of Cremora and sugar he'd taken from the diner down the street, and sat down at the little table. He had stacks of takeout menus stained with coffee rings, yesterday's paper, and, propped up against the wall, snapshots of his kids. He'd arranged them in order of age, from the oldest to the youngest. Just as he was taking his first sip of coffee, someone knocked on his door.

"It's Damon," a deep voice said. "You there, man?"

Logan got up and opened the door. "What's up?" he said, stepping aside to let Damon in.

Damon's upper arms were like hams; the back of his head was a series of hard rolls that widened until they met his shoulders. Logan wondered how he managed the creases when he shaved his head. Damon kept barbells in his room. Logan heard them clanking late at night.

"Sorry to bug you, man. Hey, you got any aspirin I can borrow?"

"Yeah, yeah. Come on in. Hey, you get that gig at the convo home?"

"Yep. I'll be working three nights a week to start. Midnight to eight. We'll see how it goes."

"Way to go." Logan found the aspirin in his shaving kit. "Your teeth still acting up on you?"

Damon nodded. He was a good-looking guy, but his teeth were so encrusted with plaque it was hard to look at him. His breath wasn't so great, either.

"Why don't you see a dentist, man?" Logan said. "You gotta take care of that."

"No way, man. There's no way in hell." Damon shook a little pile of aspirin into his hand and started chomping them like Life Savers. "One place you are *never* going to see me is the dentist."

"Why not? Those aspirin are going to do a number on your stomach."

"Already have. Sometimes it feels like I just had me a battery-acid milkshake." Damon smiled. The gold cross he wore sparkled against his white T-shirt.

"Well, lay off 'em, for Christsake."

"I try, but days like today it feels like somebody's playing drums on my molars. Sometimes I need a break. Hey, at least I won't have a heart attack. My blood's so thin you can see through it."

"There's gotta be a clinic. Someplace you can go where they'll work on you for nothing. Or at least cheap."

"It ain't the money. That's not it. I'm scared shitless, man. When I was inside, they worked on me for free. It's torture, bro," Damon said in his rapid-fire way. "They sent me to a dental school. Cuffed me to the chair, man. You see that movie *Marathon Man*? It was like that. Root canal. Stuck something in my mouth so I couldn't close it. Damn student had never done one before. Chinese son of a bitch, had to keep running to get the teacher because he didn't know what he was doing. You understand what I'm saying? I was screaming like a stuck pig, man. Out of my fucking head." He cradled his jaw in his hand tenderly, as if the ache were still there, before he went on. "No fucking way I'm ever going to a dentist again. Nope. My teeth can rot and fall out of my head for all I care. Hey, these your kids?" Damon picked up the first snapshot and inspected it close to the window.

"Yeah, they're all mine. That's Jewell, my oldest. She's at UCLA now. Smart kid. I'm counting on her to support me in my old age."

"How old is she here?"

"I don't know. Three or four." Logan took the picture and looked at it like he'd never seen it before. Jewell was about to jump from a sawed-off tree stump, her hands in the air. She had been a fierce kid, stubborn as hell and determined to do everything herself. "I gotta see her one of these days," he added. "It's been a while."

"How long?"

Logan frowned and looked out the window. His coffee had gone cold. Traffic would be bad on the way to the airport. "Jeez, I guess I haven't seen her since she was in high school." He remembered her as she'd been that last time: sullen, answering him with the least possible number of words from behind a curtain of waist-length hair. He'd been sent up not long after that, and she'd written him a few times, impersonal letters made up mostly of song lyrics and poetry written by people he'd never heard of.

"I'm going to hook up with her pretty soon, though. She's on my list. Hey, why don't you keep these," Logan said, pushing the bottle of aspirin toward Damon. "If I need any, I'll let you know."

"All right. I owe you one," Damon said, taking the pills and heading for the door. "Hang in there, buddy."

"Okay. Later."

Adrian must have turned his TV off, because when Logan locked the door behind Damon, his room was quiet. There was only the distant sound of rush hour: people hurrying to get home to houses they owned, to cooked meals and cheerful kids. Logan felt a weight come down on his chest, enough to make him sit down on the foot of the bed. The banged-up furniture and stained walls, all the people down the hall who had one story or another. Damon's aching teeth, the kids he hadn't seen, his job wiping grown men's asses. Even his damn pickup was falling apart. His life had pretty much been one fuckup after another, so why should it be any different now? He thought of his mother, who'd been dead now for almost six years. She'd never made any secret of the fact that Logan was her favorite, the baby. In her eyes he could do no wrong.

He needed money. He took off his shirt and lay back on the faded bedspread that smelled of someone else's hair oil and let the sun, which fell in a square on the bed, warm him. There was no way he could get a fresh start or change anything in his life without some cash. *Where?* he thought. *How* was he going to get it? His crotch heated up and he felt the slow pull of an erection. He unfastened his pants and masturbated halfheartedly, as the faint beat of disco started up again down the hall. A door slammed and locked, the elevator clanked. The woman he imagined now was one he'd constructed carefully over the years, an amalgam culled from advertisements and movies, from women he'd seen in the street or over coffee counters, from wives and girlfriends, women he'd known intimately and hardly at all. She was a formless creature he knew very well, a shape-shifter who changed over the years to suit his tastes, accompanying him through most of his life.

"You have the most beautiful dick," she said now, borrowing her words from Logan's first wife, Jewell's mother. "It isn't huge, but it has perfect form. I'd know it anywhere."

No matter how many times he came, it still felt great. "Remember the best orgasm you ever had? Don't you wish someone had been there to share it with you?" the woman of his dreams said now, laughing just like an actress who sold coffee on one of the TV spots he'd seen in prison. She borrowed the punchline from a woman Logan had never slept with but wished he had, the sister of a guy he shared an apartment with about four years before. "She's a dyke," the roommate had said. "Forget about it."

The jism on his stomach warmed in the sun. He thought again

about Salvetti from earlier today and wondered if he ever got off. Was it even possible? Did his wife ever sit on his face? Masturbate for him? Suck his cock? Whatever, Logan thought, scooping the mess up with his hand. It was getting late, he needed to go. Half-babies, one of his girlfriends had called it. Spunk, cosmic goo, ragout of DNA. He washed in the sink, dried his hands on a towel he'd kept in storage while he did his time.

He felt a little better. A little empty, maybe, but lighter, not so bad about himself. He was young and good looking. Optimistic. People liked him. He'd been outside for two months and he hadn't fucked up. Not yet. Something good might happen, he told himself.

You never knew.

The Lincoln Town Car drove like a cruise ship after Logan's Toyota. He kept hitting the windshield wipers instead of the blinker. He wore the long-sleeved white shirt and the Bogart jacket, a pair of brown cords pleated in the front. And the Italian shoes, of course. The guy had given him forty bucks when he picked up the car, which had a full tank. The sign they'd given him lay on the passenger's seat. STONE. And the three guys he was picking up would tip him, at least they *should*. So he was looking at a good fifty or sixty bucks, plus free gas if he finished early and wanted to run a few errands.

They were tearing up the roads around LAX. Huge pits of raw red dirt, mountains of gravel, orange cones all over the place. The place looked like a bomb had hit it. Logan inched forward in stop-and-go traffic. He thought again how he'd like to get away from all the mobs, move up to the Sierra and live the country life. He knew a few people up there. Only trouble was they were cooking meth and shipping it down south, and he had to stay away from that kind of thing. He could open a restaurant or run a ranch, except he had no experience. Live in a trailer, it didn't matter. Or maybe get a job working on the roads. At the stoplight, the woman in the next car looked at him and smiled. Logan smiled back, nodded. There were lots of possibilities in the world.

The flight Logan was to meet was delayed twenty minutes, so he had a little time to kill. The men's room was blocked off with yellow sawhorses that said WET FLOOR. Big fans were blowing on the soggy carpet outside. Beyond that was a bar; Logan wondered if it was Tommy's. Most of the barstools were taken, but he found one near the pretzel machine. The older woman tending bar looked like she could strangle you with one hand and mix a drink with the other. His napkin was on the counter before he'd settled on the stool.

"What would you like?" she said.

Logan ordered coffee.

"Say, does a guy named Wylie work here?" he asked when she brought it. "Tom Wylie?"

The woman looked him up and down. Ugly-ass shirts they made them wear. Pukey beige. Her hair was dyed shoe-polish black. GEORGETTE, it said on her name tag.

"Why, he owe you money?" she finally asked.

Logan laughed and glanced around at the others in the bar. Mostly guys by themselves, some staring down at their drinks or across the bar, others looking up at the news on the TV screen. Two women with deep tans and bleached hair were deep in conversation with each other. A couple of husband-and-wife teams.

"No, I wish he did," he said, flashing his smile. "He's my brother. My big brother."

"That right?" The woman's arms were knotty, hard. "Wylie works here, but he's not on now. Got off at three."

"I'm meeting a plane," Logan explained. "I had a little time and thought I'd drop in and see if he was here."

He looked around at the twirling pretzels and junky neon lights. This was it, then. The sad-ass place where Tommy put in his eight hours. All the people coming and going, the canned air and the loudspeaker telling someone to pick up a white courtesy telephone. So impersonal it made your heart ache. He felt a sudden sadness for his brother, remembering him as a kid. A serious boy, as Logan recalled, eager to please. The loner type, or was that just how it seemed to Logan, who was always running around in a pack, surrounded by friends? But Tommy could kick ass, he remembered that. Even though he wasn't that big, he had a reputation at school. Once his temper flared up, that was it. You were dead meat if you messed with Tommy.

"Coffee's on the house," Georgette said. "I'll tell Wylie you were here. You want anything else?"

One of the blondes was giving him the eye, or at least the once-over.

"So what's it like working with Tommy?" Logan said, loading his coffee with sugar.

Georgette shrugged. She wore several gold rings studded with lots of small, colored stones. "Nice guy, your brother. Low-key. Knows the ropes. Pretty private, you know. I wouldn't exactly call him a motormouth."

"Sounds like Tommy."

The coffee was thick and bitter, like it had been standing in the pot all day.

"You live here in town?" Georgette asked while she picked up the older couple's credit card and ran it through the machine.

Now both the blondes were staring at him. Logan made eye contact just long enough to keep them guessing. They whispered conspiratorially to each other, still glancing in his direction.

"Yeah, I got a place up in San Marino," he said. It just slipped out, but it worked. Georgette tipped her head like a spaniel listening to a strange sound and looked at him with new admiration. The Bogart jacket was working its magic. To top things off, the blondes were headed in his direction.

Georgette saw them coming. "Let me know if you need anything else," she said before heading to the other side of the bar.

The women crowded his stool, close enough for him to smell

their perfume. Even though it was November, they both wore tank tops. Little bands of stomach showed. Gold chains and lots of makeup.

"Excuse me," one of them said. "Sorry to bother you."

"No problem at all," Logan smiled, half turning on his stool.

The older couple at his side turned to watch. So did a few of the guys across the bar.

"My friend and I thought we recognized you," the spokeswoman for the duo said. "We couldn't figure out from where, though." She paused, looked at her friend, then back at Logan. "You're in the business, right?"

Logan knew better than to ask *what* business. Up close he could see the trouble the women had taken with their faces: the lip-liner and plucked eyebrows, the way their foundation ended under their chins. Hair moussed and sprayed to look tousled.

"Who wants to know?" he asked with a kidding smile.

"Oh, this is Lisa," the talkative one said. "My name is Janet."

"Logan," he said, extending his hand. "Pleased to meet you."

Their hands were narrow. Cool and limp. They were a little tipsy. He could smell the booze on their breath, possibly tequila.

The silent one snapped her fingers like she'd just remembered something. "That program about a magazine, right? You're the guy who plays a photographer. And that commercial, too. Where the guy dreams he wakes up in this giant house right on the ocean." She giggled. "He gets up and stands at the window in his underwear."

Logan pursed his lips like he was trying to remember, while he calculated how much time he had before he had to meet the plane. He had the Lincoln, which might come in handy. What if he just forgot about Stone, told the service he never showed up, and drove the women around in the car?

"No, I think it's film," the one named Janet said. "That movie with Sean Penn."

"You're both on the right track," Logan said, looking at his watch. "Trouble is, I have to meet someone whose plane is arriving in just a few minutes. How long are you ladies going to be here?"

They looked at each other.

"We have to leave in about a half hour," Janet said anxiously.

"You want to meet up later on? After I drop my friend off?"

Both of them, Logan thought. That might be nice. With any luck, one of them had a place of her own, because he sure as hell couldn't take them back to the Morningstar.

"Oh, no. We're *leaving*," Janet said. Her face looked genuinely pained. "Back home, I mean. We're flying out. Our plane leaves in a half hour. We're going back to *Phoenix*."

"Ah," Logan said slowly, nodding. That was it, then. Close, but no cigar. "Well, listen. It's been great talking to you. I've got to get going." He put a dollar on the bar for Georgette, stood, and picked up his sign, careful to keep the STONE side toward his leg. He brushed his lips lightly across each of their cheeks. Jeez, they smelled good.

"See you in the movies," he said, turning and waving as he headed off to the greeting area.

The new security made it a pain in the ass to meet anyone getting off a plane. Logan stood at the back of a mob of people who watched the trickle of passengers coming through the barrier. You couldn't tell what flight was disembarking. People came in spurts: one or two, nothing, a clot of five or six, an empty space, a short stream of ten or twelve. Logan watched their faces. He tried to guess if the flight had been smooth or bumpy, if the people were arriving in an unfamiliar city or coming home. Their eyes swept the crowd anxiously for a familiar face, broke into relief when they spotted whoever was meeting them. Others hurried past the waiting crowd with their eyes on the ground, knowing that no one would be there to put their arms around them, to kiss them and cry with joy. Weird animals, people. They held up babies, handed each other bouquets of flowers. Men in wrinkled business suits, families in sweat outfits, old ladies coming to visit their grandkids. It was still strange for Logan to see people who could get on a plane and fly wherever they wanted, who could walk out into the night and hail a cab, head down to Mexico, rent a hotel room, go out for a steak dinner. Drop in on a friend or see a movie. It probably didn't occur to any of them that at that very moment there were people who were locked up in cells, whose every movement was restricted.

Even more amazing that he was here, on the outside. He shifted his feet, looked at his watch. He held his sign at waist level and leaned against the counter behind him. There were two other men with signs, both of them in uniforms. What he had missed most while he was inside were tacos. Carne asada in a soft corn tortilla with a heap of fresh, fiery salsa. A cold beer to wash it down. He had lain in his bunk and pictured it, the same scene over and over: a wide, white beach late in the afternoon. The sound of the surf and the smell of the ocean. Him in a lounge chair, facing the water. A waitress in a bikini who worked at a stand up near the boardwalk would bring him three tacos on a big plate and an icy long-neck. Man, oh man. He could almost taste it.

Jesus, it was taking forever. What if the guy had already come through, if Logan had missed him? The crowd around him shifted impatiently. A Chicano guy with a buzzed head held the hand of a little girl with a balloon that said WELCOME HOME. She smiled up at Logan, a ring of chocolate around her mouth, and his memory fired suddenly on Jewell, how the hard white edges of her teeth had pushed through her gums when she was a baby. How he'd dipped his finger in whiskey and rubbed them, how she'd locked eyes with him while she chawed on his finger. The memory was so strong it engulfed him. That was the problem with getting clean—stuff started firing up. Everything came back to haunt you.

The Chicano guy took out a phone and flipped it open. His cell phone! Logan kept forgetting he had one. Why not kill a little time, reach out and touch someone? But who? Prison was hell on your social life. He took a chance on the speed-dial. Plugging one ear over the noise in the terminal, he listened to the electronic tones.

One, two, three.

Everything stopped when he heard the voice: his heart, his blood, his breathing in and out. He was thrown for a loop, as if his heels flew up over his head, as if he flipped, two somersaults in the air. Landing, not sure where. *His mother.* But not his mother as she'd been the last time he saw her, not as she'd be now if she were still alive. His mother when she was young, the way he remembered her as a child.

"Where are you?" she said.

His heart sank. The voice was similar, but it wasn't his mother. There was the same huskiness at the back of her throat, a reedy resonance that he hadn't heard in any other voice. But it wasn't her. For a minute he couldn't talk. It was like he'd lost her all over again. The same pain as that week after she'd died, when he'd followed the sun around on the floor of his room, sitting in the square of light, eating dry cereal out of the box and drinking warm, flat Coke from a liter bottle.

"You sound like my mother," he said bleakly.

"I don't sound anything like mom. She's from *Philadelphia.*"

"Not *your* mom. *My* mom."

Were they in an argument already? Logan watched the crowd of people surge toward him, the sea of strangers tired from their flights.

"Are you there?" his daughter asked.

"Huh?" Logan forced his eyes to focus.

"I said, *'Are you there?'*"

Good question, Logan thought. Good question.

Jewell had just closed the door on the Avon
Lady when the phone rang.

"Who?" she said into the phone. *"Who?"*

Some asshole playing a trick. Sitting there on the line breathing, beating off for all she knew. A dick, not saying anything. A psycho, not talking.

"It's me. Your *father.*"

"Oh yeah. My ass."

She knew it was, though. No one else had that ripple in his voice, as if he were talking through a grin. Her stomach froze. Now she thought the worst: he was on the run, or trying to get out of the country, or he wanted something. Why else would he call?

He chuckled. "You sound like your mother."

"What's wrong?" she asked. "Where are you?"

"Nothing's wrong. Just thought I'd say hey. I'm here at the airport."

It was like he'd pushed a button and a soundtrack came on. Now she heard the echo of big space, the noise of a crowd, a page over a loudspeaker, the beep of a courtesy cart.

"*Where?* What airport?"

"*Here.* Here in L.A. I'm at LAX."

"Where are you going?" she shouted frantically. God, her family. You don't talk to them in a couple of years, then you have a conversation like this. It was always crazy. It never made sense.

"Nowhere, babe. I'm staying right here. I'm at the airport on a job. Picking someone up. Just waiting around."

His phone broke up, and for an instant Jewell hoped that she'd lost him, that the line was severed and he'd never call back.

"Are you there?" she asked.

There was a loud pop and his voice snapped back on. "So, how're you doing? I finally tracked you down."

"How'd you get my number?"

"I had one you sent me while I was away. I called it and the guy there gave me this number."

Jewell hesitated. *Away.* That was what he called being in jail, like it was a business trip or a vacation. *The guy.* He must have called Hasani, the guy she'd been living with before she fell for Celeste. It figured he'd give out her number to anyone who called.

"Was that your guy?" Logan said when she didn't answer. His voice was youthful. *Your dad's hot,* her friends had told her the last time she'd seen him, in high school. He wasn't much older than some of the guys her more adventurous friends were dating. They'd made eyes at him, giggled.

"No, not really," Jewell said. Last time she'd seen her father, she'd been doing the straight thing. She didn't much feel like catching him up on the details of her life with Celeste. "I used to live there, that's all."

"Well, he seemed like a nice guy."

That was her dad, always upbeat. Jewell clenched the phone. All the imaginary conversations she'd had with him, all the things she'd practiced saying, and now she felt tongue-tied. "Where are you living?" she managed to ask after a tense pause.

"I've got a place downtown. Just temporary. I'm trying to get my act together so I can get settled. Find a nice place and put down a few roots. How about you? What're you up to?"

"I'm in school. UCLA." A drop of cold sweat rolled down her side.

"I know, I heard that from Tommy. I talked to him today. That's just great. That's really something. And what are you studying?"

Jesus, was she really having this conversation with her *father*? It was like a job interview, or a blind date. She stared at the stuff on the dining-room table: the project she was working on, the heaps of mail, the bag the Avon Lady had dropped off for Celeste. She hoped all the ruckus didn't wake up Rachel.

"Architecture." As if to prove it, she gestured toward the mess on the table. She had cotton mouth. It irked her that she wanted to impress him. "Urban design," she added in an offhand way.

"*Architecture!* You're kidding, right? Man, I can't believe it. Well, I'll be damned."

You could hear the hipster in his voice, the jailbird. Jewell wished she could see him. He'd come and gone so often, she didn't know how much of him she'd made up and how much was really him. She tried to remember why he'd been sent up the last time. Using, selling, or some kind of parole violation, she'd forgotten which. He always explained it away as a legal technicality that had caught him unfairly, a mistake in the system that had singled him out.

"Are you doing okay?" she asked cautiously.

He used to let her squeeze his hand with all her might, used to dare her to hurt him. She'd squeeze, dig her nails in, try to bend his fingers back. He'd just laugh into her eyes and ask her if that was the best she could do.

"Oh yeah. I'm great, fine," he said, like there was no reason for her to suspect otherwise. In the background a gong chimed and an amplified voice made an announcement. The connection broke up again, and a rushing silence washed over her like a wave. He was gone, dragged out to sea in the churn of the retreating static, nothing but foam and bubbles left behind.

"You there?" he said, his voice back, but tiny and far away.

She pictured him on the horizon, a stick figure. "Yes. Listen, this is crazy." Before she could stop herself, she added, "Do you want to get together?"

"Absolutely!" Static popped like water in hot fat. "Oh, hey," he said. "Yeah, yeah, right away."

It took her a moment to realize he was talking to someone else.

She heard another man's voice, what sounded like a palm over the receiver.

"Listen, babe," Logan said to her, "I gotta go."

"Okay, good-bye," she said, and slammed down the phone even though she knew he'd already hung up. She kicked the dining-room chair. God, she'd been stupid again! Every time he called she was like a fawning dog, happy to forget the past and come running. How many times did she have to fall for it? He never had a fucking care in his life. Just showed up whenever he felt like it, then disappeared for months and years until he cropped up out of nowhere again.

She went into the kitchen, opened the refrigerator, and stood staring inside. Mr. Goodtime Charlie. Mr. Cheerful. She wondered why her father had bothered having kids—not just her but the four who came after her, alien creatures who shared half her blood. She'd probably seen them a grand total of twenty times in her whole life, but she thought of them now as she took out the peanut butter and ate a few spoonfuls straight out of the jar. There was Stephen, the nearsighted whiner he'd had with his second wife, a small, mousy woman Jewell supposed he married in a half-assed attempt to keep himself on the straight and narrow. That hadn't worked. His next wife was a speed freak barely out of high school. Their kids, Heather and Tony, must be teenagers by now. Jewell hadn't seen them in ages; they'd gone to live with their grandparents when Logan and their mother had gotten busted at the same time. Then there was the last one, a girl named Jamie whom Jewell had seen only once, when the kid was about a year old. Logan had shown up with her and a young, silent woman who Jewell assumed was the girl's mother at Jewell's high school graduation. "Meet your little sis," Logan had said, passing her to Jewell. She was a beautiful kid, very calm. Jewell had carried her to a corner of the auditorium and stared into her face. "You're in for it, kid, did you know that?" she'd asked the smiling baby.

She screwed the lid back on the peanut butter, put it away, and drank from the faucet in the kitchen sink. You could say one thing about her father, he sure got around. For all Jewell knew, she had twenty more half brothers and sisters she'd never heard of. She was the favorite, though, she had to be. The first, the one who looked most like Logan, the one he'd had when he was young, before all the trouble started. The one he'd called on the phone.

She wandered back into the dining room and looked at her half-built project—a project, she reminded herself, that was due in two weeks. She looked at the clock on the bookshelf: 6:10. Celeste's meeting with Rachel's teacher was at 4:30, so Celeste should be home soon.

"You've got to get a grip on this," Celeste had told her that morning during their argument.

"On what?" Jewell said, as if she didn't know.

Jewell eased the staple out of the bag the Avon Lady had left. *Inez Cullen,* it said on the bill, a strange name for someone who looked Asian. Jewell looked down at the jumble of boxes and bottles. *Your daughter?* the nosy Avon Lady had asked, craning her neck to get a look into the bedroom where Rachel lay napping among the piles of laundry on the bed. She'd sniffed around the place like it was Sodom and Gomorrah while Jewell made out the check. Magenta fingernails and every hair in place, with a big cross around her neck.

Jewell pawed through the lipstick, body lotion, powder, and face cream. God knew why Celeste had to buy so much for everybody: her millions of friends who seemed to pop up wherever she went, her sneaky-eyed sisters, her mother whom she talked to almost every day. Cousins and aunts and friends of the family. Not to mention her ex-girlfriend Dana, who was practically joined at Celeste's hip. The thought of Celeste and Dana together, riding side by side in Dana's car, or possibly discussing the outcome of the meeting with Rachel's teacher in a café afterward, made the roots of Jewell's teeth ache.

Stop, she told herself. Enough already.

She was folding the bag back exactly the way it had been and bending the staple into place when Rachel appeared in the doorway.

Jewell jumped.

"What's that?" Rachel asked.

The kid had a narrow face, widely spaced eyes, translucent skin, and copper hair that stood in a crest down the middle of her head. Jewell liked her. "You're awake," she said, guilty to be caught in the act of rifling through the bag.

Rachel nodded. Her eyes were the same reddish brown as her hair. She wore only her underpants and a T-shirt decorated with owls, her favorite animal.

"That lady woke me up," she said, leaning against Jewell. She pointed at the Avon bag. "What's that?"

"That's your mom's. Aren't you cold?"

Rachel shook her head.

"Are you hungry?"

Rachel fixed Jewell with one of her extraterrestrial stares. Jewell wondered if she'd figured out where Jewell fit into this whole two-mom picture. If so, maybe she'd let Jewell in on the answer. Celeste and Dana had adopted Rachel after she'd spent her first year and a half in foster care. Jewell put down the Avon bag and hoisted Rachel onto her hip. She had the sudden desire to kidnap her, to pack a suitcase, climb in her car, and hit the road. She imagined living in a trailer in the desert with Rachel, watching her grow up as the two of them crisscrossed the country. She pictured Celeste in the supermarket, reaching for a carton of milk in the dairy section and seeing Jewell and Rachel's photos side by side on the carton. Missing, location unknown.

"Let's dance," Rachel said.

"Not now. I'm working. I'll make you a scrambled egg and you can eat here, while I work on my project. After that you can draw, okay? I'll let you use my paper and pens. You can help me."

Rachel nodded.

She understood Rachel better than Dana and Celeste did, Jewell thought as she broke an egg in a coffee mug and beat it with a fork. She'd practically grown up in other people's houses herself. Her mother the space cadet and her father the lowlife had married when they were barely eighteen, so it was no wonder they weren't exactly model parents. You can't blame a person for being depressed, but ever since Jewell could remember, her mother had spent a hefty portion of time in her darkened bedroom, watching movies on the TV balanced on a little stand at the foot of the bed, or working out complicated star charts with the aid of a thick paperback. The folds of the blankets were lined with food wrappers, pencils and paper for her astrological predictions, magazines, body lotion, and long-overdue video rentals. So Jewell was pretty much on her own. It wasn't that bad; in fact, she was the envy of the other kids. She could stay outside as late as she wanted, long after the others had been called inside. She could wear what she wanted, eat what she pleased, stay at whatever friend's house she felt like without asking permission. "Honey, don't you *ever* have to go home?" her best friend's mother had asked when Jewell was in second grade. Friends' families took care of her: fed her; put her to bed with their own children; took her to swimming lessons and softball; drove her to movies, picnics, the beach. In junior high, one friend's mother—an executive in the recording industry—had even bought her school clothes. Jewell's mother had a typically offbeat sense of what was acceptable to wear. Half the time she just pulled the bedspread off the bed when she got up and wore it like a sarong around the house or—sometimes—even to the store. But that had its advantages, too. Jewell had gotten away with wearing nothing but a vintage slip she picked up at the thrift store to high school one day, a camouflage jumpsuit from army surplus the next.

"You want catsup?" Jewell asked as she lifted the egg onto a plate.

Rachel nodded rapidly.

Yep, her mom had been clueless in a lot of ways, Jewell reflected as she dripped polka dots of catsup on the egg the way Rachel liked it. Her father, too, for that matter. In fact, now that she thought about it, the three of them pretty much had their own separate lives straight from the get-go. Logan certainly didn't know what to make of her mother's funks, which had given him a good excuse to go off and live it up on his own. Although sometimes things had clicked—like the time a friend of her parents managed to score a house down in Baja, right at the end of a dirt road near a bay where the stingrays were so thick you had to wear sneakers in the water and drag your feet when you waded out, to scatter them out of the way. You could see them below the surface, rising up like petals when you got near, fluttering away, drifting down in another spot about ten feet ahead. In the morning you felt the heat even before you opened your eyes and heard the roosters crowing, close up and farther away, like echoes of each other. For once her parents seemed to be happy right where they were, smiling at each other across the room while she and the other kids tumbled around on the tile floor and the other parents lounged on big couches, peeling the shrimp they bought by the bucket down at the little dock and washing it down with long-necked bottles of cold, pale beer. At night it was so dark. Jewell had walked between her parents down to a circle of concrete where a band played and people danced, smoke rising from a bonfire into the black sky and children chasing each other in the shadows. Her parents had danced and danced, laughing, until the sweat poured off them. All the men—both the locals and the friends who'd come down from L.A.—wanted to cut in on Logan and dance with Jewell's mother. "Man, would you look at her," Logan laughed, standing behind Jewell on the edge of the concrete as her mother followed every move of the slim, serious Mexican man who turned and twirled her. Jewell felt Logan's hands on her shoulders, smelled his warm, beery breath as he bent down and whispered next to her ear. "Just *look* at her, will you?"

"Okay, here you go," Jewell said, setting the egg down on the dining-room table. But the times when things worked out in her family were few and far between. She pushed Rachel's chair closer to the table. "Be careful, it's hot. Blow on it first."

Rachel ate a few tiny bites and pointed her fork across the table at the project Jewell had been working on for months now. "Whassat?" she said.

Rachel was the only one who was really interested in Jewell's project. Jewell was embarrassingly pleased and eager to explain. "It's a community housing plan," she said, waving her Exacto knife over the scraps of balsa wood and foam core. "See, here's where the people live, and here's where they cook dinner. Here's where they eat, all together. And when they're done, they can go outside here and watch movies. See, *outside.* If it's warm they show the movies right here on the side of the building. Get it?"

Rachel squinted her eyes. You could tell she was really thinking about it.

Jewell pointed to another building. "And they can sleep outside, too, if they want. See these balconies right outside the bedrooms? In the summer when it's hot, your bed just rolls outside on tracks. What do you think about that?"

Rachel chewed solemnly. She wasn't the kind of kid who got things on her face when she ate. Jewell wondered about her mother, the one who had given birth to her. She was fourteen when Rachel was born, Celeste had told her. Jewell had gotten pregnant herself her first year in college. Making the decision to get an abortion took about two seconds.

"Where do the children play?" Rachel asked.

Jewell laughed. *Children.* Probably a word that uptight Dana had taught her. "Right here," she said. "See, there's a place in the middle with the buildings all around. That way no cars can hit them and their moms can watch them. They're safe. And if one kid wants to come out and play, she'll know the other kids are there waiting for her."

"I want to live there," Rachel said.

"That's why I'm making it. Look, here's where they wash clothes. And the old people, they live here. They take care of the kids when their moms and dads are at work. Here's the garden where they grow food. It's *organic.*"

She pointed excitedly to everything, even though she could see the poor kid was getting bored. The problem with her project was that it was too detailed. She got all wrapped up in deciding how many cupboards there'd be in the kitchen, where the shower heads would go, and what kind of paving stones to use on the patio. In the meantime she was so behind she'd be lucky to finish it by the due date.

"It's a *utopia*," she said. "You know what that means?"

"My eggs is all gone."

"It's where everything is perfect. It's like paradise—"

"All done!"

Jewell gave up. "Okay, that's a good girl," she laughed. "You want to play now? Sit here and play while I do some work?"

"Play what?"

"I don't know. Whatever. Color or something. Play with your Barbie."

"Barbie's on vacation. She won't be back for a long, long time."

Man, this kid. She and Jewell had a stare-down. Rachel furrowed her brow and asked, "How come you're living here with my Mimi?"

Jewell choked. "Good question," she fumbled, even though she knew you shouldn't say that kind of thing to a four-year-old.

Rachel just stared.

"We love each other," Jewell ventured in what she hoped was a soothing, convincing tone. The way normal people talked to their children. "We want to be together."

"Like her and my mom?" Rachel shot back.

Who programmed this kid? Jewell grabbed Rachel's plate and glass off the table, bolted into the kitchen, and slammed the dishes in the sink.

"Let's take a bath," Rachel called sweetly from the dining room.

"Your mom didn't say you should have a bath," Jewell shouted. She ran the water full force, blasting the egg from the dish just like she did at the cafeteria. Where *was* Celeste, anyway? She should have been home by now. Maybe she and Dana were taking advantage of their sucker babysitter so that they could spend some quality time together. Maybe they had gone back to Dana's empty house and—

"Yes, she did!" Rachel shouted.

When Jewell stepped back into the dining room, Rachel gave her a shove.

"No, she didn't. And don't push."

Rachel fixed her eyes on Jewell's face and nodded solemnly. "She did. She told me to tell you."

The kid was frightening. Jewell laughed, but when she inhaled, a tender pain throbbed in the pit of her stomach. For the first time she realized she loved Rachel, too. Oh God, when did that happen? Queasiness overtook her. She grasped Rachel by the hand and led her to the bathroom, where she stuck the plug in the bath and cranked on the water.

"Okay, get undressed."

"Make it deep. I want to float," Rachel commanded as she stripped.

"You ever hear of the water shortage?"

Rachel scrambled over the side of the tub. She was so skinny you could see every knob in her spine. If Jewell kidnapped her, she'd have to flee to another country. She imagined the two of them ten years from now, herself a famous architect in Italy; Rachel a self-possessed teen. This dingy little rental would be a distant memory. She tested the water and added more hot.

"Deeper!" Rachel cried.

"No, you'll slosh water on the floor. That's deep enough."

"You get in, too."

"No, I'll sit here on the floor. Don't splash."

"Okay, watch."

Rachel held her nose and slid down on her back so that her head sank underwater. She lay faceup, as rigid as a mummy, her huge, wide-apart eyes staring at the ceiling. Seconds ticked by, then what seemed like minutes. Jewell wondered if Rachel could see her through the water.

"Okay, that's enough," Jewell shouted. "Come up!"

Rachel didn't blink. Jewell gestured frantically. Finally she plunged her arm into the water and jerked Rachel's head up.

Rachel laughed like a maniac. "I can hold my breath a long

time!" she yelled, water streaming down her face. "I can keep my eyes open underwater! Did you think I was dead!? Did I fool you!?"

Jewell's jaw trembled. She didn't know which she wanted to do more: burst into tears or shake Rachel until her teeth rattled. "Don't do that anymore," she said between clenched teeth. "You scared the shit out of me."

"That's a bad word," Rachel said. Now *she* looked ready to cry.

Jewell sighed and let her forehead rest on the edge of the tub. "I'm sorry. But you scared me."

Rachel patted her head. "You can hear a lot down there," she whispered close to Jewell's ear. "Whales, and lots of fish."

"Can you really?"

Rachel nodded. "Are you going to leave?" she asked.

It wasn't the first time Jewell had felt some strange telepathy with Rachel. Still, it took her by surprise. "Oh, Rachel. How could I ever leave *you*?" Jewell croaked. "I'm going to stay right here. I promise." She paused, wrestling with herself. Her better instincts lost, as usual, and she added, "Why do you ask?"

Rachel patted the surface of the water and avoided looking at Jewell.

"Rachel?"

"What?"

"Did you hear what I said?"

"No," Rachel said brightly.

"Why did you ask me if I was leaving?"

Rachel grimaced. "My mom said you were," she finally mumbled.

"What did she say?" Jewell demanded.

Rachel shrugged coyly.

"Which mom are you talking about?"

Rachel became absorbed in a drop suspended from the faucet.

"Your mom Dana or your Mimi Celeste?"

"Do the waterfall!" Rachel cried, grabbing the plastic bucket from the corner of the tub and thrusting it at Jewell.

Jewell forced herself to take a deep breath. It wasn't right to interrogate Rachel like that, but she had to know. "Rachel?" she prompted. "What did she say? Was it Celeste? Who said what? Tell me and I'll do the waterfall." She took the bucket and held it up enticingly.

"That you were leaving," Rachel whined. Her curls had started to dry and were springing back up on the top of her head.

"Who? Dana or Celeste?"

Rachel lunged for the bucket, but Jewell held it out of her reach. "Which one? Tell me, if you want the waterfall."

"Dana."

That bitch Dana. Too bad Jewell couldn't murder her. She was choked with rage, too mad to think. "Okay, get ready," she rasped grimly, filling the bucket. "Hold your nose and close your eyes. Tight!"

She dumped the bucket of water over Rachel's head and watched it run down her clenched eyes and puckered mouth. Rachel sputtered and gasped. "Again!" she yelled as soon as she got her breath.

"Niagara Falls!" Jewell screeched. She dumped bucket after bucket over Rachel's head, giving her just enough time to get her breath. When she stopped, Rachel was laughing hysterically.

Jewell was exhausted. She'd like to climb into the tub herself. Lie on her back as Rachel had, and feel the warm water close over her face.

"Wash," she told Rachel. "Use soap."

Rachel washed dramatically, closing her eyes and stretching her arms toward the ceiling as she lathered, the way she'd seen on TV commercials. "Tell me about my house," she said. "The one with the pool."

Jewell sighed. It would be nice to be with an adult instead of sitting there on the bathroom floor watching a four-year-old pretend to shave her armpits. She'd like to go away with Celeste, drive up the coast to San Francisco for a romantic weekend. The bay, the fog, the Golden Gate Bridge. When they'd first gotten together, just over a year ago, they'd talked all night, night after night. Their faces inches apart, whispering. Jewell had never known she had so much to say. She herself listened with amazement to the story of her own life: how she always got shuttled around to whoever would take her when her mother was having one of her freakouts. Once Jewell had lived with her father and his second wife, Stephen's mother, a high-strung hypochondriac who had cut off Jewell's beloved braids, permed her hair, and forced her to wear dresses, white ankle socks, and shoes with buckles. *Call me mother,* she had instructed Jewell, who had finally escaped by setting a series of small fires in the house. In the meantime her real mother had gotten her act together—at least temporarily—and landed a job as a live-in cook for a movie producer who raised Dalmatians as a hobby. Jewell was allowed to sleep with a pack of dogs in her bed, wear her bathing suit year-round, and grow her hair as long as she wanted.

Talking to Celeste, it had occurred to Jewell for the first time that her childhood would strike a lot of people as strange. "It's amazing that you're as normal as you are," Celeste had said. "Not that you're all that normal." They talked long past the time when the noise of the freeway died down, until the only traffic sounds they heard were the night buses grinding up faraway hills.

"Hey!" Rachel shouted. "Anybody home?" She knocked on Jewell's forehead.

"It's time to get out now," Jewell said. "Stand up and let's dry you off."

"Tell me about the house you're going to make for me," Rachel insisted.

It was an old game, one that Rachel—and Jewell, too, for that matter—never got tired of. "The house I'm going to make you has a pool in every room," Jewell began as she wrapped the towel around Rachel. Her body felt like a skinny cat, all sinew, bone, and muscle. She was feather-light to lift out of the tub. "When you wake up in the morning, you dive out of your bed and swim to the bathroom. But instead of a bathtub, you have another pool. This one is as big as a lake. It's full of pretty fish and has a waterfall and a diving board."

"And a slide," Rachel interjected. She pretended her teeth were chattering from the cold as Jewell dried her.

"And when it's time to eat your breakfast, you swim to a table outside, where there's another pool with starfish and dolphins," Jewell said.

Where *was* Celeste? She should have been home long ago. Jewell wondered how Celeste would feel if she came back to the house and found no trace of Jewell and Rachel. Just a few drops of water in the tub and a damp towel.

"Now we wrap you up like a big taco!" Jewell said, passing the towel around Rachel's body. When she picked her up, the phone rang.

"Ah, Jesus. Who is it *this* time?"

"Jesus *Christ,*" Rachel swore with alarming facility.

"I don't know if you should say that," Jewell said as she carried Rachel to the phone.

"*You* said it."

"Too bad you're so smart."

"It's Mama," Rachel said as Jewell picked up the phone.

"We're at La Palma," Celeste said. "Dana and I stopped by for something to eat before we came home. You want me to bring you something? How's Rachel doing?"

All that stopped Jewell from kicking over the table where the phone sat were Rachel's legs clamped around her waist. She listened into the phone as though listening down a well. In the echoing, black silence of the open line she heard the whispered conversations of everyone attached to the thin filament that webbed the earth. *Pick up a sixer on the way home hell yes I gave it to him what do you expect send someone over my toilet's overflowing I'm afraid you tested positive I swear baby that's what happened they'll be gone the whole week that's our chance I love you but I can't stay.* People telling lies, plotting crimes, saying good-bye.

"Do whatever you want," Jewell said, her voice dead with cold, white rage. "I don't care."

"What's wrong?" Celeste asked.

There were no restaurant sounds in the background. No conversation or clatter of dishes. Jewell could hear Dana in Celeste's voice. She was standing there beside Celeste, listening. Jewell could see them rolling their eyes at each other, Celeste shaking her head.

"I'm here with Rachel," Jewell rasped. Her mouth and throat felt as if they'd been swabbed out with fiberglass. "I've been here all afternoon."

"I'm sorry, Jules," Celeste said.

She *did* sound pained, truly sorry. She wasn't apologizing for what she'd *done*, Jewell realized, but for what she was *going* to do. Not for dumping Rachel on Jewell or leaving her a few hours too long, but for everything that was going to happen, from that moment until they parted ways.

12 Inez decided to make meatloaf instead of hamburgers, even though Rudy might not like it. She beat eggs with a fork, chopped onions, and crushed saltines with the rolling pin. Instead of spreading frozen French fries on a baking sheet, she washed three russets to bake. She hoped he didn't mind. She grated cabbage and carrots for cole slaw. Rabbit food, he called it. But there was cholesterol to think of. Fat and high blood pressure. Plus, she and Vanessa liked it. For dessert they'd have vanilla ice cream with fruit cocktail on top.

Seven hundred nineteen dollars and thirty-seven cents. Using a solar-powered calculator that had come free in the mail, she had counted up every penny of the orders from that day. A record. That put her plan on the fast track, and as she mixed mayonnaise, vinegar, and sugar for the salad dressing, she allowed herself to add a few more details to the house that she'd begun to imagine for herself and Vanessa. She would go to Oregon, she had decided after watching a show on small towns in the United States. The place she had in mind was surrounded by trees. There was a Main Street with a post office and grocery store, a coffee shop where each customer kept his very own mug, and a church with a white steeple like on calendars. Things were on a smaller scale. Everybody knew everybody else. It was far enough away that no one would know her and Rudy would never find her, but not far enough to be foreign or to require a lot of money to get there. When the time was right, she and Vanessa would go there on the train. Later she'd learn to drive.

She stabbed the potatoes with a fork, greased them with Crisco, and put them in the oven. She pictured a bar chart showing how much money had piled up in the bottom of the cedar chest. When it hit a certain notch, she'd be ready to go. They wouldn't need a lot because they'd be starting over, she thought while she mixed the meatloaf with her hands, squishing it between her fingers. Starting from scratch. Everything new, everything hers. She formed the mixture into a loaf and covered it with a layer of catsup. It was all she'd ever wanted from the very earliest time she could remember, from the time she was in foster homes when everything came to her from someone else, clothes and beds and rooms that had already belonged to strangers. In her plan she saw the house as if it already existed, waiting for her. Brand-new, with clean white walls and empty, quiet rooms. When she got there, she'd be home.

Vanessa came in and leaned on the counter next to her. Such a good girl. She'd taken a shower and changed her clothes after coming home from gymnastics practice. Her wet hair hung down her back, sending up a strawberry smell. It was hard not to tell Vanessa her plans, to let her know that they wouldn't always be living there with Rudy. *He,* Vanessa called him. *Him.* Avoiding his name like she avoided his eyes. She was too good a girl, too nice a daughter, to tell Inez how she really felt, but Inez could tell. It won't be forever, she wanted to say now, excited as she slid the meatloaf in next to the potatoes. The oven was missing one of its racks. The door didn't close all the way; she had to prop it with a broomstick. Just wait, she wanted to say. It won't be long now. Pretty soon we'll be starting our lives. Our *real* lives. Our own.

"Ground beef's disgusting," Vanessa said. "You know what's in there? They just grind up all the cows together, sometimes two thousand of them at once. Isn't it sickening to think that there's parts of that many animals in that one ball of meat? Plus they feed them things like pigs' guts and cardboard."

"Is that what you learn in school?" Inez asked sharply.

"I read it in the paper."

"So, what now? You want to be a vegetarian?"

As if in answer, Vanessa picked up one of the stubs of carrot Inez had grated and nibbled on it. She was so smart, and pretty, too. Good in science and math, especially for a girl. She went to church with Inez every Sunday, did her homework after school. It was hard for Inez not to reach out and stroke her hair, to wrap her arms around her. But those days were over. Vanessa's face had a strange, grown-up stillness to it. It was impossible to know what went on in her mind.

"He's not home yet?" she said.

Inez shook her head. It was she who insisted Vanessa call him Daddy. Sometimes she felt bad about it, but they all had a part to play. Out of the corner of her eye she watched as Vanessa went to the sink and washed her hands. Vanessa was almost the age Inez had been when she'd met Vanessa's father, her *real* father, and seeing how young her daughter was—how little, really, she knew about life—Inez was beginning to see her own life in a different way. At the time she had thought she had a choice with Vanessa's father, that she was in love with him. *Fernando.* His name sounded unfamiliar because in truth she had never thought of him by that name, had never—painful as it was now to admit—thought of him as anything other than *Mr. Vanta.* She had only been sixteen, after all, and he was almost thirty years older. The only time she'd spoken to him was at church, with everyone around. He was a respected man, a *deacon,* so why should she distrust him?

This feeling comes from God, he had told her, pressing his hand against her body through her clothes. *He means it to be this way.*

Two times, that was all! *Two times* they had been together. She didn't often allow herself to think about it. But sneaking a glance at the dreamy look on Vanessa's face as she dried her hands on the dish towel hanging on the oven door, Inez realized more clearly than ever before how Mr. Vanta had tricked her, had forced her, pushing her further and further, taking little liberties—stopping in a deserted parking lot on the way home after Bible study, pressing her hands to his crotch in the supply room at the church—until he could threaten her with the things they'd already done, using them to push her a little bit further. She remembered how the oily smell of his cologne had clung to her neck after the first time, how terrified she'd been going back to the house where she lived with her adopted family.

She had never told anyone who Vanessa's father was. *Not one soul.* "A man from the church," was all she told Vanessa. "A mistake. A big mistake." Shame had kept her silent, shame at how stupid she'd been, at how she'd been duped. If Vanessa ever got anywhere *near* anyone like that! And what man Mr. Vanta's age would come anywhere near Vanessa, Inez wondered as she opened the oven and tested the meatloaf. Her jewel, her flower, her perfect angel! So innocent, just as she herself had been. So wrong!—though at the time she had no idea. She winced, closing the oven door, wondering if Mr. Vanta had persuaded any other girls in the church, if other children had been born—children who shared Vanessa's blood.

"My bangs need to be cut," Vanessa said, tipping back her head and blinking through her hair to make her point. She stretched out her hands and felt in front of her, pretending to be blind.

"Don't act silly," Inez scolded, though she couldn't help smiling. "I can trim them after dinner," she said.

"Ah, no! You never get them even. I'd rather go to the beauty shop—" Vanessa began to object, when Rudy's key turned in the lock and both of them froze.

Inez's stomach tightened. "Set the table," she said tersely. Now the evening begins, she thought, taking a deep breath. There would be dinner, cleaning up and making lunches, watching television in the small living room, then bed. Rudy stepped into the kitchen, and Inez's guard went up. There was something different in his face. Vanessa saw it, too. She stood behind Rudy, watchful. His arms were loaded with packages. Boxes wrapped with ribbons and bows. He smiled, even kissed Inez lightly on the lips.

"Dinner's almost ready," she said.

"No, no, not tonight," he said brightly, his round face splotchy with excitement. "Tonight's different. We're all going out to dinner."

He smiled, compressing his small features into the center of his face. His hair was like fluff on a baby bird. He selected one of the gifts and held it out to Inez. She saw how he wanted to please her, and she wished, not for the first time, that she could love him. But there was something hard in her chest, as undeniable as a heartbeat.

"But I cooked," she said. The smell of meatloaf and potatoes filled the room. "It's all ready." She stared at him, trying to figure out the strange glimmer in his eye. "What happened?" she finally asked.

Rudy put the gift he'd been holding out back on the stack. It was easy to mistake him for a gentle, quiet man, the kind who always thought of others first. Once she left, people would blame her. *Ungrateful,* they'd think. *Foreign. Too demanding.*

"It's my job," Rudy said. "I got a promotion." He smiled victoriously, as if he'd beaten her in a bet.

"You got a raise?"

"A promotion, a raise, a new job title!" He gestured impatiently with his small hands. "New responsibilities. It's about time, don't you think?"

Inez nodded slowly. So did Vanessa, but Inez saw the doubt in her eyes. "That's wonderful," she said, forcing a smile. "Congratulations to you."

"Congratulations to *all* of us!" Rudy corrected. "We can start putting money away to buy our own house now. That's what you want, isn't it? And we can start thinking of Vanessa's education. You want to go to college, don't you?" he said, turning toward her. "Now we can start planning for that. Hey, look at you." He set the packages on the counter and frowned theatrically. "I thought the two of you would be glad. Overjoyed! I thought this would make you happy." He dropped his head and looked at his feet. One of his shoes was untied. "I guess it doesn't matter," he sighed. "I guess nothing I do is right."

Inez roused herself. She felt genuinely ashamed. "No, I'm happy," she said, patting him on the shoulder. "Very happy." She pulled the meatloaf from the oven, then the potatoes. "Just surprised, that's all. It's all at once. So sudden, I don't know what to say."

She smiled at Rudy, her best smile. The one that had won him over. Placid and gracious, looking him full in the eyes. It always worked. After a minute of scrutinizing her, his face relaxed and his shoulders slipped down from where they were riding around his neck. "Okay, come on then!" he called, clapping his hands like a kid. "Let's go! Let's celebrate! Let's go out to dinner! You can open the gifts there. Anything you want. Anything and everything."

It was only after they were seated that Inez realized they were in the same restaurant she and Rudy had gone to before they were married. The very one, in fact, where he'd taken her on their first date and, three months later, proposed. The White Horse, how could she forget? Made to look like an English tavern, it had big stones plastered into the walls, massive timbers overhead, rounds of colored glass set in the windows. The furniture was dark and heavy, like someone had carved it with an ax. The place was lit with rustic chandeliers, candles on each table, and a huge fireplace along one wall. In the flickering firelight you felt like you were way out in some cold, wintry countryside instead of in the middle of L.A. Everything was the same as it had been eight years ago, right down to the waiters wearing knickers and flouncy shirts and the thick steaks they carried out on wooden planks, each one sporting a metal tag that said RARE, MEDIUM, or WELL DONE. She'd been so different back then, Inez reflected, like she was only half awake. Shy, sitting across the table from Rudy, but proud to be seen in a restaurant with a man. Normal, like all the other people. Well, what did she know? He'd been living with his mother then, who'd objected to the marriage because Inez wasn't white and already had a child. She'd died a few months after she and Rudy started dating. A week later he proposed.

They got a cramped table in the corner near the salad bar. Rudy held her chair. Vanessa kept her eyes down, her arms crossed over her chest.

The menu was on a plank, too. Their waiter, Alex, set it up on the table. PRIME RIB, SIRLOIN, FILET MIGNON. Potatoes baked, mashed, or fried. As many trips as you wanted to the salad bar.

"I can't eat all this meat," Vanessa whispered to Inez, though of course Rudy heard. Vanessa nodded toward the neighboring table, where a family of four were cutting into steaks that filled their entire plates.

"Meat's good," Rudy said. He smiled, trying to be nice. "Protein. You're growing. You need that."

Vanessa wouldn't answer, she wouldn't even look at Rudy. She kept her eyes on the table until the waiter came, then she ordered the salad bar. Inez would talk to her later, after they got home. Tell her to straighten up, to make an effort. She ordered the filet mignon, medium. Rudy got the prime rib, well done. She could use the meatloaf at home for lunches, fry the potatoes up on the weekend for breakfast. She glanced around at the other diners, at the bar where a few men stood facing the dining room, drinks in hand. No matter how hard she tried, she couldn't think of a thing to say. Finally she reached out and touched Rudy's hand. "This is nice," she said. "Thank you."

"How was school?" Rudy asked Vanessa when the food came. He shook Worcestershire sauce on his meat and cut himself a hefty chunk.

"A girl got hurt at practice," Vanessa said. "She slipped on the beam and landed on her neck. It was really scary. They had to tie her to a board and take her to the hospital."

Rudy and Inez leaned forward and nodded, chewing. The meat tasted wonderful, salty and charred. And the potato, loaded with butter, sour cream, green onions, and bacon bits. No use holding back.

"You want a little bite?" Inez said to Vanessa, holding out a piece of meat on the tip of her fork.

Vanessa shook her head.

They chewed in silence, sawing through the meat, avoiding each other's eyes. The meal dragged on. What did they *used* to talk about? Rudy had been surprisingly uninterested in Inez's past life: who her parents were, how she had grown up, her relationship with Vanessa's father. He had been satisfied with the barest of answers to any of his questions, for which she had been grateful.

"We're starting over," he had told her. "Just me and you. All that matters is *now.*"

"**Open your presents**," Rudy said eagerly when the meal was over and the waiter had cleared the table.

Inez had a weakness for gifts, and when she saw the delicate gold bracelet, she felt a rush of warmth for Rudy. His face flushed and his eyes looked almost moist when she thanked him. A woman at a nearby table turned and looked, nodding her approval. And so many gifts! A kidskin wallet that she could tell wasn't cheap, and a scarf that felt like suede when she held it against her skin. Such an unusual color! Deep plum, almost black. He didn't forget Vanessa, either. But Vanessa eyed everything suspiciously. Inez would definitely have to talk to her. The scarf he'd bought Vanessa was like a beautiful tropical flower, but she barely looked at it. She thanked Rudy, laid it back in the box, and fastened her eyes once more on the table in front of her.

When Inez finished brushing her teeth and combing her hair, she took her diaphragm from the cabinet under the sink and loaded it up with spermicidal jelly. Rudy might expect something for the dinner and the gifts. As part of the celebration and the beginning of his new job. The thing was a mess and a pain to use, not to mention what came after, but once in a while it had to be expected. Less and less, though. She slipped the diaphragm in, made sure it was in place, and washed her hands. The last thing she needed right now was a baby. Even in the early days of their marriage, they had made love only once a week, almost always on Saturday night, and that was a quick and reasonably painless affair.

Rudy was a quiet lover, a little panting and grunting and he was finished. He thanked her politely afterward, and that was that. Which was fine with her. Maybe not normal, according to what she read, but people tended to exaggerate. Anyway, if he wanted it tonight, that was okay. Less trouble just to go ahead.

He was already in bed when she stepped into the bedroom and closed the door. Way over on his own side with his back to her.

"Got to get to sleep," he said when she touched his hip. He twisted around and gave her a quick kiss. "I have to go to work in the morning."

13

The first drops of rain fell as Wylie climbed the railroad-tie steps to Carolyn's house. The hillside exhaled a moist breath of eucalyptus and bay. The rain sounded like small animals scurrying through the leaves. In the mist and fading light it was easy to imagine figures darting from tree trunk to tree trunk, hiding. Wylie thought he caught just the barest glimpse of them. As he got closer, he heard pans banging and water running in the sink. Carolyn's profile showed in the yellow light of the kitchen window.

"Hey," she said. "Come in."

Her hands and the front of her jeans were wet, as if she'd been doing dishes. She was the same height as Wylie, sturdy, with a long face and big teeth. She had the complexion of a bird's egg, her body was flecked with tiny brown freckles. They'd worked out a routine during the year and a half they'd been seeing each other. Wednesday he picked up a video on the way home from work, took a shower and fed the dogs, then drove down the road to her house for dinner. She was a good cook. Roast chicken with herbs. Spinach lasagna. They ate on her couch, plates on their knees, watching the video. He stayed the night. He was happy to smell something besides his own body for a change. He felt good with her: her under him as he went inside her, her body closing around his, or her on top of him, looking down, her hair hanging across her face. They could talk while they did it, easy and comfortable. Sunday mornings he picked her up and they went out for breakfast. They took a drive: to the desert or the beach or up in the mountains. After that they went back to her place and made love, took a nap together. They had dinner and he went home to sleep, to wake up Monday morning ready for another week. It worked for him. His life hadn't exactly been easy, and right now he wanted to keep things simple.

"It's just starting to rain," Wylie said, wiping his feet on the doormat.

He embraced her and kissed her lightly on the lips. She smelled good, like the wood from the furniture she refinished.

"Go ahead. Have a seat in the living room," she said, guiding him with an arm around his shoulder. "I'll be right there."

Carolyn had inherited her house from her grandfather, whose ashes she kept in a cookie jar on the china cabinet. He'd built it himself as a weekend cabin when the area had been considered the boonies. Wylie envied it. There was wood everywhere: open beams, mahogany wainscoting to eye level, oak floors. Windows along one whole side of the house. It was furnished with Carolyn's finds: a massive couch that she'd reupholstered in what looked like a hand-woven horse blanket, a plank table polished to the deep brown of a coffee bean, cabinets with dozens of drawers, a heavy rug in the middle of the floor that mirrored the gray-greens and orange-browns of the trees outside. Despite the rustic quality, everything was amazingly comfortable. Wylie sank down onto the couch and let his head fall back, looking up at the woodwork of the ceiling. He'd be sorry if all of this had to end, if Carolyn was about to issue an ultimatum and he'd have to call it quits. He'd miss their cozy evenings, her easy laugh, and her snug bed.

"I just made some snacky things," she said, coming into the room with plates balanced on her arms like a waitress. "That okay?" She set down bowls of guacamole, bean dip, fresh salsa, tortilla chips. It wasn't Wylie's imagination: she was nervous. Fake cheery, not looking him in the eye. She came back with a bowl of black olives, a plate of sliced jicama, and two cans of ginger ale.

"You're not having a beer?" he said. He liked watching her savor it on their nights together. If he couldn't enjoy it himself, he could at least watch.

"Naw, not tonight," she said, flopping down on the couch beside him. "Go ahead. Dig in."

He nibbled cautiously, glancing at her from the corner of his eye. Carolyn was usually so relaxed she was almost goofy, which was one of the things he liked about her. But tonight she seemed tense. She stared straight ahead, absently crunching corn chips.

"Did you have a good day?" Wylie ventured.

"Oh yeah. Yeah," Carolyn said, coming back to herself. "Some old lady died, way out in the Valley. Her brother was selling her stuff. I scored. She had some amazing pieces, things that must have been in her family for generations. I was buying things right and left until her daughter showed up and called everything off. Guess she knew she could get more for it."

"Uh-huh. Too bad," Wylie said. He was getting jittery. Carolyn brought a slice of jicama halfway to her mouth and stopped, her hand in midair. She stared at the opposite wall like she'd forgotten where she was, what she was doing.

The light had faded and the room was dark. A feeling of melancholy slipped over Wylie, like his chest had just filled with cold water. Raindrops pelted the windows like gravel. Outside it was nearly black. "Maybe we should turn on some lights," he said. "You want me to close the curtains?"

Carolyn nodded. She watched him cross the room. "You're not eating much," she said when he sat down again.

"Neither are you."

She leaned forward and dipped up a mouthful of guacamole with a chip. "What happened at work today?" she asked, crunching down.

Wylie shrugged. "Same old. Made a bunch of drinks, got a lot of people sauced. Sent them on their way." The wind was picking up. Bushes at the front of the house scratched the windows like they wanted to get in. For a fleeting moment, Wylie considered telling Carolyn about the scares he'd had, the shapes moving in the periphery. Instead he took a swig of ginger ale. "Someone plugged up all the toilets in the men's room."

Carolyn was uncharacteristically quiet. She looked at him and nodded. He doubted that she was listening to him. The tension was getting on his nerves. What the hell, he thought, and added, "Oh, and someone called me at work. She said she had something she wanted to tell me."

He was relieved when Carolyn broke out into one of her grins.

"That would have been me," she said with a laugh. She took a deep swig of her drink and loaded in a few more chips. "Yep," she said, nodding. "That was me."

"Well?"

She looked at him with curiosity, as if she was trying to figure something out. Her freckles made her look young, though there were wrinkles at the corners of her eyes and a few white strands in her hair. She was a practical woman who could hang wallpaper or whip up a full meal in record time, but she had a fine, artistic side that could see the potential in an old object. Wylie had gone to garage sales with her where she'd pick out the most unlikely thing, take it home, and turn it into something fantastic, something he didn't recognize. He didn't have an eye for it. "What about this?" he'd say, hoping to impress her. She'd just shake her head. A couple of times he'd bought the things himself, just to prove her wrong, but after he lived with them awhile, he had to admit she'd been right. They had no character, no promise. They were only the thing itself, with no past, no inner life.

Carolyn raised her eyebrows mysteriously, teasing him, and drained the ginger ale. "This stuff isn't bad," she said, shaking the empty can.

"You know, I hate surprises," Wylie said. "Whatever it is, maybe you should just tell me."

"Okay. Well, let's see." Carolyn nibbled the corner of her thumbnail, then reached into her hip pocket. She handed Wylie something that looked like a cross between a toothbrush and a thermometer.

"What is it?"

"It's a pregnancy test."

He turned it over in his hands. A hunk of plastic with two little windows. He was conscious of Carolyn watching him, and for a moment he saw himself as he thought she must: a middle-aged guy with a craggy face and neat hands, the fingernails trimmed and clean. At least there was that.

His eyelid quivered.

His reaction was important. Be careful, he told himself.

"I guess you wouldn't be showing me this unless you were pregnant," he said in a measured voice.

She nodded.

"And unless it was mine."

He winced as soon as he said it, but Carolyn didn't seem to take it the wrong way. She nodded again. He kept turning the damn thing over in his hands.

"Unless one of those doves flew in my ear and I'm about to give birth to the Second Coming," she added.

"You're sure?"

"I did it twice. Plus I know. The way I feel."

He nodded.

She snatched it out of his hands to keep him from playing with it. "You're making me crazy!" she burst out. "I can't tell how you feel. Whether you're happy or pissed off or what."

"Neither can I," he said. Something was welling up from his lower gut, but it got stuck in his throat. Talking was hard. He suddenly felt sleepy, like he'd like to close his eyes and sink into a deep nap. "How do *you* feel about it?" he asked.

"God, I don't know. A lot of different ways. It changes about a hundred times a day. I guess a lot of it depends on how *you* feel."

"Uh-huh. Well," he said, stalling. "God, I don't know. I have to admit, I'm kind of stunned. I mean, when you called today, it just didn't enter my mind that anything like this could have happened. I know that's stupid, but, God—" Wylie slapped himself in the forehead. Finally he felt something—a rush of anger. "How could

I have been such an idiot?" he cried. "We were so careless! What was I thinking?"

"I just didn't think it could happen," Carolyn answered, as if he had accused her. "My period is so irregular, and my age and all that. Even the doctor said it was unlikely. *Very* unlikely. I just thought I *couldn't.* I thought it was too late."

"Forty-one isn't *that* old," Wylie said, trying not to sound like he was scolding her.

"It *is,* though. Do you know how many people my age want to get pregnant, but can't?"

Wylie scratched his chin. His temper was so close to kicking in that for a minute he didn't trust himself to talk. Instead he walked through the whole thing in his mind: screaming that she'd tricked him, kicking over the table with all the snacks, storming out of the room, slamming the door, peeling out of the driveway. "I'm a little confused," he said after a minute. His voice was thick with re- pressed fury. He cleared his throat. "I thought you told me it was okay. I thought you said you *couldn't* get pregnant."

Carolyn shook her head. "No, I told you what I just said. That it was *unlikely.* That's what the doctor said. We were sloppy. Noth- ing happened this whole year we've been sleeping together. But I never told you it was *impossible.*"

"Well, I guess I misunderstood."

Now Carolyn heated up. "Come on, Wylie," she said. "Don't act like I put one over on you. You had the same information I did. For whatever reason, this happened. It just did. That's what we have to deal with. If you want to point fingers, fine. But it's not going to solve anything."

He'd never seen her angry before, at least not at him. For some reason it calmed him down. "I'm not pointing fingers," he said in a conciliatory voice. "I'm just surprised, that's all. I'm kind of in shock, if you want to know the truth."

But Carolyn didn't back down. "If you want to get mad, get mad!" Her face had gone white. Her nostrils flared. "Why don't you let it out for once? Tell me what you're feeling. I can't read your mind."

"I don't want to get mad. You don't want it, either, believe me."

"Is that some kind of threat?"

"Not at all. I'm just trying to be adult about this. For a change."

Carolyn let her head fall back on the couch. Rain hit the windows, harder now. She rubbed her face with her hands. "The last thing I want to do is fight about this," she said in a tired voice. "Can we just go to bed? I'd really like to be prone. Let's continue this conversation between the sheets."

Wylie took his time undressing. When he'd taken off his shirt and shoes, he sat at the edge of the bed and massaged his feet, which hurt from standing all day. Carolyn had shed all of her clothes in a heap on the floor and was already in bed with the blankets pulled up to her chin. Wylie could just make out her face in the faint light from the big window that looked out over the trees.

"Got any beer in the fridge?" he said. When she didn't answer, he added, "Just kidding."

"Very funny."

"Lame, I know." He watched the branches bouncing in the wind. Far beyond, fuzzy in the mist, he could see a line of yellow lights. "Have you ever thought about this? You know, having kids," he said. "Have you ever wanted them?"

"I thought about it for a while. Once, in my early thirties or so. But things weren't right, you know." From the sound of her voice, Wylie could tell she was looking out the window, too. "I kept thinking later, later, later. I could always do it later if I wanted. I'd see how I felt and how things went. Then, all of a sudden, it *was* later. There wasn't any more time. So I thought okay, it's not going to happen. It wasn't meant to be. I was a little sad, but mostly it was a relief. I didn't have to think about it anymore. Then this happens."

Wylie nodded in the dark. His feet gave off a cabbagey smell, and he wondered if he should go wash them. The rain sounded nice on the roof. He was reluctant to get into bed.

"What about you?" Carolyn said. "Did you ever want kids? I mean, you were married and all. Didn't you ever think about having them?"

"Twice. I was married twice."

"I know. So?"

Wylie sighed. Continuing the conversation was like forcing himself to run when he was tired, or lifting something heavy. Hard, painful. He searched his mind. There was so much to say, it seemed useless to start. After all this time. Be brave, he told himself. Just launch right in.

"There was this woman, after I got out of college. When I came out to San Francisco. My first love, I guess you'd call her. Anyway, I fell pretty hard."

That got Carolyn's attention. She sat up in bed.

"What was her name?"

"Coral." It felt strange, a little embarrassing, to say her name after all this time. He saw her perfectly: her crescent eyes, her quick way of moving, her prehensile feet.

"For real? Or was that a name she gave herself?"

"It was for real, but I called her 'Corral.' For fun, you know."

"And the two of you thought about having kids?"

"No, not really. Well, once she thought she was pregnant. She might have been, in fact. But there was no question, then. I mean, there was no way she would have had the baby. She was going to have an abortion. But it turned out she wasn't pregnant, or she had a miscarriage, or something. In any case, she didn't want a baby. I didn't either, I don't think." He scratched his chin. His eyelid flickered and he was glad for the dark. "But the funny thing was, after that, every time I thought about having a kid, I thought about having it with her. Even when I was married. Both times. I guess I was still holding out in some way. She was in the back of my mind, even though I didn't really know it." He paused, amazed at the simple realization that Coral was probably the reason that both of his marriages had failed. Well, *part* of the reason. "With my wives, it didn't seem right. I mean, I was crazy then. Boozing it up, you name it. I was mixed up. And they weren't the right people. Besides, I was in no shape to be a father. I'm still not, if you want to know the truth."

Carolyn chose to ignore his last remark. "What happened to her? To Coral?"

The inside of the window was fogging. Eucalyptus leaves slapped wetly against the glass. Even though Wylie was shivering, cold sweat ran down his sides. He still didn't want to get in bed.

"Who knows? We were only together a couple of years. She dumped me. I don't blame her. I was fucked up then, royally. Unlike now." He laughed. "I don't know what happened to her, or where she went. When I picture her, it's always like she was then. Sometimes I think I see her in a store or something, and I have to remind myself that she's different now, that I probably wouldn't recognize her. She must be married to someone else. Maybe she has a bunch of kids with him, who knows?"

He heard Carolyn swallow in the dark. It couldn't be pleasant listening to him talk about an old girlfriend this way, but then she was the one who'd asked.

"What was it about her?" she asked in a flat voice.

If Carolyn wanted to be a glutton for punishment, who was he to stop her?

"I was just fascinated by her, from the first time I saw her. I don't know what it was. She just seemed so sure of herself. Everything she did, it was perfect. I just watched her, all the time. I couldn't get enough of looking at her, no matter what she was doing. That was part of the problem, I guess. She always used her feet to do things: pick clothes off the floor, throw paper in the trash. I wouldn't have been surprised if she could type with them, dial the phone." He gave a little laugh. "She was like a place I couldn't leave, even after she was long gone. I never felt like that again. When I got married the first time, it was like we were playing house. Honey, I'm home and what's for dinner. We had some good times, don't get me wrong, but it was never in the same class as Coral."

Well, he'd done it now. For better or worse, Wylie sat back to see what would happen. He felt a little better, like he'd taken some control over the situation.

"Is that how it is with me?" Carolyn asked, predictably. "Like playing house?"

"I shouldn't have told you all that," Wylie said, larding his voice with concern.

"No, I'm glad you did. Really. It's better."

"Really?" Wylie said, a little hurt. Was she trying to get back at him by acting like she didn't care? No woman could have liked what he'd told her.

"Yeah, really. It makes it more real, for both of us. I mean, I hear where you're coming from. And you hear it, too. Besides, the more you tell me about her, Coral, the more real she becomes. As in less powerful. Sounds like she takes up a lot of space in your life, but how long has it been since you've seen her?"

The fluttering eyelid thing was really getting on his nerves. He chewed his lips before he answered. "Twenty, twenty-five years." Even then he was cutting it short.

"Right. So maybe you'll start getting over it if you don't keep it all to yourself. Maybe you'll get on with things."

"That's not really for you to say," he started in. "Like I said, I was wrong to tell you all that—"

"Oh Jesus," Carolyn interrupted in an exasperated voice. "Let's just give it a rest, can we? What are you doing out there? I'm freezing. Get in bed."

He took off his Levi's, folded them carefully, and put them on the seat of the chair. He hung his shirt over the back and placed his shoes underneath. As soon as he slipped between the sheets, she glommed onto him. She threw her thigh over his, her arms across his chest.

"What's with the undies?" she said.

"What?"

"Take them off," she ordered, tugging on the waistband.

"Jesus, wait a minute," Wylie said, rolling away from her.

They wrestled a moment, Wylie feeling odd and priggish as he fought Carolyn, who pulled his briefs down to his knees, hooked her toe around the top, and finally stripped them all the way off.

"Much better," she said, winding her legs around him again. She pushed her pelvis suggestively against his hip and took his dick in her hand.

Wylie breathed heavily, but not because he was turned on. In fact, he could hardly remember ever having been *less* aroused. He forced himself to lie still, though he would have loved to jump up, get dressed, and walk out into the wet, leaf-smelling darkness, to climb into the familiar coffee-scented capsule of his car and drive away. He pulled her insinuating hand away from his numb, flaccid dick and trapped it against his chest.

"What's wrong?" she whispered, her lips brushing his ear.

"I just—I don't know. This whole thing has been kind of a bombshell, you know. I need to think about it. We need to talk."

"We can talk—in a little while," Carolyn said. She straddled his leg and began licking his nipple.

Wylie couldn't help but laugh. "What's up with you?" he said, taking her head between his hands and bringing her face to his. "Am I that irresistible?"

"Absolutely," she said. "Plus I seem to be having some kind of hormone surge."

Her lips slipped down from his nipple to his stomach, lingered on the skin just above his pubic hair. She cupped his balls in her hand, nuzzled his penis. Wylie looked at the ceiling, listened to the rain. Even when he was boozed to the gills, this had never happened. He'd always managed, somehow.

"This is serious, isn't it?" Carolyn said, lifting her head. Her hair brushed his thighs. "Is it that I'm pregnant, is that what's freaking you out?"

He groaned and pulled her up to him. "Shit, I don't know," he said. "I don't think so. My body's just shut down for some reason.

Or maybe it *is* freaking me out. That something, *someone,* is in there."

"For Christsake, Wylie. It's as big as a sesame seed. Nothing's going to happen. We did it last week and I was pregnant then, if that makes any difference to you."

"Look, I'm not saying it's rational. This is kind of a big thing, you know."

"Okay, whatever. Jesus, I'm not going to beg you." She flopped over on her back, her hands over her head.

The rain was getting fiercer. For a moment they lay listening to it. A tree screeched and groaned like a boat moored to a wooden pier. Then Carolyn snuggled closer, nestling into Wylie's side.

"It's just that you're so good," she whispered.

"Oh, *please.*"

"I mean it. Didn't I ever tell you that? From the very first time, I wondered where you learned your tricks. Who taught you that stuff?"

"My second wife, the ball buster," he answered truthfully. "She told me exactly what she wanted, then she showed me how to do it. She was a taskmaster. Very demanding." With Coral, he'd kept it simple, he reflected. He'd been such an idiot. Now he wondered. If he'd had his moves down then . . .

"Well, I guess I owe her. She should go into business," Carolyn purred. Her hand sneaked back to his crotch. "For some reason, you being standoffish like this is really turning me on."

"Great. I'll have to remember it for the future."

"Really. It's driving me wild. The more you resist, the hotter I get."

"That's twisted."

"I know!" she laughed.

"Listen," Wylie said, taking her hand once again and clasping it in his own, where it couldn't get into trouble. "I feel like a schmuck, but I really think we need to get serious. How long do we have to think about this?"

Carolyn sighed and pulled her hand away, giving up. "Well, I just missed one period. So we have time, but I guess the sooner we decide, the better."

"Okay," Wylie said, relieved that she'd laid off him. He went on in a reasonable voice. "You know, the thing is that we didn't plan this at all. We didn't sit down and decide we wanted to have a kid. We never even talked about it. That doesn't seem like a good way to bring a new life into this world."

"Unless we did it accidentally on purpose."

He gave an exasperated huff. She was getting on his nerves in more ways than one. Deep breath, he told himself. "I don't think so," he said in a stern voice. "At least that wasn't *my* intention."

"So you're saying no."

"I'm not saying no absolutely. I'm just leaning toward it."

It was her turn to give an irritated sigh.

"Why?" Wylie said. "Do you want to keep it?" Something else occurred to him. "Does it matter what I do? Would you want to keep it even if I didn't?"

"I thought about that. This is my last chance, you know. It's now or never. But the thing is, I really don't want to be a single parent. I know that might not sound fair, like I'm giving you an ultimatum or something. Really, I'm not. But I do have to admit that I don't want to do this on my own. So it makes a difference if you're into it or not. That's just the way it is."

Wylie felt like someone had tied tourniquets around both wrists and squeezed the blood to his fingertips, where it thumped painfully. He cursed himself again for getting involved in the whole mess. At the same time a thought flashed across his mind like a fish breaking the surface of the water, leaping, flipping, and disappearing once again. *What if?* For a second Wylie pictured a child, his child. Himself as a father. Just as quickly he dismissed the thought. It wasn't for him, all things considered.

"It's just a hell of a lot of responsibility," he said. "Your whole life changes. I mean, I'm a bartender. You have your own business. We're both pretty independent."

"Yeah, but that's no big deal. We wouldn't have to change that much. I own this place. We don't need a lot of money. We wouldn't have to get married or even live together."

"We wouldn't?" Wylie said. He didn't know whether he was relieved or hurt.

"No, why should we? We don't have to do things by the book. We could carry on like we have been. There'd just be a kid around, that's all."

"I could never see how people just did these things without thinking," Wylie said. "Like Logan, my half brother. The guy has never had a real job in his life. He isn't even forty yet, and he has five kids by three different women. *At least* five kids. It's no big deal to him. Years go by and he doesn't see them. Just like our old man. He was in and out, back and forth. Hang around for a couple of years, then go take a so-called job on the East Coast. In the meantime he got together with Logan's mother, had him, left them, too. Went back and forth between us. I don't want to be like that. I couldn't do it."

"You wouldn't."

"I might. Or maybe I wouldn't. Maybe I'd go too far in the other direction. *Over*protective, you know. I could see that happening. Not let the kid out of the house. Always worrying. What if something happened to him?"

"Or her."

"Or her. Whatever. You know, it would really scare me just to watch him play on the jungle gym or something. Jesus. I could see myself going nuts, trying to make sure he didn't kill himself." Wylie held a finger over his eyelid to stop it from twitching. "It's just not the kind of thing you do lightly. I mean, we can't just say, 'Oops got pregnant. Okay, let's go with it.'"

"You worry a lot," Carolyn said.

Wylie squeezed his lips together to keep from snapping back at her. If she only knew. "I guess so," he forced himself to admit. "I guess I do."

"It's funny," she said, stroking his calf with her toes. "You seem like such an easygoing guy in so many ways. But at the same time you're really uptight." She paused, and Wylie had the feeling she was debating whether or not to ask him the next question. "Is it the war thing?" she finally said.

How easy it would be to say yes. Wylie was tempted. Everybody understood that. It was a syndrome, with its own name. It would explain everything. Except how things really were.

"Part, maybe," he began. "But you know, I was always uptight. My old man, you never knew what was going to set him off. Might be because I forgot to put the milk away, or the electric bill was too high."

He ran his hands over his face and tried to imagine a life without fear. Wouldn't it be amazing? As it was, a large part of his life was frozen into black and white. Stills. That was the only way he could handle it.

"You poor thing," Carolyn said, stroking his cheek.

"Ah, no," Wylie said, embarrassed. "That stuff's all in the past."

"Come on."

"Okay, maybe it bothers me once in a while. God, what time is it?" he said, straining to see the clock radio that sat on the table beside the bed. "Not even eleven yet. Jesus, I'm whipped. I feel like it's three in the morning. All this talking. What do you say we just go to sleep?"

"All right. I'll let you off the hook."

They kissed, and Wylie turned on his side, facing the window. All he saw was black, like a churning, inky sea. Carolyn slipped her arm around his waist. It was the first time he'd stayed with her that they didn't have sex, he realized.

What kind of milestone was that?

14

A tall guy with pale, freckled skin and russet hair that clung to his head like fuzz on a tennis ball walked up to Logan and handed him his suitcase. "Here you go, buddy," he said.

"Stone party?" Logan asked. He dropped the phone in his pocket. Too bad he had to cut Jewell off like that. He looked Stone over. Not really fat, though he gave that impression. Khaki pants that bagged at the crotch, fly halfway down. Shirt untucked in the back, toes turned inward. Gold-rimmed glasses. Still, you could tell he was a take-charge kind of guy. Two underlings trailed behind him, dragging luggage.

"Jerry Stone," the guy said, not bothering to hold out his hand. He wore a fat gold wedding band. Probably lived in a big, new house with his wife and kids, the kind of guy who picked up his own Skivvies and washed them, too. Drove his kids around, helped them with their homework. Took his wife to a plush weekend getaway on their anniversary. A nerd.

"Teagle and I will wait out front while you go get the car," Stone told Logan. "Aaron, go get the bags and bring them out there."

Logan watched the guy swagger in front of the other two, who stumbled over each other to follow his orders. Mutt and Jeff. Logan smelled money. Free and clear, with no deductions for child support or taxes. He shifted Jerry's carry-on to his own shoulder, took his laptop. An easy mark. Something clicked on in Logan's chest, the predatory instinct. He couldn't help it, it was an animal thing. A wolf chasing down a deer. Fleece the guy and get out of there.

Logan clapped him on the shoulder and gave him a Hollywood smile. "Meet you out front," he said.

It was raining pretty hard as they headed for the hotel on Wilshire. The asphalt was slippery. Light reflected on the street and the glass sides of the big buildings, silver on black. Mutt, the short, stocky lackey with dark hair, was in front with Logan. Jerry Stone and the willowy lackey with wispy blond hair were in back.

Logan glanced in the rearview mirror. "So, what business are you all in?" he asked.

"Software," Stone barked. "R&D."

Logan nodded, meeting his eyes in the mirror. "How's life in Atlanta?"

Stone scooted up on the seat. "It's fine."

The windshield wipers thwacked back and forth. Water sprayed under the tires. Logan could feel Stone thinking. He wondered if his hair felt like it looked, rough and springy.

"So," Stone said, looking out the side window. "Los An-gel-eese. You know the area?"

"Grew up here."

"Uh-huh." Stone sucked his teeth.

"Great place," Logan said. "Lots to do."

Logan could feel Mutt and Jeff getting nervous. Stone scraped his fingers on his chin stubble. "Listen, you know where we can have some fun around here?" he said. "Get a little action?"

Stone talked like he'd been in cold storage for forty years. The guys inside would eat him for breakfast. "Sure," Logan answered. "What're you looking for?"

The lackeys looked at Stone, who choked. Logan smirked. Stone wanted to act up but didn't know how. Logan knew the type. Once he got him tight, he'd make a killing. And Stone would be too embarrassed the next day to make a stink about it.

"I've got to tell you, though," Logan said. "This isn't really my car. I'm an actor, you know. I just do this between gigs. I rent the car by the hour, and I was planning to take it back once I'd dropped you off. And then there's my time, too. You understand, right?" He looked at Stone in the rearview mirror.

"Sure, no prob," Stone said, acting tough in front of the lackeys. "Don't worry about the money. We'll take care of you. Tell me your name again."

"Logan."

"Logan. Kind of unusual, isn't it? How'd you get that name?"

"My grandma gave it to me, Jerry. It's some kind of rock or something. A rock that moves, something like that. I forget exactly. Druids or something." *Carte blanche,* he thought. A big haul. "Okay, so I'll take you around. Show you a few places."

He held his open palm over his shoulder. It took Stone a minute to figure out he was supposed to slap it. Once he did, he relaxed. The lackeys took it easier, too.

"You guys hungry?" Logan asked. "Want to get something to eat? Maybe a little surf and turf, with a view of the ocean?"

They did.

Logan took them to a place near Malibu where they got a table close to the window. Not that they could see anything in the dark with the rain streaking down, but the guys seemed impressed that the ocean was just there, outside. Logan had the full steak-and-lobster treatment with a big baked potato. His own bottle of fancy mineral water. Jesus H. Christ, it was good. It sure as hell beat the Chinese noodle place. The others started with cocktails, then ordered a bottle of red wine. Then another. They got frisky as the meal progressed, talking and laughing like boys. Stone warmed up. By the time he picked up the tab he was ignoring the other two, treating Logan like his best buddy. As they walked back to the car, Mutt and Jeff trailed behind like two sulky kids. Stone slid into the front seat.

"Where to, James?" he said, laughing up a storm.

They stopped at a bar in Santa Monica that Logan had heard about. Lanterns made of handmade paper cast a golden glow on the crowd of slim young women wearing short, tight dresses and unshaven men with strategically rumpled clothes. The women showed a lot of tan, toned flesh. The Atlanta gang looked out of place, dowdy and pale.

"So, this is the real L.A.?" Stone asked.

"The real deal," Logan replied. You had to yell over the noise. The women were hot. He hadn't seen anything like this for a long time. He wondered if his Bogart jacket and Italian shoes were cutting it.

"What'll you have?" Logan asked before a waitress could make her way over. Stone pulled a hundred-dollar bill out of his money clip. *Money clip.*

"You choose," Stone said.

The thing to do was get them sauced without spending too much of the hundred Stone had handed over, since he was probably feeling too buddy-buddy to ask for change. Logan pushed through the crowd, ordered a beer and a shooter for each of them, and got a glass of water for himself. That ate up more than half the money, but he figured his investment would pay off later. Waiters carried tiny servings of sushi on giant platters. He could smell the beer, sweet as nectar. This was the first time he'd been in a bar since he'd been out. *If you don't want to fall, don't go where it's slippery,* someone in his program had said. But Logan had it hammered. There was no way. Besides, this was work, not play.

"So, what do you think of the ladies?" Logan shouted.

He'd managed to get another round down them, to get another hundred and keep the change.

Stone's forehead was moist. "Nice," he nodded. "Top grade."

After that they headed toward The I-Beam, where one of the residents at the Morningstar worked as a sometime bouncer, but first they stopped at an ATM for Stone to get more cash, then at a liquor store for a bottle of Scotch. Stone and the lackeys passed it around in the car. The smell of the booze started to get under Logan's skin. Things sure looked different when you were straight, especially when you were with people who were in the process of getting loaded. Logan clenched his jaw. If he was lit, this would be different. It was easy to hang out with *anybody* then, to have a good time. Sober, it was grim work, a job like any other.

The parking lot at The I-Beam was full of cars; a few people were standing around smoking joints or making out. The place looked like a warehouse. You could hear the music booming a block away.

Logan cut the engine and turned toward Stone.

"Listen, this place has a cover, plus they don't let just anyone in. I know the doorman, but you got to make it worth his while. It's a great place, but they're pretty selective. You'll have fun once you're there, but it's going to cost a little. The women here are righteous. Are you up for it?"

Logan had never been to the place before. He kept his fingers crossed that there was some truth to what he was saying. He was getting a jumpy, tweaky feeling. The skin on his elbows and shins itched. The backs of his knees ached. He wanted to move his toes, to stretch his legs, to—

"Sure," Stone said, taking out his money. "No problem. How much?" His speech was starting to slur. The other two were giggling in the back, wrestling over the Scotch bottle.

Logan told himself to take it easy. Fleece the lugnuts and go home flush. "About fifty for each of you," he said. "I'll take care of myself. Don't worry, it'll be worth it."

"No, no. I'll pay for you. How much for all of us? We're all in this together. I insist."

Near the corner of the building, Logan spotted two men with a crack pipe. The lighter flared, they bent over the flame. He could almost smell it. "You know, I think I'll wait this one out," he said. "I'm feeling a little tired. I'll get you guys in and wait for you out here. You take your time. I'll just wait for you in the car. Maybe catch a few winks."

Stone affectionately grabbed the back of Logan's neck. "Are you kidding? There's absolutely no way. It wouldn't be the same. Come on. Don't poop out on us now." He took a handful of bills from his wallet and shook them in Logan's face. "Come on, just tell me. Tell me how much."

The bills were twenties, fresh from the machine. Stone must have gotten the max. "Okay, okay," Logan said. Stone fumbled with the money, trying to count it out. "Here, just take it," he said, pushing a wad at Logan. "You're a good guy, you know it?" He patted him on the shoulder. "I'm really glad I met you."

"Same here," Logan said, taking the money. "How're you doing back there?" he said, turning to the other two. "You guys ready to tear it up?"

"Let us at 'em!" the stocky one yelled. He was further gone than Logan had thought. He slumped against the wispy one, who sat with a bewildered look on his face, the bottle still in his hand.

"Okay, wait here."

The rain had dwindled to a mist. The fresh air felt good. It was a relief to be away from the others, if only for a minute. Hands in his pockets, Logan crossed the parking lot to the door, where a bouncer sat on a tall stool. His lips and ears sported heavy hardware.

"How's it going?" Logan said.

"Not bad."

"What's the cover?"

"Ten."

"Got some friends in the car back there, three of them. Here's for all of us." He peeled two twenties off the stack Stone had given him. "You know a guy named Patterson? Works here?"

"Bartender?"

"No. Works the door, I think."

"I don't know. He must be here the nights I'm off."

"Probably."

Chances were the others were watching him from the car. Logan made a show of slapping the guy on the shoulder. "Listen, these guys I'm with are from out of town," he said, leaning close and peeling off another twenty. "Do you mind doing it up a little with the royal treatment? Just a little?"

"Sure. No problem."

Logan walked back to the car. "Okay, we're all set," he said, opening Stone's door.

"Let's roll," Stone said, stumbling out of the car.

Logan steadied him with one hand. "Your zipper," he said, pointing to his fly.

Stone grinned and swayed as he retucked his shirt and zipped up.

"Glad to see you here tonight, gentlemen," the bouncer said as he opened the door with a flourish. "You're all taken care of. Enjoy yourselves." He winked at Logan.

The place was like an airplane hanger, with catwalks overhead and scaffolding against the walls. Noise and lights bounced in all directions. Go-go dancers shimmied on the scaffolding, the dance floor was packed body to body. There was a kidney-shaped bar in the center of the room where people stood three deep and another bar along the far wall.

Logan wondered what in the hell he was doing there. The bass boomed in his chest like a too-big heart. The Atlanta group clung to him like kids on a field trip. They trailed him to the bar, where he slid between the bodies and got them their drinks. They followed him over to a corner where Logan sipped his mineral water as he looked up at two dancers dressed only in the briefest of cut-off jeans. Thank God it was too loud to talk. The women danced athletically, twining their bodies around each other, dipping to their knees, arching against the poles of the scaffolding.

Jesus God, Logan thought. It had been a long time. Ten months inside and two more since he'd been released. A whole fucking year, he realized with a shock, since he'd even touched a woman. The song changed and the tempo slowed. The tune was familiar; something in Logan's stomach leaped up and grabbed him by the throat. He watched the dancer nearest the bar, a woman with tawny skin and plush thighs who danced with her eyes closed like she was there just for her own enjoyment. To wake up next to that,

Logan thought, to feel her body next to him in the bed. God, she was fine. You could melt right into her. His throat burned and his eyes started to smart. He was lonely, he realized, desperately lonely, and he'd been that way for a long time. The beat pumped up, and he had to look down to hide the tears that filled his eyes. Everything, everything that he'd lost. He went down the list again, as he'd done countless times when he was inside. His mother, who'd died just a few days after her sixtieth birthday. She'd always been his best defender, his biggest fan. No matter what he'd done—come home drunk, been suspended from school, or gotten hauled in by the law—she was always on his side. He'd been inside when she passed on, just six weeks after they'd diagnosed her with cancer. And his own kids, growing up on their own. Jewell's mother, who *still* came to him in his dreams, giving him the same warm rush of joy that he'd felt when they were first married. The women after her who'd accompanied him on camping trips, drug buys, nights on the town, breakfasts in bed. Cletus, best man at his second wedding, who was found OD'd in the parking lot down at the beach in Malibu. *Gone,* he thought bitterly. *All gone.* The first bike he'd ever had, stolen out of his own garage by a bunch of hellraisers up the street. The canyons he'd played in as a kid. Even his fucking fox terrier Mitch, who ate rat poison. What was left? Nothing, just him standing there in a place he didn't want to be with three dickweeds, trying to scrounge a few bucks.

The number changed and the dancer sauntered away across the scaffolding. That was it. Logan was having a drink. What difference did it make? Just a beer, because alcohol wasn't his real problem, or at least not his main problem. As long as he stayed away from the other stuff, especially the speed, he'd be okay. Big fucking deal. He could taste it already.

The bar was a zoo. People with sweaty hair clinging to their necks, trying to get drinks. Bartenders with bare, shapely arms moving as fast as they could, but not fast enough. He could call his sponsor. He could just walk out of the place, get in the car, and drive away. Leave those three asswipes here. He had the keys, the cash. Women in midriff tops, men in sleeveless tees. The smell of bodies and cosmetics. Lots of them high, he could tell. The thump of music. Man, he was sick of it. Of people like them, not a care in the world, who had all the breaks. Not a clue what it feels like to be in the hole without one person giving a damn. Parents to pay for their school or buy them a car, set them up for good. He pushed his way forward, finally got a piece of the bar. The bartender closest to him, a young woman with an elaborate necklace tattooed on her neck, was lining up a long row of shots. Logan was determined now, no matter what. Just get it over with because he was sick of fighting it off. It would be a relief to feel the moment of no return. Then he would know where he stood. Then things would be easy.

"Be right with you," the bartender said as she sped past him to the other end of the bar. People leaning over, holding up their money. A guy with dreads was passing out the shots to a group behind him. They knocked them back, slammed the glasses on the bar, and reached for another. The bartender opened a handful of beers, carried the bottles by the necks past Logan.

He had to pee. All that fizzy water.

Another bartender with thick black hair on his arms, a red bandana on his head, and heavy silver hoops in his ears rushed to Logan's side of the bar.

"Excuse me," Logan called out.

"Be right there," the guy replied without looking up from the glasses he was frantically filling with ice.

Just go to the bathroom, Logan told himself. When he was inside, he learned to break things down into the smallest parts. You didn't look at the whole time you had to do, just the few moments in front of your face. Get through chow, take a shower, watch a little TV, go to group. One day. Concentrate on five-minute blocks. So he'd take a leak. When he came back he could have the beer.

The bathroom was dim, almost dark, lit by candles set in niches in the walls, which were covered in sheets of steel held in place by dime-sized rivets. A long zinc trough on one side served as the urinal. An identical one, except with faucets, ran down the middle of the room. Guys hung around washing their hands or waiting for one of the two stalls at the end of the room. The relative quiet was a comfort. Logan peed. A guy at the end of the trough gave him the eye. Logan turned away, went to the sink, washed his hands. He bent over and splashed water on his face, wet the back of his neck, rotated his head to ease the tension. When he finished drying his face with a paper towel, the wispy lackey, the one he called Jeff, was standing in front of him.

"Oh, hey, Logan," he said, out of breath and relieved. "I've been looking for you. Listen, Aaron's sick. Jerry thinks maybe we should call it a night."

Logan pulled over on the freeway. He ran around to the passenger side and jerked the door open. "Hold it, man! Just hold it a second!" he yelled over the traffic noise. He didn't want to have to clean the car up. He got Mutt under the arms and dragged him to the edge of the shoulder where the asphalt ended and a ditch separated the road from a big tract of empty land. It was raining again. Logan stood behind Mutt and wrapped his arms around his stomach so that he wouldn't pitch forward onto his face.

"All right," he yelled. "Let 'er rip. Heave-ho."

The guy retched so hard that Logan stumbled, almost falling on top of him. He hoisted him back and braced for the next heave. The vomit splashed like a waterfall: steak, lobster, red wine. Mutt didn't hold back on the sound effects, either. He sounded like he was being turned inside out.

"Watch my shoes, man," Logan shouted. "This is genuine Italian leather. Aim for the ditch, buddy. Don't get my shoes!"

When Mutt was all puked out, Logan pushed him against the side of the car. They were both wet, rain streaming down their faces. "You got a hankie?" he asked. "Something to wipe off your face?" Mutt was too stupefied to answer. Logan signaled for Stone to roll down the window. Fucker sitting pretty in there all cozy with the radio on. The other lackey was lying across the backseat, passed out.

"You got a hankie? Something I can clean him up with?"

Stone was smashed, too. His face was moist and paler than ever, except for a slash of brilliant red on each cheek. He gave Logan a shitfaced grin as he passed his handkerchief. Logan wondered if he'd gotten hold of anything at the club. Ecstasy or something. But who cared, it wasn't his problem. At this point he didn't give a rat's ass what happened to any of them, as long as he dumped them at their hotel first.

Mutt closed his eyes while Logan wiped his face. "Those guys are shits," he slurred, almost crying. "Teagle's a fudgepacker and Stone's a son of a bitch. Everybody hates his fucking guts. High and mighty prick. He can suck my cock."

"Hold still," Logan said. "You can tell him that as soon as you get back." Why did he spend so much time washing grown men's faces?

"You're okay. You're all right," Mutt went on. He slid sideways off the car and Logan had to grab him by the jacket to stop him from falling. "I really appreciate it. You're a real pal. I mean it."

"Nada," Logan said. He helped him back inside the car and stood there a minute, buffeted by the wall of air from a semi blowing past. The traffic had thinned out. He could smell the wet weeds in the field, the dirt. The Bogart jacket was soaked through. He remembered that he'd talked to his daughter earlier that evening, though now it seemed like days ago. Jesus, she'd sounded like his mother. He'd been a fuckup where his kids were concerned. Christ, it was a shame. But that was the story of his life, wasn't it?

"What are you in?" Stone asked as soon as Logan got back in the car.

Logan glanced into the backseat before he started the engine and pulled back onto the freeway. The two lackeys could have been corpses the way they were slung all over each other.

"What do you mean?" he said, merging farther to the left.

"I mean when you're not doing this. As an actor. Are you in films, or what?"

"Oh, commercials mostly." It didn't feel right between him and

Stone, now that the other two had passed out. The rain made it worse, enclosing them in the car. "You see that spot where the guy wakes up in a house right next to the ocean? That was my most recent. I get some bit work on a TV series now and then. I played a photographer in that show about the magazine. You catch that?"

Stone nodded. He was trying not to act as drunk as he was. Logan felt something bad coming. Stone took out his wallet and fumbled in it awhile. He pulled out a photo and held it near the steering wheel so that Logan could see.

"What's that?"

"My kids. A picture of my kids." Stone took the picture back and looked at it himself. "You got any kids?" he slurred.

Logan nodded. Not too much farther, he told himself.

"You with somebody? Got a wife? A girlfriend? I don't want to get personal or anything, just wondering."

The windshield wipers slapped back and forth. Logan concentrated on the rhythm and kept his eyes on the red taillights ahead. "No," he said quietly. "Not right now."

His exit came, finally. He rolled down his window as he turned onto the surface road and listened to the water spray up from the tires. There weren't many cars on Wilshire.

"It's boring, Logan. It's a boring life," Stone burst out. "Don't get me wrong. I love my wife and kids. But it's all over. There's nowhere to go from here. It's kind of lonely, know what I mean? Like that song."

Logan clenched his teeth as Stone sang "Is That All There Is?" He cursed at a red light that prolonged his agony.

"Not like you," Stone said in a pleading voice. "Not like your life, Logan. God, I admire you. I really do. I envy you. You've got it made. And I'm stuck. I'm just stuck."

What a relief to pull up in front of the hotel. Logan turned off the engine and popped the trunk. The sooner he got rid of these losers, the better.

"You get what I'm saying?" Stone whined. "Do you understand what I mean?"

"Sure," Logan said. "Of course I do."

A doorman unloaded the trunk while Logan dragged Mutt and Jeff out of the backseat. He led them to a bench near the door, where he propped them into sitting positions. Stone was waiting back at the car. He started fumbling in his wallet again when Logan came back.

"Here, here's my card. It's got my work number if you want to call me there, and my e-mail address. Just to shoot the shit or whatever. Or anytime you're in Atlanta, be sure to look me up."

"Will do." Logan took the card. The money Stone had given him at the club was still in his pocket. It had to be a few hundred. He was sure Stone had forgotten he'd handed it over.

"You're a good guy," Stone went on. He gave Logan a few thumps on the shoulder. "I'm really glad I met you. I wish we lived closer so we could hang out sometimes. Go round, take in the sights. Like we did tonight."

Logan nodded, waiting to see if the wallet was going to come back out. Stone looked at him uncertainly, then offered his hand. They shook. VICE PRESIDENT, it said on Stone's business card.

"Well, I guess this is it," Stone said, glancing at his co-workers slumped on the bench. A bellhop had loaded their bags on a cart. "Take care, buddy. It's been a great night." He turned and lurched toward the hotel.

"Hey, Jerry!" Logan called when Stone had gone a few steps.

Stone turned around with an expectant smile, like he had been hoping that Logan would call him back, like he'd been waiting for this moment all night.

"You forgot to pay me, pal. Remember?"

Stone opened and closed his mouth like a fish sucking air. The red streaks on his cheeks spread to the roots of his hair. He took out his wallet and looked at his watch. "About seven hours," he said in a flat voice. "Here's eighty dollars. Thanks for your time." Without a backward glance he slouched off toward the big revolving door and the brightly lit lobby. Mutt and Jeff followed him like puppies.

Logan started the Lincoln. Eighty bucks, the fuck. Chump change, at least to Stone. What about the gas? It just went to show you: get it while you can. No one was going to hand it over, you had to take it for yourself. Logan turned the radio on, but the music grated on his nerves. He punched it off. He turned right on Wilshire, headed east. He felt edgy—jumpy but tired. Be glad, he told himself. Just that morning he'd been worried about five bucks to gas up his truck, and now look at him. He had enough money to live it up that night, to do almost anything he wanted.

And what was that?

Get high. Feel the stuff hit his veins and then the sensation of flying up, higher and higher with each breath, lighter than air. When everything snapped into crystal-clear focus, when you knew what you wanted to do and, even better, knew you could do it. Right then. Your blood singing. Happy. Free. He could do it. He had the means, the will, the knowledge. He even had the cash to pick up a woman. They could rent a room, a nice one, maybe even in the hotel where he'd just dropped off Stone and his friends. Stay up all night, fuck and get high, catch the first morning light. The sweet pink dawn. Head up to Mulholland, look out over the city, the ocean in the distance.

Logan stopped at a red light, even though there was no one else at the intersection. He tapped his finger against the steering wheel. Sometimes it could be so quiet in the middle of the city, like you just hit a pocket of secret air. A warm current in the cold ocean. *Help me,* he pleaded, to no one in particular. *What am I going to do?*

The answer came from the black sky, the drizzle lit into flurries around the street lamps.

There was only this minute to get through. This minute, and the next minute, and the minute after that.

| 15 | To keep herself from going to the window every time a car came down the street, Jewell turned on the television. Celeste had called again, around ten, to |

To keep herself from going to the window every time a car came down the street, Jewell turned on the television. Celeste had called again, around ten, to say that she was dropping Dana off at her house and that she'd be home soon, but that had been over an hour ago. Rachel had been asleep for hours. Rain pattered against the window. Jewell got off the couch, went over to the phone, and pressed number three, which was programmed to Celeste's cell. Her voice mail picked up right away. The phone was switched off.

The weathercaster, a petite woman with a freakishly pronounced widow's peak, pointed to the massive storm system on the satellite map. "A Pineapple Express is blowing in from the southern Pacific," she announced, "We'll be seeing lots of moisture." They had reporters out in the field: Beatrice Tran in a yellow slicker on the Santa Monica pier and Emilio Noriega with an umbrella on Wilshire. Wind whipped their hair. Already there were flash floods, flight delays, a small mudslide. A seventy-four-year-old man had drowned on his way home from a late-night trip to the supermarket. The live footage showed the roadblock he'd evaded, the place where his car had been struck by the torrent that flowed across the washed-out road. He'd panicked, opened his door, and been swept away. The camera zoomed in on the rain-soaked grocery bag squashed in the mud, on the frozen pizza and pint of ice cream.

"The storm door is open," the weathercaster said. "Systems are lined up all the way to Japan."

Jewell switched off the TV and put on her shoes. She dug her jacket out from under the pile of books on the dining room chair, found her wallet and keys. Her fingernails throbbed at the quick. Each fingertip pulsed. Her face felt numb and rubbery.

She went into the dark bedroom, wrapped Rachel in a blanket to protect her from the rain, and carried her out to the car. The rain was coming down in sheets now, warm, like the weatherwoman had said. Rachel didn't wake up when Jewell laid her in the backseat, when she shut the door and started the car.

Jewell drove grimly, turning the wheel, applying the brakes. The headlights cut two silver cones through the rain. She drove too close to the curb and water pummeled the underside of the chassis. The car fishtailed. She went through a red light on Sunset Boulevard. A pickup screeched to a halt, blaring its horn.

As she drove north, the ground swelled into gentle hills. She crested one rise and there was Silver Lake, glowing like mercury spilled into a bowl. She turned without thinking, first right, then left, then left again. Spanish-style stucco houses with tile roofs and arched windows stood along the residential streets. A few porch lights were on, yellow to keep the moths away.

She recognized Dana's house, no problem. There was a banana tree on one side, a three-legged stool on the porch. Dana's car was parked in the driveway, Celeste's at the curb. Jewell switched off the motor. Lights were on in the house, front and back. A sudden cloudburst hammered the car from all directions, and Jewell thought of the time she and her father had ridden through the car wash in his dented-up gas hog. Brushes spinning on the windows, the whirlwind of soap suds and blasted water. He'd laughed his ass off, enjoying it as much as she did.

The rain was loud on the windshield, like gravel thrown up from the road. It was hard to think. She could drive up on the lawn, spin a few doughnuts. Plow right through the front window. Or write a note, slide it through the mail slot. Then take off and never come back. She wished she could turn the radio on, but she didn't want to wake Rachel.

She turned and looked into the backseat. Rachel was on her back, her arms thrown over her head. Sound asleep. Jewell tucked the blanket more snugly around her, opened the door as quietly as possible, got out, and gently closed the door. She dashed across the yard, trying to shield her face with her arm, but the rain pelted her anyway, making it hard to see. The lawn squelched beneath her feet. The windows were low to the ground, covered with blinds. She ducked down next to the one in front and, from the edge, was able to make out the end of a sofa and a floor lamp that gleamed on a honey-colored wood floor. There was a glass coffee table. On it was Celeste's purse.

Jewell crept to the side of the house, slipping in the muddy flowerbeds that made a sucking sound when she lifted her feet. The room on that side was dark. Farther back was a redwood fence with a gate that led to the backyard. The banana tree tossed, its fronds gleaming like a fish. The gate was locked. Rain soaked the shoulders of her jacket, seeped through her shoes. Her hair was plastered to her head. She pressed her eye to a crack in the fence. A square of light fell over the back lawn. The bedroom. A flower she couldn't place released its scent into the wet night. It was tropical, cloying.

Rage churned so violently in her chest that her breath tore out of her throat with a ragged wheeze. The yellow light from the bedroom taunted her. Rain ran down her face, into the collar of her shirt, between her breasts. It was pathetic to be standing outside like this, drenched, peeping in. She gritted her teeth. Rachel was okay in the car, she reassured herself. Again she thought of driving away and never coming back. But then, in a silence that seemed to come between raindrops, she heard Celeste's laugh. There was no mistaking it. No one else laughed like that.

Jewell ran toward the front of the house. She slipped in the wet flowerbed and knocked her shoulder against the stucco wall. She leaped onto the porch and started pounding on the door, her fist keeping up a steady beat until a light came on in one window and feet thumped across the hardwood floors. The curtain in the front window moved, and Jewell caught a quick flash of Dana's face looking like she'd just witnessed a car wreck.

The deadbolt clicked and the door swung open.

Dana gasped. She brought her hands to her mouth in an exaggerated gesture straight from the silent screen. "Where's Rachel?!" she shrieked hysterically. "What have you done with my daughter?!"

Jewell glared at her through the water running down her face. She realized that her chest was heaving up and down, that her neck felt as if it were swelling, Hulk-like. "She's fine," she choked.

"*Where is she?!*" Dana wailed in a high-pitched screech.

Jewell wanted to put her hands around Dana's throat and slowly squeeze off her air. Her pulse raced in her throat, high, thin, and dry. "She's in the car, sleeping," she rasped. Seeing Dana's face go ashen with horror, she added, "*You're* the one who left her at *my* house, remember?"

Dana, who was a good half-foot shorter than Jewell, lunged forward and knocked Jewell out of her way. She rushed down the walkway toward Jewell's car, rain pocking the cement around her like someone was taking potshots at her feet.

"Rachel needs her bed!" Jewell called after her. "She needs to be in her *own* place!"

Dana struggled with the car door, the rain pelting her.

"Where's Celeste?" Jewell shouted toward the street, even though she knew the rain would swallow her words. "Where the hell is she?"

When she turned around, Celeste was standing in the doorway. For some crazy reason, Jewell broke out in a grin. Despite everything, she was glad to see Celeste. Her heart surged. Celeste looked back at her, and Jewell thought—for an instant at least—that she might laugh, that they might laugh together. Celeste might shake her head, put her arm around Jewell's shoulder, and the two of them might walk away, get in the car, and drive home. But the instant passed quickly.

"What the hell is going on?" Celeste demanded. She squinted out into the rain, toward Jewell's car, where Dana was bent into the backseat, before she turned back to Jewell and asked, "What are *you* doing here?"

For a second Jewell was dumbfounded. Then rage blazed up in her chest and hit the back of her throat. *"Me?"* she choked. *"Me!?* What am *I* doing here? What about you? What the fuck are *you* doing here?"

Before Celeste had a chance to answer, Dana bustled up the walk carrying Rachel wrapped in the blanket. She knocked past Jewell again and stood with her bundle like a fireman who'd just rescued a child from a burning building. "She left her in the car!" she wailed. "All alone, out there! Sleeping out there in the dark at this time of night!"

"Oh, come on!" Jewell responded. "She was fine! I was right here! It was only for a minute!"

Dana turned to Celeste melodramatically, the indignant, self-righteous mother. "She left her," she whispered, as if her voice had failed her. *"Alone."*

"That's a load of crap," Jewell appealed to Celeste. Her heart banged against her ribs with fury. "Rachel's fine!"

Rachel raised her head and looked at each of them. When she had assessed the situation, her face crumpled and she started to cry.

"Take her to bed," Celeste ordered in her sternest schoolteacher's voice.

Jewell felt a tiny shiver of pleasure, hearing Celeste speak so harshly to Dana, who stood with her mouth hanging open in disbelief that her bereaved-mother act had fallen flat. She pushed into the house and headed down the hall. Rachel waved good-bye to Jewell as she passed.

"What are you doing, Celeste?" Jewell began in a low voice when Dana was out of earshot. "What are you doing, huh?" she repeated, louder this time. She smacked the doorjamb with the flat of her hand. It felt good and she smacked it again, this time with her fist. "What the fuck are you doing?" she yelled, full voice. *"What are you doing?!"* She kicked the doorjamb. "What, Celeste?! *What?!"*

"Stop it!"

They locked eyes. Once again, just for a instant, Jewell thought that they might be able to forget the whole thing, to never mention it again. But then her eyes drifted to the buttons of Celeste's cardigan. It was her coral-colored one, the one with wide ribbing at the wrists and waist. Something was off. Jewell's eyes slid up the buttons and down again. With a shock of recognition, she took in the incriminating pucker between Celeste's breasts where she'd missed a buttonhole. A patch of golden skin showed in the gap. She glanced at Celeste's frightened face, looked back down. Sure enough, the last button was unbuttoned, bereft of its corresponding buttonhole. It blinked there alone, indecent and irrefutable, like the punchline to some horrible joke.

This was how it was going to happen, Jewell realized. It was happening *now.*

"You missed a button," she spat. "Guess you were in a hurry."

Celeste blanched. She looked down and splayed her hands over the uneven closure.

Nausea rose to Jewell's throat. Watery spit filled her mouth. She was going to be sick. She was going to vomit all over the porch. "You're *disgusting.* You make me *sick,*" she choked.

"Jewell—" Celeste began. Her eyes gave it away. They admitted everything.

"Shut the fuck up," Jewell hissed. "Just shut your lying, filthy mouth."

Celeste turned and looked behind her, down the hall. Jewell looked, too. The house with its potted plants and polished floor. The armchair and stereo speakers. Dana and Rachel at the back of the house, waiting. When Celeste turned around again, her eyes were brimming.

"Don't come home tonight," Jewell gasped. Talking was like twisting a wooden peg in a tight socket; her voice was squeaky and dry. "I can't talk right now. I can't even look at you."

But the truth was she couldn't take her eyes off Celeste. Every time she looked at her, it was like the first time. She had never gotten over her cheekbones, the folds of her eyelids, the corners of her mouth. She watched until the tears in Celeste's eyes spilled over and ran down her face.

"God, Jewell. Stop looking at me like that," Celeste pleaded. "I can't stand it. What can I say? I'm sorry." Celeste covered her eyes.

"Close the door, then," Jewell rasped. Her own tears were cauterized by rage. "Why don't you close it, Celeste? Go on, close the fucking door!"

She slammed the flat of her hand against the doorjamb again, close to Celeste's face.

Celeste jumped, her eyes wide. "Stop it, Jewell!" she cried. "What the hell is wrong with you?"

Jewell felt her shoulders sink, her arms drop to her sides. The nausea subsided, leaving a wide, empty space in her stomach. She watched as Celeste lowered her face into her hands. Celeste's shoulders rose and heaved. She sobbed into her palms. Jewell didn't move, didn't say a word. Celeste cried energetically, dramatically, her cries escaping in measured sobs. Tears squeezed out between her fingers and tumbled down the front of her telltale sweater.

"Look at me, Celeste," Jewell rasped. "Look at me. *Look at me!*" Her own chest felt like a parched stump, heavy and twisted.

Celeste's face was battered when she finally raised it and looked at Jewell.

Jewell felt the ugliness of her own expression, the rage and the humiliation. "You see me?" she shouted. "I'm an idiot! I'm a fucking fool!"

An idiot! she repeated to herself as she turned and walked off across the wet lawn into the dark and the rain. *A fucking fool!*

16

Rudy checked the ground around the foundation of the house. It wasn't quite midnight. He used a rake to pull the tall grass back from the stucco and shined his flashlight down at the damp earth. He found a hubcap, a mousetrap, a piece of hose. If only he knew what to look for. Wires, most likely, but also freshly dug earth, or footprints, or pipes. Anything suspicious. Out front, the battered white van parked two houses away caught his eye. He'd noticed it a couple of days running. It was just the kind of thing they'd use. Old and dinged-up outside, inside equipped with the most sophisticated listening devices money could buy. Two guys with headphones, cameras pointed his way. He hurried up the walkway, rain soaking his flannel pajamas.

It had all come to him that night at dinner. How big the whole thing was, how everything was connected. He'd spotted the first guy on his trip to the salad bar, the sandy-haired man with a scrappy beard who sold newspapers and candy at a stand right before you got to baggage claim. Coincidence, he'd thought, until—at the other end of the dining room—he'd seen the scrawny barmaid with the shoe-polish hair who was working the cocktail lounge every night when he got off work. She was pretending to eat with a younger couple, but when he looked up from his steak, he caught her staring right at him. That's when he started to catch on. All his suspicions came to a head when, just two tables over, he saw the bald Filipino gent who sat behind the X-ray machine at the security check. The Filipino glanced at the barmaid, the barmaid at the bearded guy, the bearded guy back at the Filipino. Like a net around him. He hadn't let on that he'd noticed. But once he was out of there, he had to act fast.

First secure the house. He'd had a quick look around the bedroom while Inez was in the bathroom. Once she was asleep, he checked the pipes under the sink in the bathroom, the window over the tub. The closet in the hall where Inez kept the vacuum cleaner, the laundry hamper, and an assortment of coats and jackets. The loveseat upholstered in a large floral print, the floor heater, the light fixtures and electrical outlets. Nothing behind the couch, the TV looked okay. Even as he searched, he felt someone watching him. He cursed himself for being so blind, because he realized, the more he thought of it, that this had started long, long ago. Signs were everywhere. Remarks dropped at work, little things that seemed like nothing at the time. Looks his crew had given him, little nods between the higher-ups. Every piece that fell into place revealed a bigger piece. A web. Not just his dismissal, but business falling off at the airline, the supposed increase in security and terrorist threats. *A ruse.* All this time and he'd finally tripped over it. He opened cupboards in the kitchen, checked inside the oven, under the sink. The jars of spices, cans of food, and bottles of oil. Things he'd never looked at before, though he lived with them every day. His gut twisted into a knot. Was there *anyone* he could contact, *anyone* he could trust?

Vanessa's room was the only place he hadn't checked. Some self-imposed rule had always made it off limits to him. But now he wondered. They could use her to get to him, they could take advantage of the respect he'd shown her. Her closet, her bed, her desk. Anything could be hidden there. He'd look later, when no one was home. Sundays they went to church, Wednesdays to Bible study. He'd find a way.

He had to get organized. It was a short dash from the kitchen door to the garage. He'd make it command central, his nerve center. The smell of gasoline and dried grass reassured him. He started to work methodically, laying things in place. Once he had a plan, he'd feel better. Thoughts bubbled while he worked: how his co-workers always kissed ass at the same time they were backstabbing. Incompetent, all of them. No wonder the airline, the whole country, was in such a state. Jesus Christ! Part of him was tempted just to let it all go to hell, to stand back and watch it happen. But then it was his duty to open their eyes, to show them where things were headed. Not just by telling them, because the idiots wouldn't listen to reason. You had to show them. That's what he meant to do.

He was shivering when he headed back inside, his pajamas damp and icy, clinging to his goose-pimpled skin. He needed his rest. All his strength and brain power. They'd do everything they could to discredit him, to spread the rumors around. Even to his family. He had to expect it, to keep it in mind. And he had to work fast. Little things counted. Details. He remembered how Inez and Vanessa had looked at him when he came home, and later, again, at dinner. Guarded, like they suspected something.

The minute he opened the back door, the flash hit him in the face like a searchlight, like a beam from an interrogation lamp.

And there she was.

Oh God. God, oh God.

His knees could barely hold him. A spasm jolted his hands, scattering the things he was carrying across the floor.

She was in on it, too.

Wylie was having a heart attack. The more he tried to breathe normally, the harder it became. He forced himself to take deep, regular breaths, but his chest felt as if it were bound by thick elastic bands. Beside him, Carolyn slept peacefully on her back, as if their little chat, their predicament, didn't bother her at all. It was only nerves, he told himself, though considering his age and diet and the stress in his life, he couldn't rule out a coronary. In that case it was important to act quickly. He'd read that in the paper. Mortality rates and muscle damage were directly related to how long you waited before getting help. Should he wake Carolyn? Tell her to dial 911, take him to the hospital? He checked carefully for other signs. No stabbing pains, though he *did* feel slightly nauseated. No pain in his left arm, though his jaw ached, especially on the left side. He was clenching his teeth, he realized. *Relax,* he told himself. *Relax and breathe.*

He'd been lying there for hours.

He needed air. It was stifling upstairs, under the roof beams. Carolyn slept so soundly it was easy to slip out of bed and pull on his shirt and pants, to tiptoe down the stairs and unlatch the front door. His breath came in shallow gasps. What if she found him sprawled on the kitchen floor, or in a heap at the bottom of the steps? His face blue—who knew what? Would she still have the baby, raise it without him? "Your dad died right here," he pictured Carolyn saying, pointing to the very spot where he was standing. "A long time ago, before you were born." He saw the child, recognized the bewildered expression on his face. It was his *own* face, he realized.

Cripes.

The wooden steps were slick with rain. He descended carefully in his bare feet, the cold biting his skin. The menthol smell of eucalyptus rose up. Branches creaked and swayed. He made his way slowly over the wet leaves, following the path that led to the back of the house. There, between a coiled garden hose and a pile of empty clay pots, he squatted down and leaned against the side of the house. He breathed, pulling in the moist air. The elastic bands squeezed his chest front and back. His ribs were caving in, his lungs collapsing. What would Carolyn think if she found him there, crouching behind the house like a spooked dog?

It was like an X-ray when the flash came. A brilliant second of whiteness. The space between the stark, straight tree trunks burned at regular intervals across the background of pure light. Black on white. Wylie's breath caught. His heart paused. The rumble rolled across the sky, shaking the earth and reverberating in his chest. The bands eased then, like they had been shaken loose by a profound cough that began deep in the earth and rattled up through his bare feet to the pit of his stomach and then to his throat, where it exploded out of him in a gasp of relief. The sharp crack of the thunder was followed by a deluge of rain. A fever breaking, a release from pain. Wylie looked up at the sky, letting the water drench his hair and face.

Inez was hot and restless in the bed. Maybe it was the steak she'd eaten, or the wind that whistled around the house and caused the screen to slam like someone pounding on the front door. Rain pelted the roof and windows. In her fitful sleep she worried that the ceiling in the living room would leak again, that she should get up and put a bucket under it so it wouldn't drip on the loveseat. She slipped back into a jumble of fragmented dreams that merged like a series of unrelated movies spliced haphazardly together. She was on the bicycle again, flying effortlessly up and down hills, traveling miles and miles. The landscape changed from green countryside to burned-out cities, but people were nowhere to be seen. Then she dreamed she was making deliveries, but when she opened the bags it was food, not Avon products, she handed out—chicken wings, pork ribs, and chocolate cake that her customers devoured hungrily, smearing their faces and hands. She dreamed that she gave birth to a monkey, that she discovered a secret passage in the bedroom closet that led to the house of her dreams, that Rudy had a disease that caused his bones to soften into taffy. It was a relief when she finally started awake, her heart beating hard, her chest and neck wet with perspiration. She looked at the clock next to the bed. 1:43. She breathed deeply and listened to the rain, a comforting sound. Gradually she felt the presence of God, His nearness, as if He were right there in the room watching over her. It was a great peace, a blissful feeling of rest that both surrounded her and filled her body.

When she turned toward Rudy, she saw that the blankets were thrown back, that the sheet reflected light from the street lamp outside. There was an indentation in his pillow, a pool of shadow where his head should have been.

It seemed to take Jewell forever to drive home from Dana's house in Silver Lake, but when she pulled up in front of her own house, all she could remember of the trip was the yellow line of the freeway racing past her. She had glanced at the speedometer once, and though it felt like she was moving at a suicidal speed, the needle pointed to forty-five. She sat in the car with the motor running, the windshield wipers thwacking back and forth. Rain hammered the car. Her house looked dark and empty, as if it had already been abandoned. Now it was just one more place she'd have to leave.

Her strength left her when she turned off the engine. She slumped forward until her forehead rested on the steering wheel. She closed her eyes and cried copiously, monotonously, clinging to the steering wheel, shaking it like the bars of a cell. Snot ran down the back of her throat and big, warm tears fell on the thighs of her jeans.

When the flash came, her first thought was that someone had taken a picture of her through the window of the car. It was the same blue-white light as a camera strobe, and for an instant—as thunder rumbled down the street like a battalion of tanks—she saw herself in immediate exposure, frozen in that moment, like a snapshot. Curled in a **C** around the steering column, her head down as she cried, watering her own body. Her skin absorbed the tears so that her bloodstream could move them back up to her eyes so she could cry again. Her own little biosphere, the same old story.

Wet and tired, Logan nodded to other residents as he made his way up the stairs of the Morningstar. The hotel came alive at night. Doors swung open and slammed shut, footsteps sounded in the halls, the old elevator clanked up and down like a ghost dragging its chains. People shouted, toilets flushed, music played. As if suddenly everyone had somewhere to go.

Cockroaches scattered when he opened his door and turned on the light. He'd left the window open. He took off the Bogart jacket, the Italian shoes. Thank God the guy hadn't puked on them. A shopping cart rattled past outside; bass boomed from a car idling on the corner. A shower would be nice. He remembered Sylvia Salvetti's bathroom from that morning. My God, was this *still* the same day? But at least he was home. Still on the straight and narrow and with a wad of money in his pocket. He took his towel, his shower shoes, a change of underwear, and headed down the hall.

Wonder of wonders, the shower was free. His lucky day. The whole room was tiled in pale blue. The grout was mildewed and the drain clogged with hair, but the water came on full force. Logan opened the little window and stood under the hot spray while cool air from outside blew on his face. A heavenly combination. No one to tell him his time was up, get back to his cell. Nothing to worry about until the next day. He lathered his head with the bar of soap, worked down from his shoulders to the soles of his feet. A wad of money. He would go out for breakfast the next day, he promised himself. A place in Hollywood he hadn't been for years. Pork chops, eggs, and toast—no holds barred. The newspaper and cups of steaming coffee.

He didn't meet anyone in the hall on the way back to his room; things had quieted down. He pulled the curtains closed so he could sleep late, laid his clothes over the chair at the desk, drank from the sink in the corner. He might not have the finest linen in the world, but it sure felt good to get in bed. He found the hollow like a nest in the middle of the mattress and lay on his back, his arms at his sides, his legs crossed at the ankle, listening to the rain. Another day. The muscles in his back and shoulders loosened luxuriously. *Thank you,* he said to the rain-freshened air that blew in through his window.

Damon's weights clanged next door. Endless repetitions, like someone striking an anvil. Poor son of a bitch with his aching teeth. The worst hurt in the world, at least physically. Logan began to drift. The cracks in his ceiling became rivers branching through a delta. His eyes closed, flickered open, closed again. When the flash came, it burned through his eyelids like sun through a window shade. He remembered an experiment: the retina of a rabbit carried the image of what it had seen at the moment of its death. What picture was that? A raised ax? The open yaw of a coyote?

Confused, caught between consciousness and sleep, Logan followed the turns and forks of the afterimage traced on his eyelids, not sure whether he was navigating the complicated geography of his ceiling through deep gorges and ancient estuaries, or whether he was gazing at the spidery network of his own veins, the waterways along which his platelets bounced and bubbled, carrying him deep into the night.

Inez checked Vanessa's room first. The door was closed. She pressed her ear against it and listened, remembering her delight and wonder when, in the first years of Vanessa's life, she had woken at night in the facility for mothers who were still in high school, crossed the tiny room she shared with Vanessa, and leaned over the crib to breathe in her daughter's sleep. The atmosphere had been like nectar, outside of everything else in Inez's life. It hadn't mattered that there had been outrage in her church, that her adoptive family had arranged for her to leave their house for the sake of their own two daughters, that the man who had fathered Vanessa pretended she didn't exist. For once she had somebody she belonged to, and who belonged to her. Flesh and blood. Even now, with Inez's bare feet cold against the worn carpet in the hall, the silence on the other side of the door felt alive with Vanessa's breathing, with her dreams and growing body, with the person she would one day become. The cedar chest was safe, Inez was sure. Nothing wrong in there.

The living room was a different story. The furniture looked sinister, hunched along the walls in the half-light from the streetlamp. Rain sheeted the windows. The screen door continued its desolate banging. Inez stepped to the window and saw that Rudy's car was still parked at the curb in front of the house. The palms of her hands itched with apprehension. The sad street, the rickety houses. Where was he? The bathroom was empty; she'd checked. She hurried to the kitchen and looked out the window over the sink. Lights in the garage. There was a line of yellow around the door, a glow in the window. Her stomach tensed and gurgled. She burped, bringing up the bloody taste of steak.

As she watched, the door at the corner of the garage opened and Rudy stepped out. There was no mistaking his wide behind and his striped flannel pajamas. Inez had a strange feeling of fascination and guilt as she watched him turn and close the door, check that it was locked, and start across the lawn toward the house. Her heart beat faster. Was it the bike? Had he gone out to see if she'd been riding it? Her mind raced foolishly, trying to remember if she'd left any sign of where she'd been. Would he know from the tires, from the rack over the wheel? Thank God the money was in Vanessa's room. He was carrying something. Inez leaned over the sink, squinted through the rain-clouded window. How strange that this man with skim-milk skin, a shambling walk, and the small paws of a rodent was her husband. His feet were bare, she saw as he got closer to the house. He was talking to himself.

It happened quickly. The door opened. Rudy saw her before he could step inside. She opened her mouth to speak, but just then the lightning flashed and, startled, Rudy dropped what he was carrying. It flew across the cracked linoleum in all directions. In the rumble and crack of thunder that followed, his eyes opened wide in terror and his hands grasped at the air in front of him as if he were trying to grab a lifeline.

Inez switched on the light.

Rudy pressed his lips tightly together. His hands were balled now in front of his chest, opening and closing like beating hearts. Inez could see the pulse racing in a vein on his forehead.

"What are you doing up?" he hissed, looking like he was about to lunge at her.

"I woke up. You were gone."

She tried to put it all together. The storm. Rudy's panting, seething face. The things scattered on the floor.

"The rain," he said. "I heard it raining and I remembered there was a leak in the garage. I went out there to fix it."

Inez nodded slowly. She looked down at what Rudy had dropped. The swirls in the linoleum eddied and spun, curled against the metal cupboards, the greasy oven, the chipped leg of the kitchen table. Red, green, black, and yellow, the design seemed to twist and curl like constellations spinning in deep space.

"The roof," Rudy said. "Water coming right into the garage." He bent and picked them up.

A roll of tape.

A pair of scissors.

A box of sandwich bags.

A folded newspaper.

A can of baking powder.

Tuesday, December 3

17 Rudy didn't eat his usual fried eggs and toast before he left in the morning. "Executive breakfast," he told Inez, because that way he could kill at least an hour in a coffee shop somewhere. It had been two weeks since that big sap Waller had laid him off, and Rudy had learned that being out on the street all day was no picnic. Sure, he'd visited lots of places he'd never seen before: Hollywood Boulevard, Griffith Park, Grauman's Chinese Theater, the Santa Monica Pier. They were places you'd go on vacation, but instead of being fun, they gave him a lonely feeling. If only Inez could be there so he could point things out to her, stop and have a Coke, watch the world go by. But he couldn't let on. He took his keys and wallet, kissed her on the cheek, and headed for the door. Once his plan was in place, everything would be okay. He'd have his job back, this whole mess would be straightened out. "See you tonight," he called out before stepping onto the porch to face eight hours alone in the world.

His appetite had changed since he lost his job. Now the thought of runny egg yolks and butter-soaked toast turned his stomach, while he craved sweets with a hunger that made him gnaw the corners of his fingernails. As he started the Buick, he ran through the list of possibilities for breakfast: a creamy cheese Danish from the Red Ribbon Bake Shop, a chocolate éclair from Sweet Sue's, or one of the fabulous maple bars from Dick's Donuts. The Sugar Bowl had really wonderful Napoleons: more layers than you could count of flaky pastry filled with vanilla. Or the King of Tarts, where the bear claws were heavy and rich with almond paste, covered with toasted slivers of crunchy nuts. Since it was important not to establish any predictable pattern of his whereabouts, he never went to the same place two days in a row. Pulling away from the curb, he decided on the Jolt N Bolt down near Union Station. They made a cinnamon bun that was a meal in itself, a big, fluffy affair with a hot pool of thick frosting ladled over the top. He was going to the airport today to get his job back, so he needed his strength. A big breakfast for a big day.

When he was a few blocks from home, he took off his tie and laid it on the seat beside him. If Inez asked, he could describe the executive lounge of the airport where he'd tell her he met with suited men like himself about airport security and labor problems, about protecting the public while guarding profits for the airlines. He would describe the meetings and decisions that took up his days, he'd talk about city commissioners, the FAA, and a whole range of government agencies that the average person didn't even know existed. As he crept through rush-hour traffic, he pictured the other men listening while he talked, nodding respectfully as they sipped their coffee. He could see it all so clearly, it almost seemed real.

"Look who's here!" Hilda, the woman behind the counter, shouted when he walked into the Jolt N Bolt. She was a big woman with long gray braids. Her orange lipstick was always smeared on her teeth. Rudy grinned, proud that she remembered him. His mouth watered in anticipation of the cinnamon roll. He imagined Hilda arriving in the wee hours of the morning to do the baking herself, though behind her in the kitchen he could see two Mexican men rolling out dough and sliding baking sheets into the oven.

"The usual?" Hilda boomed, reaching for the tongs.

"Make it two scoops," Rudy said as she ladled the frosting from a machine near the cash register. He held up a crumpled bill. "I'll pay extra."

She waggled her finger to show the extra was free. Flirting with him, if you asked Rudy. "Now, are you going to have the hot chocolate, or the coffee?"

Rudy pursed his lips and pretended to debate. It didn't hurt to flirt a little in return. The thick, sweet hot chocolate was so good with the cinnamon roll, but with coffee you got free refills and a reason to stay as long as you wanted. Still, he'd been craving chocolate. If he wanted more, there was no reason he couldn't buy another cup.

He was the only one in the place. He settled into his favorite table near the window, his stomach growling and his mouth gushing. The cinnamon roll came apart like flesh in his hands, sending up a luscious, steamy cloud of spice, sugar, and yeast. The taste was more than a flavor, it was happiness itself, like a perfect circle. He chewed rapturously, the warm syrup and slushy dough sliding down his throat like nectar. He let himself enjoy it. Just now, everything was fine. The sun coming through the window was warm, the smell of coffee and pastry filled the shop, Hilda clinked dishes behind the counter. Across the street, the train station rose from its parking lot like a cathedral. The tall, skinny palms that surrounded it tossed in the wind. Light bounced off the pools of rainwater that stood in the parking lot. Rudy blinked. He liked the train station with its intricate, inlaid floor. The high wood ceilings where pigeons flew from beam to beam, just like they were outside, and the patios splashed with bougainvillea. Only problem was, the class of people there wasn't so good. Lowlifes tended to hang around, looking for trouble.

He licked each finger when he was finished, then drained the hot chocolate to the final dregs. It was gone way too fast. He would like to have another cup, maybe even another roll, while he read the newspaper that someone had left in a basket near the door. But his work was cut out for him. This was the day he'd planned: December 3. December was the twelfth month, and if you added the two numbers that made twelve together, one and two, you got three and today was the third, exactly two weeks since he'd been laid off. Which proved it was the right day for him to make his move. He wiped his fingers on his napkin, set his mug on his plate, and brushed the crumbs out of his lap. He'd been dreading this moment, but it had to come. If you didn't stand up for yourself, no one would.

When the glass doors slid open and Rudy stepped into the terminal at LAX, it seemed like ages since he'd last been there. Ages and ages, not just two weeks. Another lifetime, like he was going back now to his old elementary school, or to a family reunion with relatives he'd known only in childhood. Was it possible that he'd come here every day for years, that he'd walked through these doors wearing his name tag and carrying his lunch? Innocently going to work, unsuspecting. Just like all the people here now: standing in lines like cattle, dragging their children and belongings behind them, happily going about their business like nothing in the world was ever going to happen to them.

Weak sunlight filtered through the high glass windows, making everyone look like they were moving through the cloudy water of a dirty fishbowl. Colors were bleached like old Polaroids; people looked insubstantial, casting long shadows. Rudy sat down on a bench near the arrival and departure screens and looked at the long ticketing counters, the agents in their uniforms, the luggage moving on conveyor belts. He rehearsed the lines he'd concocted over the past weeks. But the movement and light distracted him. The baby screaming at the top of her lungs while her mother tried to zip up her jacket. The Chinese family wrestling with a cart of enormous boxes. Two young women in skirts that barely covered their behinds yakking not far from where he was sitting. What was he going to say? The speech, all the points he wanted to make to his boss, slipped from his mind. He should have written them down, stupid idiot. Wait, he *had* written them down. What was he thinking? He reached into the pockets of his jacket and felt the papers—the napkins and pieces of torn cardboard, the bits of newspaper, old stationery, and recycled circulars—on which he'd built his case. The plastic bag was there, along with a few of the turnovers he'd bought at the Sunbeam day-old bakery. And of course his ID tag.

Best to walk around a little. Get the lay of the land and gather his thoughts. He wished he'd brought a duffel bag or a small piece of luggage so he would blend in with the other passengers, but chances were no one would guess he was undercover, that while he pretended to look at key chains in the gift shop he was really watching the crowd headed for the security check, or that while he glanced at the headlines in the newspaper racks he had the baggage handlers under surveillance, alert to any irregularities.

The old Filipino man who'd spied on him at the steak place was nowhere in sight. Neither was the sandy-haired guy who usually sold newspapers next to the flower stand. He wondered about the stringy woman bartender with the shoe-polish hair, and—since he didn't feel quite ready to talk to the bosses yet—he decided to rest a little and scope things out at the bar. Not that he'd drink. Not at that hour, or any hour for that matter. He had to stay in control, keep his wits about him.

Rudy walked past the candy cart, the espresso wagon, and the machines that sold travel insurance. Near the security check, the terminal opened up into a big bulb where people in rows of black vinyl seats waited for the passengers they were meeting to come from the gate area. There was a shop that sold pet gifts: refrigerator magnets of every breed you could imagine, coffee mugs, food bowls, rain slickers for poodles and pugs. There was a music store, and a Mexican restaurant that had painted chairs with straw seats, and piñatas that hung from the ceiling. The bar was right in the middle. Beyond was the metal detector. People entered the chutes that snaked back and forth, making their way to the machines where they took off their shoes, emptied their pockets, removed their belts. Right now it wasn't too busy. The security officer who checked the boarding passes, a black woman with bright orange hair, was chatting to the janitor who was sweeping up the waiting area.

But the bar was loaded. Not even noon yet, and every stool was taken by someone sloshing down booze. Rudy approached cautiously, his hands resting on the supplies in the pockets of his jacket. The skinny woman bartender wasn't there; instead it was the guy with bad skin who looked like he'd probably been tipping back a few himself. He had an attitude; Rudy had never liked the look of him. Still, with his view of the terminal, he probably had a pretty good idea of what was going on. A businessman talking on his cell phone slid off his stool and walked away. Rudy took his place.

Scarface was right there to wipe the counter. He gave Rudy a noncommittal nod, as if he might recognize him or he might not. Who was he trying to fool? Or had someone been around, talking to the airport employees?

"You have root beer?" Rudy asked.

The guy's deepset eyes gave him a shifty look. "Sorry. Coke, Diet Coke, 7-Up, Dr Pepper."

All that and no root beer. "Gimme a Coke, then," Rudy said with disgust. "Skip the ice."

Worse yet, it was from a machine, served in a paper cup. Foaming on top, not even filled to the brim. "Okay if I eat this here?" Rudy said. He didn't wait for an answer, but pulled one of the turnovers from his pocket. Let the guy try to stop him. Lowlife smartass. Go ahead, make my day, he thought as he peeled off the paper and took a big bite.

Scarface watched him, wincing like something hurt. Rudy wondered what had made his skin like that: smallpox, or a fire, or just a bad case of acne. The turnover was berry, Rudy's favorite. They were four for a dollar at the day-old place, and you couldn't tell the difference from the ones in the store. Perfect for eating in the car during the day, or out in the garage at night. He kept a cache in both places, and he found that two or three were a meal in themselves. Even if you had four at once, it was only a dollar. The berry was definitely the best, but the chocolate pudding wasn't bad, either. Rudy ate greedily, leaning over the bar so he wouldn't drop any of the filling on his pants. The fizzy Coke cut the greasy feeling in his mouth. When he finished, the bartender pushed a napkin toward him.

"Where's your partner?" Rudy asked as he wiped his face and hands. The only problem with the berry was that it had tiny round seeds. He felt several of them lodged in his teeth.

"Who's that?"

Rudy pulled the second turnover from his pocket and opened it. Vanilla custard. "You know who I'm talking about," he said, once he'd taken a bite. Who did the guy take him for? "Your *partner*. Slender lady. Dark hair. Might be Mexican." He chomped on the creamy custard. Just *let* Scarface try to say something about it.

"You mean Georgette? The other bartender who works here?"

Rudy waved his hand in the air. A dollop of custard landed with a blop on the bar. "Yeah, whatever her name is. You know who I mean." He leaned closer and looked the bartender right in the eye to show him he knew what was what. "I *saw* her at the restaurant. I *know* she's in on this thing."

Scarface stared a minute with his sneaky eyes.

"She's on at three. Excuse me," he said, and beat it to the other side of the bar.

Now Scarface was going to ignore him. Rudy knew *that* game. He finished the second turnover and used a cocktail napkin to wipe the custard that had dropped on the bar. It left a swirled chalky film, like polish on a car. A face like the bartender's had to have a past. Watching the guy pretend to cut celery stalks, to wash glasses and busy himself with customers who already had full drinks, Rudy wondered what he had to hide. He wouldn't trust a type like that around Vanessa, that was for sure.

"Excuse me!" Rudy said, snapping his fingers when the bartender came back to his side of the bar.

The guy didn't smile, didn't even talk. He just stood in front of him.

"This cup was only half full when you gave it to me. The rest was foam. Better check your machine. There's no excuse for this."

Something about the guy's stillness as he stood on the other side of the bar caused Rudy's heart to pick up and forced him to look down at the crumpled napkins and turnover wrappers. If Scarface reached out and grabbed him by the jacket, if he punched him in the face as Rudy had a feeling he was about to, then it was all over. No reason for Rudy to worry about any more jobs because the lawsuit he'd file against LAX would keep him in the green for the rest of his life.

"You work here, right?" the bartender said in a low voice.

Rudy nodded, still not raising his eyes.

The guy took Rudy's cup, topped it off, and set it down without a word. He picked up the crumpled papers and tossed them in the trash. He wiped the custardy film off the bar. "Anything else?" he said.

Maybe he wasn't so bad after all.

"Listen," Rudy said in a low voice, leaning forward so no one else could hear. "Anything out of the ordinary going on around here? Anybody acting funny?" He pulled his ID tag halfway out of his pocket, tapped it with his index finger, and gave Scarface a knowing nod. "Just checking up."

The bartender raised his eyebrows. He studied Rudy a moment, then his face broke out in a smartass grin.

"Oh yeah," he said. "People act funny all the time."

Rudy put his ID tag around his neck as he headed toward the administrative offices. You can do this, he told himself. Stay calm, be reasonable. Move your arms, pick up your feet. He was almost there. The ceiling reeled for a minute; his scalp buzzed. He pinched one of his earlobes in an effort to get his balance back. It was all a misunderstanding. He pulled open the door to a long hallway with offices opening up on both sides. The floors and walls were white, with pools of light reflected in them like patches of ice. Everything white, white, white, but dirty white and scuffed—like the banged-up inside of an old refrigerator. He had a perfectly good case. Once he explained it, they'd all apologize and he'd go back to work. Rudy concentrated on his breathing. Office workers shuffled listlessly beneath fluorescent lights in the small, messy offices. None of them glanced up as he passed.

Glenn Waller was there, in his messy office near the end of the hall. Not only that, but Waller's boss, the head of the department, was there too. Srinivasa, Srinivasata, Srinivasan—something like that. An Indian from India: a compact man with a perfectly round bald head, thick glasses, and skin—if you really looked at it—as dark as a black man's. He always dressed the same: gray slacks, white shirt, red tie. Rudy had never seen him smile. The two of them were leaning over Waller's desk, looking down at a stack of papers.

Something in Rudy's chest lurched and swirled, propelling him forward. He gulped a lungful of air, threw back his shoulders, and plunged into the office. To his amazement, the two bosses jumped back! Rudy couldn't believe the looks on their faces! Waller's mouth dropped open, and the color drained from his saggy jowls. Sriniwhatever, on the other hand, tightened. He clenched his mouth so hard you could see the muscles in his jaw swell. They were *afraid* of him! Of *him*! It only lasted a moment, but long enough for Rudy to see. His first urge was to step forward and reassure them, to tell him he was just there to talk, to straighten everything out. But as Waller and the Indian recovered, their faces hardened into suspicion and disgust. Plain as day. That's when Rudy changed his mind. Right then. About everything. That was it: from then on everything had to go forward.

"Glenn," he said with a smile, stepping into the office. "How are you?"

"I'm fine, Rudy," Waller said, moving forward with his arms extended, as if to push Rudy out the door. "Sanjay, this is Rudy Cullen—"

"I know who he is," the Indian interrupted. His eyes were fastened on Rudy. He didn't say hello or crack a smile.

Rudy said hello as normally as he could, but in his brain a string of realizations popped off like fireworks. The Indian! That was it! Everything fit together, fell into place. Why hadn't he thought of it before? Rudy made an effort to stay composed, to keep a poker face, but in Sanjay Srinivasa's stony stare he could see that it was too late, that the Indian knew that Rudy knew.

"What can I do for you, Rudy?" Waller said, glancing nervously at Srinivasa, back at Rudy, at the door, at the phone on his desk. Rudy wondered if Waller was in on it, too. The patsy. It wouldn't surprise him.

"Just checking in like you told me, Glenn. I came by to see if something's opened up for me."

Waller kept glancing at Rudy's chest. Probably trying to see if he was wearing a wire or maybe a weapon. The big, inept walrus. "It's only been a couple of weeks, Rudy," he said. "Nothing's changed."

"Listen, Glenn," Rudy said firmly. "You need to understand about this whole thing. I've—"

"Glenn, why is Mr. Cullen still wearing his ID tag?" Srinivasa interrupted. He had a clipped way of talking, his words curling up at the ends.

Rudy turned and looked at him. Hatred bubbled in his throat like a thick, hot liquid. Oh boy. This whole thing was deep, so deep. There was definitely something military about the stiff way Srinivasa stood, the abrupt way he moved. He didn't even try to hide it. He was obviously high level, very high.

"I'm authorized to wear this," Rudy sneered, covering the tag with his hand.

"Glenn, please take the tag and escort Mr. Cullen out of the terminal," Srinivasa said, like Rudy wasn't even there.

Waller fumbled. Either he was good at playing dumb or he was out of the loop. "You'll have to give me the tag, Rudy," he said, holding his hand out timidly. "Come on, now. Don't make a big deal out of this."

"Listen, this is a security issue!" Rudy shrilled. He clenched the tag in his hand in case they tried to snatch it from him. It was only fair to give them one more chance. "That's what this is all about! That's why I'm here!"

The Indian picked up the phone, dialed calmly, and spoke a few quiet sentences. He crossed his arms over his chest, leaned against the desk, and waited. Cool as a cucumber. Waller, on the other hand, was sweating like a pig.

"You're making a mistake! A big mistake!" Rudy shouted, looking wildly from one of them to the other.

One of their goons burst into the office. Waller nodded toward Rudy. The Judas! The lowlife patsy! The goon took one of Rudy's elbows, Waller the other. "Come on, Rudy," Waller said. "Let's go."

Rudy didn't fight it. What was the point? Now was not the time. He walked between Waller and the goon back out through the terminal. Before he knew it, they were out front, where a river of cars jockeyed for position near the curb. People hugged and kissed, taxi drivers unloaded luggage, skycaps eased through the crowd with loaded carts.

"Listen, Rudy," Waller said. "I'm talking to you as a friend here. Do yourself a favor, okay? Just let this whole thing drop. I know it's hard, and you've had a tough break. Nobody's disputing that. But these are hard times. The sooner you accept it and move on, the better it's going to be for everybody."

In the bright outdoor light, Rudy noticed that a tiny drop of oil stood in each craterlike pore on Waller's face. Worse, a flake of crumbly yellow wax was speared on a hair in his ear.

"You get me? You could get in trouble, Rudy. A lot of trouble."

Rudy watched Waller shamble back to the terminal, his khaki slacks riding up his ass. Well, he'd tried to tell them. You can lead a horse to water, but you can't make it drink. The clouds were moving quickly, rolling across the sky like time-lapse photography. Cars pulled up to the curb, then pulled away. The glass doors slid opened and closed. Rudy stood there. He had the sensation of being the only thing in the world that was still, the center around which everything else moved, coming and going.

He almost cried out when he looked down at the front of his shirt. The ID tag was gone. Instead, just over his left breast—right where you put your hand when you pledge allegiance—was a bullet hole. Perfectly round, glistening with ruby gore. He frantically backed away from himself while he tried to signal to the people who came and went heedlessly around him. But there was no pain. No weakness, no symptoms at all. Was he dreaming? He didn't remember anything. Rudy put his finger to the wound, probed it gently. Still wet, but—

He brought it to his nose, sniffed. Shook his head and laughed. Looked around to see if anyone had noticed. What the heck, he thought, and sucked his finger.

The sweet berry taste, the two tiny seeds.

18 The fetus curled in Wylie's brain like a cutworm. As he cleaned celery stalks for Bloody Marys, he pictured it salamander-like, breathing through gills that opened and closed as it floated in his cerebral fluid, bouncing softly against the walls of his skull. Its transparent fingers flexed and grasped. Its tiny, segmented spine coiled like a lasso. It nudged the edges of his cranium like a minnow nibbling, floating up to him with enormous, blind eyes. An alien, straight out of Roswell. But there was something familiar about it too, something he recognized. The moment his mind was unoccupied, the larval curl bobbed to the surface of his consciousness.

"It's a little limp, don't you think?" the guy who'd ordered the Bloody Mary said. He looked like he'd shaved with a lawnmower. There was a spot of blood in front of his ear, one in the cleft in his chin, another on his neck that bled down onto the crisp collar of his white shirt. "The celery," he said, flicking it with the back of his hand. "Looks like it's made of rubber."

Wylie retrieved the entire bunch from its compartment and held it up. It was curved like a crippled hand. "This is how it came this morning," he said in a flat voice. "Somebody must have shoved it in a plastic bag or something." Since his fist was itching to connect with the guy's jaw, he laid the celery down and fastened his hands behind his back. "I can remove it if you prefer," he said, drilling the guy with his eyes.

The guy backed down and took a big slug of his drink. "No, no. It's okay," he said. He smacked his lips in an unappetizing way. "You'll never guess what happened to me last night."

Like Wylie really wanted to know. The things he'd listened to. People who were left, battered in love. Stepped on and walked over, cheated, lied to, abandoned because their lovers needed space or a nicer house or a younger lover. Or no reason at all. Just left. You come home and they're gone, out of the clear blue sky. Bam. He'd listened to stories of people deserted as children, of pets lost but never forgotten, of fortunes made and squandered, of mean grandmothers and schemes gone awry, of bowling games and slights suffered in childhood. You name it. He'd listened to hundreds and hundreds of jokes, conspiracy theories, elaborate plans for making money. Every pickup line in the book. Every excuse for having another drink or not paying for the ones you'd already had. He'd seen the panics at last call, when men and women scrambled for each other like musical chairs. And fights: over spilled drinks, songs played on the jukebox, money left on the bar. The whole gamut. And now here was another one, a guy with a story.

The guy leaned forward, his shoulders hunched up around his ears. One of the cuts was still bleeding. "Last night," he said, looking first over one shoulder and then the other, as if someone might be listening in, "I went out to pick up a woman, you know. It was my last night in town and all. I'd had a few drinks, so I went out to Sunset and had a look around."

Wylie wondered why people thought bartenders were different from anybody else. Why they could tell them anything and it didn't matter. What if the tables were turned? What if he went up to a customer and said, "You know what, buddy? I'm fifty-one years old. I've got this kid in my head like an idea that just won't go away. Like when you wake up in the middle of the night and keep thinking the same thing over and over."

The guy tapped Wylie's wrist to keep his attention, to prevent him from looking around the bar and seeing who needed service.

"I found this gal. She was beautiful, man. Tall, hair down to here. Just gorgeous. When we got back to her place—"

The guy lowered his face in his hands and rubbed his eyes as if trying to wake himself from a bad dream. Wylie had an idea of what was coming. What if, instead of listening, he told the guy, *I keep thinking of when I was a kid myself. I don't know why, but all of a sudden things are coming back to me. The pencil-shaving-and-bologna smell of the cloakroom at my elementary school, the night my father loaded us all in the car and drove us out of town because we owed months and months of back rent. Left everything, including my cat. Woke us up and took us, right in the middle of the night.*

"She was a man. A *man*."

The guy looked bug-eyed at Wylie, as if begging him to argue, to tell him he was wrong. But Wylie just stood there.

"I mean this guy was *gorgeous*. Long hair. Tits out to here. You would have never known. I mean it. It wouldn't have crossed your mind."

Wylie shrugged. "I guess things aren't always what they seem—" he began to say. That's when he became aware of some commotion on the other side of the bar.

"Holy shit, something's happening!" the guy who'd picked up a man said.

People were crowded around a spot at the other end of the bar. The ones standing up strained to see past the ones sitting down.

"I've got it on my hands, all over my hands!" a woman with pale skin and hair the color and texture of an orangutan's fur cried when Wylie came over. She held her hands up as if he'd pulled a gun on her. The crowd fell back. There was a general murmur, a few startled exclamations.

For the life of him, Wylie couldn't figure what was happening.

"Call security!" someone shouted. "Get somebody over here!"

"Oh my God!" another woman cried. "It's here, too. It's all over!"

"Stand back!" a beefy guy in a Dodgers cap shouted. "Get away from the bar! Don't touch anything!"

A couple of stools went over with a metallic clang. The woman with the orangutan hair stumbled against the bar while a thin, mousy man with sleepy eyes tripped over one of the downed stools and fell on the floor. People from the other side of the bar rushed over to see what was happening. A few people walking through the terminal slowed down and looked over with curiosity.

"It's you!" the beefy guy shouted, pointing to the mousy man who still lay meekly on the floor. "You were the one! You were sitting here when I came!"

"Hold on!" Wylie yelled over the noise. Someone had to take control. "Everybody settle down."

Wylie's breath caught when he saw the white powder scattered across the black Formica of the bar. His first thought was that someone had been doing drugs right there. It wouldn't be the first time. Some of the places he'd worked, people didn't bother going to the bathroom to cut their lines on the back of the toilet. He'd even sniffed a little off the bar himself, courtesy of his customers, back in his day.

"What is it?" he said to the ring of faces whose eyes were fixed on him, waiting for some kind of response.

"It's *white powder*, man," the beefy guy with the baseball cap said angrily, like Wylie was an idiot. He seemed to have appointed himself leader. He was massive, with a beer gut and fleshy hands. Funny how the biggest male tended to seize power that way, Wylie reflected. So animal kingdom.

"It could be anything!" a woman behind the beefy guy shouted. "It could be anthrax!"

"Anthrax!"

"Anthrax!"

"Anthrax!"

The word echoed in expanding rings out into the terminal.

"It's anthrax!" Wylie heard someone yell over by the stand with the umbrella where they sold espresso drinks. "Someone put it on the bar!"

"Let's all stay calm," Wylie said.

"My glass was sitting right in it!" a woman with very short bangs and a necklace that spelled NANCY shouted at him. "It's all over the floor! It's on my suitcase and shoes!"

As if it was Wylie's fault.

"He did it!" the beefy guy said, hoisting up the man who was *still* on the floor. "This guy right here! I saw him! *This* is the dude!"

The mousy guy's legs were tangled in the barstool. When he was on his feet he blinked his sleepy eyes like he'd just woken up and didn't have a clue what was going on.

"Hey, man. What are you?" the big guy shouted, shaking him by his collar. "Are you an Arab? Do you speak English?" He held him up by his jacket for everyone to see. "Look at him! He's an Arab! He was sitting right there!"

"I ain't no Arab," the mousy guy said, knocking the beefy hands off his collar. "I'm Chicano, man."

"I saw you! You were right here."

"Fuck off! I was sitting there, but I didn't do it."

"Oh yeah?" the beefy guy said. "Well, look at this lady here. She's got it all over her hands."

"Hold on!" Wylie shouted. He waited for the crowd to get quiet. "Everybody stay right where they are. I'm going to call security."

"I already called," a male voice said from the back of the crowd. "They're on their way."

"Well, then. We just wait," Wylie said, embarrassed that the attention was now on him. The beefy guy let go of the Chicano, pissed that he'd lost his chance to play hero. The crowd shifted restlessly. Wylie looked down at the bar. The white powder had dissolved in the wet places. In others there were little chunks the size of match heads. He tried to remember who'd been sitting in that spot at the bar, but the day came back to him in disjointed fragments with large patches missing. The businesswoman who'd cried during her cell-phone call, the two longhairs who'd played poker, the cheerful mother and her sullen daughter. The pudgy guy chowing down pastries, the bodybuilder who'd spilled his drink. The three guys wearing gold chains, who drank orange juice. They really *had* looked like Arabs.

Wylie was relieved when security got there. They swept in, cordoned off the area with yellow tape, herded all the people to the side.

"I'll miss my plane," the woman with orangutan hair yelped.

"How long is this going to take?" the guy who'd picked up a man asked.

There was a lot of bustle around the bar. Some of the security people began inspecting the area while others tried to quell the objections of the patrons. Wylie noticed that somehow during the scuffle he'd cut his thumb. A line of blood ran down to his wrist.

"Everybody take a deep breath," said a man with a silver mustache who seemed to be in charge, raising his voice above the din. "We want to get you out of here as soon as we can, but it's going to take some time. If everyone could step over to the side of the bar, these gentlemen here will take care of you."

Three men in suits herded the others away. "You can stay here," one of them said to Wylie.

"We had some other trouble, over in the gift shop," the head guy told Wylie confidentially when his officers began to question the others. "Somebody left a threatening note. A gal found it while she was picking out a key chain."

The guy took out a notepad, wet his finger, flipped back the first page. Just like in the movies. His chest muscles looked firm beneath his white shirt, like he worked out. He took Wylie's name, his contact info, who he worked for, the time he'd gotten there that morning.

"Okay, now. Relax a minute. Let's backtrack. I want you to try to remember. Just let your mind drift. Any details. Anything that comes to you. Let's start with now and work our way back."

The embryo bobbed to the surface of Wylie's mind like a dolphin. Bumped him with its rubbery head, stared with its octopus eye. Wylie had the feeling, startling in its intensity, that it was trying to signal him. To send him a message like the printed words that float up on the bottom of the Magic 8 Ball. An answer to a question: TRY AGAIN. FOR SURE. BEWARE.

Wylie laughed, shook his head. If only he knew the question.

The policeman looked up, his pencil poised above the paper.

The little fish grinned, safe in its capsule of fluid, its embryonic nectar, its dark private sea.

19

Jewell lay in the big hall closet and listened to Celeste go about her morning routine. Water running in the bathroom, the toilet flushing, steps down the hall, dishes rattling in the kitchen sink. She was washing out her coffee cup, so it wouldn't be long before she left. Jewell wondered what Celeste was wearing, pictured the preoccupied look on her face as she hurried around the house, gathering her things. Would she say good-bye, call out something to the accordion door of the closet? Celeste's keys jangled, her shoes clicked to the door, the lock turned. The door opened, closed, and locked. Then it was quiet. Celeste was gone. There was only the morning and the silence of another day. The dull, aching throb in the pit of Jewell's stomach.

She had been sleeping in the closet for almost two weeks now, ever since the night she'd driven to Dana's and found Celeste there. The futon, which she'd dragged off the frame in the living room, almost filled the space, which was basically the size of a jail cell. She'd stacked her folded clothes around one of the baseboards, plugged a crook-necked lamp into the one socket, and filled a plastic liter bottle with water to drink at night. Up near the ceiling was a handkerchief-sized window, on one wall were shelves that held furniture polish, folded paper bags, plastic knives and forks, crap they hardly ever used. It was pitiful. At night Jewell pulled the accordion door shut, stared at the square of dark sky, and cried.

She threw back the sleeping bag she was using as a blanket and forced herself to get up. She had the breakfast shift that morning. After that, she'd go look at more apartments. She felt like a prowler creeping around the empty apartment, seeing the clothes Celeste had left on the bed the night before, the book open on the coffee table next to an empty mug. All the evidence that Celeste's life was proceeding as normal: numbers she'd scribbled down near the phone, makeup in the bathroom on the back of the toilet, crusts of toast on a saucer in the kitchen. Jewell brushed her teeth. She still couldn't believe it was over, that they'd reached the end of their road together and were about to part ways. In the meantime, living like this was torture. Sleeping in the closet; listening to Celeste move around the house; nodding to her in the hall; the raw, swollen silence. Jewell looked at herself in the mirror. She'd gotten paranoid, straining her ears to make out Celeste's phone conversations, going through her things when she wasn't home. Her face looked pale, shipwrecked, bewildered. She was a fucking zombie. *Night of the Living Dead.*

She let the shower hit her on the back of the neck and played through the apartments she'd looked at so far. She was practically broke, so of course she couldn't stay in this place alone, and the places she *could* afford were dives. She scanned the apartment-for-rent ads relentlessly. They whispered in her head all day long, speaking in secret code: *w/w remod, clean, nu cpt, avail now, dntwn vu, prkg, lndry.* It was like a prayer, language distilled to its essence. She washed her sad, unloved arms and legs; soaped and rinsed her untouched breasts and belly. *nu pnt, snny dck, sm grdn, tp fl, hi ceil.* The vowel-starved language hinted that, after all this was over, life might go on. There might be other rooms, other streets, other lovers. The broken syllables gave her hope.

Jewell went to the kitchen and opened the refrigerator, but since the incident at Dana's, she felt sick whenever she thought of eating. Pounds were dropping off; her pants bagged around her waist. She didn't mind. It gave the look of reproach she shot Celeste whenever they saw each other that much more bite.

She nosed through the garbage. *Celeste* was having no problem eating. Jewell found the remains of Vietnamese takeout from their favorite place near Chinatown. The order was written on the paper bag: *sp rlls, 5 sp chkn.* How could Celeste stand to go to the very place where she and Jewell had met so often at the end of the day, where they'd laughed and talked over steaming bowls of pho? Celeste's dishes were washed, drying in the rack. Just like nothing was happening. Jewell choked down a glass of water. She looked out at the gray sky, the soggy yard. Already it seemed like years since she and Celeste had slept in the same bed, shared a meal, made love, or ridden in the car with the radio on. *fpl, wlk-in clst, pet ok* Jewell reminded herself. She felt skinned, open to the elements. Her organs—her heart, lungs, and kidneys—were tender, as though they'd been dropped in boiling water. Giblets. Stop, she told herself. Enough. *lg rms, wd fl, gd lite.* Her place was out there somewhere, she just had to find it. But right now she was late for work.

She parked at the loading dock behind the cafeteria and sat for a minute in her dented red Nissan. A jet broke through the heavy clouds, and she watched it move like an arrowhead across the sky until it pierced another pocket of gray and disappeared. She thought of her father, who must have spent time sleeping in a space about the same size as the one she was sleeping in now. She yearned suddenly to see him. He lived here, in the same city. For all she knew, he could be blocks away. She could run into him by accident today. She shivered and pulled her sweater tighter around her neck. The loading dock was wet; a thick hose stretched like a python across it. The warm smell of frying doughnuts threaded the cold morning air that flowed through the Nissan's window. Yellow light fell through the open double doors of the cafeteria.

Jewell locked her car and walked up the steps on the side of the loading dock, careful not to slip on the greasy concrete. As soon as she stepped through the doors the warm air engulfed her, smelling of mass-produced food and sour rags. There was the clash of baking sheets and tub-sized pots, the groan of the huge ovens whose shelves revolved like Ferris wheels, the clatter of silverware and dishes being stacked. After the long, lonely night, the noise and light comforted her. She punched in, then went into the locker room to tie back her hair and put on her grungy shoes.

The head cook stopped her on her way to the dish room. "Hey, Jewell. Where you been? Vicki's out today," he said. "We need you on the hotline."

Jewell hated the hotline. It was cleaner and less work than the dish room, but you had to stand there in a hairnet and a plastic apron and serve hash browns and French toast to your classmates.

"Who's in the dish room?" she asked.

"Eli's finished in the pot room. He can cover the dish room himself. Come on, hustle. They're lined up all the way out to the dining room."

The steam table was loaded with pans of sausages, hash browns, Cream of Wheat, scrambled eggs, and French toast. Jewell pulled on latex gloves. Behind her was a grill. As the cook had said, a line of students with puffy eyes and wet hair, dressed in sweat clothes and flip-flops, snaked around the serving bay. They picked up trays that they loaded with drinks, silverware, and napkins before they came up to the hotline and told her what they wanted.

She tonged the sausage and French toast onto their plates. Doled out scrambled eggs with an ice cream scoop. Over easy, sunny-side up: she worked the grill with quick snaps of the wrist, ladling out the egg for omelets, flipping the finished products expertly onto the plates. *Logan,* she thought as she jerked an empty pan from the steam table and added a new one of hash browns. *Dad.*

Maybe it was the season, with Christmas coming on, or maybe it was breaking up with Celeste, but he was on her mind. The last time she'd seen him, at her high school graduation, he'd left his youngest daughter in her mother's arms and motioned Jewell away from the crowd that had gathered in front of the auditorium.

"C'mon. C'mon over here," Logan had said, taking her by the hand and leading her down the street a little. When they reached the corner, he leaned against one of the parked cars and jammed his hands deep in his pockets.

"So, how're you doing?" he'd asked, glancing up and down the street, jittery. "You look good." He grinned and nodded. "You turned out pretty good. You okay?"

He was twisting the program in his hands. Jewell saw that he had it open to the honor roll, that he'd circled her name, the last one in the column, in shaky ballpoint.

"I'm doing okay, Dad. I'm fine."

She peered into his face, half curious, half shy. He looked gaunter than usual, with hollow cheeks and stubble glinting on his face. The little patch of beard beneath his lower lip bristled like a small, furry animal when he chewed his lips. She sensed there was something he wanted to tell her, and she shifted her feet nervously, glancing across the street at a circle of boys with shaved heads who were passing around a joint while they talked, looking over in her and Logan's direction now and then. In truth, Jewell felt hungover, having spent the night before partying with some of the very friends who were now hugging grandparents and receiving pats on the back, who were getting into cars, slamming doors, and driving away.

"I'm proud of you, baby," Logan said, gnawing at his lip. He pulled his wallet from his back pocket. "Here, I want to give you a little something."

"Oh no," Jewell objected. "You don't have to do that." She tried to push his hands away before he could reach for the money. She laughed when she saw his wallet. "God, what happened to that thing? It looks like roadkill."

"What?" Logan said innocently, holding up his tattered wallet, which was stuffed with papers but flattened so that it *did* look like a squashed animal with its guts hanging out.

"What's all that stuff in there?"

"This is my office, man," Logan shrugged. "This is where I file important documents."

"Like what?" Jewell joked, feeling suddenly at ease with him.

They knew practically nothing about each other, but just then her father felt familiar, as if they'd never been apart. "Let's see what's in there," she said as she made a grab for the wallet.

Logan dodged away. "Hey, hold on there," he said, hiding it behind his back.

"Come on, let me see."

They scuffled while the boys across the street watched with interest. Jewell managed to get hold of Logan's wrist. "Show me!" she demanded.

Logan laughed. "Okay, okay! I give up!"

"Got any pictures?" Jewell said.

"Well, let's see."

Logan began to thumb through the wad of papers. "Bunch a shit, really," he said. "Even *I* don't even know what's in here."

There was an article torn from a newspaper, yellow and crumpled. A receipt from Save-On, $3.47. A list squeezed onto a Post-it note. A small stack of photos that he didn't bother taking out. "I guess everybody has one of these. It's a—whadyacallit—a cliché," Logan said, holding up a napkin with a name and phone number written on it. He pulled out a business card with a woman's picture and scowled at it a minute. "Real estate agent. Guess somebody wanted to sell me a house," he mumbled, crumpling the card in his fist. Then his face brightened. "Hey, here's something you might be interested in," he said, pulling out a color snapshot. One of the corners was bent. "What do you think about this?" he beamed, passing it to Jewell.

She squinted down at it. It was a kid in a carnival ride, four boats attached to arms that went round and round a little pool of water. The kid looked about three. Wearing a hooded sweatshirt, she leaned over the side of the boat, looking into the water.

"Is it me?" Jewell asked.

"Sure it is. Who'd you think?"

Jewell studied the picture. Never having seen it before, she felt like she'd just discovered some new part of herself. The fact that Logan was carrying it around, that he might even have been carrying it around all this time, made her feel dangerously close to crying.

"See how you're looking at the water?" he asked. "Me and your mom told you not to lean over the side and to keep your hands inside the boat. But you waited until it went around to the other side, behind that machine there in the middle. You thought we couldn't see you. The minute you thought you were out of sight, *bam,* your hand went in the water. Then, when you came back around to where we were standing, you pulled your hand back in. See how you're hiding your hand with the other hand? We laughed and laughed."

Jewell looked at him with amazement. Had he really been standing there, watching her, with her mother at his side? It seemed so *normal,* so unlike how she always imagined her family. And he *remembered* every detail.

"Didn't you get mad?" she ventured.

Logan shrugged. "I guess we should've. You know, be consistent and all that. But you were just so damn cute, you know." He took the photo from her, took one last look, and slid it back in his wallet. "I probably thought you took after me or something. You know, wanting to do something just because someone told you not to. Hey? Hey, what's up?"

Jewell's chin quivered, then her chest heaved. Oh no. Her throat burned. There was no turning back, she realized, she'd gone too far. The tears seemed to leap from her eyes. They splashed over her lashes, gushed down her face, even hit her knee on the way down, darkening the sheeny polyester of her rented gown. School colors, crimson and gold.

Logan put his arm across her shoulder and drew her into his side. She felt his warmth, smelled his unknown life clinging to his clothes. What was it? Baked beans from a can, the sun-warmed upholstery of his car, laundry detergent bought from a machine at the coin-op, the scent of the woman who slept next to him? She'd never know. To her own horror she sobbed, pressing her face into his shoulder.

"What is it, baby?" Logan pleaded, peeling her away so that he could see her face. "What's wrong?"

It passed quickly, a sudden squall. Jewell shook her head and wiped her eyes. She felt calmer, but now she wanted to be away from him. Still, she managed to smile. "Just, you know. Kind of an emotional moment or something."

Logan smiled back. He still had the wallet out and now he fished in it again, drew out two stuck-together twenties.

"I wish it was more, but you take this."

"No. It's okay," she insisted. She was pretty sure Logan didn't have much to spare. "Really. You don't have to."

"Go on." He poked it into her fist with his forefinger like a magician stuffing scarves into his hand. "Go out with your friends, have a drink on me."

Jewell laughed. "I'm eighteen. We'd get busted."

"Oh, okay. Minor detail. Well, how about this? Lemme buy you something. Is there anything you want?"

"How about a car?" Jewell joked. "Or a condo?" Before she could suggest anything else, the woman who had come with Logan walked up and stood impatiently about twenty feet away, watching them. She was holding the baby on her hip; a diaper bag and a big purse dangled from her shoulders, weighing her down. The little girl, whom Jewell had held and admired earlier, was fretful now, squirming in her mother's arms. The woman wrestled with her, shifted her to the other hip, struggled with the diaper bag.

"Uh, I think that woman might be waiting for you. I forgot her name."

"Tonya?" Logan turned and looked over his shoulder. "Uh-oh," he said. "I guess I better get going."

As she stood in her graduation gown, watching Logan walk back to two more people who would probably never get a big enough piece of him, Jewell had felt him slip away, disappearing back into the part of his life that she knew so little about. She had wondered when he might pop up again—in a week, several years, maybe never. But now, three years later, as she slid a spatula under an omelet and transferred it to a plate, she sensed him drawing near. She would see him again soon, she could almost feel it.

"*Way* too much cheese," a ponytailed sorority type said as Jewell handed the omelet over the glass partition. Jewell knew the breed: snotty and fresh-faced, the kind who worked the Stairmaster while reading glamour mags in the gym, fucked her meat-headed boyfriend on the weekends, and was headed for a public relations job in some corporation, a husband who golfed, and two kids with a live-in nanny.

"It's an *omelet*. This is how they come," Jewell said.

"I asked for *light* cheese. You must not have heard me."

Too bad Jewell wasn't in the dish room, where she could have blasted this bimbo right in her peaches-and-cream face with the overhead sprayer. Instead she gritted her teeth and gestured peevishly with the spatula. "Look, this is the fucking cafeteria. Not Sunday brunch at the Ritz."

"I can't eat this much cheese. I'm *sorry*." The sorority girl maintained her tight smile. They always did.

"Fine." Jewell slid the spatula under the omelet like she was slitting a throat. She catapulted it into the garbage behind her, where it landed with the dull thud of a dead body. "Anything else? Sausage?" She picked one up with the tongs and held it so the girl could inspect its turd-like profile. "Look, not a speck of cheese."

The woman paled. "I don't eat meat."

"Oh, really? Why not?"

It wasn't worth getting obnoxious over, but Jewell was starting to hit the wall. She hadn't eaten or slept much for several days now. She felt lightheaded and belligerent. The plate she held felt like concrete.

"Forget it," the sorority girl said, looking at Jewell with frank disdain. "I'm just going to have cereal."

Jewell shrugged. Her father had never had a real job, she reflected as she ladled maple syrup over the next student's French toast. Nothing where you punched a clock and got a regular paycheck. It was always some get-rich-quick scheme or legally questionable scam that was supposed to pay off big. Then it would be high-rolling for the rest of their lives, don't bother working. For a while they'd talked about moving to Tahiti, to Mexico, to New Zealand, paradises where houses with lots of land were dirt cheap. But the farthest they ever got was a double-wide near Palm Springs where Logan planned to cash in on an egg farm. Two weeks after they moved, raccoons wiped out the whole flock of chickens.

"Hello? *Excuse* me?"

Another twit. This one had *two* ponytails, one on either side of her head.

"These eggs aren't done. They're, like, almost raw." The girl jiggled them on the plate. "Could you put them back on the grill for a little while longer? Just, like, thirty seconds?"

Jewell didn't have the energy to be snide. She slid the eggs onto the grill and cooked them until the yolks were solid. "Enjoy your breakfast," she chirped as she passed the plate back.

She sleepwalked through the rest of her shift, daydreaming about the apartments she might find: a cottage in Laurel Canyon owned by a wealthy old lady crazy enough to rent it out for peanuts; a bungalow in Santa Monica, steps from the beach, offered in exchange for minimal yard work; a rambling rancher in the Hollywood Hills with views to forever. The first place she could remember living in, when Logan was still around, was the top floor of a two-story wooden house owned by two old Italian sisters who lived downstairs. She remembered only a few things about it—a tile painted with a black-and-white striped angelfish set into the wall near the tub, the metal cupboard under the sink in the kitchen where she was allowed to stick her magnetic alphabet, and the avocado tree in the backyard where the skunks came after dark to eat the fallen fruit. Logan had taken her out of bed one night to watch them. From the top floor she could barely make out the white stripes on three or four of them as they snuffled in the grass. *Shhh!* her parents said if Jewell jumped or ran on the bare floors. It riled up the old sisters, who would bang on the ceiling with a broomstick. When that happened, the three of them—Jewell and her mother and father—would freeze in place, look at each other, and—with their hands over their mouths—laugh.

It was downhill from there. There was a succession of lifeless apartments alike in their dreariness, with sliding glass doors that led out to slabs of concrete, buzzing squares of fluorescent lights set into the ceilings, walls so thin you could hear people clearing their throats next door. Downy, Whittier, Pomona. A place in Torrance built so close to the sidewalk that people seemed to be passing through their living room at all hours of the day and night. Another in Inglewood that smelled so pervasively of cat piss that Jewell and her mother always ate their dinner sitting on the front step, staring out into the wide, treeless street. The one in a city-subsidized housing project where fuses were always blowing, where a fire had started inside the wall. Houses that were more like dentists' offices, banquet rooms, tool sheds. Shower stalls with sordid pasts, cupboards saturated with odors of despair. Throughout her childhood and adolescence, Jewell dreamed about returning to the first place she'd lived, the one the sisters owned. She daydreamed about the thick wood windowsills, the arched doorway between the living and dining rooms, the swirls of plaster that had been troweled onto the walls. *Listen!* Logan had said, crouching on all fours and putting his ear to the floor. Jewell had pressed her cheek to the floorboards and heard, traveling up from downstairs, the deranged wheeze of an accordion and, accompanying it, the shrill warble of an old lady's vibrato. *The old coots are sauced,* Logan had laughed. *Drunk as sailors.*

Jewell slung a gluey scoop of Cream of Wheat into a bowl and handed it over the counter. Who in their right mind would eat that shit? While she doled out strips of bacon, she furnished, landscaped, and painted the houses she dreamed of finding and inhabiting, right down to the faucet on the bathroom sink. And when it was all finished, when she was settling back near the fireplace in a room with a one-eighty-degree view of the whole city, when the dark was coming down and the lights were coming up, that's when the phone would ring. That's when Celeste would call to say what a mistake she'd made. That's when she would cry and beg, when she would plead with Jewell to give her one more chance. And since the house was big, since there were bedrooms and bedrooms, who wouldn't want to live there, well—Jewell would reconsider. There was even room for Rachel. And so they'd start again, and this time it would be different. This time—

"Hey, homey. Jules! *Jules!*"

Standing on the other side of the hotline was Eli. He was fresh from the dish room, wearing his hairnet like a beret and with his billygoat beard strung through a chunky wooden bead.

"How's it going? You look totally spaced. What's up?"

Jewell shook off her daydream. Eli had already loaded his tray with four milks and two cups of coffee. "Jesus, what time is it?" Jewell said.

"Time to close down, girlfriend."

Jewell glanced at the clock. "Shit! I'm supposed to look at an apartment in a half hour. You want the usual?"

"Yeah, the works."

Jewell loaded a plate with a mountain of scrambled eggs and a heap of sausage and bacon. "French toast?" she asked.

"Yeah, why not? I'll take a couple of pieces."

As soon as she served Eli, Jewell started jerking the pans of stray sausages and stiff hash browns out of the steam table.

"So you haven't found a place yet, huh? What's up with Miss Priss?" Eli had never liked Celeste.

"Nothing. We're still living in the house together. I'm sleeping in the closet. I run into her in the hallway on the way to the bathroom once in a while."

"Sounds harsh," Eli said, munching on his third strip of bacon.

"It sucks. I need to get out of there. It's hard, though, not having much money. It's not like I have a whole lot to choose from." She pulled a rag from under the counter and started wiping down the stainless steel. "Keep your eyes open, will you?"

"Yeah, sure."

"Old men with big houses who're circling the drain, summer places down on the beach where I can hole up during the off-season."

The bead on Eli's beard swung when he nodded, thumping him on the Adam's apple. "Don't worry. You'll find something."

"You think so? It just seems so unreal. I mean, I can't believe this is happening." Jewell paused. The rag had a sour smell. Her stomach did a queasy flop. "I guess part of me thinks there's still a chance something will happen," she admitted. "That we'll get it together somehow."

Eli had eaten almost everything on his tray while he stood there. Now he paused with a strip of bacon halfway to his mouth. "You mean you're still thinking you can patch it up with Celeste?" he asked incredulously.

Jewell gave a slow, guilty nod.

"Jules, you're better off without her," Eli said emphatically. "Trust me, she doesn't appreciate you. You deserve better."

Jewell nodded, even though she wasn't convinced. Eli didn't understand. On the other hand, things were miserable at home. Intolerable. She couldn't take it much longer.

"Hey, I'm going to ask around," Eli said. "I might have a lead on a place. Really, I mean it. Friends of mine mentioned they might be moving." He wiped his face with the back of his hand. The only thing left on his plate was the pile of scrambled eggs. "You gotta get out of there."

"This is *it*?" Jewell asked the landlord.

He was a healthy-looking blond guy in chino shorts and a polo shirt who lived in the huge, sunny house on top of the renovated garage he'd listed for rent. He'd divided it into three tiny, windowless rooms. You dropped the mail through a slot in the big double door and it fell onto the linoleum floor. But the landlord could afford to look smug because there was a buzz of competition among other would-be tenants who were poking into the closet-sized bathroom and running their hands over the Formica counter that was supposed to pass as a kitchen. While the others crowded the landlord for applications, Jewell escaped through a side door. It was a bad start, she told herself. It had to get better.

The next apartment had shag carpet halfway up the walls. The windows faced a four-lane thoroughfare. Jewell had to shout at the manager, whose eyes kept shifting to her breasts.

"You get used to the noise," he said with a shrug. "Just turn up the stereo."

By the time she looked at the third place, one that the ad had listed as "furnished," but that turned out to be a storehouse for the landlord's old furniture, Jewell felt that she was carrying a bowling-ball-sized lump around in her chest.

"What if I wanted to get rid of some of this stuff?" she asked the landlord as she looked over the living room packed wall-to-wall with old sofas, government-issue desks, and armchairs that smelled of cat piss.

"Then you wouldn't be the right person for this apartment," he replied with a sniff, as if the place were the Taj Majal.

The last place on her list sounded like a flophouse, but it was cheap. *dntwn, cls to all, lg closet, share bath.* She thought again of her father as she headed downtown, thought of the houses where she'd lived with him when she was young, the stained carpets and banged-up walls, the gouged floors and the smells of other people's lives: dirty socks, baby powder, cigarettes, stale perfume, fried hamburger. But when Logan was around, it hadn't seemed to matter. He was the kind of guy who could feel at home anyplace. Where was he now? She exited the freeway near the Civic Center, turned down a one-way street, and added a few more details to the house she was building for herself in her dreams. She might make a little addition for her father, a place where he could live in the back. She was an architect, after all. Her place would be Zenned-out. Feng-shuied to the max. Bamboo floors, smooth lines. Lots of windows, lots of wood. No curtains, carpets, or clutter.

She pulled up in front of a three-story brick building with a laundromat on the ground floor. When she buzzed, a wiry old man with a German accent and thick white hair that stood straight up on his head answered the door. He took her to the top floor and led her down a hall that smelled of Pine-Sol. They walked past doors with panes of wavy, frosted glass set in the top half like in old detective movies. She imagined her name painted on one: JEWELL WYLIE, P.I. The manager stopped at the end of the hall. While he was working the key in the lock, an older woman wearing a bathrobe, men's athletic socks, and plastic sandals cracked the door across the hall and watched them.

The place was one big bare room with a window that looked out on the buildings across the street. The manager crossed the room, opened a wide closet door, and pulled down a bed that lowered to the floor with a metallic clank. There was a chipped porcelain sink in one corner, a tiny refrigerator, and a small range with two gas rings. Jewell crossed the room and looked out the window. There was some kind of church or rescue mission across the street. On its roof a blue neon cross glowed weakly against the gray sky. It looked more medical than religious, like something you'd see on an ambulance.

When she turned, the manager was watching her. His huge white eyebrows curled over his forehead. "What happened to your old apartment?" he asked suspiciously. His accent made her think of Nazi interrogations. "Why are you leaving?"

Jewell choked. She and Celeste had known the minute they walked into their house that it was the right place for them. "This is it, Jewell!" Celeste had beamed. "This is *our* house."

"I'm getting divorced," Jewell told the manager. The queasy feeling rose up into her throat. She could feel her jaw loosening, the spit gathering in her mouth. "I have to leave, find a new place."

There was something creepy about the old dude, who kept his watery blue eyes fastened on her. In an effort to pull herself together, Jewell walked over to the sink and opened the medicine cabinet above it. She felt raw, like there was no insulation covering her nerves. Anything might set her off, even the chip in the porcelain sink, black on white. No one had cleaned out the medicine cabinet. The shelves were stained with rust from razor blades. There were a couple of old Band-Aids and a few cotton swabs.

She clamped her hand over her mouth.

"Bathroom's down the hall," the manager said.

The places where they'd lived when she was a kid had driven her mother crazy. All her father's so-called friends coming and going, sharing places with other families and all their kids, who mixed like litters of dogs who'd forgotten who their own mother was. *Her* mom was always moving cast-off furniture around, building tables out of milk crates, and hanging bedspreads on the walls. No wonder she'd gone round the bend.

gd lite, sm grdn, quiet Jewell told herself. The room blurred as her eyes filled with tears.

"You want to see?" the manager asked.

Jewell shook her head.

Outside, the rain started, pocking the window with hollow taps.

20 Rain sputtered against the window like buckshot. Logan groaned when he opened his eyes and saw the heavy sky hanging outside. The dense, suffocating gray. Just under his breastbone, at the very top of his stomach, the dime-sized hole was acting up. He could feel himself leaking out of it: his soul, his energy, every want and desire, every reason for living bleeding out with a low hiss like a pinprick in an inner tube. They'd find him like that: flat, a pelt in a broken-down bed.

He felt so bad, what was the point? Of holding off any longer, one day at a time, saying *no no no* when all he wanted to do was say *yes.* Get it over with. Feel the thrum in his veins, higher and higher, the power and the knowledge and everything sliding into place. Outside, cars roared down the streets, up one way and down the other. Horns honking, valets chirping for cabs in front of hotels, planes taking off and landing. All the people outside and not one he could call then and there, say how're you doing, what's going on. No one he wanted to see and who wanted to see him. No one to love. Not one. The women were gone, he'd blown that. His mother was dead. His kids had gone their separate ways.

Yeah, he felt sorry for himself.

One of the guys inside, a Muslim who was doing time for embezzlement, said that in his religion you didn't have to believe. All you had to do was go through the motions: pray, fast, play by the rules. Morning, noon, and night, just go through the motions and pretty soon the belief would come, almost without your knowing it. So Logan got up. He took a leak in the sink, washed and shaved, got dressed. One thing they forgot to tell you was, once you get clean, there's still life to deal with. Minor detail. It's still here and you're still here, the same loser you always were. He was sober and clean, but so what? He was still a thirty-nine-year-old ex-con who basically had no skills no interests no direction few friends no family who was working a shit job and who seemed to be thinking more and more of the old ways: scoring, using, selling.

Logan combed his hair and pulled it back with a rubber band. He put on his jacket and a baseball cap and tried to push away the bad thoughts. At least a little way away, at least for now. First have breakfast, he told himself, then you can score. Easy does it, one thing at a time.

He took the stairs down. The cinnamon-roll smell was strong today and he took that as a good sign, a signal that things might get better. Salem the manager was reading the paper in the little cage in the lobby and the big fat guy with bandaged feet was sitting in one of the armchairs watching the rain fall. The hole in Logan's chest whistled like wind through a broken window, emptying him out. That same tender spot like someone pressing a fingertip just below the place where his ribs joined over his heart. It was an old feeling, he'd had it as long as he could remember. The sound of the house when the door closed and you were all alone. The buzz of fluorescent lights, the smell of warm bologna, the look of the dirty dawn when you couldn't go to sleep. Ah, jeez. He pressed his hand over the spot to staunch the flow.

When he stepped outside the rain blew in his face. Breakfast, he reminded himself. Just get through breakfast and worry about the rest later. Down at the Olympic Flame on Figueroa you got two eggs, two strips of bacon, hash browns, and toast for $2.99, which was a good deal but it was still over three bucks with tip, and money was another thing, wasn't it? Cash was low. He got so sick of it: the scraping and saving, counting his dimes. Six dollars an hour. Whoa. Big deal. If he was lucky enough to work five hours a day he earned a whopping thirty dollars, not even enough to pay for his goddamned room, his little fleabag hole-in-the-wall with the broken down bed and the who-knows-what stains on the fuzzy-ass rug. The room where hundreds of poor bastards before him had gotten drunk or stared at the walls or, if they were lucky and had a little money, got their rocks off for maybe ten minutes before going back to their miserable lives. Meanwhile some jerkoff was sitting at a desk making thirty bucks *an hour* pushing paper around on his desk, or, even worse, thirty bucks *in five minutes* signing his name to some deal or a thousand other things that were a hell of a lot less work than grunting and straining and wiping the ass of some poor schmuck who couldn't lift a finger of his own hand.

How? How was he ever going to get any money? He turned the corner at Four Brothers Furniture and the rain hit him in the back of the neck, sending icy shivers down his spine. At this rate, he was never going to have a goddamned thing. Even if he worked *twenty hours a day* he'd only make a colossal $120 *before taxes,* big fucking deal. Simba, the guy who sold incense and scented oils, was at his table under the awning of the Bodega Santa Maria. Logan slapped palms with him. Plenty of people would front him some stuff right now, no cash down. All he had to do was say the word. He could unload it fast, make a nice wad, and clear the hell out. Take off down to Mexico or out East to the boonies, get a sweet little place. Start over.

Man, he was in a bad way.

The Olympic Flame was long and narrow, with a counter running the length of the place and a row of two-spot tables along the wall. The thick, homey smell of hot grease hit Logan's nose before he got to the door. The light was low inside. Four or five guys were hunched at the counter. Gus, the Greek owner, was working the grill while he kept his eye on his bleach-blond wife, who was waiting tables. She had a fine, tight little ass. Oso, a big, slumping guy who lived and breathed the Lakers, was sweating over the sports page at the end of the counter nearest the door. Logan hurried past him. The last thing he wanted to do was listen to a character analysis of each and every player.

"Logan, my man," Gus said.

Irene, the wife, poured his coffee.

Logan ordered eggs over easy with rye toast. He sipped his coffee and watched Gus flip pancakes. Why couldn't he be more like other people? Why didn't he care about the goddamn Lakers or a wife with a tight ass or Jesus in heaven or low gas mileage or drought-resistant plants? *Something.* The trouble with being clean was that things kept coming up in your mind. Crazy things, things from the past. Technicolor. You had no control. It was like an article he'd read in an old magazine lying around in the lobby at the Morningstar: some researcher touched a guy's brain with a fine-haired paintbrush and every time he touched a different spot, the poor bastard remembered something that had happened fifteen or thirty years ago like it was yesterday. What the experiment proved was that everything, *every little thing,* was all stored there in your brain, waiting to creep up on you. It was almost like tripping. And that was what had been happening to Logan, what had been setting his nerves on edge. Just that morning, out of the blue, he'd remembered climbing the fence of an empty lot, jumping down on the other side where someone had left a board with a nail hammered through the end. He must have been nine or ten years old. The pain shot all the way up his leg to the base of his spine. And when he'd looked down there was the nail coming through the top of his foot. He hadn't thought of it for eons, but that morning it was as vivid as the moment it happened.

And that was just the tip of the iceberg.

"More for you?" Irene said, holding up the coffeepot. She had a lot of mascara on. Each eyelash was the diameter of a toothpick.

Logan nodded, even though the coffee wasn't doing the hole in his chest any favors. He pictured it like a cigarette burn in a blanket, the edges scorched and crisp, the pink mouth in the middle open, juicy.

"You wanna take this home? Want me to wrap it up?" Irene said. She gave him the eye as she pointed to his plate, dipped her head, smiled. All that was left were the hash browns and a half slice of toast. Jeez, how bad off did she think he was?

"No, you can take it away. I'm done."

"Anything else?" she asked. She gave a sneaky glance at her husband, then patted Logan's hand. "Anything else I can do for you?"

The rain had stopped and the sun was trying to push through the clouds when he stepped outside. He decided then and there that he would go to a meeting. The New Way Tabernacle over on Broadway had one that started at eleven, in five minutes. Logan turned in that direction and stepped up his pace. You couldn't say he wasn't trying. The hole in his chest was a *yearning* feeling, he decided. As if something inside him was *reaching*. He pulled the bill of his cap low over his face, and put his hands in his pockets. He crossed the street thinking how he was going to lay it all out on the table once he got to the meeting. He was going to let go of his problems and hope for some help.

"Hey, hey, hey!" someone called behind him. "Hey! You! *Psst! Psst!*"

Logan turned and saw a gangly figure in a thigh-length sweater and a stocking cap pulled over half his face waving his arms in the air.

"Wait!" he called. "Come here!"

Some kind of street crazy. But just as Logan was about to turn and keep walking he realized it was Wally, the guy who worked the register at K&M Liquors, where he sometimes bought Lotto tickets. He hadn't recognized him outside of the little cubbyhole behind the counter where he usually sat watching a toaster-size TV.

"Hey, where you been?" Wally called. "I look for you."

Logan didn't know whether Wally had a language problem or if he was just simple. He couldn't figure out where he came from, either. Serbia or Croatia or one of those places that fell apart? Iraq or Iran or Afghanistan or one of those Middle Eastern places where they were always blowing the shit out of each other? Anyway, the guy knew about three words of English. He was super-friendly, though, like Logan was a long-lost friend. Logan walked back to where Wally was standing in front of the store.

"Hey, how's it going, man?" Logan said.

Wally pounded him on the chest with the palm of his hand, right where the hole was. "Hey, you win, you win!" he beamed.

"Who, man? What're you talking about?"

Wally looked at Logan with wide eyes, like *he* was the one who was crazy. "Yeah, they come! They say me! They say me your name!"

Logan's pulse picked up. He didn't know whether he was scared or excited. "I won the Lotto?" he asked cautiously.

Wally shook his head furiously. "Here!" He grabbed Logan's wrist and pulled him into the store. "Here! Here, see!"

Wally ducked behind the crowded counter, punched a button to open the register, and fished out a stub of paper. "See!" he said, thrusting it at Logan. "Look!"

GRAND PRIZE: TRIP TO MEXICO it said across the top. It took Logan a minute to recognize his own shaky handwriting: name, address, and phone number. Then he remembered the fishbowl on the counter, the raffle ticket he'd filled out weeks ago, on a day when he was feeling flush.

Wally snatched the ticket away from him. "Phone no work. They try."

"Yeah, the phone's at the end of the hall where I live. Pay phone. That was before I got my cell. Nobody ever takes a message."

Wally fished under the counter and came up with an envelope. "You win!" he said. "Call here."

Bang, just like that.

Logan forgot about his meeting. Mexico. *Mexico.* In his early twenties, he'd spent almost a year crisscrossing it with his friend Bellamy. They'd slept on the beach or in the bed of the pickup.

There was nothing like it: the rich charred smell in the air, roosters crowing in the morning. The beer and the beach. The sun. And the water. Blue, baby. *Blue.*

A bus rumbled past, churning out diesel fumes. Logan paused under the awning of a Shoe Pavilion and opened the envelope. He'd won a one-week vacation to Cancún, all expenses paid. *Un-fucking-believable.* He'd been to the Yucatán on his other trip. He and Bellamy had spent weeks living in a palapa village on a little bay near Tulum, selling pot to gringos who came to get drunk and laid. One of the best memories of his life was floating in the turquoise water with the sun blazing down on him. Everything was *right there.* There was nothing more to want. If he could go back to that—

But he couldn't. It would violate his parole, big time.

As Logan stood staring down at the ticket with all the people passing, the sneakers and boots lining the windows of the Shoe Pavilion behind him, the gum stuck to the sidewalk, the grit flying up behind the cars, who should walk up but Pete Cortez? Pete, *Petey,* his buddy from way back. They'd gone to high school to-gether, partied through their teens and into their twenties. For a while they'd even had a landscape business and really kicked ass, wiping up big bucks from the hoity-toity set down in Laguna Beach. Petey was a wizard with plants; he could turn anything into the fucking Garden of Eden. All the big shots wanted him. Logan threw back his head and laughed. God, it must have been ten, twelve years.

"Oh my God. Logan!" Petey cried, his face breaking into a grin. "Where you been, man? Where the hell you been?"

"Around," Logan laughed. "I been around."

"You living downtown?" Petey asked. "I am. Just a few blocks away."

"Yeah, I'm staying at the Morningstar? You know it? What a trip! What do you know? We're still homies!"

They embraced, pounding each other on the back. Up close, Petey smelled like beer. He looked a little scruffy, like he could use a shave, a wash for his jean jacket and Levi's. But he was the same soft-spoken, sweet guy. Skinny as a snake and loose-strung; he moved like a puppet. He had spaniel eyes: deep brown, gentle.

"I'm heading up to The Fuse," he said, pointing up the street. "Come join me. I'll buy you a drink."

Here we go, Logan thought. He stuck his hands in his pockets, looked down at the cigarette butts smashed on the sidewalk. *I'm not drinking. I don't drink. I quit drinking,* he rehearsed to himself. He couldn't decide which one to use. He looked at his watch. Five past noon. "What's The Fuse?" he asked.

"Place up the street. Nothing special, just a good place to hang out. Cheap." Petey had the nicest, warmest smile. "I'm a regular." He grinned, clapping Logan on the shoulder.

Just because you go to a bar doesn't mean you have to drink. Hadn't Logan already proved that to himself? Drinking wasn't his real problem, anyway. And how often do you run into an old buddy on a day you're feeling blue? How often, for that matter, do you win an all-expenses-paid trip, even if you can't use it?

"Vamonos," Logan said.

The place was dark inside. It took your eyes a while to adjust enough to see the few guys at the bar, chatting with each other or with the bartender, who had sideburns that looped over his jaws, then curved up into a thatchy mustache. Pete was right, it was friendly. He ordered a Miller Draft. Logan got a Coke.

"This is my lucky day," Logan said, crunching ice. "You'll never guess what happened."

He took the prize information out of the envelope and showed it to Petey. "Only trouble is, I can't leave the country," he said.

"How come?"

Pete drank like he was thirsty. He finished the first pint in a few gulps and ordered another.

"Little problem with the law," Logan said with a grin. "I'm on probation."

They talked awhile about Mexico, about what a fucking different world it was—closer to life, and closer to death. *More real.* Logan tried to explain what the water was like there on the Caribbean coast, how it was like that movie *Liquid Sky*. Brilliant and clear. They decided that Logan could go if he wanted to, that you didn't need a visa to go to Mexico, that chances were he could be gone a week and no one would notice. That luck was on his side. It'd be worth it, man. On the other hand, if he didn't want to go, he could probably sell the ticket. Might be good for five or six hundred, which wasn't bad. Logan's hands itched. There was something important he wanted to tell Petey, something big and deep, but he couldn't put his finger on what it was. His legs felt twitchy. The hole in his chest fluttered like a tight muscle.

"I'll have the same," he said when Petey ordered his third beer.

It didn't feel strange to drink it. It felt normal. Which just went to show you. It was him, after all. That's who he was. Just like his dad and his grandfather before that. Like his brothers and all his friends. His confidence came back, the loose, easy feeling. He breathed a sigh of relief. How long had it been since he'd had someone to talk to? Petey was different than the losers Logan usually met. He had a brain, and he really cared. At two beers, Logan stopped. Which also went to show you. *If you don't want to fall, don't go where it's slippery.* He was on shaky ground, he fully admitted it. Still, at two beers he climbed off the stool, gave Pete a last pat on the back, and walked out the door.

His mind was a pleasant blank as he walked back to the Morningstar. He felt calm. He noticed the parking valets who stood around the lot, trying to look tough in their white jackets as they flicked cigarette butts at each other's feet. He noticed how quickly the clouds were moving across the sky, the white limo parked in front of the rescue mission a couple of blocks from his place, the waifish girl at the bus stop who lifted her eyes and smiled at him when he passed.

It started to pour right when he got to the Morningstar. The cleaning woman was vacuuming the lobby. He couldn't stand the monotonous drone of the machine. He took his cap off and shook the rain from the shoulders of his jacket. The elevator was there, waiting, so he took it, but when the door slid closed, he panicked. It was the same fucking size as some of the cells he'd been in. He forced himself to stand still, not to hammer at the walls. The elevator inched its way to the third floor. He burst out, gasping for breath, when the door slid open. The radiators were blasting; the hall was like an oven.

TVs blared from behind closed doors: game shows, talk shows, soap operas. He strode past them. The hole in his chest was like an aching tooth, like a cavity when you eat something sweet. Someone was shouting in the room next to the bathroom. Jesus, it was hot in here! Like a goddamn sauna. Not that he'd ever been in one. You'd think they'd want to save energy. He turned the corner and headed down to the end of the hall, where his own room was. He stood outside his door and looked at the three innocent numbers, 3-1-2. All the lonely times he'd spent there came down on him, the nights he'd lain in the bed staring at the ceiling, the mornings he'd woken up and looked past his own feet to the open window and into the wide, empty Los Angeles sky. Trying, *trying* to stay on the straight and narrow. He didn't put the key in the lock. He felt like he might never go inside that room again. Like someone else might be living there already.

Instead he tapped lightly on the door of the next room. Damon opened it immediately, as if he'd been waiting. Strung out. Logan wasn't surprised: he knew Damon had been holed up in there for almost a week now. He hadn't heard Damon's weights clanking late at night, hadn't heard the radio, hadn't heard Damon going out to his job in the morning or coming back in the evening. Hell, Logan had even *smelled* the stuff coming through his open window.

"Hey," Damon said.

Inside was the chemical smell of a human body cranked up high, the caustic reek of someone who had traded lowly animal pleasures like food and sex and sleep for the high-flying burn and whir of a mind vibrating to a different frequency. Logan didn't waste any time. Damon's stuff was spread out right there on the table near the window.

"Got a bump?" Logan said.

Two hours later Logan sat on the foot of his bed facing the window with a hand over each kneecap. One thing had led to another. Didn't it always? It was really fucking amazing. A chain reaction. First he'd won the contest, then he'd run into Pete. If he hadn't run into Pete, he wouldn't have had the beer. If he hadn't had the beer, he wouldn't have had the bump. If he hadn't had the first bump, he wouldn't have had the second. And then the third and fourth and fifth, then the crack, then on and on, and now here he was. And if the phone rang right this minute, if his PO called him in for a test, that was it. He'd be right back where he started: back inside with the smell of funk and BO, noise bouncing off the bare walls like rocks rattling in a tin can. He was a goddamn son-of-a-bitch asshole! A motherfucking asswipe idiot! Jesus, Jesus, *Jesus*! What the hell had he been thinking?

He tried to think of an excuse, a way out. He fought the urge to get under the bed, to duck and cover, put his hands over his ears. Don't let his caseworker call now, don't let him knock on the door. His mind raced: the dirty test, the look on the booking clerk's face when they brought him back. With a twist of his guts, he realized how good he'd had it. Now he'd blown it all. Good-bye to his room at the Morningstar, coffee and the paper around the corner, $1.99 bowl of Chinese noodles at the Jade Kitchen. No more evening strolls on the gum-scarred sidewalks, aimless jaunts in the pinging Toyota, mornings sitting on the wall down at the boardwalk, nodding at women who jogged by in shorts. Salvetti and his skinny wife, they'd have to do without him. He wouldn't see Jewell.

If only he hadn't had the two beers. Then none of the rest would have happened. Or maybe it would have, you never know. Maybe it was bound to happen, maybe it was just in his stars. One little slipup and everything goes to hell. There's no turning back. You're fucked.

At least it was over now. At least he'd gone and done it so he could stop worrying about when it was going to happen. But he just couldn't go back inside. Couldn't, couldn't, couldn't. It was no joke when you got older. And he was different now. Despite this slipup, something in him had shifted. One thing was sure, he had to drop out of sight before they caught him dirty. Leave the Morningstar, make himself scarce.

Then he remembered the trip. *Of course!* Now he got it. He laughed, shook his head. It was all there, as big as life. All he had to do was take a step back, see the big picture. The plan, how every piece fit together. *Wow!* It all made such perfect sense. All this time he'd thought he was lost, and someone else was calling the shots.

It was all a plant: the way he'd felt when he woke that morning, winning the contest, running into Pete, drinking the beers. Doing the crank, smoking the crack, falling off the wagon. It was all a way to get him out of there. To force him to use the winning ticket to start fresh. *In Mexico.* Wasn't it a new place, with new rules? Where life was more real? With none of the bad influences he had here? Where things were cheap and he could afford a house, get a good start, get his act together?

A flood of relief washed over him. Thankfulness. *Mexico.* The healing heat of the blazing sun. The amazing sparkle of the blue, blue water.

He'd go, then. Make a break for it.

21 It was only when he saw the tusks rising out of the water, the massive trunk trumpeting in agony, that Rudy realized where he was. Surrounded by spires of glass and steel that rose up into the moving sky, the jagged hole of black tar breached the crust of the earth like a cavity in a molar. A memory from his childhood stirred: the mammoth family at the edge of the pond, the fountain splashing forlornly on the gray water. *La Brea.* Even now the name tugged at the pit of his stomach. He slowed the car, turned left, circled the block. The second time around, damned if there wasn't a parking space. Why not? Rudy wondered. He still had the whole afternoon to kill.

He fed the meter and zipped his jacket. The wind was picking up. He walked along the iron railing that circled the pond until he got as close as he could to the three mammoths: the biggest one submerged up to its shoulders in water, its head thrown back and mouth opened to the sky as if begging for mercy. Safe on the bank, the mother and baby mammoth watched placidly, either oblivious or unconcerned. That's what had bothered him as a kid: the two mammoths standing dumbly by while the father thrashed, trapped by the tar. Beneath him were the bones of all the other animals who had met the same fate—dire wolves, giant sloths, sabertooth tigers, huge vultures, and tiny horses who had been sucked one by one into the oozing asphalt.

Rudy realized now that he used to think they were real. That La Brea was a sanctuary right there on Wilshire where all the animals and land were kept exactly as they'd been since prehistoric times. That each time he passed by, the family trio was there: the father still struggling, the mother and child still grazing tranquilly nearby. Pressing his face against the iron railings, he saw L.A. as it had once been: steamy and verdant, teaming with the animals whose bones lay under the sidewalk where he stood. A sense of desolation lingered over the mass grave that had been covered, season after season, with a new layer of carnage. Even now it gave Rudy a lonely feeling, a dull awareness of peril.

But the place was also shabby in an ordinary way, like a worn carnival ride. In the reeds near the shore smashed paper cups, plastic bags, and soft-drink containers floated. The paint on the mammoths was chipped and faded. Bare spots were worn in the grass that ringed the pond. The water itself was a lurid greenish brown, and Rudy could see bulbs of algae clinging to the mucky bottom. Streams of bubbles rose from the mud, making the surface of the pond boil. In Rudy's mind they were the exhalations of the long-sleeping animals, sighs breathed by skeletons of bison and coyotes laid side by side in the ooze.

When the rain peppered his back and blew in squalls across the surface of the lake, Rudy pulled his jacket tighter and turned toward the car. But as he got nearer he realized that he couldn't face more aimless driving, and the thought of drifting haphazardly through the city filled him with such despair that he whimpered as he wiped his wet face with the palms of his hands. He wanted to sit down on the sidewalk, to cry out. More than ever he yearned for his bed, the sweet dark room where no one could see him, where all he had to do was curl up and pull the blankets around his shoulders. He should have brought a pillow, he told himself, a blanket. He could stretch out in the back seat of his car and take a nap while the rain popped comfortingly on the roof.

Instead he headed up the slight incline to the museum itself, a low, bunkerlike building. He'd never been inside before, and he figured he could at least sit down, be out of the rain. Few people were around. Inside was a ticket counter, beyond, a gift shop.

Rudy unzipped his jacket. The entrance fee was far from cheap, but he decided to splurge.

When he held out the money, the young, fragile-looking woman at the register gasped and covered her mouth with her hand.

"Oh, sir! What happened?"

Rudy followed her eyes to the berry stain on his chest. It had dried to a purplish black. He looked at it a moment, then covered it with his hand. "It's all right," he said. "Nothing to worry about."

Once he was inside, it was hard to concentrate. There was so much: mechanical beasts that moved and roared when you pressed a button, dioramas of wolf packs and feasting vultures, vats of oil with interactive levers so you could feel what it was like to be stuck in the tar. Skeletons and skeletons and skeletons. So many bones. Rudy ran his hand over a mammoth tooth the size of a footstool. He read bits from signs that described how leaves and water disguised the surface of the tar, how animals trapped in the asphalt lured others in after them. Flocks of schoolchildren raced through the museum, shrieking like parrots. Guards in blue uniforms watched from the doorways.

A slow ache built at the base of Rudy's spine, like the muscle was twisting in a knot. His temples and the back of his neck throbbed. He went to a bench near a window and rested a minute, trying to pull the room into focus. He was tired, so tired. The room expanded and contracted. The ceiling was dizzyingly high. The walls lost their perpendicularity and leaned at crazy angles. For a moment it was hard to tell which way was up, and Rudy slammed his hands down on his thighs in an effort to stabilize himself. What was wrong? It could be food, he told himself. Maybe he needed to eat. The floor dipped. The room was too big. Horizons spread endlessly in all directions. If he didn't get into a smaller space soon, Rudy felt that he would be swept into oblivion.

Somehow he made it to the restroom. What a blessing: the light was dim. The stainless-steel doors and cool porcelain sinks calmed him. Rudy stepped into a stall and emptied his bladder. That was a relief, too. He'd been holding it all day, and that had added to his anxiety. At the sink he gave himself a stern talking-to. Everything was okay, there was no need to worry. Nothing was wrong with him. Everything was under control. He smoothed back his hair. Go out there and enjoy yourself. Take a break. Learn something. Have some fun.

He tried to distract himself at the glass booth where men and women in white jackets worked with paintbrushes and solvents, cleaning bones. They worked with their heads down, their latex gloves and white coats stained with tar. Rudy watched them dip and clean, holding the tiny bones with tweezers, numbering them meticulously. Nearest him, a storklike man laid tiny bones on a paper towel. The sign said they were mouse teeth. Rudy tapped the glass and waved. The man nodded and went back to work. When Rudy knocked again, the man ignored him. *Mouse* teeth. It figured. When Rudy knocked louder, the guy got up and moved across the room. Did he think he was some kind of fancy scientist, sitting there all day dipping what looked like grains of rice in turpentine? Sheesh. Rudy walked away, shaking his head.

Rudy was about to leave when he noticed a group of schoolchildren gathered around a display on one side of the room. He edged to the front of the pack until his hands rested against the glass panel. There, at the back of a small black cave, a short human skeleton stood upright, facing Rudy as if it were ready to walk toward him.

"I can't see," one of the kids said behind him.

"Hey, fat ass!" another called. "Get out of the way!"

Titters. Giggles. Laughter.

Rudy didn't turn around. The crowd of kids had a smell: bubble gum and laundry detergent. He read the placard to the side of the glass. The only human skeleton found in La Brea, though scientists didn't think it was the tar that got her. *Her.* Rudy looked back at the skeleton. A young woman, the placard said, probably killed by a blow to the head. Sure enough, there it was: a star-shaped fissure in her skull, like a cracked egg. Her empty eye sockets stared at

Rudy, her too-long arms dangled at her sides. She was slightly pigeon-toed, with an unsure grimace. She'd probably been killed elsewhere and thrown into the tar, the caption went on to explain. Probably murder, one of the earliest ever discovered.

"Push the button!" one of the kids called from behind. An older boy, you could tell by his voice.

"Push it!"

Rudy looked down. To his right, at waist level, a girl with scrawny arms and bangs cut jaggedly across her forehead looked up at him. Her front teeth were missing. Grinning, she brought her finger up to the large black button on the wall and pushed. There was a murmur from behind him, some shuffling as the kids surged forward.

To Rudy's amazement, the skeleton began to change. First a faint glow surrounded it, then flesh grew on the bones in a reverse process of decay. Within seconds a squat aboriginal woman wearing a tattered brown hide stood in front of him. She had a dazed expression, as if she knew the fate that would befall her.

"Looks like your mama!" one of the boys called out.

"No, like yours!" another shouted. "I saw her wearing that same dress this morning!"

There were squeals and laughter and pushing. Rudy got an elbow in the side. Floating in the glass above the woman's head, he saw the ghostly reflection of his own face. Pale and bewildered, his mouth a small, pinched circle.

"She was murdered!" he shouted, spinning around. "They killed her!"

There was an immediate and complete hush. The children's faces were uniform, each one staring at him with wide-eyed terror.

"They bashed her head in," Rudy said, looking at each of them in turn. "How do you like that?"

The children's mouths hung open. Their eyes shifted with horror from Rudy to the murder victim behind him. That sobered them up, made them think for a change. See that life wasn't all fun and games. But too soon the spell was broken. Across the room, someone pressed the button for the moth-eaten woolly mammoth. The machine ground audibly into action, the animal's trunk cranked jerkily into the air, and a garbled trumpet sounded across the room. A few of the kids turned and looked. Rudy looked back over his shoulder at the prehistoric woman. The ragged dress slowly disappeared, the flesh evaporated from the bones. Only the skeleton remained, stained as if it been dipped in motor oil, the joints wired clumsily together.

"You're sick, mister," one of the kids said.

That's when Rudy noticed the guard. The same one, the *same* damn one who worked at the security check in the airport, the one who had pretended to be eating in the restaurant. Watching him. He should have known.

"Watch out," Rudy said, pushing through the crowd of kids. "All of you."

Outside, the rain had stopped. Rudy felt like Noah stepping off the Ark after the floodwaters had receded. All the pavements were wet; water streamed down the gutters, the wide lawn was churned up and muddy. The little fountain still sputtered and the three mammoths stayed frozen in place.

He walked a ways to make sure he wasn't being followed. He was a little hungry. There was a phone booth not far from his car. He knew better than to call from home or any other place where the calls could be traced, and this place was as good as any. He'd taken the quarters from the jelly jar that Inez kept for the laundromat. All the information he needed was on the scraps of paper he kept in his pockets. It hadn't been hard to find the numbers and addresses. To get warmed up, he ordered a pizza for Glenn Waller in his office, then sent the Roto-Rooter truck to his house once he got home that evening. He scheduled a cabinet refacer to come out on the weekend for an estimate. Sanjay Srinivasa was in the book: Rudy left his name and number with several businesses, including an escort service and an adult bookstore. Then there was his staff:

Latasha, Imogene, Maria. He called Waller a few times and hung up when he answered, then tried Srinivasa, but he wasn't there.

By the time he got to the trickier calls, his quarters were getting low. Some idiot put him on hold. While he waited, Rudy glanced around at the new subdivision of townhouses that was going up right there within sight of the tar pits. New concrete walkways split off from the sidewalk and led to the doors of beige and green buildings, which were piled like a jumble of rectangles on top of each other. THREE BEDROOMS/TWO BATHS the sign in the front said. ATTACHED TWO-CAR GARAGE. Once things got straightened out, maybe he would buy a place there. An all-new townhouse, right in the middle of things. Inez would like that: she and Vanessa could walk to the fancy stores, could spend an afternoon at the art museum. He wondered if beneath the courtyards and patios there were layers and layers of bones like he'd seen in the photos inside the museum. In his own yard at home, the only artifacts he'd found were a perfectly clear marble and a green army soldier. But who knew? There might be pebble choppers and shards of pottery, maybe even skeletons of prehistoric people like the one inside. The lawns around the townhouses were just coming in, sprouting tiny blades of grass like down on a newborn's head. They'd installed a sprinkler system at the edge of the sidewalk. The spigot nearest the phone booth floated in a glistening pool of black tar.

"I assure you that this is no joke!" Rudy said when he was finally taken off hold. People were so incompetent! "That's right," he said after listening a moment. "That's correct." A heavy truck passed, making it hard to hear. Rudy plugged one ear. "Well, how about this? When this whole thing is reported in the papers tomorrow, I'd hate to be the one who thought it was a joke. If I was you, I'd take it serious. *Very* serious."

He slammed down the phone.

God, he was tired. Hungry, too. He really should eat something healthy. Vegetables, or something hot. An apple maybe, but only sweet things sounded good to him. His feet hurt as he headed back to his car. The ache in his lower back had spread up to his shoulders and down to his hips. What if he just went home and told Inez what had happened? He closed his eyes a moment, imagined her arms around his neck, her whispering that everything was going to be all right. But then he remembered the look on Waller's face earlier that day, how the kids inside the museum had taunted him just a few moments ago. Even Inez couldn't be trusted, especially the way she'd been behaving lately. So watchful, so distant. And if she found out he'd lost his job . . . There was no need for her to know. Things were going to change soon, anyway.

His car looked cleaner after the rain. If he absolutely *had* to, he could always live in it, at least for a while. The sky was clearing. When he opened the car door, a wall of warm air hit him pleasantly in the face. The wrappers and napkins that littered the backseat and floor of the car scented it with a sugary fragrance, like a bakery. He slipped behind the steering wheel and took a box of six miniature doughnuts from the console between the seats. Only $1.49 at the Sunbeam day-old.

It was so nice to relax a minute. The sun coming through the windshield warmed him like a soft blanket. He took his time with the doughnuts, enjoying the powdered sugar on the outside, the way the whole thing melted to a velvety mash as he chewed. They were small; it was easy to eat all six. He tossed the box on the floor with the rest of the stuff: the newspapers he read to kill time, the crumpled napkins, packets of catsup, and crushed soft-drink cans. Too bad he didn't have any milk.

Did any of the animals manage to escape the tar once they were stuck? Pull themselves loose and live another day, thinking what a close call it had been? Rudy didn't know, but it certainly seemed possible. He started the engine. Even though it was warm and stuffy inside the car, he kept the windows up so he could enjoy the safe, toasty feeling. If he drove slowly, staying on surface roads with all their red lights, it wouldn't be too early to head home.

Home.

As he pulled into traffic, he thought of the woman with the bashed skull. The eyes of the wolves glowing at night. The flapping of gigantic wings. All on the same streets where legions of people now pushed their shopping carts full of their earthly belongings, where they slept in doorways and ranted to themselves, the contents of their minds spilling out into the open like stuffing from a dirty mattress. Lining up at church basements for their dinners. Hanging out all day long on the sidewalks, their empty hands extended. Groundless. At sea. Ships without anchors.

Not him. Rudy was going *home.* He pictured everything in the small square house. The chairs and furniture. The table in the kitchen, set with place mats, glasses, silverware. Food. He had a wife and daughter. A bed with sheets, blankets, and pillows. He had a bathtub, a garage, a refrigerator.

He would do anything, *anything,* to keep them.

22

Inez turned the burner off under Vanessa's cauliflower when she heard Rudy's car door slam. She drained the vegetable in the sink and sprinkled on the cheese she'd grated.

Rudy started his rant the minute he walked through the door. It was the mail this time that set him off, the little pile of bills: gas and electric, telephone, the second statement from Penney's. "How many times do I have to tell you," he said, coming into the kitchen with the torn envelopes, the statements trembling in his dainty hands.

He'd gained weight, Inez noticed: a pouch of flesh quivered under his chin, giving him a grandmotherly look.

"You can't keep spending money like this. The phone bill is sky high. The gas and lights are—" He gestured toward the ceiling, as if to say that there were no words to express the enormity of the bill. "I work and work and work, and all you do is spend. There's got to be a limit to how much money goes out of this house. They keep raising the rates, too, in case you didn't notice, and with you spending and them milking me for every last dime there's no way we can keep our heads above water if this goes on. I know Vanessa's in there gabbing on that phone every spare minute, and with all the clothes and shoes and whatever else it is you buy at the department store, we're going to be out of house and home before you know it. There's only so much I can do. With bills like this coming in every day—"

He paused for breath and gave the papers in his hand a disgusted backhanded slap.

"Dinner's ready," Inez said. "Tonight's Bible study at the church."

He kept it up all through the meal, his voice rising and falling, on and on. The bills and his job and the meat, which wasn't cooked enough. "I don't like it to bite me back," he said, though the hamburger was grayish, cooked through and through. "Look at this, there's a puddle of blood on my plate." The people at work who couldn't tell their asses from their elbows, how he was always covering for them, how—if it weren't for him—the whole place would go down the tubes. He couldn't stop. Names she'd never heard of. Everybody a moron. And Vanessa. The way kids dress and talk and never do a damn thing worthwhile. They'll be sorry later, you watch. I had a job at your age, pointing his fork at her. My eye on the future. What do you do in there in your room all the time, anyway? Vanessa, her face closed, her fork moving back and forth.

"The potatoes," he said, turning up his nose. "Soggy."

When did he start talking so much? Inez wondered. When they'd first met, he was so quiet she'd squirm uncomfortably when they were out together, waiting for him to say something. They could eat an entire meal exchanging only a few remarks on the food. She even felt like other people in the restaurant were looking at them, wondering why they didn't speak. She'd thought he'd loosen up once they were married, but he'd kept up his polite, distant manner, mildly commenting on something now and then, but hardly ever telling her what he liked or didn't like, what he wanted or feared. He seemed perfectly happy that way and she'd gotten used to it, had come to expect it from him. Now, after all those years of silence the dam had burst and he couldn't stop talking. Inez watched the finicky way he cut his food, his pinkie fingers raised delicately. There were dimples on his elbows. His clothes looked rumpled, as if he'd been sleeping in them. When she met him he'd been fastidious: his shirts perfectly ironed and his hair frequently cut. Now it hung in wisps on his collar, with a matted spot on the back of his head.

"Did you want any more potatoes?" Inez asked Vanessa.

Rudy slammed his silverware down. "Excuse me, but I was talking," he huffed, his eyes bulging. His face pinkened. "Did you not hear me? Does anyone care whether I'm talking or not?"

"I heard you," Inez said. "I'm listening."

In the car it was more of the same. Rain pelted the windshield, the wipers slapped. "You got Waller and that Arab or whatever he is and between the two of them and that lazy crew they don't do a damn thing all day," Rudy went on. He drove erratically, accelerating when his argument got more heated, slamming on the brakes when he got to the end of a sentence. Inez clutched her Bible in her lap. The car smelled funny. The heater was up high and the air was stifling. Inez's mind wandered. She made a mental calculation of the Avon money that would come in during the next week. With the fruitcake girl who lived with the other girl who had to buy for every Tom, Dick, and Harry in her family, it would be a big haul. As she did more and more often, she began to dream of the house in Oregon, of the life she and Vanessa would lead once she slipped away and left Rudy behind. The rooms she imagined were almost familiar to her now, with their bare wood floors and white walls. She pictured herself behind the wheel of a small, reliable car that got good mileage. Vanessa in the passenger seat, the two of them chatting as they drove through the tree-lined streets of the small town she'd seen on the television special. Happy and carefree, their lives moving forward.

She was so carried away that it surprised her when the car stopped in front of the old movie theater that now served as their church.

"I'll be back here at eight sharp to pick you up," Rudy said.

Neither Inez nor Vanessa had said a single word during the trip.

The thought of escaping from Rudy's constant babble was such a relief that Inez threw open the door and already had one leg out when Rudy called her back. Vanessa was already standing on the sidewalk, about to slam the door closed.

"Wait a minute, wait a minute," Rudy said, motioning them back inside.

Vanessa, who had spent the whole ride in a black hole of silence, now stamped her foot with impatience. "We have to *go!*" she said, "We're going to be *late!*"

Inez stayed as she was, with one leg still in the car, the other extended toward the curb. She looked at the peeling paint of the church. The marquee was still there, but instead of announcing movies, the big black letters now spelled out HE IS RISEN. EVERYONE WELCOME.

"Get back in the car," Rudy said through clenched teeth. "Now."

Vanessa hurled herself into the back seat. Inez pulled her leg in.

"Close the door. *Close. The. Door.*" It was the pauses between the words that scared Inez. Tight, raging silences.

She pulled the door closed.

Vanessa slammed her door with such fury the whole car shook. What had gotten into her? Inez kept her eyes forward. Ahead of them a car pulled to the curb and two teenage boys got out, one with a guitar case. They were in Vanessa's class, gangly kids with pimples. They ran through the rain to the overhang under the marquee and slipped through the door into the theater.

Rudy grunted, shifting in the seat to face Vanessa.

"I don't like that," he said in a flat voice. "I won't tolerate it."

Inez sneaked a look over her shoulder. Vanessa sat with her arms crossed over her chest, staring defiantly back at Rudy. At times like this, Inez felt she didn't know her daughter at all. She was struck by the sudden fear that Vanessa might leave, that she might have her *own* plans that had nothing to do with the house in Oregon.

"Could we go now?" Vanessa said tightly. "They don't like us to show up late."

Rudy sighed like the weight of the world was on his shoulders. "Go on. But remember, eight o'clock sharp." He tapped his watch. "Don't keep me waiting out here."

They used the big theater downstairs for services: the old upholstered seats for pews, the pastor and choir up on the stage where the heavy, faded curtains still hung. Inez remembered the day years ago when she'd accepted the Lord Jesus Christ into her heart as her personal savior, how she'd stood up from her seat at the end of the service and, while the choir sang "Just As I Am," walked down the long aisle toward the stage. The old ladies nodding their approval, everyone's eyes on *her.* She'd walked up the stairs at the corner of the stage as if she were going to give a performance. The pastor had welcomed her, his arms outstretched as the organ began to play. He'd clasped her hands in his, congratulating her on her decision to devote her life to Christ, and then turned her to face the congregation. Fourteen years old, Vanessa's age. They'd all looked up to where she stood on the edge of the stage: kids her own age, babies in their mothers' laps, her foster family in the middle of the auditorium and, in the front row where the deacons sat, the man who would become Vanessa's father.

"I'll meet you out here," Inez said to Vanessa, once they were in the lobby. The church used the former snack bar for the library: pamphlets and flyers littered the glass counter where concessionaires had once sold candy bars and popcorn. The carpet, huge pink hibiscus blossoms on a black background, was worn in front of the counter and in paths to the double doors that opened into the auditorium. The whole place smelled of dust and mildewed socks. On the walls were felt decorations of flowers and doves along with posters that said WALK WITH THE LORD and TRUST IN JESUS.

While Vanessa headed off to the room behind the stage where the youth group met to play guitar and sing folksongs, Inez climbed the carpeted stairs to what used to be the projection booth. The adult Bible study group was already assembled.

Tonight there were only four others, with Bibles in their laps. Inez said hello and took her place in the ring of banged-up wooden chairs. Sister Murdock was leading the group that night. She nodded eagerly toward Inez, smiling so the wide spaces between her teeth showed, as if every other tooth were missing. It made her look like a jack-o'-lantern. She always wore the same thing: a huge black skirt ironed with the creases on the sides so she looked like she'd been pressed in a book and a men's denim work shirt with a pocket over the breast. With coarse salt-and-pepper hair, a flat nose, and breath so bad it gave you a shock, Sister Murdock was one of the most devout members of the church. She witnessed in the neighborhoods, vacuumed the lobby carpet, and attended to people in the congregation who were sick or dying. But she wasn't popular. After Sunday services, when most members of the congregation shook hands and chatted in the lobby, Sister Murdock often stood by herself, looking shyly on. She lived in one of the residence hotels downtown. A member of the congregation who visited her said the only food in her cupboard was cat chow, even though Sister Murdock had no pets.

"The lesson for tonight is Ruth," Sister Murdock announced.

Inez opened her Bible. Hers was white, given to her by her foster family when she was baptized. Back then it was a brilliant, blinding white, soft and supple as kid leather, but now the cover had yellowed and hardened, cracking around the edges like an old cardboard box. The gold embossed letters that spelled out HOLY BIBLE on the front used to stand out like jewels. Now they faded into the nicotine-colored background. She used to be proud of the white Bible, but now she wished hers was black or navy, like the others around the circle.

"Say, I heard what happened at the airport," Luella Springs leaned over and whispered to Inez. Her clothes smelled like fried food. The way her hair started far back on her forehead reminded Inez of a picture she'd seen of Queen Elizabeth I, back in the olden days.

"What?" Inez whispered back. She knew the books of the Old Testament by heart and had already found Ruth.

Sister Springs drew back with surprise. "Well, your husband works there, don't he? They shut the whole thing down. Didn't he say anything about it? It was all over the news."

Inez shook her head. She wished they'd get started. She'd seen a few red Bibles, and one that was forest green. But black was best, more official. Like the words inside were more apt to be true.

"Well, Sister Cullen, I can't believe you didn't hear about it. They shut the whole thing down. Anthrax scare. Turned out to be baking powder, but still. Somebody playing tricks, probably a kid. Sure caused a mess, though."

"All right now. Everybody got it?" Sister Murdock said, glancing around the circle. Luella stopped talking and started riffling through the pages. Duane, a young white man with large jaw muscles that gave him a chipmunklike appearance, was way off. He was thumbing around in the back, in the New Testament. You could tell it bothered Brother Lacy, who was one of the deacons. A thin black man with a perfectly trimmed mustache and a booming voice, Brother Lacy reached across the circle and flipped Duane's pages toward the front.

"Joshua, Judges, *Ruth*," he said, his bass so deep Inez could feel it vibrate in her chest. "It's one of the books of history, son. In the front. Right after the laws of Moses."

"All right," Sister Murdock said. You could tell she didn't want Brother Lacy taking over. "Let's start. Roof."

Roof? That's what she said. Inez heard it.

Ruth was short so they took turns reading the whole thing out loud. Duane stumbled over the words and had to be helped by Brother Lacy, who read his section in a loud, dramatic voice, like he was preaching a sermon. Inez was shy at first, but warmed up to her part, the words and the story drawing her on. The Bible was strange when you actually read it. People did funny things. Like Ruth sleeping next to Boaz when she wasn't married to him, and uncovering his feet, whatever that meant, and him giving her grain. Or Ruth refusing to leave Naomi and telling her your people will be my people and your God my God—the same wedding vows Inez had exchanged with Rudy right there in that very church, not the kind of thing you'd imagine a young woman saying to her mother-in-law. All the men died in the story, Naomi's husband and two sons, and while Brother Lacy read on in his pompous voice, Inez imagined Rudy dying—in the airport from anthrax or at home in bed from a heart attack or in a car crash on the way to work. A sinful thing to think about, especially in a church, and as soon as she realized she was thinking it she told herself to stop, but not before she wondered how much she'd get from his life insurance if he died. It would certainly solve all her problems, especially if she could buy the house in Oregon and be free of Rudy without doing a thing. Wrong, wrong, wrong, and sinful even to imagine. The devil was always there, just waiting to put thoughts in her head.

She asked forgiveness.

At ten minutes until eight they closed their Bibles and said a prayer. Inez lowered her head and pressed her eyelids together, her hands clasped on the white Bible as Sister Murdock rambled on about having faith in the Lord and knowing that things will turn out right in the end, just like Ruth, who went into a strange foreign country and trusted other people to help her. Sister Murdock's bad breath filled the stuffy little room, and Inez's bottom ached from sitting on the hard wooden chair. Brother Lacy cleared his throat. Inez said a short, private prayer for God to look down on her and guide her thoughts, for Him to clear the confusion from her mind. *And help me,* she added just before Sister Murdock said amen. *Please, please help me.*

Rudy wasn't there when they went outside. Vanessa came out with a group of kids from her class, talking and laughing. Inez seldom saw her like that: noisy, full of life. She shoved one of the boys playfully and the rest of the group squealed like monkeys. As they stood a ways off saying good-bye to each other, it occurred to Inez that her daughter had a life of her own that Inez knew very little about, that Vanessa had a personality she kept hidden away. A strange envy welled up in Inez as she stood on the curb pretending to look for Rudy's headlights while she sneaked glances at Vanessa and her friends. By the time the other kids went to their cars and Vanessa joined her at the curb, Inez was stiff and tight-lipped.

"Edward brought crackers and grape juice and we had kind of like communion," Vanessa said with a laugh, still talkative and excited. "We went around the circle and everybody had some, then there was a lot left over, so Edward said, 'Who wants seconds on Jesus?'" Vanessa threw back her head and laughed, not noticing that Inez stood silent, a scowl on her face. "So of course we *all* did. We all had more and then we even had *thirds*. We porked out on Jesus!" She laughed again, the rain sparkling on her face.

"That's not very nice, Vanessa," Inez said stiffly. "I don't think it's right of you to say that."

"It was just fun. We were just being silly."

"Jesus isn't silly. Communion isn't a game."

"Edward's the assistant pastor. He wouldn't do it if it wasn't right."

"I don't care who he is, that's not a respectful way to talk about Jesus."

The rain sliding down Inez's neck made her feel desolate and tired. Vanessa sighed dramatically and crossed her arms over her chest. They watched for Rudy's car without talking while a streetlight buzzed overhead. Something was wrong with it. It dimmed and brightened, flickered, then glowed back on.

"I wonder where your father is," Inez said to fill the silence.

"I do too," Vanessa said in a too-casual voice. "I've wondered that my whole life."

Inez's hands turned ice cold. Flustered, she looked at Vanessa, but could only meet her eyes for a second. What had made her bring *this* up after all these years?

"We read about Ruth tonight," Inez said. "You really have to wonder what it was about Naomi that made Ruth love her so much. You just know that Naomi must have been something really special."

Garish light from the streetlamp reflected in the water on the asphalt, making the whole world look white and black. Inez counted the times Vanessa blinked. "But Naomi was a Jew," she said, hoping to break Vanessa's stare. "They all were in the Old Testament."

"He's up to something, you know," Vanessa said.

"Who?" It was more an exhalation of breath than a word.

"Your husband. Haven't you noticed? Didn't you see his car?"

Your husband. Had Vanessa really said that? Where was Rudy? Inez leaned far out into the street to look for him. "What about his car?" she asked casually.

"It's a mess! There's stuff all over the floor! It looks like a trashcan, like he's been living in it. It even smells!"

"His car's a little dirty," Inez shrugged. "He just needs to clean it up, that's all. Take it to a car wash on the way home from work."

Vanessa's eyes widened. It was no way to look at your mother. "He's not *going* to work, Mom. He just drives around all day. I know, I've seen him go past my school in the middle of the day. I've seen him parked down by the mall when I come home."

It was so cold out in the rain, Inez started to shiver. She had never really spanked Vanessa—just a pat on the bottom or a slap on the hands when she was very young—but now she would have liked to smack her right across the face. Such lies. "What in the world are you talking about?" she exclaimed. "What's gotten into you? Why are you saying these things?"

"Because it's true!" Vanessa shouted back. There was no stopping her now. "He's doing something out in the garage. At night, haven't you heard him?" She talked faster and faster, not even lowering her voice when Duane and Brother Lacy came out of the door behind them. "He walks around the house and out in the yard at three in the morning. How can you *not* know? And he's been in my room! I swear! I haven't seen him, but I can tell. I know he's been in there."

"Sister Cullen," Deacon Lacy said, laying his hand on Inez's shoulder. He nodded at Vanessa, who made no attempt to hide her wild eyes.

"It's true, Mom. I swear," she pleaded, as if Duane and the deacon weren't standing right there. Inez had never been so ashamed.

"What are you doing standing out in this rain? Do you have a ride?" Deacon Lacy said in his deep voice.

"We're fine, Deacon. Fine," Inez said hurriedly. "My husband's coming to pick us up." She smiled and nodded at him, then shot Vanessa a warning glance.

Lacy looked at his watch. "It's wet, and getting late. I don't like to see you two ladies standing out here. What time is he coming?" He frowned, the busybody. So stubborn.

"Really, really. It's okay," Inez said, patting his shoulder. "Don't worry about us. Go ahead. Go on home before you get wet." She grinned uneasily at him as she secretly squeezed Vanessa's arm. The young guy, Duane, was eyeing her daughter.

"Sister Cullen, this is not the best neighborhood," Deacon Lacy went on, like a dog with a bone. "Now please don't argue with me. We'll just wait here until your husband comes."

There was no getting rid of him. Cars drove past, spraying water, but none of them was Rudy. Inez was suddenly terrified that he knew about the Avon money, that at that very moment he was in Vanessa's room, digging in the cedar chest past the layers of sweaters, the blankets and afghans, to find the envelope. She tried to keep her face neutral, to hide her rising panic. Brother Lacy blinked into the rain. Duane glanced out of the corner of his eye at Vanessa, who stared savagely at her feet. It occurred to Inez that if Rudy found the money it might not be safe to go home. Her heart raced. She wondered whether she should tell Brother Lacy, whether she should go to the church for help. An oily, foul-smelling shame welled up in her stomach. A car rounded the corner, its headlights washing over the four of them. It pulled to the curb. *Him.*

He didn't turn the engine off. Brother Lacy opened the door and leaned into the car.

"Haven't seen you at services for a while, Brother Cullen," he said.

If Rudy responded, Inez didn't hear it. She was eager to disappear into the car, to get away, no matter what happened. When Brother Lacy straightened up and looked at her, his face was confused.

Inez slid into the passenger seat. Rudy's hair was rumpled, like he'd just gotten up from bed. "Get in, get in, get in, get in," he mumbled, not looking at them but keeping his eyes fixed on the windshield. His hands were locked on the steering wheel. Vanessa got in, slammed the door. The heater was turned up high, stifling after the rain-laden air outside. Without a word, Rudy pulled away from the curb, leaving Duane and Brother Lacy standing on the curb.

Inez knew then that Vanessa was right. More than that, she realized that she'd known it for a while. Something was up. In the stifling heat that smelled of burnt sugar and sweat, the scalpy funk of unwashed hair, she said a prayer. For God's guidance. For Jesus' protection. She was the lamb, he was the shepherd. So often, she reflected as Rudy accelerated around a corner, his lips pressed into an angry scowl, you didn't get what you prayed for. Later you realized that was because you asked for the wrong thing. Because you couldn't grasp the big picture, the plan God had for your life. Rudy cursed under his breath, sucked air through his teeth with a hissing sound. Later you might understand. Might see the story laid out for you, beginning to end, the reasons why, the place you were headed all along.

23 The frozen raviolis Wylie got at Trader Joe's were pretty good. He ate them in front of the TV as he watched the evening news. After that he had a bowl of Chunky Monkey. Small, because he was watching his gut. The dogs sat in front of his easy chair and begged, so he let Murphy lick the plate and Elsa the bowl. When they were finished, Elsa rolled over to have her belly rubbed and Wylie saw she had a tick right where her back leg connected to her body. It looked like a lentil, mud-colored and flat. He got the tweezers and for once it came away clean, head and all. At least that had gone right. That was *one* thing to be thankful for.

Elsa lay in front of him as he watched the next program, a PBS documentary about Louis Armstrong. He rubbed her chest absent-mindedly with his bare feet. Murphy went over by the furnace and jibbled at the dry patch on his back. Wylie had almost made up his mind about the baby. All he had to do was work up the nerve to tell Carolyn. Jesus, what did she expect? He was getting on in life. Fifty-one, for Christsake, and she was no spring chicken, either. The poor kid would barely be out of diapers before he'd be changing *theirs*. Ha-ha, very funny. Satchmo had four wives. None of them understood that his horn came first. The program didn't mention whether *he* had any kids.

Having a kid would be like starting all over, and Wylie was closer to retirement than embarking on a whole new life. There were plenty of things he wanted to do, plenty he was interested in.

Fishing. Cabinetry. Adult school classes in history, maybe. Life drawing, why not? His dogs. Just sitting. The peace, after all the work he'd done in his life. All the drinking and wives and getting up early and coming home late. The struggling to make ends meet and stay sober and just get through one day after another. Now he could get his house and yard into shape. Travel. He'd always wanted to drive cross-country, stopping wherever he wanted, taking his time. Carolyn could come. But not with a kid. Oh no. *No, no, no.* You could forget about your own life then. Kiss your plans good-bye. Sleepless nights and feedings, always tied to schedules. The three of them stuck in the house day after day. The routine. The worry. All the stuff they'd have to buy: car seats, high chairs, cribs, and toys. Mountains of pastel plastic. Where would they put it all? The clutter and noise. *No.* Snot, puke, fevers, and shit. Rashes. Falling down and drowning. Not to mention diseases. Choking. That's *if* the baby was born normal in the first place, a big if considering their ages *plus* all the drugs and booze he personally had consumed. Who knew what *that* did to your chromosomes? And wouldn't that be nice, to be saddled with a child who had *special needs,* who would never be able to take care of himself, who would have to be cleaned, fed, and carried around for the rest of his life, or rather the rest of *their* lives, his own and Carolyn's, which wouldn't be long since they were so old. Then the poor kid would have to be *institutionalized,* and considering Wylie's savings, which were practically zilch, it wouldn't be the Ritz, either.

No, thank you.

He got up and switched the TV off. His heart was racing, his eye was twitching, his underarms tingled with sweat. What a fucking idiot he'd been. All the times in his life he could've gotten someone knocked up and he goes and does it now, when he should have known better, when he's a fucking old man who can hardly get out of his chair, sitting around with itching dogs eating ice cream in front of the TV.

Elsa lifted her head and watched him pace back and forth.

"What should I do?" he asked her. "Tell me."

She let her head drop back to the floor and closed her eyes. That did it. He went in the bathroom and brushed his teeth, changed his shirt, locked up the house, and drove to Carolyn's.

Her car was there, but she didn't answer his knock so he walked around the back of the house to her workshop. The storm had picked up and the eucalyptus trees were tossing wildly, their branches screaming and creaking. The workshop was blazing with light; one of the double doors was open. Among the stripped-down tables, broken chairs, iron bedsteads, chests of drawers, and the cans of stain and solvent, Carolyn was sitting on a wooden box with her head between her knees.

Wylie approached cautiously. "Hey," he called. "What's up?"

"I'm having a little spell."

Inside it smelled of wood and turpentine. Even though the door was open, an electric heater glowed next to the table Carolyn was sanding. The fragrance of wet eucalyptus blew in from outside. Wylie stood in the doorway dripping. "You look green," he said. "You okay?"

Carolyn nodded miserably. She wiped her forehead with the back of her hand. "Ugh. You know. It's better not to talk about it right now." She took a deep breath and exhaled loudly. "What are *you* doing here?"

Wylie shrugged. He hitched his pants up, ran his hands through his hair, and shrugged again. He felt shy and awkward. "Just came to talk, I guess," he said, shoving his hands in his pockets and looking at the wet, black night outside the door. "Just thought we ought to."

"What time is it?"

"Around nine."

Carolyn jumped up as if startled, and Wylie stumbled back against a bedstead.

"I'm going to barf," she announced, heading for the door.

Wylie followed her to the side of the workshop, where she put her hands on her knees and lowered her head. He averted his eyes. There were tall weeds back there: thistle and mustard, some kind of wild pea. It was a hell of a fix, he told himself. A hell of a fix. When she was finished, he laid his hand on her back.

"You okay?" he asked. "You want anything?"

"No, I'm okay. I feel better now."

Jesus, she was good-natured.

"You sure?"

"Yeah, really. I'm almost hungry, believe it or not. That's one of my three states: hungry, sick, or tired."

"Isn't this supposed to happen in the *morning*?"

"I think so. I guess no one's really keeping track in my case."

Wylie's stomach knotted. "I guess we need to talk about this, huh?"

She nodded grimly. "Yeah, we do. We need to decide."

"You want to go in the house?" He fumbled with her elbow in a lame attempt to support her.

Carolyn straightened up and flipped her hair back. Despite everything, she looked pretty good. Strapping, robust. "Let's stay out here," she said.

She flashed her goofy smile and he caught himself grinning back at her. "We're in a pickle, aren't we?" he said.

"Christ, don't say *pickle*," she laughed. "I wouldn't mind something to drink. How about getting me a ginger ale from the fridge? There's more in there if you want one, too."

The kitchen smelled like beans. The radio was on, tuned to NPR. The newspaper, along with the remains of Carolyn's dinner—an almost-empty bowl of bean soup and a few bites of cornbread—were on the little table near the window. Who would want to give this up? He got two ginger ales out of the refrigerator and headed back out to the workshop, where Carolyn had pulled a couple of chairs together so they could look down at the city. Wylie sat down and popped the tabs on the sodas.

"Nice color," he said, pointing to a cushion she'd covered in lichen-green corduroy. "I like that." He pretended to inspect the label on his can of soda. "We had a scare out at the airport today. Some joker left a bunch of powder on the bar. They were afraid it was anthrax."

"Was it?"

Wylie shook his head. "Baking powder. Everybody went nuts for nothing."

Carolyn took a long drink of her ginger ale. She covered her mouth to hide a burp, watched the rainfall a moment, and said quietly, "Look, Wylie. Enough chitchat, okay? Let's cut to the chase."

He scanned her body out of the corner of his eye to see if there were any changes. Nothing so far. It seemed amazing, really. Hardly possible. Such a common occurrence, yet the more he thought about it, the stranger it seemed.

"I keep thinking and thinking, but the more I think, the less I can make up my mind," he said. Better to start off slow.

She nodded encouragement.

"I just keep thinking about my family, my own family," he went on. "Mostly the *men* in my family. A bunch of boozers. My half brother's in the program, thank God. Just like me. But he's been in and out of the pen, I don't know how many times. Same as my father. A boozer. A loser, with a capital *L*. And his old man, too. Coming and going, moved all over the damn country, and even my great-grandfather, who, from what I can tell, had to get the hell out of Ireland or they were going to put him away, too. So I just figure the buck should stop here, you know? Why pass all this on? Break the chain."

Wylie had been staring at a Folgers can of paintbrushes on the floor while he talked; when he looked up, Carolyn was watching him.

"You know what my dad did once?" he asked with a little laugh. It was funny that he remembered this story now. He felt slightly ashamed telling it, as if he felt sorry for himself and was asking for sympathy. Which he wasn't. But the night sky and the falling rain made him feel hidden, like it was safe to talk, so he went on. "I think I was about nine or ten. My mom's mother was dying and she'd flown up to San Francisco to be with her. We couldn't afford airline tickets for all of us, so my dad was going to drive me and my sisters up in time for the funeral. Well, we didn't make it far. Just outside Bakersfield he met up with some long-lost buddies and started drinking. My sisters and I waited in the car for what seemed like forever, until after dark. They were just little kids, probably five and seven or something like that. Finally the old man came out, loaded of course, and said that he had business to take care of and we kids were taking the bus up to Frisco."

Carolyn bent over and set the soda can on the ground.

"You okay?" Wylie asked. "You feel sick again?"

"No, I feel fine."

"You bored?"

"No. Finish the story."

"Well, he drove us to the Greyhound station, gave me some cash, and told me to take the girls to San Francisco," Wylie said matter-of-factly. He took a sip of ginger ale. "Didn't even get out of the damn car. I was totally freaked out. When I asked him what I was supposed to do, you know—which ticket to buy and what bus to take, he just said, 'Figure it out.' Can you believe that? I'll never forget him saying that." Wylie shook his head. "'Figure it out.'"

"Wow," Carolyn said quietly. "I can't believe it. How could he have done that?"

"I don't know. Something in him was missing, I guess. He just didn't care. Or maybe he thought it wasn't a big deal. Maybe he just thought we'd get there, no problem."

"Did you?"

"Yeah, I guess we did," Wylie chuckled. "I asked someone what to do and we made it to San Francisco. Probably safer on the bus than riding all the way up there with my dad, come to think of it."

Carolyn nodded thoughtfully. Only half of her face was lit by the drop lamp that hung from the rafters behind her and he remembered the first time he'd seen her, at a garage sale near the grocery store where he shopped on Saturdays. She'd been on all fours, her head under a table as she pawed through a box of odds and ends. "Whoa! Look at this!" she'd crowed, standing up suddenly and holding up a metal lamp with its cord hanging down like the tail of a slain beast. She'd turned to him with a triumphant grin, and he'd been struck by how happy she looked, for no good reason at all. "Score!" she'd said. "Luck be a lady." He'd wanted to kiss her then and there, to soak up some of her joy.

Now she pursed her lips and turned toward him. Sometimes he caught a glimpse of the girl she'd been, gawky and sweet. "But you're not like that," she said slowly. "Not at all. That's not what you're thinking, is it?"

"No. Well, not that bad. But— Jesus." All this talking. Really, did it ever get you anywhere? And was there any way to cram what you felt into words? He tried. "I don't know. I just don't know. I mean, can you see me as a father? Can you picture me as that kind of person?"

Carolyn chewed her lips. To Wylie's horror, tears brimmed in her eyes and spilled down her face. "You're a great guy, Wylie," she said. "Too bad everybody knows it but you."

Wylie was stunned. He'd never even imagined such a thing. He suddenly felt like crying himself. "You think so?" he said, shocked at how high and thin his voice sounded. He craved a cigarette, though he'd quit smoking over ten years ago. "I don't know." He shook his head and looked at his useless hands lying in his lap. He picked at the Band-Aid that covered the cut he'd got during the anthrax scare that afternoon. "I just don't know. I think it's too late. Too damn late."

"It's never as late as you think it is," Carolyn said. "You never know how much time is left."

"We've never really talked, you know," he stammered. He gritted his teeth. Clenched and unclenched his hands. Carolyn watched him steadily. He knew so little about what went on inside her head and, until now, that had been just fine. "About us. You know, you and me."

"Yeah, I know," she said. She leaned back in the chair and

surveyed the rafters where she stored lumber and spare parts: chair legs, spindles, drawers, cushions. "I guess we're kind of chicken-shit. Both of us."

Wylie squirmed. The whole second part of his life had consisted of getting over the first part. Now what? Words stuck in his throat. Rather than getting a grip on things, he seemed to have gotten *more* inept as time went on. He needed to pull himself together, to remember what he'd decided back at his place. Did he always have to be such a wimp?

"I can't do this, Carolyn."

She leaned forward and put her index finger on his kneecap. "Do I need to tell you I love you, Wylie?" she asked with the concern of a doctor questioning her patient about his illness. "Because I do. In case you didn't know. I might as well just say it." He noticed the spokes in her eyes, rods of yellow laid over the brown. "I love you, that's all."

It was the most amazing thing he'd ever heard. More incredible than the fact that she was pregnant with his child. It seemed ages ago that she'd taken out the pregnancy test, showed it to him.

"You never told me," he said.

She shook her head. "That's just the way this thing has worked with us, isn't it? I guess I was afraid to tell you. Afraid if I did, that would be it. That I'd scare you away."

She was probably right, but he didn't let on. His own inadequacy gaped before him like a black pit. She had told him she loved him. It was his turn, now. That much he knew. That was the script: one person says *I love you,* the other answers *I love you, too.* Simple. But he couldn't, just couldn't. He was a chunk of meat. Limp, numb, mute.

A gust of wind whipped through the eucalyptus trees, making it sound like they were applauding. Wylie felt mocked.

"You don't have to say anything," Carolyn said. "I just decided to tell you." She pursed her lips and scrutinized him. "What's wrong with your eyelid?"

He put his hand over it to stop the jumping. "It's like there's something in there trying to hatch out. Damn thing's driving me crazy. I'm a mess. A nervous wreck."

They laughed and things relaxed a little. He felt better, good enough to say, "It's just kind of hard, the whole thing being up to me."

Oops. Wrong move. Carolyn colored and flared. "It's *my* choice, Wylie. I know that. I'm not some *chick* waiting for you to make the decision. I told you I want this kid, but not if I have to raise him or her alone. I just don't want to do that. I can't. So that's the situation and we both have to live with it."

"I know, I know," Wylie said. Jesus, she could go from I love you to pissed off in five seconds. He got up and put his arms around her.

She pushed him away. "Are you saying you want me to go ahead with it then? To go ahead and get rid of it?"

"For Christsake, Carolyn. Do you have to say it like that?"

"Well, what *should* I say?" Her nose turned red when she was mad.

"It just sounds so *brutal*. I mean, I don't think about it like it's a *thing*, like I don't have feelings for it. I—I think about it all the time." If you only knew, he thought.

"*It!?*"

"*Her,* then. Or him. Whatever."

"Can you give me some idea of where you're headed with this? And could you please quit saying *whatever?*"

Now was his chance. Just lay it on the line. Be honest. She was breathing heavily, her chest rising and falling. She didn't have much hope for him, he realized. The mournful look in her eyes was not for their predicament, but for *him*. Was he *that* pathetic?

"We didn't plan this," he said, more like a question than anything else.

"No, we didn't," she confirmed. She watched him gulp air a minute, then said, "Listen, don't decide yet. Give it a little more time. A week or so. We can wait that long. I want you to be sure."

"But that just makes it harder," he wailed. God, what a whiner.

"Harder on you," he added in a firmer voice. "You know, the longer we wait. It's not fair to you."

Carolyn rolled her eyes. "God knows we have to be fair."

He bent down and pressed his face into her hair. It felt damp, warm near her scalp. Was it the eucalyptus or the turpentine he smelled? Maybe it was her shampoo.

"You want me to stay?" he whispered against her neck.

She shook her head. "No, I think you better go. I'm tired. I'm about ready to hit the hay." She took his hand and pressed the palm to her lips.

He kissed her cheek, then her mouth. Without looking at her again, he got up and stumbled away, floundering along the path in the dark, the slick eucalyptus leaves sliding under his feet.

The phone was ringing when he got back to his house. He struggled with the lock, cursing. He was sure it was Carolyn, calling to tell him, on second thought, to go fuck himself. Who could blame her? The dogs mobbed him when he got inside, Elsa tangling in his feet and Murphy launching himself at his stomach. "Get down!" Wylie shouted. The damned dog had never learned not to jump up. They'd also torn something up on the rug under the table. The ice cream carton and the ravioli box, it looked like. Shredded to confetti. The icing on the cake was the indentation in his chair. Someone, Elsa most likely, had been sleeping there.

"Bad dogs!" he yelled before picking up the phone.

"Hey, hey, hey!" a male voice said. "I was ready to give up on you."

"Hi," Wylie said tentatively. His heart thumped—wildly, painfully, irregularly. He probably needed bypass surgery, triple or even quadruple.

"What's up, man? How're you doing?"

Whoever it was obviously thought he needed no introduction. The voice was familiar, but Wylie couldn't place it. "I'm doing okay," he said, playing along in hopes that he'd recognize the guy if he spoke a little more. "How're you?"

"I'm great, man. Doing fine. That's why I'm calling. I won this contest and I'll be taking a little trip. To *Mexico,* man. Can you believe that? All expenses paid. I'm going to set up down there, really put some roots down, and turn everything around—"

Whoever it was was flying high. Wylie glanced at the clock: ten minutes until eleven. The guy was a motormouth, talking a mile a minute. Maybe it was a wrong number.

"And these jobs, they're just not getting me anywhere. Same thing, day in day out. Working for peanuts, man. Can't save a *dime,* and I'm living in a *dive,* and where's that going to get me? It's like I'm going nowhere, fast. It's not *me,* you know? I really want to do something with my life, turn it around, and if I stay here doing this I'm just sinking deeper and deeper into a hole. You get me? You know what I'm saying?"

Elsa stood in front of Wylie wagging her tail. He pointed to the phone, shook his head, and shrugged.

"Tommy? You there, man?"

As soon as he heard his first name, Wylie knew it was Logan. The fact that it had taken him so long to recognize his voice showed how far his half brother was from his thoughts. Wylie's guard went up immediately. When it came to Logan, you were usually talking trouble. He was a sweet guy, a fun guy, but trouble. Always had been. And Wylie had been around enough users to know when someone was high. "You're going to *Mexico?*" he interrupted.

"Yeah, that's what I'm *saying,* bro. That's why I'm *calling.* I thought maybe we could hook up before I left. I don't know how long I'll be gone and I really want to see you. You were always there for me, man. You're my bro, you know? So before I take off I'd like to get together."

Poor guy. To Wylie, their brotherly relationship consisted mostly of him getting Logan out of scrapes when there was no one else around to do it. It's not like they'd been raised together. "When are you leaving?" he asked.

"Week from Friday. Friday the thirteenth! Think that's bad luck?"

"Nah, I wouldn't worry about that." Wylie hesitated before asking, "Listen, Logan. Is everything okay? I mean, is it okay for you to take a trip? You know, leave the country and all?"

"I won this contest, like I said," Logan answered brightly, ever the con man. "All expenses paid. How often does that happen? I think it's a sign for me to pack up and move on, you know what I mean? I really gave it a try here, you know? Tried to stick with things, but they just weren't working out. I think this is my big chance. Like I can really turn the corner here. You know what I'm saying?"

"Wait a minute. Are you talking about a vacation, or leaving for good? I'm not really getting what you have in mind."

Logan paused in his rapid-fire barrage, and in that moment's hesitation Wylie felt just how lost his brother was. The dumb shit.

"Because if you're talking about leaving for good, about *moving* to Mexico, I really think you could be making a mistake," Wylie said as kindly as he could. At the same time he wondered why he was bothering. If Logan left, he'd be one less thing to worry about. One less bad-news phone call.

"It's a lot harder than you think to just go and set up down there," Wylie went on, despite his better instincts. "For one thing, it's probably not even legal. I'm pretty sure that if you try something like that, they're going to lock you up again, Logan."

"They're *not* going to lock me up again, Tommy," Logan snarled in a menacing tone. He was definitely high, probably strung out. "I am *not* breaking the law, they are *not* going to catch me, and they're definitely *not* going to lock me up." He huffed audibly several times. When he spoke again he was calmer. "I just need a change of scenery, that's all. I'm going to play it by ear. See what happens. That's all." He heaved a huge sigh. "So, do you want to get together or not?"

Wylie sighed, too. He looked down at Elsa, who was staring toward the kitchen. Murphy was back under the table, licking the pieces of torn-up paper.

"Sure, Logan. Sure I want to see you. When do you want to get together?" *I've got a kid on the way,* he thought of saying. *Any advice?*

"Great, that's just great, because I really want to see you. You mean a lot to me, you know, Tommy."

Logan, the man of many moods. Wylie just wanted to get off the phone.

"I thought maybe I could see you on my way out," Logan said. "You know, at the airport. I could come a little early and stop by the bar."

"Fine," Wylie said. "What time will you be there?"

"Well, my plane leaves at eight, so I figure around six-thirty or seven. How's that?"

"I can't. I work days, Logan. Seven to three. I'll have to meet you some other time."

"Shit, man. Too bad. Let's see—"

"Wait, not this Friday, right?" Wylie interrupted him. "You said *next* Friday, didn't you?"

"Right, the *thirteenth,* remember?"

"Yeah, how could I forget? It just so happens I traded shifts with the other bartender that day. She has her daughter's birthday party or something. So I'll be there, believe it or not." Wylie laughed. "I *never* work nights. You *always* get your way. You're a lucky son of a bitch, Logan. Always were."

Logan laughed, too. "That's right. How do you think I won this contest? Things always work out for me. One way or another, they always do."

Friday, December 13

24 Jewell didn't see Eli's car, so she parked in front of the address he'd given her and waited. It was a hilly section of Boyle Heights: the street in front of her rose like a hump on a rollercoaster. The houses were wood frame, three stories, unusual for L.A. The house at 2624 must have been yellow once, but now it was faded to the color of old parchment, the trim a brownish red. Fallen berries from a big eugenia bush on one side of the house had stained the driveway purple. At this hour, two o'clock, the only person in sight was the mailwoman who walked with a slow, deliberate pace up to each house. She was tea-colored, large, wearing shorts that showed off her sturdy legs. Sunk in the driver's seat, studying the scraggy lawns and the sagging faces of the sun-bleached houses, Jewell felt like she was on a stakeout. She wondered how people ever decided to fold up and clear out, how they managed to leave each other, find new homes, start new lives. She wondered how she would ever do it.

Eli's car appeared in her rearview mirror, and she watched it slide down the hill and pull up behind her. Just a couple of weeks before Christmas and he had on shorts, too, like the mailwoman. Flip-flops, sunglasses, a Hawaiian print shirt.

She got out of her car and leaned against the side.

"So, what do you think?" Eli said when he walked up.

Jewell shrugged. "Looks nice. Seems like a quiet street and everything."

"Wait till you see it. My friend, the guy who just moved out, lived here three years. It's funky, but cool. There's something special about it."

"That's good, because I'm scraping the bottom of the barrel. You wouldn't believe what's out there. Yesterday I looked at a place with this woman named peregrine. *peregrine.* Small p. You can't believe the rules. No meat, no scents, no booze or drugs *of course.*"

"No tuna, no sugar, no men with penises?" Eli added.

"Right." Jewell managed to laugh.

"You still living in the closet?"

Jewell shook her head. "Celeste has more or less moved out. She stays at Dana's almost all the time. Stops by to pick up her mail or get some clothes, but she never spends the night. She already gave notice. She'll be back with her happy little family in no time."

Jewell stared down at the street and watched the asphalt blur as her eyes filled. She pressed her lips together to keep her chin from quivering and waited until the blacktop came back into focus. She was so sick of crying.

"Well, shall we go have a look?" Eli said, too cheerfully. "I have the key."

"You know I've never even lived by myself?" For some reason Jewell didn't want to go inside. The sky was overcast and there was a light wind, but during the lulls between the gusts, the weak sun pushed through the clouds. The warmth felt good.

"You haven't?"

"Nope, I just realized it the other night. Either I've lived in a house with a bunch of people, or I've gone from one person to another. You know, I was living with Hasani when I met Celeste, and I moved straight in with her. I always think that this one's going to be different, but they're all the same. And worst of all I realize that *I'm* the same, that I've done it again."

"Well, maybe this time it'll be different. Shall we go?" Eli indicated the house with his chin. "Sorry, but I have a shift later today, so I don't have a lot of time."

They walked down a driveway that ran around the side of the house, to a rickety wooden stairway strung against the outside wall.

"Remember these berries?" Eli said when they passed the eugenia tree. "Did you used to eat them when you were a kid?"

"Yeah. We used to write on the sidewalk with them." She bent down and scraped a message on the driveway with the biggest berry she could find: *SOS.* "Hey, it still works."

"Better not come home too wasted if you live here," Eli said as they climbed. "One false step and you're roadkill on these stairs."

"Yeah, too bad. I don't think I'll be able to make it when I'm an old lady."

At the top of the stairs, the porch felt like a pile of matchsticks fastened to the side of the building with four nails, max.

"Fucking hell, is this safe?" Jewell asked.

They were three stories up; the door was just under the roof. From the porch you could see over the other rooftops. In the next yard a fat kid was bouncing a ball against the back of the house. He looked up and waved.

"You get used to it," Eli said. "Besides, that's what makes it so *affordable.* If it was a legal apartment, *everybody* would be swarming the place. Here we go."

He pushed the door open and Jewell caught the smell of sun-warmed hay. She peered into the long, narrow space. The ceiling sloped; the beams were open. There were three windows, a wood floor. Something stirred in her chest. At the far end of the room, looking down on the backyard, was a makeshift kitchen with a tiny fridge, a stovetop, and a small sink.

"Bathroom's there," Eli said, pointing to the other end of the room, toward the street. "And Jules, come here. Check this out. You put your mattress right here," he said when she'd joined him under a skylight. "At night you see the stars."

Jewell looked up at the naked sky. Had it really come to this? "I don't know," she said after a long pause.

"Ah, Jules. Come on! What's not to like?"

"When do I have to let the landlady know whether I want it or not?"

"You snooze, you lose, girlfriend. It's already Friday. Chriselda needs the money pronto, and there are plenty of people who'll take it. She wants to know before the weekend's over."

"Why're you pressuring me?" she snapped.

With a look of amazement, Eli held up his hands. Jewell watched the emotions pass over his face: surprise, disappointment, and finally dismissal. "Hey, no pressure," he said. "Do whatever you want."

"I just don't want to give up if it's not really over. Relationships aren't easy, you know. They take work," Jewell recited. She realized how lame she sounded, but she couldn't stop. "And there's Rachel, too—her little girl. And Celeste. I still, you know—" She looked at Eli, watched him blur around the edges. "I still—have feelings for her."

"Look, Jewell. I'm not telling you what to do," Eli said in a tired voice. "If you don't want the apartment, don't take it."

She walked to the window in the little kitchen and looked down into the yard. There was a clothesline, a barbecue, a weather-beaten lawn chair. *Now or never,* she told herself.

"I need time to think," she told Eli.

"Okay, let's go, then."

Jewell felt like she should hold on to the rain gutter while Eli locked up, in case the porch gave way. The fat boy with the ball was gone. You could see a lot from that height: billboards a few streets over, telephone wires, the freeway overpass, trees.

"The river's right over there," Eli said.

"Where?"

"Just there, on the other side of the freeway."

"Wow," Jewell said, picturing it not as it was now, a brown spill imprisoned between concrete walls, but as it had been: a *real* river lush with cattails, twisting and turning.

"Thanks, Eli. I'll let you know," she said, resting her hand on his shoulder as they made their way back down the wobbly stairs.

Celeste's car was parked out front when Jewell got home. It had been over a week since they'd seen each other face-to-face. A wave of joy washed over her. Idiotic and definitely not a good sign, but she rushed to get out of her car all the same, as excited as if they were newly in love, as if they'd been involuntarily separated for some time and were about to have a happy reunion. When she got to the sidewalk there was a racket and a clatter. She turned just as the Avon Lady bumped over the curb on her crazy bike.

"Hi. We don't need anything today," Jewell called out as cordially as she could manage. She was desperate to have Celeste to herself.

The Avon Lady dismounted. How anyone who just rode a bike from who knew where could look so perfectly manicured, Jewell had no idea. The woman's black, intricately styled, and heavily sprayed hair was perfectly in place; her cream-colored slacks had crisp creases and not a spot of road dirt or chain oil anywhere. A gold brooch was fastened to the lapel of her plaid blazer, and she wore shiny pumps with chunky black heels.

"How about your friend?"

"I don't think so."

The woman wheeled her bike alongside Jewell, bumping it over the unkempt lawn. "There's still time to buy for Christmas."

"She doesn't celebrate Christmas. She's *Jewish*."

"Nieces and nephews. She likes to buy for everyone."

Jewell stopped short and turned. The woman flinched. A flash of fear passed over her face. Jewell glanced down and noticed her engagement ring: a big gold setting with a tiny little diamond. The ring and the wedding band looked like it had been bought in a boxed set with the gold cross she wore around her neck. "I don't mean to be rude, but Celeste is moving," Jewell said. "We both are."

"Is she home?"

The Avon Lady might be scared, but she was also stubborn. Very stubborn. There was no getting rid of her. Celeste appeared at the door with the laundry basket under one arm and her purse draped over the other. Jewell's breath caught. It felt so good just to *see* her. It was like in the very beginning, when the sight of Celeste used to knock her into a kind of stupor.

The Avon Lady clicked down her kickstand and bustled up to Celeste before Jewell could move. They chatted on the porch while Jewell stood on the walkway near the bike. When had the two of them gotten to be such good friends? Celeste kept glancing at Jewell while she nodded and smiled at the Avon Lady, who took out her brochure and thumbed through the pages. Jewell shifted her feet restlessly. My god, Celeste was gorgeous. She'd pulled her hair straight back so that she looked like a flamenco dancer: elegant and fiery.

"All right Inez, thanks for everything," Celeste said. "I'll miss you."

Finally. The Avon Lady turned and came back down the walk. She shot Jewell a not-very-friendly look as she passed.

Jewell had to tell each muscle and tendon what to do in order to walk the short distance to the porch. Even then she felt spastic: her legs kicked out at odd angles, her arms jerked in irregular motion. Her face was out of control, too. It hung like a rubbery mask from her skull, contorting from a shit-eating grin to a grotesque grimace. "Hi," she managed to say as she struggled up.

All the hairs stood up on Jewell's arm when Celeste laid her hand on it. Celeste looked into her eyes and gave her a warm smile. What was up?

"Hi, Jewell. I'm just leaving. I'm on my way out."

"Uh," Jewell muttered. "Um." Her throat had closed up. Her eyes played over and over Celeste's face. She was hungry for it. God, what a state. The important thing was to keep her there as long as possible so she could keep looking at her. "Isn't it strange that the Avon Lady rides a bike?" she finally managed.

Celeste laughed. *Laughed!* Jewell had forgotten the precious way Celeste's narrow bottom teeth jumbled against each other. And her throat when she tilted her head back! Jewell was in a bad way, even she knew it. But she laughed, too, a strangled gurgle that made her throat burn. Not too much, though, because that might open her tear ducts again.

"She's a strange one, all right," Celeste said. "I don't know where she comes from or how far she rides that bike. I don't think she can drive. I get a weird vibe from her, like something freaky's going on—even though she looks normal, or pretty conservative." She shrugged. "Maybe it's just the Christian thing. That cross around her neck."

The small talk loosened Jewell up enough to suggest they go inside for a minute. Celeste set the laundry basket down by the dining room table, her purse on top of it. She was wearing a long, loose-knit sweater Jewell had never seen before. Very flattering. It felt good to be in the house together, the place where they'd loved each other with such joy, where they'd had so many laughs.

"My God, Jewell. How much weight have you lost?" Celeste said when she turned and looked at her.

Jewell lifted her shirt and pulled out the waistband of her sagging jeans. "Guess I dropped a few," she said. Celeste's eyes fixed on her bare stomach. She still wanted her, Jewell could tell. That frumpy Dana couldn't hold a candle to her, at least in the looks department. Jewell took a step closer. She softly touched Celeste's neck, then her face. She saw the fear in Celeste's eyes, the heat. Still, she was surprised when Celeste leaned toward her, met her halfway.

For the first few moments they kissed, Jewell felt like her ears were plugged, like she was underwater. There was pure silence, then there were only muffled sounds, vague rustlings and distant murmurs. After what seemed like a long time she began to surface. She heard the refrigerator kick on in the kitchen, a car door slam out in the street. She couldn't tell her own breathing from Celeste's. Still they kissed. Jewell felt like she could go on forever. She sensed their concentration, Celeste's and her own, like they were traveling a treacherous road together and had to pay strict attention. Celeste's kisses became more frantic. In just a moment, Jewell was sure, she would feel the click in Celeste's desire that meant there was no turning back. The increased urgency that meant Celeste had taken the first step on a trajectory that wouldn't end until she lay sweaty and exhausted beside Jewell, a smirk on her face.

Anticipation of that moment so excited Jewell that she slid her hands up the front of Celeste's sweater, under her bra, to the warmth of her breasts. Celeste's nipples hardened immediately. She gasped, moaned, and fell against Jewell, pressing her pelvis against her thigh. Now it was Jewell who was frantic. She pulled her hands from under Celeste's sweater and grabbed her ass instead, pulling her against her. Her sadness, the raw grief of the past few weeks, boiled up into a voracious craving. She felt like she had to hold tight to the seat of Celeste's jeans to keep her hands from shredding the denim to tatters.

Then Celeste pushed her away.

They stared at each other like two wrestlers about to close in the ring, panting.

"I can't do this, Jewell. I just can't."

Jewell's ears popped. Her eyes slowly focused. Her mouth filled with spit like she was going to be sick.

"Don't do this to me, Jules," Celeste rasped. "I can't take it. Please don't do it."

Jewell felt like her stomach was being hauled out through her mouth. She moved her jaw as if she were trying to clear her ears, adjust to a different altitude. She couldn't talk, she didn't even try. All she could do was kick the laundry basket. The clothes went flying, then lay strewn across the floor like bodies washed up on a beach.

"Just leave," Jewell said.

She listened to the door close, Celeste's car starting, the motor accelerating as she drove away. Then there was just the house again. Water gurgling in the leaky toilet tank, a creak as the wall settled.

She went into the bedroom and lay at the foot of the bed. Like a dog, like Lassie. For a while she kept her mind a blank and stared out the window over the bed. Then she turned her face toward the bed, pressed it into the bedspread, and sobbed, alternately kneading the blankets and pounding her open palm against the mattress. She let herself go, wailing as she rubbed her wet, hot face against the blankets. She cursed herself, Celeste, and Dana. But then, just as she was really getting into her tears, they dried up. It always happened that way: the mood passed before she was ready to stop crying. *Despite* her. She sat up, wiped her face. She felt lucid, strangely calm. Not optimistic, but resigned. Some kind of Zen state, she supposed. Beyond suffering. She wrinkled up her face, contracted her chest, tried to force another sob. More, she wanted more. No good. Nothing came. She was finished.

She spied her backpack on the floor next to the bed. She pulled out her wallet and searched through four crumpled one-dollar bills, a receipt for the balsa wood she'd bought for her project, and a coupon for a free cup of coffee from a shop on the north side of campus, until she found the corner of notebook paper where she'd written the number her Uncle Tommy had given her.

She pulled out her cell phone and dialed. No wonder she was fucked up, she thought bitterly as she listened to the phone ring. She'd learned from the master. With her parents as role models, it was a wonder she would even *try* to be in a relationship. She pressed her face into the bedspread and imagined she could smell the commingling of her own and Celeste's bodies—the hours they'd spent dreaming side by side, the warmth of their entangled limbs. She loved to wake when the faintest light was just starting to come through the window over the bed, when the folds and peaks of the blankets shimmered with a glacial blueness and Celeste was sunk in her deepest sleep, her hair spilling over the pillow. There was still time to go back to sleep, time for just the two of them before they'd have to get up and start their days, go their separate ways.

Normally she would have hung up after so many rings, but somehow she expected this from her father, so she stayed on the line. No telling where he was: if he was still in town, still out of jail, dead or alive. Señor Love 'em and Leave 'em. While she listened to the rings, she stared blankly at the wooden crate that served as Celeste's nightstand, at the cigar box where Celeste kept all the

polishes and potions for her feet and hands. Celeste was the ultimate multitasker, reading a magazine, drinking tea, talking on the
phone, and giving herself a pedicure all at once while she leaned
against the headboard of the bed and winked at Jewell, pointing to
the place beside her, telling her to come and sit down.

Jewell didn't bother wondering why she was calling her father
now, of all times. She knew it was messed up. What difference did
it make? It wasn't like she had a whole lot to lose. The phone
seemed to ring forever. Then there was a click, and it stopped
ringing.

Jewell sat up on the bed.

"Yeah?" Logan said.

His voice was familiar, like she'd heard it a day or two ago.

"Hello?" he said.

Jewell just listened. To the static on the line, to his breathing, to
the low buzz of the current that connected them. It's *him*, she
thought. Logan, her father.

"Hello?" he repeated, pissed that no one was answering.

"Hi, Dad."

He laughed, a liquid, bubbling sound. "I don't believe it!" he
cried gleefully. "You read my mind!"

25 | Logan was a little funny on the rent, so he carried his things down to his truck on the sly, a little at a time. With any luck, no one would break a window and rip off his gear before he left; with a little more luck he'd say *adios* to the Morningstar without Salem, the manager, noticing he was gone. He'd told Damon next door that he could use the Toyota while he was away; all he had to do was drive Logan to the airport. So things were pretty much set. If everything went off without a hitch, this time tomorrow he'd be feasting his eyes on that blue, blue water.

He took it as a sign that Jewell had called him today of all days, right before he left. Though he didn't like to play favorites, he had to admit that of all his children, she felt the most *his*. His first. The day he'd brought her home from the hospital he'd felt like he'd pulled one over on everyone, like he'd really gotten away with something. Like he should get her home as fast as possible and hide her away, his precious thing, before someone realized what he had and tried to take it away from him. Best of all, he'd get to see her before he left, since she'd agreed to meet him that night at the airport. With her and Tommy there, it would be a real send-off party.

He looked under the bed and in the drawer of the table to make sure he hadn't left anything behind. The room look scuffed and desolate without his things spread around. He'd had some good times here; he'd miss the place. Some damn lonely times, too, but on the whole a lot of good. He never *did* get around to Sylvia Salvetti, he thought with a chuckle. That surprised him. Didn't matter though, because where he was going they'd be lining up at his door. Not only the *señoritas,* but *gringas* there on vacation, wanting to cut loose a little before they headed back home. A lot of them had money. After a while maybe he'd come back with one of them, live the high life.

He jumped when his phone rang. Beethoven's Fifth. Fate knocking at his door. What an idiot to choose that ring when he could have had *La Cucaracha, Louie Louie,* or the *Blue* fucking *Danube.* Jesus Christ, if they caught him now, wouldn't that be the shit to end all shits? He'd already talked to the Salvettis, Tommy, and Jewell, so it *had* to be his caseworker, the prick, telling him that his number had come up, to come in and get tested. It was all over. Logan started sweating bullets. Don't answer, he told himself. It'd stop ringing and by the time they came to get him he'd be gone, out of the country. He was way too small potatoes for them to check the airports. If he didn't answer, everything would be cool.

The phone kept bleating. The trouble was, he was jumpy as hell. Except for a few times he'd lain down in his clothes and dozed, he'd been up for two nights running. Getting high, coming down, getting high again. Thinking about crazy things he hadn't thought about for years. How his mother had complained for months and months about a backache before they found her cancer. How his son Stephen had sent him handmade cards—Christmas, birthday, Father's Day—year after year, and Logan hadn't done squat. Nothing, not jack shit, not even a phone call to say thanks, even though the kid was a regular Hallmark factory—glue, sequins, the whole nine yards. It hurt to think about it. He thought about his uncle Vance, his father's brother, who took him fishing for catfish in the canals over by El Centro. After Logan had sat the whole day in the blazing sun and not caught a thing, Vance—who'd lost his thumb to a chainsaw and talked with a bad stutter—had told him to go over to the car and bring him a beer. When Logan returned and his uncle handed his pole back, he'd reeled it in to find a good-sized catfish hanging on the line. Didn't matter that the damn thing was as limp as—well, a dead fish. It had taken Logan a long time, years, to figure out that's exactly what it was, that his uncle had taken pity on him and tied it on the line. He thought about Mrs. Keezer, the old lady who lived next door to him and his mother when he was in junior high. Her thing was gardening in the middle of the night. She'd drag a pole lamp out on an extension cord, put a little radio beside her, and dig away, down on her hands and knees in a house dress under the moon and stars. All the jaw-grinding, moaning, farting, and snoring he'd listened to while locked up. The sweet spells he'd had, holed up with some woman. He thought about his mother and father, the people he'd known who'd checked out one way or another. Lying awake, clench-jawed and cotton-mouthed, watching his life played out on the ceiling of his room. Old feelings coming back. It tired him out. Made him feel like an old man.

"I'm not here, you motherfucker!" he yelled at the phone.

Who in their right mind would let the damn thing ring so many times? Then he realized it wouldn't matter if he answered. He could tell his caseworker fine, he'd be right in, and by the time they figured out he wasn't coming, he'd be gone. Even if they showed up at his goddamn door it'd be too late. By the time they got their act together to pick him up, he'd be kicking back down in Mexico.

"Come get me, you sons of bitches," he said, flipping open the phone.

It was Damon, wanting to know what time they were leaving.

"I told you, man, we leave at *five-thirty*. I'm counting on you."

He hung up and settled down. Just one more hour, then it was *sayonara*. He thought of praying, but it didn't feel right. He'd saved one hit to do just before he left. Then he'd have to tough it out because there was no way he was taking anything across the border. That was a whole different kettle of fish, federal offense, and while he might indulge in risky behavior, he wasn't stupid.

Someone had left a flat box of good paper in the drawer of the table near the window. *Onion skin* it said on the cover. Logan sat down and took out a sheet. It was brittle and yellowed around the edges, but that didn't matter. The aged paper seemed right for what he was going to write: better than the yellow pad of lined paper he'd bought in the prison commissary, or the white Xerox paper he'd filched from the place where he cashed his checks. He got the Sunset Savings & Loan ballpoint off the windowsill, took a deep breath, and started writing.

To whom it may concern, he printed in official-looking capital letters. He scratched it out. What the hell, he tore the paper up and took a whole new piece. It was a legal document, after all. Last will and testament of logan paul wylie, he began, centering the line at the top of the page. He cracked his knuckles. He didn't have a whole lot to give away. He chewed on the pen. Time ticked by. Damon could keep the truck, if worse came to worse. Good luck to him. He had two rings: a big chunk of turquoise he'd won from an Arizona Navajo he'd served time with, and a Celtic cross given to him by a woman he'd lived with out by San Bernardino. He left one each to his sons, Stephen and Tony. To Heather, his second daughter and Tony's sister, he left the collection of Indian-head nickels he'd had since he was a boy. It was in his storage locker; he gave instructions on how to retrieve it. And to Jamie, his youngest daughter, he left a clay sculpture of a reclining woman that he'd made when he was a senior in high school. That was in storage, too.

His wedding rings were gone. The first one, from his marriage to Jewell's mother, he'd pitched off the Santa Monica Pier late one night about a year after they divorced. He had no idea what had happened to the other two. He left his father's wristwatch, a big silver clunker, to Tommy. The only thing he had from his mother was a sad little filigree locket with her parents' pictures inside. It had blackened with age; the chain was knotted and crimped. Worth about twenty bucks, tops. Still, it was precious, because in many ways his mother was the love of his life. No one had ever loved him like that again, come hell or high water. He left the locket to Jewell.

He didn't kid himself about the other crap: no one would want it. Just a few bunged-up power tools, his high school yearbooks, and a stack of LPs from when he was a kid. Santana, Springsteen, Eric Clapton. Still, he didn't feel satisfied. He cracked his knuckles again, rolled his head to try to work out some of the kinks in his shoulders, gripped the pen with extra force, and wrote:

My dear family and friends,
    This is what I have Left. Please don't ever fight about Money or Material Things. I have always done my Best in Life, even though it might not come out the way I planned. Its the Thought that Counts. To my Children, please always be True to Yourselfs. That is most Important. I love Each and Every one of you.
                                Your Father/Logan Wylie

He signed his name, folded the paper carefully, and put it in the envelope that Wally from the liquor store had given him with the letter saying he'd won the contest. OPEN ONLY IN THE EVENT OF MY DEATH, he printed on the outside. He waved the envelope as if the ink were wet and put it in the inside pocket of his Bogart jacket.

Then, sitting at the little table and looking over the familiar rooftops of downtown, he did the dope. Rush hour was gearing up; everybody racing their engines to get the hell out of Dodge, get a jump on the weekend. *Here's to Friday the thirteenth,* he toasted, raising an imaginary glass to the city outside. The speed hit his veins like thick, golden fire. He felt himself swell, straighten, converge.

Everything was cool.

He sniffed and wiped his nose, stood up and pushed the chair in, put on his Bogart jacket.

He was ready to go.

26 Inez pushed the bike to the back of the house and locked it to the banister of the porch. She took the plastic cover from the box under the steps and fitted it over the bike. It was going to rust out there, cover or not, but this was just one more of Rudy's new rules. It was cluttering up the garage where he was trying to keep things in order, he had explained, his eyes bulging. Right. Sure. What did Rudy think she was, stupid? Something was going on in there, just like Vanessa had said.

Inez tiptoed across the thick, soggy crabgrass to the garage. Rudy had been keeping it locked, but she twisted the knob anyway, throwing her weight against the door. Nope. He'd taped newspaper over the window in the upper half of the door, so she couldn't see in. She crept around to the side of the garage. That window was covered, too. What he was up to? She couldn't imagine. But she didn't want to get caught snooping around out there.

The truth was, she was getting more and more afraid of him. The way he talked all the time, whether to himself or to her—it no longer seemed to make much difference. Anything could set him off: the way she arranged the food on his plate, if she opened a window for some air, a remark she made while they were watching TV. His eyes bugged, his face went red, spit flew from his lips. And his personal hygiene. He wasn't changing his clothes very often; she could tell by how much was in the laundry. And his dandruff was worse than ever: flakes fell from his fine red hair and clung to his oily eyelashes. Worst of all was the smell he gave off, acrid and vomity, like an unwashed baby.

She just needed to hold on a few more weeks. All the money from the Christmas orders would soon be in, and that would be enough. It was too bad about Celeste, the one who lived with the other woman, but even without her order, Inez would meet her goal. Just wait for that, then for the holidays to be over, and then—as soon as the new year started—she'd be on her way. She had already picked the town in Oregon. She didn't need a lot, just her nest egg and one suitcase each for Vanessa and herself. They'd pay cash, take a taxi to the train. She'd already contacted the Avon people; they'd help her set up a new route. She didn't want any of the things in the house anyway. It was a lot of trash. A load of bad memories. What she wanted was a fresh start.

She crossed the yard back to the house and took her things from where she'd left them on the step. Vanessa had gymnastics practice after school today; after that she'd go to a friend's house, where she'd stay until the mother got home and drove her back. At the thought of Vanessa, Inez's hands stopped rummaging in her purse for a moment. Her eyes went soft and blurry. Her daughter. Maybe she loved her so much because she was her only child. Maybe because she'd had her when she was a child herself. Sometimes she couldn't take her eyes off Vanessa; she could barely prevent her hands running through her hair, squeezing her shoulders, caressing her face.

And him, Vanessa's father. It was funny how fresh he was in her mind after all these years: his matter-of-fact ways, his neat suits, his clove smell. The brutal way he'd used her. The lies he'd told the others. Who would have thought that such a beautiful girl could come from *him*? Inez had drawn a lesson from it, one that she remembered often during these hard times with Rudy. *Good can come from bad.* God had given her the trial of Vanessa's father, but from it came Vanessa. And through Vanessa, all of Inez's family came to live with her—her mother and father, all the aunts, uncles, and grandparents she'd never known. Vanessa had their eyes, their hands, their voices. The man was just the instrument that had brought Vanessa to her, the tool that had allowed Inez to create her lost past out of her own body.

Inez found her key in her purse. The lock on the back door was sticky; she jiggled the key in it. She couldn't help imagining the day Rudy would come home and find the empty house, her and Vanessa gone without a trace. Picturing his rage was terrifying; she had to remind herself that she wouldn't be there to experience it. No, she and Vanessa would be on the train, chatting as they ate a picnic lunch and watched the scenery go by. While he trashed the house, ranting and raving, they'd be in the dining car ordering dinner. By the time he figured things out, got in his car to go looking for them—maybe even with the gun he kept behind his shoeshine kit in the closet—they'd be climbing into the bunks of their sleeping compartment, the train clackety-clacking toward their new home.

The door stuck, too. Once she finally got the lock to open, she gave the door a hard kick and stumbled inside. Suddenly her breath stuck in her throat. The hair rose on the back of her neck. Before her brain could even form the words, her heart started pounding. *Someone had been there.* She didn't know how she knew, she could just feel it. The air, the sound in the house. Something had been disturbed. She threw her Avon things on the kitchen counter and rushed into the living room. She looked wildly around: at the floral-print loveseat, the lumpy couch, the dead eye of the television. Through the window, she could see the phone wires swaying in the wind. Everything looked the same, but that didn't fool her. The air was charged. She smelled something.

She felt like a panther stalking its prey as she walked down the hall to Vanessa's bedroom. The minute she opened the door she knew. *Oh no!* she cried as she ran to the closet. *Oh no! Oh no!* The lid was down on the cedar chest, but a puff of blanket was caught in the crack, spilling out like rising dough. Her knees went loose and flimsy. She had to hold on to the edge of the chest to keep herself from collapsing. The most surprising thing was that she wasn't surprised. She'd been waiting for this, she realized. She'd dreamed it over and over. Every time she'd lifted the lid on the chest, she'd pictured it just the way it was now: the delicate lock broken; the blankets tangled instead of neatly stacked; the once-tidy layers churned up like a wild animal had dug through them. She reached down, her hand making its way to the bottom of the chest, and yes, sure enough, it was gone. Not just the money—all of it. Her pictures, her bundle of papers, her birth certificate. Everything. *Gone.*

Yes, she'd been waiting.

She closed the lid. The room was quiet. Her chest, neck, and arms felt like they were swelling, inflating with each outraged breath, like someone was pumping them up with air. Her nest had been robbed and fouled. She wrung her hands as she glared at the seam where the wall met the ceiling. His filthy hands had pawed through her things, had stolen them, had hidden them away. It hurt to breathe. His pink, prissy fingers. His piggish, lying eyes. *Her* things. Her plan was demolished! Everything was ruined! She moaned, and then she roared. She screeched until the tendons in her neck felt like they'd pop, until her hands, clenching the edge of the chest, felt like they'd been smashed with a hammer. *And my wrath will burn, and I will kill you with the sword.* Her nest: the money, the only pictures she had of her family, the papers that might someday lead her to them.

Help me, Lord, she prayed desperately, her eyes clenched tight. *Help me. Help me. Help me.* She repeated those two words until she was exhausted, until her breathing slowed to match her chant, until she was calm. *Let justice roll down like waters,* she recited, *and righteousness like an everflowing stream.*

She went to the phone and called Vanessa, told her to stay at her friend's house. "Everything's fine," she told her. "Don't ask questions." *His wrath is poured out like fire, and the rocks are broken asunder.* She recrossed the living room, went back through the kitchen where the clock over the oven said 3:55. The door was stuck again; she kicked it open. She stomped down the stairs, back across the grass, over to the fence where someone had dumped a pile of broken cinder blocks. She found one that was still in one piece, hoisted it up, and carried it over to the door. *My God the rock of my refuge,* she panted as she heaved it through the window.

Inside it smelled of dried grass and gasoline from the lawnmower. Light filtered in from the open door and from a small window near the workbench. She walked across the broken glass and stood in the middle of the room. For the second time the hair rose on the back of her neck, and suddenly she felt in real danger, as if something were lurking in the garage. She was thunderstruck, rooted to the spot. Rudy had taped things to the walls: news articles, pages torn from the phone book, sheets of notebook paper covered with his writing—line upon line of cramped scrawl that grew more compressed as it reached the bottom of the page. There were sketches complicated by arrows and blocks of words scratched in pencil. Inez couldn't make out what they were. Taped to a wall stud over the light switch was a floor plan. LAX, Inez read, recognizing the layout of the terminals as panic sent her into a slow, dizzy spin. There were seating charts from different aircraft, emergency instruction cards with evacuation routes from the seat pockets of the airplanes. Timetables of arrivals and departures; catalog pages of weapons, camouflage uniforms, ammunition.

Oh my God, oh my God, oh my God! Inez repeated to herself. She shut her eyes tight, pushed her fists against the sockets. *This* was what he'd been doing. All this time! How long? My God, was this really happening? It was, she told herself. It had to be.

The worktable was scattered with wires and screws, rolls of electrical tape, paper bags twisted shut. A cardboard box of long red sticks that *had* to be dynamite was sitting on the floor. The first few layers were gone. There was a lot more stuff, but she couldn't take it all in. Scattered everywhere—on the floor and on all the surfaces like a flock of butterflies come to rest—were empty bags and packages, twists of cellophane and smudged tissue paper from the food he'd eaten. Chips, cookies, doughnuts, cupcakes. The same smell of scalp and sugar that filled his car now lingered near the workbench.

Inez looked at the ceiling as if she might see straight through the dusty rafters, the curled pigeon-gray shingles, the disconnected television antennas, the sagging telephone wires, the low ceiling of battleship-colored clouds, right to God Himself. The whole world had tilted; she felt like she might slide off the edge. *What?* she pleaded out loud, stretching her arms up to heaven as she breathed the suffocating air. *Tell me!*

She closed her eyes and listened for an answer. Just when she thought that God had forsaken her, the words of Isaiah rang in her heart with crystal clarity: *For the day of vengeance was in my heart, and my year of redemption has come.*

27 At four-thirty, Rudy pulled into the Arco station he'd chosen the week before. He drove around to the back, near the hoses for air and water. He'd found Inez's stash, like a rat's nest covered with blankets and pillows, shawls that smelled of dried flowers and mothballs, down at the bottom of the cedar chest. Years and years of her filthy secrets in a fur-lined pouch like the rotten spot in her brain that had betrayed him, decaying their marriage like cancer. The pile of money she'd stored up, the lists of names, blueprints for her future. Yup, he'd finally zeroed in on its signals, tiny beeps high as a dog whistle that he'd tracked until they led him there, to Vanessa's room. An old photograph of a child and a man with a bike; Vanessa's birth certificate, father unknown; immigration papers with Inez's other name, Santos. The foreignness of her. The conniving. The Yes, Rudy, nothing's wrong and What can I do for you? and all the time she was plotting, storing up, sneaking. Lying cheating and deceiving. Through her teeth. With her eyes wide open. Lying next to him in bed. She and all the rest of them and he should have known all along, but at least in the end the joke was going to be on her. He put the car in park and killed the motor. He had her now. Carefully, holding his breath, he had robbed the infected nest of its putrid contents. Placed it in a paper bag. *Evidence.* Hidden it in the garage for safekeeping.

The Arco station was right off the freeway, not far from the airport. From where he parked, Rudy could see the solitary person sitting at the register in the white cinder-block booth where people paid for their gas. He'd rehearsed everything because everything had to be just right. Every detail planned, like taking a trip. The trouble was, just when he needed all his concentration, his mind kept going back to Inez. *Where had she been when he'd come home?* It was a double betrayal: keeping those things, then not being home to answer for them. It enraged him, but it also unsettled him because it meant that the first part of his plan had fallen apart. She wasn't there, she wasn't there. *Where was she?* His mind kept going back to it. But he couldn't let it throw the rest of the plan off track. Commandos are trained to be disciplined, to perform under the toughest circumstances. Concentrate, he told himself. Stay focused.

The restrooms were around back: one for men, one for women. One-seaters with deadbolts on the doors. Perfect. Soon everyone would know. He got out of the car and locked the door. It was a special day today: Friday. The day he was born. He knew because his mother had told him that was the day she did her weekly grocery shopping. The pains had started in the parking lot, with a trunkful of perishables: ice cream, milk, ground chuck. Three weeks overdue, she'd told him, which was why, according to her, he was born with a thick head of reddish hair and fingernails so long his little newborn face was as nicked and scratched as an old dinner plate.

He went around to the back of the car and opened the trunk. Everything had built up to today. Not just these last few weeks of long, lonely hours in his car; the mornings and afternoons figuring things out in cafés; the late nights in the garage—but his whole life. Researching, collecting, planning. He took the satchel out of the trunk. It was caramel-colored, with handles on top like an old-fashioned doctor's case. It had been his mother's; he'd taken it with him when he went in the navy. He felt important carrying it across the short stretch of blacktop. Inez had her schemes, he thought as he glanced at the few people filling their cars at the pumps, but he had his. By the time this day was over, she'd know what he was capable of, and so would everyone else. But by that time it would be too late.

He pushed open the door of the men's room. It was vacant: so far, so good. He locked the door behind him and set down the satchel. The hospital smell of disinfectant and pee was strong. The room was about the size of a jail cell; there was even a small barred window over the sink that let in a square of dirty gray light. The concrete floor had a brass drain in the middle. There was a toilet, a sink, a trashcan, and a machine that dispensed condoms and combs. On the wall next to the mirror was another machine with a big roll of white linen to dry your hands on. It was broken, though, and the cotton towel hung down to the floor, wet and wrinkled like a soiled bandage. When the big trucks pounded by on the freeway outside, the room seemed to sway. The sink dripped. Still, it was peaceful in here, cool and quiet. So quiet Rudy could hear himself breathe.

Someone had pissed without flushing. They'd left the toilet seat up. Using a piece of toilet paper so he wouldn't have to touch anything, Rudy lowered the lid. He took off his jacket and unzipped the bag, then he laid everything carefully on the lid of the toilet and the edge of the sink. The explosives, the scissors, the duct tape. He took off his shirt and patiently worked his way around his waist, carefully taping each stick. The growing weight and stiffness reassured him. When all ten sticks were in place around his belly, he wrapped a few extra loops of duct tape round and round his middle to make sure everything was snug. He could hear cars coming and going outside, doors slamming, engines starting. No one came to use the restroom. It was like fate was on his side, like everything was working *with* him. He lost track of time. Stay calm, he told himself. Work it through. When he was finished, he felt the satisfaction of someone who's good at his job, who takes pride in it.

The detonator was the tricky part. He had taped it to his left arm so the trigger dangled exactly into his palm without showing any excess wire. Doing it with one hand was hard, but he managed. The lightness of it, its simplicity, excited him. If only his luck held out. He cut the last piece of tape, pressed it into place, and stepped over in front of the mirror. Wow! It took his breath away. He was a machine, a commando, a comet about to blaze across the sky. The thing to do was to believe in it, he told himself as he put everything back in the bag. That would get him past the obstacles.

He pushed open the door and stepped out into the bright light. He blinked. The ground was unsteady under his feet. The awnings of the gas station, the big blue sign, the cars and trucks streaming by on the freeway, all seemed unreal. It didn't matter about Inez now; he had bigger fish to fry. The phone booth was right there, just outside the restroom. His call would distract security, pull them to one side of the terminal so he could come in the other. Good thing he'd been a baggage handler and knew all the ropes. That crappy job was finally paying off.

He walked stiffly, like he was wearing a body cast. He dropped in the coins, dialed, and stared at the ground while he listened to the rings. The blacktop was broken around the base of the phone booth. A single dandelion had pushed its way through a crack in the asphalt. The yellow petals radiated against the tar like a drop of gold fallen from the sun. Rudy took it as a sign.

"Listen carefully," he said calmly, concentrating on the flower as intensely as a prayer. "It's very important you do like I say."

28

Damon was steamed that he had to drive to the airport during rush hour. He'd been back on the wagon for three days, and everything was getting under his skin. Sweat poured down his face and neck as he navigated through freeway traffic.

"What a dumb fucking time to go to the airport," he complained for the hundredth time.

"It's a *charter,* man," Logan replied. "I couldn't *pick* the damn time I wanted to go. Take it easy, will you?"

"Charters suck, Logan. The planes are shit. They have about two of them and they fly them back and forth, over and over. You ever hear of metal fatigue? That's what happens, going up and down all the time. Like a fucking tin can. They're held together with duct tape. You wait and see."

"Nothing's going to happen."

"Oh yeah. How do you know?"

"I just know. It's safe to fly on planes. Safer than riding in this truck like we are right now."

As if to prove him right, Damon swerved and laid on the horn. He signaled and changed lanes, the road buttons bumping under the tires. Logan was scared shitless. He wished Damon would shut the fuck up. The dusk sky was the same color as the asphalt. It sucked all but a trace of color from the cars and houses. Logan looked at the dingy crackerboxes that backed onto the freeway. At the mountains in the distance and the cars pouring onto the interstate like ants. *So long,* he said in his heart. *Nice knowing you.*

"And another thing, Logan," Damon went on. The poor bastard was gritting his sore, rotten teeth. "I still don't see how you think you're going to get away with this. You can't travel out of the country, man. What the hell are you thinking? They're going to pick you up and put you away before you can say suck my dick. I mean, what's the story?"

Logan took a deep breath. "I told you," he said, trying to stay calm. "I checked everything out. You don't *need* a passport to go to Mexico, especially on one of these charters. All you have to do is prove you're an American citizen. I got a driver's license. I need to get out of here, man, in case you forgot. If I get caught dirty, my ass is grass. I got to get it *together.*"

"Yeah, but how do you think you're—"

"Damon, can you give it a rest, buddy?" Logan interrupted. "You're really working my last nerve here. I'm letting you use my fucking truck. What more do you want? It's a pretty sweet deal if you ask me. All you have to do is drop me at the goddamn airport. Jesus Christ. Is that asking too much?"

"Where am I going to park it while I'm staying downtown? It's going to be a bitch finding a place to keep it."

"Don't take it then, man! I wish you woulda told me. I coulda loaned it to somebody else."

That shut Damon up for a few minutes. He drove with his lips puckered up and his shoulders hunched around his ears. He'd sweated out big circles under his arms. Logan wished to hell he could have one more pop before he walked into the airport. He was getting more and more antsy.

"I just hope whoever moves in next door is as good as you been," Damon said after a while. "I ain't going to be there much longer, anyway. They're getting me that job. I'm going to school. They're even going to fix my fucking teeth. But I'm still going to miss you, man."

"Maybe they'll give you something to take the edge off," Logan laughed. "A few 'ludes so you won't shit your pants while you get those new choppers."

"No way. I'm done with that." Damon smiled back. Things were okay between them again. "Not a chance in hell."

"Yeah, it's going to be sweet, man. I'll have my little cabaña on the beach and a *bad* mamacita to keep me warm at night. You'll have to come visit. Check out that righteous blue water I've been telling you about."

"Dream on, Logan. Dream on."

"Hey, watch it." Logan laughed, faking a punch.

"*You* watch it."

They reached the airport exit, curved off the freeway, and joined the bumper-to-bumper lanes headed toward the terminal. Good thing they'd left plenty of time. Damon inched ahead, keeping the truck in first.

"If it starts missing, clean the plugs," Logan said. "If you hear a lot of pinging or it's burning too much oil, I know this guy over in Inglewood who's worked on it before."

"Don't worry about it, bro. My brother-in-law's a mechanic. He'll fix me up."

"Okay, cool. That's good, man. That's good."

Damon followed the signs to the drop-off area. Cars wove in and out, pulled suddenly to the curb as if by magnets. Three cop cars shrieked past, lights flashing and sirens screaming. They cut through the traffic and disappeared around the curve ahead. People slammed trunks, honked horns, shouted. Ran in and out of the lines of triple-parked cars, dragging luggage, hugging each other, yelling for porters.

"Which airline is it?" Damon yelled. "What's the name of the goddamned airline?"

"Sun Treks," Logan shouted over the din. "Up there, past the taxis."

Damon gunned it and cut to the curb in front of another car.

Logan felt a stab of grief about leaving his truck, as if he were abandoning a pet.

"Not here!" he shouted. "It's red."

Damon parked anyway. Logan had let him drive so that he wouldn't have to stop the truck, but Damon killed the engine, got out, and went around to the back where Logan's duffel bag was stowed in the bed.

"I got it!" Logan cried. Things were suddenly crazy. "You don't have to stop. Thanks for everything—"

"There's no stopping here," an airport cop shouted. "Sir, no stopping!"

Damon ignored him. He took Logan's bag out of the truck and set it on the curb.

"I guess this is it," Logan said.

"Sir, you'll have to move your vehicle!" the cop said, striding up. "There's absolutely no stopping here!"

When Damon squared his shoulders and stood up to his full height, he looked like a linebacker. The cop piped down.

"Take it easy, Logan," Damon said. He hooked his arm around Logan's neck and pulled him close.

Logan hugged him, sweat and all. "Thanks for everything," he said. "Take care of yourself, brother."

"Sir, I'm *sorry*. This is a security zone," the cop said. He'd taken out his walkie-talkie. "If you don't move immediately, I'm going to cite you."

"Yeah, yeah, yeah," Damon sneered. "Adios, amigo," he called to Logan before he got in the truck and drove away.

Logan watched his Toyota thread its way through the traffic, pull into the left lane, and disappear. He took one last look at the gray sky, the flowing sea of cars, the families huddled like refugees at the curb. Then he picked up his bag and headed for the glass doors. They opened eagerly, as if they'd been waiting for him, and closed silently and efficiently behind him, as if some small measure of fate had been satisfied.

29

God had given Inez a tool.

She switched on the news, and sure enough, there was Beth Fong—who had just resumed her duties as anchor after having a baby—live at the airport. A swarm of police cars and official vehicles were down near the baggage claim. Beth had to shout to be heard over the confusion. A bomb threat had been phoned in not long before, she announced. Parts of the terminal were closed, the canine unit and bomb squad had been called in, SWAT teams were being deployed.

Inez got the portable phone and dialed as she watched. She was sure now, of everything. Beth handed off to Darrell Jackson, who was inside the terminal. The emergency line rang seven times before the dispatcher picked up. Inez told the story as simply as she could: how Rudy had been acting, how he'd come home when she wasn't there, what she'd found in the garage. All the time she kept her eyes on the screen. Darrell Jackson was talking to an airport official, who mentioned threats that had taken place over the past three weeks. They suspected a hoax, he said, though it was better to be safe than sorry.

"Ma'am, could you go through that one more time, please?" the dispatcher asked. She had a southern accent.

Inez repeated her story. This was really happening, she had to remind herself. It wasn't a dream.

When she was finished, the dispatcher sighed.

"Everything I say is true," Inez said. "It's him, my husband. I'm very afraid."

"Well, I'm going to go ahead and take you seriously," the dispatcher said, though she sounded doubtful. "Stay on the line, please. I need to transfer your call."

Men in green uniforms carried machine guns, electric carts zipped back and forth. Darrell Jackson interviewed passengers who had just flown in from Florida. Did they ever dream something like this would be going on when they landed in L.A.? They did not, not in a thousand years. In the meantime, some flights were being held on the ground, while others were diverted to nearby airports. Inez waited forever for her call to be transferred. Considering what she had to say, you'd think they'd hurry. She needed to get away from the house, just in case they didn't catch him. She'd leave as soon as she'd made the call. She knew he'd come for her if he got away.

The same dispatcher came back on. "Ma'am, are you still there?"

"Yes, but—"

"Okay, please hold on." She sounded more concerned this time, like somebody had clued her in. But she *still* put Inez on hold.

Now Beth Fong was inside, standing in front of a cordoned-off area. So far, no sign of any explosive device had been found, she said, but no sooner had she made the announcement than a small squadron of armed men in jumpsuits ran through the barricade. Beth jumped back; even *she* was alarmed.

"However, judging from what we just saw, I think we can conclude that no one really knows what's happening," she announced.

Hurry, Inez prayed. She wondered if she should try hanging up and calling again. At the same time her mind raced forward. She couldn't help but wonder: if Rudy went to jail, would she be entitled to their small savings account? He must have hidden her things *somewhere.* With him out of the picture, she'd be able to find them. She might even consider staying right there, in L.A.

There was a click and the connection opened. An official-sounding man came on, and his attitude was a whole lot different than the dispatcher's. He was very polite, and he took her seriously. He asked lots of questions, which she was glad to answer. When she told him that Rudy worked at the airport but that her daughter said he hadn't been going to work, he *really* got his attention. And when she told him about the cut-up newspapers, the notes she'd found hanging on the wall, the rolls of wire, and the box of what looked like explosives, his breathing got short and quick.

"You have a photograph of him?" the man interrupted.

She did.

"Stay right where you are. I'm going to transfer you to someone, and I want you to stay on the line with her until we get there. We'll have someone at your house in a few minutes."

For a moment, as she waited to be transferred, Inez felt terror, deep guilt. She had betrayed Rudy, her husband. *A wife is bound to her husband as long as he lives.* But the Lord had made Rudy an instrument, she reminded herself. He had used the bad to reveal the good. As if to comfort her, the words of Isaiah sounded once again: *You will forget the shame of your youth . . . For your Maker is your husband, the Lord of Hosts is His name.* Her *Maker* was her husband, not Rudy.

"Hang tight, ma'am," a new woman said on the other end of the line. "Our agents are on their way."

"Oh, my good Lord," Inez gasped. "There he is."

"What is it, ma'am? Ma'am, are you there?" the woman on the line shrieked. "Pick up! Pick up!" Inez heard her call to someone else.

In childhood photos of his school or family, Rudy was always the one cut halfway off by the edge of the frame, or obscured by someone else standing in front of him. "See, that's my foot there, and that's the side of my head," he would show her. A vague shape, fractured or out of focus. That's how it was now. Only she knew it was him. Standing right there on the edge of the crowd like an onlooker, his face in profile. She got up from the chair, carried the phone closer to the TV to get a better look.

"Stand by," the woman on the phone shouted. "She's not responding."

They say the camera adds ten pounds, but this was different. Rudy was wearing his jacket, but he looked swollen, stiff. Inez got within two feet of the screen, stared. She saw him objectively now, with amazement. He was her husband, but he was a stranger. He watched as the team of searchers walked through the baggage-claim area with dogs that strained at the ends of their leashes. He watched like an arsonist who stands in the crowd and watches his fire burn.

Inez dropped the phone, though she could still hear the woman's voice shouting from the receiver on the floor. Rudy turned his head. Even from that distance, Inez could make out his pointed nose and small, bunched-up features. He looked straight at the camera. Inez's heart fluttered wildly, beating against her chest. He smiled. Rudy stared at the camera and smiled, as if he were looking *right at her*. As if he could see her there in their living room, crouched in terror.

30

Friday evening was like the shifting of the tide in an estuary. The flood of people headed out for the weekend—eager to escape to beaches, golf courses, ski slopes, and casinos—converged with the rush of people coming back home to their own beds and familiar routines. Wylie watched the two streams crash and mingle in the pavilion in front of the bar. From there, departing passengers funneled into the chutes that siphoned through the metal detectors, while arriving passengers were presented with hugs and kisses, Mylar balloons, bouquets of carnations, and crying babies by the people who waited for them in the black plastic chairs. At this hour, just after six, the windows reflected the scene inside. Lights from outside—from the runways, the service vehicles that zipped silently back and forth, and the flashlights the ground crews used to guide the jets to their gates—were superimposed on the moving crowds, the banks of seats, the rows of bottles in the bar, and the pink neon sign of the La Paz Cantina. Only when you stood close to the glass could you see the shapes of the planes drifting like whales in black water.

The bar was busy. After working days for so long, Wylie had forgotten how different the night vibe was. A group of paunchy men in T-shirts and windbreakers were watching sports highlights as they shouted and laughed over in the corner. Men and women in suits sat at the high single tables, sipping drinks as they worked on their laptops. *Tahoe* he heard people in sweat suits and shorts tell each other. *Vegas.* Fresh out of work, ready to party. There was lots of coming and going—a quick turnover of the stools at the bar. Except one, where a Chicano dude in an Angels cap had been sitting near the register for going on two hours, getting toasted. Every time Wylie came over to ring up a sale, the guy had something to say.

"This plane I was on, the one I was telling you about," he picked up where he left off. "The one that couldn't get its landing gear down?"

Wylie nodded. The connection for credit card approval was slow. Every time he had to ring up a sale, he had to stand there and wait.

"You know what they decided to do?"

"Nope, no idea."

"Well, they decided to climb, then dive. Climb and dive. They thought the force of that might loosen something up. You know, knock something loose."

The guy was starting to slur.

"That right?" Wylie said.

"Honest to God. The funny thing is, it worked. Landing gear popped down and we were able to land. When they opened up the cabin, the smell of puke and shit was so strong the ground crew choked. Know what I did? First thing I did when I got off the plane?"

A crowd of party boys—tanned twentysomethings in muscle shirts and knee-length baggy shorts—walked into the bar like a flock of parrots, making a shitload of noise.

"What did you do?" Wylie said. He poured three Buds while he waited for the answer.

"Went right out and divorced my wife. She was waiting to pick me up. Told her right in the airport. *Bam,* just like that. *I want a divorce.* Know why?"

"Why?"

"I realized up there I didn't love her. When the plane was diving and I thought I was going to die. It's a shame, I thought, because all this time I've been married to a woman I don't love. So when we landed, I didn't waste any time." The guy tossed back his drink. "Never regretted it for a second. Never looked back."

"That's some story," Wylie said. "Excuse me."

The party boys were going to Cancún. They all wanted margaritas. Probably on Logan's flight, Wylie thought as he measured out the tequila and added the mix. God help the Mexicans when that pack landed.

A tall, big-boned young woman with long chestnut hair and baggy jeans pushed her way up to the bar and grinned at Wylie. He wiped the counter in front of her, set the napkin down, and took her order. Beer. When he asked for her ID, a grin broke out across her face.

"I can't believe you don't recognize me, Uncle Tommy."

"Oh my God," he said. He grinned back at her, at a loss for words. The last time he'd seen Jewell, she'd been a sullen teenager. Now she was magnificent, completely grown up. He could still see a lot of the kid she'd been, though. A tough little brat with a lot of energy, always asking questions.

"Jeez, you look like your old man," Wylie said. "Here, let me get you a seat." He turned to an older man whose luggage was piled on the stool next to him. "Excuse me. Could you move your things, please?" he asked. "The lady here would like to sit down."

Jewell apologized to the man and sat down. "That's why I'm here," she told Wylie. "I'm supposed to meet my dad."

"Yeah, he told me he was coming by. Guess he got lucky again, huh? Your old man specializes in being in the right place at the right time."

Wylie stopped, not sure how much he should say about Logan. He was conscious of his paunch and bad skin. The poor kid had gotten dragged around from one place to another her whole life. It was good to see she'd survived. There had been times he'd wondered about her.

"I haven't seen him for a couple of years," Jewell said. "Since I was in high school, I think." She leaned forward and said in a low voice, "I'm kind of nervous. I don't know what to expect."

Wylie put his hand over hers. "Don't worry. It's good you're seeing him. Here, let me get you that drink. What kind of beer do you want?"

She raised up on her stool to get a better look at the taps. "Foster's is fine."

He glanced at her while he filled her glass. She was looking around nervously, checking the terminal behind her. A big, strong girl with the assured, easy manner of her dad. She grinned at him as he walked back with the beer.

"He's late," she said, taking a drink. "What a surprise. In fact, I'll bet he doesn't show up at all."

The bar was packed. Wylie felt customers glaring at him from every direction. Probably thinking he was ignoring all of them while he made time with this youngster.

"Come on," he said. "He'll be here."

"It wouldn't be the first time he didn't show up."

"You got me there," he laughed. He couldn't bring himself to leave her sitting alone.

"Something was going on, though," Jewell said. "Out in the terminal."

She pushed the hair back from her face and frowned so that her eyebrows almost met. If he had a daughter, would she grow up to be like this? Ah, God, Wylie thought. Back to that. He'd actually managed to put the baby out of his brain for five minutes, and here it was again.

"Some kind of commotion," Jewell went on. "There were a bunch of cops and military guys near the ticket counter. And out front where you pick people up, the TV station had a van with a big antenna. Newscasters and a bunch of cameras. Maybe he got stuck in that."

Wylie wished he could tell her how wonderful she'd been as a kid. She'd lean against your leg as she talked to you, as warm and floppy as a pup. Look right in your face.

"Could we get a drink over here?" a guy with a goatee shouted from the other side of the bar. Wylie turned and saw a whole line of pissed-off faces.

"Listen, the natives are restless. I gotta serve these jokers," he apologized, patting her hand again. "You want a pretzel or a piece of pizza? Something to eat?"

She shook her head. Who could blame her for wondering if Logan would show up? Wylie had doubts himself. "Okay, hang tight. I'm sure your dad'll be here any minute. I'll be right back."

Wylie got busy. People were testy, trying to push through the crowd to get to the bar. It was even louder than before, if that was possible. People who had already ordered were sitting there with empty glasses, another army waited for their first drink. The damn company he worked for should have two bartenders on Friday nights, the cheap asses. But Wylie was good. He put his head down and worked his way through, one order at a time. At least it took his mind off his predicament with Carolyn. Now and then he glanced at Jewell, who sipped anxiously, scanning the group for her dad. Wylie filled glasses, sliced limes, speared olives. He watched his own hands: no motion was wasted. The rhythm was comforting. He took money, made change. Glasses piled up in the sink. The Amber Ale sputtered, hissed, and spit foam. Wylie tossed a plastic cup over the handle.

"Doing okay?" he called across the bar to Jewell.

She nodded.

The group of party boys left and the noise notched down a little. He caught a glimpse of the TV. It looked like news crews were there, at the airport. Must be over on the other side, in a different terminal. He didn't have time to figure out what was going on. Whiskey sour, Bloody Mary, cosmopolitan. He scraped tips off the bar, wiped the counter, tossed out napkins. The next time he glanced over at Jewell, Logan was there, his hands in his pockets, talking to her.

31

The sticks taped around Rudy's waist made him stand up straight and tall and walk in a slow, dignified way that he felt was right for the occasion. As he approached the pavilion in front of the security check, the importance of what he was about to do filled him with a sense that he was on the verge of walking straight into history. The stiff bindings girded him for battle, like a knight in armor. The secret of what was about to happen sang in his heart and a smile played over his lips. He enjoyed looking into the faces of people absorbed with their own petty concerns and knowing that in a few moments everything was going to change.

There were even more people in the pavilion than he'd expected. The place was hopping: a long line waiting to pay for gum and magazines in the gift shop, people with trays of nachos and enchiladas trying to find an empty table at the Mexican restaurant, a crowd on the black plastic chairs waiting for arriving passengers, drinkers standing three deep at the crowded bar. Noise from the big-screen TVs in the lounge, from the wheels of suitcases skating over the white floor, and from the clamor of hundreds of voices crashed in Rudy's ears like a waterfall.

It was hot. Rudy wiped the sweat off his forehead and upper lip with the sleeve of his jacket. It was sweaty under the tape, too. His armpits prickled and itched. Worse, the ends of the sticks had rubbed a raw line across his stomach where the flesh pouched out above the waistband of his pants. It stung like a blister worn on his heel. Next time he should tape them *over* his T-shirt, he told himself, and giggled.

"Look, Mommy!" a little girl pulling a pink Hello Kitty suitcase said, pointing at him. "That man."

Rudy felt a flash of alarm, but the girl's mother jerked the girl's arm impatiently and pulled her along. The little girl's head swiveled and she looked back, keeping her eyes fixed on Rudy until she disappeared into the crowd. But she was the only one. Everyone else walked by like he didn't exist, oblivious of the fact that in a few short moments all eyes would be on him. *You wait,* Rudy thought, enjoying himself. *You wait.* He worried that the TV crew down by the baggage claim wouldn't be able to get up here in time, that they might miss getting everything on tape. He thought of the people who might see him on the news. His boss, Glenn Waller. His slacker crew. Maybe a few of the losers from his high school. He imagined them casually watching the news, noticing him, doing a double-take. Could it be? they'd think. Then they'd see. Yes, it was. He chuckled. That'd surprise them. That would *really* throw them for a loop.

He paused by the newsstand to get the lay of the land. The moment was so big. Bigger than when he'd walked to the podium to get his high school diploma, bigger than when he'd climbed onto the stage of the converted movie theater and taken Inez to be his lawfully wedded wife. He'd felt like fainting as he looked down at the congregation staring up at him in his rented powder-blue tuxedo. He'd thought he was going to pitch down headfirst right into the front row of red upholstered chairs. A courtesy cart zipped past. Now it all seemed so long ago, so unimportant.

Standing near the checkout line at the gift shop, Rudy chose a spot roughly in the middle of the pavilion to make his stand. It was a natural clearing, far enough from the shops and the security check to be seen by everyone. This was it. He took a last look around and noticed the bartender with the bad skin who was moving like lightning, sweeping empty glasses off the bar, setting up full ones. Long lines were threading their way toward the metal detectors. Kids were crawling around on the floor under the black chairs in the waiting area. He felt a surge of nostalgia for all the time he'd spent here at the airport. All the mornings he'd shown up faithfully, bright and early, to clean the planes. All the passengers who had entered the cabin and looked out at the fresh aisles and clean seats, the seatbelts just so. Not that it mattered, when push came to shove. In the end, they'd cut him off without a second thought. All the time and effort he'd given, all the years he'd strived, working in good faith, trusting them to do their part, and then they'd kicked him in the gut. In the groin! Stuck it up his ass! Two weeks notice, after everything he'd done!

No pension, no party, no nothing.

Just like that.

A lump formed in Rudy's throat. Sweat ran into the raw places where the sticks had chafed him, stinging. All his dreams and hopes, everything he'd wanted to do with his life, it had all brought him here. This moment. He fingered the pull on the zipper of his jacket, unzipped it a few inches for a test run, zipped it back up. His breath was quick and shallow. Sweat ran down his temples and neck, into the collar of his shirt. He was finished talking. That was over. He was ready now to explain in a way that didn't use words, a way that made people *see*. That woke them up. That showed everyone.

Once he started walking, he moved quickly—or at least as quickly as the gear taped to his torso allowed. It was unbearably hot. As he advanced toward the center of the pavilion, noise was amplified: it bounced off the big windows that looked out onto the runways, off the high ceiling and bare floor. People in a hurry bumped into him, jostled him, practically spun him around. Rudy blinked. Sweat ran into his eyes, almost blinding him. He wiped them frantically, tried to gauge his position. The space seemed to spin with the movement of people around him. Finally he came to what he judged to be the center of the pavilion, equidistant from everything on the outside walls. Ground zero. He closed his eyes and pulled himself together.

"Now," he panted. *"Now."*

32

Jewell spotted Logan walking through the crowd wearing a tatty linen jacket and a pair of shoes that looked like he'd found them at Goodwill. He had a duffel bag over his shoulder, his hands in his pockets, and a big grin on his face.

"Look at you," he said, putting his arms around her and touching his lips to her cheek. He *smelled* like a secondhand store, too, though she caught a whiff of his soap as well—sandalwood or something spicy. When he leaned back to look at her, she saw there was a little gray at his temples, but most of his hair was honey brown streaked with blond highlights, like he'd been out in the sun. It was coming out of the ponytail that hung down his back, curling at the nape of his neck and around his ears. He looked a little worn out, like he'd been tumbled and kicked around, with crinkles under his eyes and a soul patch on his lower lip, but basically he looked good. If you shined him up and gave him some nice clothes he'd be awesome, straight out of the movies.

"So, you're going to Mexico?" Jewell said. Lame, but she felt shy, practically tongue-tied.

"Yeah, I thought I'd go down there, check it out. You ever been?"

"Just across the border. Down to Tijuana, Ensenada. You know, the usual."

"Well, maybe I can take you sometime. Or maybe you can visit me, after I get settled."

Jewell started. "You're *staying* down there?"

Logan gave his cool-cat shrug. "Never know. I might. Depends on what happens."

They smiled at each other. He was checking her out, too, she could tell. She had to keep reminding herself that this was her *father*, that she was actually looking at him. There was something likable about him, believe it or not, like you might want to spend time hanging out with him. Not that he wasn't a fuckup, someone who never should have had kids, but an okay guy, despite everything. The trouble was, she couldn't think of anything to say. The small talk was getting on her nerves, but she didn't know him well enough to get into anything heavy. All she could do was grin.

"So, heard from your mom?" he asked.

"No, I'm taking a little break from her. She's just too crazy for me right now, you know? I got enough things going on in my life."

Wylie came over and leaned across the bar, clapped Logan on the shoulder.

"Hey, can you believe this kid?" Logan cried as he pumped Wylie's hand. "Didn't I do good, Tommy? Doesn't she knock you out?"

"She's pretty amazing, Logan," Wylie said, winking at Jewell. "You sure she's your daughter?"

"You bet your ass she's mine," Logan said proudly.

He put his arm around her. Jewell was embarrassed, but pleased. She felt strangely proud of Logan, too, like she'd like to show him to someone, Celeste or maybe Eli. Not that he'd done anything fabulous, she just wanted someone to *see* him.

"And she's in college, Tommy. *College,*" Logan gushed. "What do you think about that?"

"I think you got lucky, all things considered," Wylie said. "You want something to drink, Logan? Jewell, another beer?"

"Yeah, I'll have another one," Jewell said quickly. The whole deal was giving her the jitters.

"What're you drinking?" Logan asked her.

"Foster's."

"Yeah, I'll have one of those," he said casually.

So much for the clean-and-sober routine, Jewell thought, meeting her uncle's eye. Wylie paused a minute, apparently decided to keep quiet, and went for the drinks. The couple next to Jewell left, and Logan grabbed a seat.

"You look so much like my mother," Logan said. "I just can't get over it."

He laid his hand over hers. A small *x* was tattooed between his thumb and first finger, like the *x* marks the spot on a treasure map. It was homemade, like he'd scratched it there himself. Jewell wondered where the treasure trail came from, what it led to. She imagined a dotted line winding up his arm and across his chest, to his heart.

Wylie brought the beers.

"Hey, Tommy. Did you ever see my mother?" Logan asked. "You remember what she looked like?"

"Kind of," Wylie said. "I think so."

"Don't you think Jewell looks *just* like her? When she was young, I mean."

"That would have been when Dad was still married to *my* mom, so *yours* was probably a little bit of a secret," Wylie said. "Plus I was still a kid. I don't think I knew her then."

"Yeah, I guess you're right," Logan admitted.

"Listen, you two," Wylie said. "I feel real bad that I can't stand here and chew the fat, but you see how crazy it is in here. Plus I know you have a lot of catching up to do. So I'm going to leave you alone. Be sure you call me over to say good-bye before you take off, Logan."

"Will do, bro. Go on. I know you're busy. We're just getting reacquainted here. We can take care of ourselves."

Jewell wished she could do something other than sit there mute, but it didn't seem to matter because her father was such a chatterbox. He turned to her and started in again about his mother.

"Yeah, I sure wish you could have known your grandma. Or I wish *she* could have known *you*. That she could see you now. Man, oh man. She would have loved the living daylights out of you. She would have really thought you were something."

Jewell nodded and stared for a minute at her lap. Logan had almost knocked off his beer already.

"I've thought about you," she said quietly. "I've wondered, lots of times, how you were doing."

Logan finally shut up. He seemed surprised by what she said. He leaned back on his stool and looked at her.

"So, how're *you* doing?" he said slowly, once he recovered. "You with somebody? Are you happy?"

Jewell choked. "I, ah—I'm actually in the process of breaking up with someone," she said. Her throat constricted. "I guess I'm pretty miserable right now."

"Who's the guy?"

Might as well go for it, Jewell thought. God knows *when* she'd see him again.

"It's not a guy, it's a girl."

"Whoa! I didn't see that one coming," Logan exclaimed. He braced himself against the bar. "Hold on a minute. Just give me a little time. This has to sink in." He stared at the foam sliding down the inside of his glass, nodding like he was having a conversation with himself. "Okay, okay," he nodded, and finished the beer. "Guess there's no chance we're going to get another one of these with this crowd," he said, inspecting the empty glass. He huffed a few times, like he was recovering his breath after a long run, rolled his head, and shook out his shoulders. "Okay, I think I'm getting it. All right. Okay, so what's the story?" he said, turning back to her.

She had to laugh. So did he. It felt good to laugh together.

"I guess I'm in love with her," she said with a shrug. "The funny thing is, she doesn't love me. At least not enough."

"Well, nothing you can do about that."

"You don't think so?"

"Nope. Someone wants to leave you, there's nothing you can do."

"Don't you believe in working on things, working them out?"

"Nope."

Jewell laughed again. She couldn't believe that she was having this conversation with her *father*. But she was beginning to feel strangely at ease with him.

"But in advice columns they always say that you have to work on a relationship, on staying together. It doesn't just happen by itself," she said.

"It shouldn't be so much work. If somebody wants to leave you, it's too late. You might postpone the inevitable, but what's the point of that?" He leaned in closer. "I have to tell you something, sweetheart. I'm not saying I haven't messed up, because I have. I've done a lot of things I never should have done and not done a lot of things I should have. But I *do* know that you can't make somebody love you. No matter what you do. No matter how bad you want it. I learned the hard way."

Interesting. Jewell wasn't used to parental advice. She blinked at her father in bewilderment. She couldn't help wondering what had happened to him to make him feel this way. Was he was talking about her *mother,* or was it one of the fifty million other women who'd probably passed through his life?

"Just like you can't make yourself love somebody if you don't feel it in your heart," he added. "No matter what you tell yourself, how hard you try. You're just wasting your time. Man, I sure wish we could get another beer."

"So, what should I do?" Jewell asked.

"Accept it. Move on. It doesn't mean you stop loving them. You always will. You carry them in your heart. And we got a lot of stubborn hearts in our family, believe me. They don't listen to common sense. But it doesn't mean you get what you want. *Who* you want."

Jewell was about to respond when she noticed the racket of voices in the waiting area near the security check. She turned just as three men in business suits sprinted in front of the window that looked onto the runway. People standing in line to go through the metal detector scattered like startled birds. A woman stumbled over her luggage and caused a spontaneous pileup of people and belongings. Suddenly everyone in the waiting area near the gate was running. It sounded like a stampede. Someone shouted. Another screamed.

"Jesus, what's going on?" Logan asked, cranking his head around.

Everyone at the bar turned at once. There was a communal gasp.

The last clear picture Jewell had was of her uncle, who stood frozen in place, a glass of ice in each hand.

33 Wylie set the glasses on the bar, looked up, and saw people running, first one way, then another. Like a scrimmage where no one knew who had the ball. At first he thought there was trouble at the security check, but then he saw the commotion was more toward the center of the pavilion, to one side of the black plastic chairs. He stood on his tiptoes to try to see over the heads at the bar. People charged like panicked cattle. They grabbed children, knocked over luggage, shoved each other out of the way. *Oh Jesus,* he thought. This was no joke. Something serious was happening. His heart pounding, Wylie crossed the bar and stood near Logan and Jewell.

Someone shouted, someone else screamed. People eating at the La Paz Cantina cranked their necks around and stared. Shoppers ran out of the pet gift store with coffee mugs and dog sweaters in their hands to see what was happening. The gift-shop cashier came out from behind the register. All the noise—loudspeakers, voices, carts, and footfalls—blended into a dull roar. Then, after a moment, Wylie could hear one voice rising above the others. It shouted the same command, over and over. Gradually the other noise died down and people stopped running. Finally, Wylie could make out the words.

"*Stop! Stand still! Don't move!*"

Everyone fell back from a point in the middle of the pavilion. One person stood in the center of the ring, like in a children's game. The cheese stands alone, Wylie thought. He had a sudden, unsettling sense—like remembering a recurrent dream—that all of this had already happened. *This* was what had been bothering him, he realized, as the hair stood up on his forearms. *This* was the thing that had been making him jumpy for weeks. Strangest of all, now that it was finally happening, he felt oddly calm.

"Stop! Stand still! Don't move!"

Wylie recognized him right away. The goofy guy who used to clean the planes, the one who had left a mess on the bar not that long ago. Of course! That's the way it always was, wasn't it? The loser. The outcast. The one with a grudge. Like a dime-store thriller. The quiet one. Pear-shaped, awkward, soft. The one no one suspected. Incredibly, Wylie remembered his name, even though he'd only seen it a couple of times on his ID tag. *Rudy.*

"Stand back! Nobody move!" Rudy shouted like a bad actor who had rehearsed his line many times but still delivered it flat and wooden.

The crowd around him froze. Some crouched, others sheltered their children or clutched their hands to their chests. As he unzipped his jacket, he smirked at the people who encircled him, and slowly raised his arms. There was something graceful about the way he did it, Wylie thought, like a cormorant sunning itself. He had a sleepy, contented look on his face, like he was basking in everyone's gaze.

An electric jolt shot up Wylie's spine, from his sacrum to the root of his skull. Taped around Rudy's chest like a corrugated life vest was a row of red explosives. A wire ran up his arm. There was a trigger in his hand. He leered, twisting his torso slowly, so that everyone could see.

There was nothing anybody could do, Wylie realized. Not a goddamn thing. He calculated quickly, wondering how much punch the ammo would pack, how far the explosion would reach. To him? He clenched the bar, waiting for the blast.

"Please!" a woman shrieked. *"Please don't do it!"*

People dropped to the ground and covered their heads with their arms. A baby began to cry, then another. Rudy looked wildly around, his arms still out, taunting them with the trigger in his hand. Any minute now the blast would shatter the crowd, would spray people, luggage, glass, and seats against the walls. Wylie braced, waiting for it.

The crowd waited, too. Speechless, breathless, and unmoving as they counted the seconds before the moment of annihilation. Waited, waited, waited. Waited too long. As Rudy surveyed the ring of faces surrounding him, the defiant jeer on his face melted. He opened his mouth as if to say something, then shook his head. Something in Wylie lifted its head. Perked up. Looked around. A glimmer of hope. Was it possible? Yes. Slowly at first, but then unmistakably, the balance shifted.

The crowd stirred.

A voice rang out from somewhere near the black plastic chairs. *"Get him!"*

The ring around Rudy pulled back, then surged in, like a giant drawing breath.

"Get him!" a woman near the bar cried.

A tall black man with cornrowed hair ripped through the crowd toward Rudy, pulling others in his wake. He broke the inner circle, launched himself into the air, and hit Rudy in the chest with his shoulder. The last thing Wylie saw was the surprised look on Rudy's face, the small, confused *O* of his mouth. Then he was down. The crowd rushed in, mobbing him.

"The cops are coming! They're on their way!" someone shouted.

The center of the circle churned with bodies that had piled on Rudy, like piranhas feeding on a cow. People on the edge of the crowd shouted, stood on tiptoe. Suddenly the man with cornrows rose up in the center, holding Rudy by the collar off his jacket. He hoisted him up like a prize, so everyone could see.

"These are road flares!" he screamed. "Nothing but road flares!" He shook Rudy so fiercely that his head snapped back and forth. The cornrowed man bellowed, "They can't blow up a damn thing! I got some in my own trunk just like this! They're just *road flares!*"

Wylie was about to breathe a sigh of relief when there was a huge commotion: the pounding of running feet, shouts, screams. Cops were suddenly everywhere. Soldiers with automatic weapons. They charged past the bar and into the middle of the crowd. Another squad of green-uniformed soldiers, guns drawn, exploded into the pavilion from the other direction. People screamed and dove for cover.

A surge of icy dread hit Wylie's veins. He'd been in situations like this before. Someone was going to shoot. He could feel it, could smell it in the overcharged air that vibrated with potential destruction. Any movement could trigger it, any sudden noise or false step. The gunmen swept their rifles over the crowd, searching for targets. A few of them trained their rifles on Rudy while others swiveled from the hips, trigger fingers cocked, muscles twitching.

Wylie clenched his jaw, held his breath. As if on cue, there was a scuffle on the side of the bar, just to his right, not ten feet away. He heard a murmur, a scrape, and—sure enough—one of the metal barstools went over with a loud bang, clattering to the floor. The nearest soldier, young and gaunt, reacted. He swung toward the noise, his gun at his shoulder. Wylie could see how terrified he was by the jerky way he moved.

Another stool crashed to the floor.

The soldier planted his feet, leveled his gun, and aimed.

Though he was a good fifty feet away, Wylie felt like he was looking down the barrel of the gun. He saw it up close, a small black circle, perfectly aligned with the middle of his chest. Two points determine a line, he remembered. These were the points, beginning and end: the muzzle of the gun, the middle of his chest. This was it, he realized. His last moment. This was how it was going to end. He only had to wait for the bullet's geometry, for it to travel the shortest distance between two points.

Hyped on adrenaline, the young soldier didn't dare wait to see what would happen next. His finger flinched on the trigger.

The shot rang out, the blast reverberated.

It took Wylie a moment to realize he was still standing. He had miscalculated the trajectory, he saw. The bullet was heading for Jewell. But in the silver silence that followed the blast he realized that it wasn't him, and it wasn't Jewell.

Logan was on the ground.

34

Jewell watched Logan slide off the barstool, square his shoulders, and step into the path of the bullet. Calmly, cheerfully, as if he were walking through a door. What made him stand up right at that moment? She saw the back of his head, the fabric of his scruffy linen jacket stretched between his shoulder blades. Then he was gone, fallen at her feet.

There was so much commotion in the waiting area, hardly anyone seemed to notice Logan. Only a few amazed faces at the bar turned toward him. Jewell looked past them, out into the terminal where the young, skinny soldier who had fired the gun stood with an expression of blank disbelief on his face.

"No!" Jewell screamed. "No! No! No! No! No!"

Screaming it was the only way she could get through those first few moments. She sank to her knees beside her father. Bar patrons rushed over and pressed in, but Jewell leaned over Logan and shut them out with her hair, which closed around the two of them like a curtain.

He writhed, twisting from side to side.

"Get someone," she pleaded, raising her head only for the time it took to say those two words.

He stopped moving and opened his eyes. For the first time she realized who her father was. Not a face or a body, or a collection of memories. Not what he'd said or done, but only this moment as she looked into his eyes. It felt so familiar. Pure recognition. She felt his full attention. Each of her cells, every hair follicle, was alert, a receptor, drinking it in. She couldn't remember a time when words weren't necessary, but now everything they needed to say passed between them without a syllable. She had never experienced such fullness of expression. The air between them felt thick with words, with understanding. His eyes rested on her, unmoving. She felt bathed by his gaze, fed and caressed.

His hand closed around her finger.

The moment lasted and lasted. It was faceted, broken down into hundreds of pieces. It contained every moment that had come before: the first classroom Jewell had ever walked into, all the houses she'd lived in, every tear she'd shed, the first time she'd laid eyes on Celeste.

As if *she* were the one who was dying, her life passed before her eyes, but her life *to come,* not her past. She understood that it was over between her and Celeste, that she would never stop loving her but that they would never be together, and that her love didn't have all that much to do with Celeste, anyway. It was more her own stuff, all her own stuff. Still, she saw possibilities. She might live in the house under the eaves with the smell of warm hay. She might finish school. After a while she might leave this basin of smog and jittery earth, her home. She might love someone else, and they might love her in return. Life would go on.

"Hey!" someone in the crowd shouted. "There's a guy down over here!"

As the attention of the crowd shifted away from Rudy and over to the bar, Logan squeezed Jewell's finger one last time, hard, before the pressure relaxed. The moment was almost over. But before it ended, Jewell realized how amazing it was to live and how easy to die. The line that separated the two was remarkably thin, she learned as she watched the life pass peacefully, almost imperceptibly, from her father's face.

35

In the river of pain were little islands of relief, a few seconds when the searing agony in Logan's chest subsided and he was flooded with well-being. He rested then, floating in comfort until it was time to move on and the torment started again. When the pain was too much, just as he was about to go over the edge, relief engulfed him. Not for long, though. Still, he was grateful for those few merciful moments.

He heard the shouts around him, the confusion. He was frightened, terrified, breathing in short gasps, trying to hold on to his breath, to keep his life in the confines of his body, to not let go. He clenched his eyes and concentrated on the pain, got inside of it, and sure enough it started to ebb away, to leave him. His body lightened, his fear dissipated. It wasn't going to be that bad, he realized. It was almost a relief, the blood running out of him, because with it went all his desire. How amazing: this was really, *finally* happening. It was a mistake, but it was meant to be. It had been coming, always coming, since the moment he was born. And now here it was. Coming.

As the pain and fear subsided, he opened his eyes and looked at Jewell. So much like his mother. He smelled her hair where it fell around him, soft on his face like the most tender grass when you lie on the ground. Finally he was able to look at her, to get his fill. To look and look. They spoke the language they knew before there were words.

A shiver passed through him. His hands and feet were cold, his nose and lips tingled. He thought of the water—the clear, blue water. He could see it in the distance, sparkling against the sand like liquid glass. He was light, so light. What a great feeling, just to lie there and do nothing. Not a care in the world. Not a god-damned thing to worry about: where the next buck was coming from, what the guy in the next cell might do, or how some cop might come to put his ass away. Nothing. It all left him. Love, hu-miliation, desire. All gone. The years he'd worked. The children he'd had. The lust and resentment. Couldn't touch him. The hurts he'd suffered and the names he'd been called. The laughs. The moments of peace. The disappointments. None of it mattered. He'd never felt so good. So rested.

He could hear the water lapping, its wet slap on the creamy sand. He felt sorry for the people who were shouting and milling around him, working themselves up for nothing. He thought of his mother again, how her love had been like the warm sun on his face. The water—the blue, blue water—lapped gently over his feet. It was the most wonderful feeling as it slipped over his toes and then his an-kles, as it inched up his legs to his knees. It was the perfect body temperature, neither warm nor cold. When it reached his thighs, every last care flowed out of him. Even Jewell didn't matter any-more, not his mother or any of his wives, anyone he had ever loved or hoped to love, because all of them had their own lives and now he had his before him. This last thing was his and only his, the water, the tide coming in until he was floating, his body the most delicious weight, every ounce of him bobbing in the most amazing uncaring.

"I'm going," Logan said, whether aloud or to himself he couldn't tell.

Time stood still and then it moved quickly. For one brief flash he felt exactly as he had when he was a child. A forgotten feeling when he raised his head and said *Here I am*. Then his legs flipped up, up over his head, and he tumbled. Over and over and over. Be-neath him and over him was the blue, so clear you could see the sand below, the sky above. Finally he reached deep water where it was only the blue—the bright, bright blue.

36

The suspect had been apprehended in the terminal, Beth Fong reported. Her hair was mussed on one side, as if she herself had helped with the capture. Shots had been fired. It was unclear who the assailant was, who had been wounded, what the motivation had been. Viewers should stand by for more details, Beth advised. As soon as there was more information, she would give the full report.

Inez switched off the television and hurried across the room to the phone. Things had suddenly become very simple.

She had to get away.

She dialed the home of Vanessa's friend and waited for the mother to call Vanessa to the phone. Inez heard water running into a sink while she waited. The ping of an electronic game and the laughter of a younger child. Normal sounds of a normal family.

"Come home," she said when Vanessa answered. *"Now."*

Two agents were out in the garage, another parked in an unmarked car across the street. What happened to Rudy wasn't her concern. Not anymore.

She made another call, remembering the number from the jingle they played on TV. *Dial 234-6161 and here comes the Yellow on the run.* Funny how things stick in your mind. The dispatcher answered the phone, took the information, said she'd send the cab. It was also funny how easy things were when you broke them down into little steps. All she had to do was grab a few things, wait for Vanessa, leave the house, get to the station.

Rise and enter the city, the Lord had told Saul when he was struck blind on the road to Damascus, *and you will be told what to do.*

She didn't need much. Wherever she went in this country, people would need Avon. The money would pile up, just like it had before. And until then? There were shelters for people like her, weren't there? Churches? Women left men all the time with nothing but the clothes on their backs. Hadn't her own father left his country and everything he knew with nothing to rely on but his own mind and body? She hurried into the bedroom and pulled the suitcase off the top shelf of her closet.

She felt confident as she packed a few essentials. Underwear, jeans, sweaters. As she was tucking in a tube of toothpaste, his voice came to her, as clear as if he were right there in the room. *His* voice, Vanessa's father. *God has given me this feeling,* he told her, just as he had so many years ago. *He has put this feeling for you in my heart. He wouldn't put it there if it wasn't right. He means for us to do this, to be together like this, to do what we are doing. It is God's will. We must obey Him.*

That was a lie, Inez realized as she snapped the suitcase shut. The revelation was so clear and simple that, despite the peril of the moment, a smile spread across her face. And that wasn't the only one, either. The lies she'd been told and the ones she'd told herself. About so many things, even about God himself. She picked up the suitcase and headed for the door. Now that she saw them for what they were, lies spread out before her all the way to the horizon.

For everything there is a season and a time for every matter under heaven. Now it was time to get away, to leave. That was all that mattered. Later, there would be plenty of time for everything else. She had the rest of her life to figure it out.

The back door slammed in the kitchen. Inez looked wildly at the front door, measuring the distance, her heart pounding. Where in the world was Vanessa? She had to leave! She couldn't spend another moment in this house!

It was one of the agents. A Filipino of all things, a soft-spoken young man with caramel skin and thick black hair cut so that it lay smoothly against his head. He wore a stylish, olive-green pullover. Nothing like you'd expect from a government agent. He was holding a brown grocery bag from Albertson's.

"Mrs. Cullen, we've found something here. Could you have a look?"

Inez crossed the living room. When she got near the agent, she could smell his cologne. Something bracing and fresh, with a citrus base. He held open the Albertson's bag. She looked down into it and there, nestled at the bottom, were her things: the stack of Avon receipts, the packet of photographs, the envelope of money.

"Mrs. Cullen, is this you?" the agent asked, holding out a piece of paper.

"Certificate of Live Birth," Inez read.

Sex: Female.

Name: Santos.

"Santos," she pronounced, looking up at him with a questioning stare.

"Is that you, ma'am?" the young man asked. He had such lovely eyes.

She handed the certificate back to him. "Yes. That's me. Santos," she proclaimed, shaking her head with wonder, amazed that she'd found everything, that she had it all back again.

37

The ambulance crew came running, pushing through the crowd with their tubes and pumps and paddles, but Wylie could tell by the look on Jewell's face when she turned and looked up at him that it was too late.

"Stand aside! Please stand aside!" the lead paramedic shouted, shouldering his way in. When he got to where Wylie was kneeling beside Jewell, he took hold of Wylie's arm and pulled him away. "Make room, please! Let us in!" he commanded. "Let us do our work!"

Wylie stood. He felt the crowd behind him, the curious pressing in. Jewell was still bent over Logan, her hair hiding his face and chest. Wylie could only see Logan's hand, curled as if in sleep, his splayed legs, his feet with the toes pointing out. The shoes were frayed, scuffed on the heels. One was untied.

Logan had never gotten it quite right, Wylie thought to himself. He'd never really gotten the hang of this world.

"Come on! Move it!" a short, slight paramedic shouted right next to him. A woman, he saw, with kinky black hair hanging down her back. Tough as nails.

Wylie stepped aside. The phone was ringing behind the bar.

He elbowed his way through the crowd, made his way back to the bar, lifted the counter, and stepped behind it. He looked at the place where Logan had been sitting just a few minutes before. His empty glass was still on the bar. Wylie gazed absently at it. Logan had held it in his hand, had raised it to his lips. And now those lips would never take another drink or speak another word or kiss another mouth. No. Logan was done with that. He had no use for it anymore. There was a space where Logan had been. An empty place.

It occurred to Wylie to take a drink himself. To pour three or four fingers of Scotch and knock it straight back. Instead he walked over to the phone and picked up the receiver.

He knew it would be her.

"Jesus Christ, Wylie!" Carolyn burst out. "I was watching the news! I saw the whole thing! Are you okay?"

It was only when he tried to speak that he realized he couldn't. He strained, and his throat emitted a dry croak—half grunt, half moan, like he was straining to pick up something very heavy. He clenched his jaw and the tears squeezed out the corners of his eyes. They burned as they trickled down his face. He felt their warmth as they made their way over his lips and into his mouth. He tasted their salt. It had been years since he'd cried. Years and years.

"Wylie!" Carolyn gasped into the receiver. *"Are you there? Are you okay?"*

All he could do was nod.

"If you're there, say something, for God's sake!"

He managed to squeak, to gurgle, to gag. He was like the Tin Man who had rusted into place. *Oil me.* His chest heaved. Finally he managed to take a deep breath. It took every bit of his willpower to gasp, "Yes, I'm here. I'm okay."

"Thank God, Wylie! Jesus, I was scared! When I saw where it was, I couldn't believe it! I just happened to switch the TV on and—"

"My brother got shot," Wylie interrupted. "Logan."

"What? What in the hell are you talking about? Are you kidding? Wylie, what do you mean?"

The pain in Wylie's throat reached down into his chest and up into his ears. He swallowed, wet his lips, and struggled with his tongue. "I'll have to tell you later," he managed to choke out. "Listen, Carolyn. I have to say this."

"What?" she asked anxiously.

"I love you," he said.

The voice didn't seem to come from him. It sounded familiar, though, as if it belonged to a person he once had been, or might become.

"And I want to—"

There was silence on the end of the line. A listening silence. Wylie wondered if the line had gone dead, if Carolyn was there at all.

"I want—"

She *still* didn't say anything. No one was going to help him out.

"Let's," he finally stammered. "Let's."

Acknowledgments

My deep gratitude to Rebecca Lowen for the many years she has encouraged me, offered judicious advice, and worked long and hard on my manuscripts. Your generosity still takes me by surprise. My warm thanks to Nina Friedman, who for decades has given her unwavering support to practically every word I've ever written—and who has generously shared her gift for pointing out inconsistencies and errors in reasoning. I'm grateful to Michelle Echenique for being what every writer should be so lucky to have—an inspired partner in crime, a sympathetic ear, and a joyful and intelligent reader. Sandra Cisneros has guided me in many ways, both large and small. For helping me hear those voices in our hearts that make us writers, and for tending my work with such care, I will always be grateful.

Thank you to my friends and colleagues at the University of California Press, who have not only read and commented on my writing but who have also cheered me on and enabled me, one way or another, to create these stories while holding down a full-time job—in particular Hillary Hansen, Joan Parsons, Jim Clark, Mari Coates, Julie Christiansen, and Shira Weisbach.

To my fellow Macondistas—my loving, dedicated, and wildly talented writing comrades—thank you for building a place where we can bring our most secret and precious things. Thank you to Marcia Donahue for her keen perceptions and for catching all those "who knews." To Steve Johnson, who simply stepped into my path one morning, asked to see my manuscript, and went on to make a series of brilliant suggestions that greatly improved the end result. To Erasmo Guerra, who so generously took time from his own writing to help with mine. To Alex Espinoza, for his loving spirit and for being the first to bring a part of this novel to print. And to my family, where many of these stories begin.

Space is lacking to describe the many fine qualities of my agent, Stuart Bernstein, for whom I feel an enormous sense of warmth and gratitude. Sally Kim has nurtured this book with her abundant energy, intelligence, persistence, and vision. Many thanks to her and to everyone at Shaye Areheart Books who gave these characters and this story such a fine home.

I am grateful to Hedgebrook, where I completed this novel during a writer's residency, and to the John Templeton Foundation Power of Purpose Awards for its generous gift.

Thanks finally to Carla Trujillo—for all the big things and the many little things and everything in between, and for all the fun we have on the way.

About the Author

Leslie Larson was born in San Diego, California. Her work has appeared in *Faultline*, the *East Bay Express*, and *The Women's Review of Books*, among other publications. She lives in Berkeley, California.

About the Type

This book was set in Adobe Garamond, a typeface designed by Robert Slimbach in 1989. It is based on Claude Garamond's sixteenth-century type samples found at the Plantin-Moretus Museum in Antwerp, Belgium.

Composition by Stratford Publishing Services
Brattleboro, Vermont

Printing and binding by Berryville Graphics
Berryville, Virginia